RAMSEY CAMPBELL

BORN TO
THE DARK

The Second Book of the
Three Births of Daoloth Trilogy

This is a **FLAME TREE PRESS** book

Text copyright © 2021 Ramsey Campbell

FLAME TREE PRESS
6 Melbray Mews, London, SW6 3NS, UK
flametreepress.com

US sales, distribution and warehouse:
Simon & Schuster
simonandschuster.biz

UK distribution and warehouse:
Marston Book Services Ltd
marston.co.uk

Thanks to the Flame Tree Press team, including:
Taylor Bentley, Frances Bodiam, Federica Ciaravella, Don D'Auria,
Chris Herbert, Josie Karani, Molly Rosevear, Mike Spender,
Cat Taylor, Maria Tissot, Nick Wells, Gillian Whitaker.

The cover is created by Flame Tree Studio with
thanks to Nik Keevil and Shutterstock.com.
The font families used are Avenir and Bembo.

Flame Tree Press is an imprint of Flame Tree Publishing Ltd
flametreepublishing.com

A copy of the CIP data for this book is available from the British Library
and the Library of Congress.

HB ISBN: 978-1-78758-563-8
US PB ISBN:978-1-78758-561-4
UK PB ISBN: 978-1-78758-562-1
ebook ISBN: 978-1-78758-564-5

Printed in the USA by Integrated Books International

RAMSEY CAMPBELL

BORN TO THE DARK

The Second Book of the
Three Births of Daoloth Trilogy

FLAME TREE PRESS
London & New York

"There's a place past all the stars that's so dark you have to make your eyes light up to see," Toby said. "There's a creature that lives in the dark, only maybe the dark's what he is. Or maybe the dark is his mouth that's like a black hole or what black holes are trying to be. Maybe they're just thoughts he has, bits of the universe he's thinking about. And he's so big and hungry, if you even think about him too much he'll get hold of you with one of them and carry you off into the dark ..."

More than thirty years have passed since the events of *The Searching Dead*. Now married with a young son, Dominic Sheldrake believes that he and his family are free of the occult influence of Christian Noble. Although Toby is experiencing nocturnal seizures and strange dreams, Dominic and Lesley have found a facility that deals with children suffering from his condition, which appears to be growing widespread. Are their visions simply dreams, or truths few people dare envisage? How may Christian Noble be affecting the world now, and how has his daughter grown up? Soon Dominic will have to confront the figures from his past once more and call on his old friends for aid against forces that may overwhelm them all. As he learns the truth behind Toby's experiences, not just his family is threatened but his assumptions about the world...

For Tammy and Sam – the past creeps closer

'Gaze not too long upon the outer dark, lest it turn upon you.'
Revelations of Glaaki, volume 4, *Of the Secrets behind the Stars*
(Matterhorn Press, 1863?)

Stop Press, 11 April 1955
Eric Wharton, the popular newspaper columnist, was today drowned in a fall from New Brighton ferry.

From an editorial, 13 April 1955
So Eric Wharton has gone on his way; on the way we must all one day follow. He will leave a gap in many lives. Popular alike with his colleagues and his many readers, he was a true man of the people who told the truth as he saw it without fear or favour. Liverpool-born, he travelled the world but always stayed true to his roots. He was admired by most, and even those he criticised in his column respected him. He once famously wrote that if he were a stick of seaside rock, the word he would want to be printed all the way through him would be Honesty. He need not have feared, and surely now that quality has earned him his place in Heaven.

NEWSPAPERMAN'S LAST WORDS DISPUTED.
JOURNALIST "DISTRACTED" BEFORE DEATH.
The Liverpool coroner today recorded a verdict of accidental death in the case of newspaper columnist Eric Wharton.

On the afternoon of the 11th of April, Mr. Wharton fell overboard from the Royal Iris ferry. Crewmen were alerted by members of the public, but were unable to rescue Mr. Wharton. His body was subsequently recovered by the Liverpool coastguard.

In court, colleagues of the journalist described how he had seemed "preoccupied" or "distracted" in the weeks preceding the accident, to the extent that he became unable to write his popular newspaper column. An unfinished draft was found in his typewriter, complaining of his inability to think and ending with the apparently random words "looking over my shoulder."

Passengers on the ferry, on which Mr. Wharton regularly used to travel to his home in New Brighton, observed that he gave the impression of "looking or listening" for someone on board. Several passengers reported that he appeared to be trying to brush ash or some other substance from his clothes, though he had apparently not been smoking. His preoccupation may have left him unaware that he was dangerously close to the rail, where his actions caused him to lose his balance. While a number of witnesses agreed that he uttered a cry as he fell, there was dispute as to whether the word was "leave" or "believe."

Mr. Wharton's housekeeper, Mrs. Kitty Malone, was overcome by emotion several times while giving an account of her employer's mental condition. She described how Mr. Wharton became critical of her tidiness, which he had previously praised in his column, and would straighten the bed she had made "as if he thought I'd left some nasty thing in it." She further testified that Mr. Wharton seemed to grow determined to embrace his faith in his final days, frequently repeating the word "Christian" to himself.

The coroner concluded that while the balance of Mr. Wharton's mind may have been to some extent disturbed, there was no evidence of intent for suicide, and insufficient reason for a verdict of death by misadventure.

Eric Wharton was born in Liverpool in 1904. He attended St. Edward's College and subsequently went up to Oxford. In the Second World War he was awarded the DSO...

1985

CHAPTER ONE

The Reunion

You and a guest are cordially invited to the launch of Roberta Parkin's new book The Entitlement Trap *at Texts in Tottenham Court Road. 18.00–19.30, 15 February 1985. RSVP…*

The train from Liverpool broke down less than halfway to London. It loitered between stations while the fields that isolated it grew dark and distant windows lit up as the first stars did. By the time a replacement engine arrived I was by no means the only passenger who would have walked to the nearest transport if the guard hadn't kept the doors locked. Well before the train crawled into London, Bobby's bookshop event was over.

I thought of going home to Lesley, and now I know I should have gone. As a voice encased in static announced that the train was outside Euston I retrieved the invitation from my bag. The large white card embossed in gold bore a postscript in Bobby's small but elaborate handwriting. *Eats afterwards at Yellow Sea in Chinatown. Hope you and Jim can make it! Let's be three again!* I couldn't resist that appeal, and as soon as the guard released the doors I jumped onto the platform and sprinted to the underground.

The escalators were as crowded as the subterranean platform, which was populated mostly by smokers. At least smoking on the trains themselves had been banned last year, and so the atmosphere was no longer quite as stifling, especially once someone opened a window to let in a draught, along with the shrill roar of the dark. At Leicester Square I struggled up an escalator with a commuter on every step to emerge onto Charing Cross Road. By the time I left some of the crowd behind by dodging into Chinatown my hip ached with the insistent thumps of the luggage strapped over my shoulder. Competitively coloured neon signs glared in my eyes and put out the sky as I searched for the restaurant I was growing desperate to find. I had to retrace my steps before I caught sight of most of an illuminated word at the far end of an alley. **YE OW**, the brightest letters said.

The place looked like just another Chinese café dangling headless poultry in its window. Opening the door let out more noise than I would have imagined the place could contain. Though the front was narrow, the room gilded with paintings of dragons stretched back several times that width. Every table was occupied by Chinese diners, all of whom seemed to be talking at once. No, in the far corner an occidental woman was facing me, but she was nobody I knew. As I wondered where I'd gone wrong an unsmiling waiter came up to me. His face made it plain that the restaurant was fully booked, but I couldn't leave without saying "Parkin."

He shook his head, which failed to shift his frown. "No parking here."

"No, Parkin."

"I say that." He plainly felt I didn't understand English. "I say no parking."

"No, I'm saying Parkin. The Parkin party, they're meant to be here."

The woman in the corner was staring at me as if the waiter's scrutiny wasn't enough. "Parking party," he said, and I was about to spell the name at the top of my voice when the woman's companion turned around. "Dom," she shouted and sprang to her feet. "We're over here."

How could I have failed to recognise her broad straight shoulders, even if we and Jim hadn't met for decades? As she raised her face to greet me, her long nose and indomitable chin helped resolve her smile. The waiter flung his hands apart, using one to wave me onwards, and I was edging between the tables with my bag pressed against my side when the door to the toilets let out Jim. "Jim," Bobby called, "he's come after all."

He was slimmer than I remembered, and half a head taller than me. He caught me before I reached the table, and shook my hand with both of his. "Great you made it," he said. "Bob was starting to be disappointed."

"I would have been too. I was stuck on the train." As we sidled to the table I said "Have you brought your wife?"

"No," Bobby said, "Carole's mine."

I'd forgotten how red my face could grow. I hadn't really noticed the way Bobby and the other woman could have been competing for the tersest hairstyle. Bobby gave me a prolonged fierce hug and kissed my cheek, none of which left me less aware of her partner. Carole's small face looked concentrated around watchfulness – you could have called the features delicate or sharp – and her scrutiny hadn't relented. "Sorry," I said hardly loud enough to be heard over the hubbub of diners, and took her cold limp hand.

"Why?"

"Not if you don't think I need to be."

"What you feel ought to be your choice," Carole said and dealt my hand a solitary shake.

"I feel happy for you both," I said but suspected that she thought I was being too deft with language. As soon as I let go of her hand I was worried my swiftness could seem like aversion. The punch Bobby dealt me would have come as a relief even if it had been less affectionate. I shrugged off my bag as she poured me a glass of Sauvignon so pale it earned its adjective. "Here's to the book," I said, raising the glass.

Along with hers Bobby lifted her face as if her smile had buoyed it up. "And here's to us."

Carole waited until Bobby met her gaze. "Yes, to us."

Jim seemed to think he needed to improve on this. "Old times," he said.

When we all clinked our glasses Carole's gesture felt qualified, not far from withdrawn. As a waiter ladled soup into our bowls I said "How did the book launch go?"

"Plenty of arguments." I gathered Bobby welcomed this. "So long as they buy the book," she said, "but we always know half of them won't, don't we, Carole? Half's the target, which we nearly reached."

"Maybe if you hadn't given them your definition of a socialist..." Carole said.

"Someone who cares so much for other people," Bobby let me know, "that they want to spend other people's money on them."

Though I knew her journalism well enough for her views not to come as a shock, I was still prompted to ask "What does your father think of your book?"

"He's disowned me." She jerked her chin up in the gesture I remembered, and then laid a hand on Carole's wrist. "My mother nearly did," she said, "for the rest of who I am."

"We haven't, though," Jim said.

I could tell he would have liked to plant a hand on Bobby's, and for an ignominious moment I recalled spying on them in the cinema more than thirty years ago. That revived memories of Christian Noble, of his family and the secrets beneath his church. How long had it been since I'd thought of them? The memories seemed so remote they felt close to unreal, and just now they were no more than an intrusion. "I'm sure we never will," I said.

None of us spoke while we finished the soup, but as the waiter bore the bowls away in the tureen Bobby retrieved her capacious canvas bag from the floor and took out two copies of her book. "Here you are, both of you," she said with untypical awkwardness.

I was about to ask her to inscribe my copy when I saw she had, and more than that. *For Dom and Jim with love*, the dedication said, *we're still three.* "Bobby, thank you," I said, which Jim topped with "Thanks a lot, Bob." We both took her hands, and I was put in mind of a séance, which revived memories of Christian Noble once again. I squeezed her hand as the waiter brought a platter of dim sum. "Tuck in, boys," Bobby urged. "It's on us."

As we all set about it, she said "When are you going to bring a book out, Dom?"

"I'll leave that to the writer at the table. My family and lecturing, they're really all I have time for."

"I thought you'd end up writing. You inspired me to."

"You're one reason I joined the police," Jim told me, "the way you were always trying to make us investigate things and do good."

I was surprised and touched, but felt Bobby's partner was being left out. "What do you do, Carole?"

"Oh," Carole said with a trace of resentment, "I'm a journalist as well."

"Is that how you two met?"

"No." As if my suggestion were somehow improper she said "We met in the sort of bar we used to frequent."

I'd begun to wish Jim would have more to say for himself, but presumably he had while they were waiting for me. The arrival of the rest of the banquet gave me time to find a topic that seemed neutral, though perhaps I wanted to resolve an insistent memory. "Speaking of journalism, did you two hear what happened to Eric Wharton?"

Jim glanced up from spooning steak off a hot metal platter onto his bowl of rice. "Remind us, Dom."

"You read about it, then."

Bobby put Jim's blank look into words. "I think Jim's saying we don't know who he is."

"The columnist who exposed Christian Noble and his church."

"Oh, him." Before I could decide which of them she was dismissing, Bobby said "So what did happen to whatever you said his name was?"

"Eric Wharton. He drowned less than a year after he wrote that column."

With a hint of his profession Jim said "Are you saying there was foul play, Dom?"

"The coroner didn't think so. Accidental death, he said. Only some of the witnesses made it sound as if Wharton was trying to fight something off and that's why he fell overboard."

"Did any of them see anything?"

"Not that the reports said, but I don't need to tell you what I think."

"You might need to tell me," Carole said.

"Christian Noble used to teach at our school, Jim's and mine. They didn't know he was a spiritualist, well, rather more than that. He went in for raising the dead."

"Presumably you mean he believed he did."

"I think you'll find some people here do as well."

As Jim and Bobby exchanged glances Carole said "Are you seriously suggesting this journalist you mentioned was killed by a ghost?"

"Perhaps he thought one was after him," Bobby said. "Noble seemed to have a knack of getting inside people's heads."

"You know he did more than that," I protested. "Remember what you saw by the bridge that night in the fog."

"Dom, I told you at the time I wasn't sure if I saw anything."

"What was Bob supposed to have seen?" Carole said.

"Something Noble sent after me because I'd been watching his house." I felt reckless with wine and combative too. "It used to be his father," I declared.

I saw Carole refrain from uttering her first thought. "How old were you?" she asked her partner.

"We were all thirteen."

"I'd guess that explains it, then."

Bobby looked close to agreeing but reluctant on my behalf. "Explains what?" I demanded.

"Bob's told me how active your imagination was. Is still, I'm guessing. Perhaps you used to do what you say this Noble person did, put your fancies into other people's heads."

Carole was scrutinising me again, and now I realised that her watchfulness was concern for her partner. Even so, I was about to retort when Jim said "Dom, did you read about Wharton's death at the time?"

"I did, and I've still got all the clippings."

More like a policeman than I found appropriate Jim said "Why didn't you tell us then?"

"Because you both seemed to have lost interest." For a moment I was on the edge of revealing how I'd caught them in the cinema. "And all right," I said to preclude that, "I was nervous of saying."

"Why would you be nervous?" Carole said.

"Back then I thought talking about those things might bring them after me."

"You don't now." Before I could respond Carole said "Well, you were only thirteen. I suppose it was a kind of fun."

"You wouldn't say that if you knew what happened at the end."

"When someone wrecked his church, you mean," Bobby said, explaining to her partner "Noble had started a church he told people could bring back the dead."

"More than wrecked." Once I'd said this there was no point in not saying "I never told you two what happened."

"Why didn't you?" Jim said, which sounded only slightly less interrogative for adding "Dom."

"As Carole says, I was just a child. I'm afraid I was angry with you both for leaving me to deal with the Noble business by myself."

"You do seem to have kept a lot to yourself," Carole said.

"I did wish we'd done more, Dom." I was tempted to enquire at what point Bobby had started feeling that way, but she said "Are you going to tell us what happened, then?"

"You know I went to Noble's church while you two were at the cinema. I told you I went in the crypt, but I found more than I said. He was keeping plants down there, and herbs. His congregation brought them, you remember, and maybe he did too. Only—" Although taking a drink failed to help me decide how much it would be wise to say, perhaps it made me careless. "They weren't just vegetation any more," I said.

"What on earth can you mean by that?" Carole said.

I felt bound to laugh, though not to suggest I was joking. "They'd mutated somehow. They weren't species anyone would recognise."

"You didn't say you were a botanist."

"That'll be because I'm not one. I'm just a lecturer on cinema, but I think even you would have agreed with me if you'd been there." For Bobby's sake I tried to be less hostile as I said "They were worse than deformed, believe me. They were moving."

Carole met this with an unimpressed look. "Moving in what way?"

"Twisting their stems. Opening their flowers."

"Isn't that quite common? Plants like that are called carnivorous."

"And why would somebody keep anything like that under a church?"

"Perhaps he was more of a botanist than we are."

Even if she meant to make peace by associating me with her, I found her comment absurd and patronising. "You must have taken some away with you," Bobby said, "mustn't you, Dom?"

"I didn't. I destroyed the lot of them."

Jim looked disappointed, very possibly with me. "That doesn't sound like you, Dom. Why did you behave like that?"

"I was bringing one away when it tried to get hold of me. I knocked a table over and those plants started moving as well, and I'm afraid I lost it. Somebody had left an axe, and I chopped them all to bits."

As I did my best to forget how much of my disgust had related to Bobby and Jim, Carole said "So did anyone else see the evidence?"

Was this another sly gibe? "Not that I ever heard."

"I'm sorry we didn't come with you, Dom," Bobby said.

"Make that both of us," Jim said. "At least it's over with and long gone."

"If you think it is," I said.

Until that moment this hadn't occurred to me, at any rate for many years. "Why," Jim said, "have you heard any more about him?"

"No, but you know what he was like. Can you imagine him just giving up? Wherever he is, he'll be up to something."

"If anybody hears," Bobby said, "we should let the others know."

"At least his daughter will have grown up," Jim said.

"Yes," I said, "but there could be other children involved in whatever he's doing."

"I don't suppose that'll be against the law." All the same, Jim said "Keep me posted if he shows up anywhere."

"Does that exhaust the subject?" Carole hoped aloud.

Sensing that Jim and Bobby felt it should, I thought it best to let it go. I produced interested comments while Carole described the series she was writing about homophobia in various ethnic communities and assorted workplaces. "My publishers say it'll make a book as well," Bobby said with pride. Though I'd done my best to leave Carole in the spotlight, when we all left the restaurant I felt compelled to say "Sorry if I let an old obsession take over."

"Better caring too much," Carole said, "than not enough," and clasped Bobby's hand.

"I expect it was too much," I said, and just then I believed that Christian Noble was no longer our concern. I suppose that was a kind of faith. I might as well have put my trust in the neon signs that lit up the streets – in imagining they had done away with the infinite darkness that surrounded us, when they couldn't even hold it back.

CHAPTER TWO

Shaped by the Snow

As I let myself into the hotel room a crimson shard glared at me out of the dark. I groped for the switches on the wall of the unfamiliar room, and when I managed to turn on a lamp above the bed around the corner of the vestibule I wondered if I'd extinguished the red light somehow. It took me several drunken moments to grasp that I could still see its enfeebled image in the dressing-table mirror. The light belonged to the bedside phone, showing that someone had left me a message.

I dumped my luggage on the bed and dialled nine as a card beside the phone directed. I was hoping this would take me to the message, but a voice said "Operator."

"Yes, hello. You've got a message for me."

"One moment, sir. What room are you again?"

I almost asked him how he couldn't know. "Two one four," I still remember saying.

"Just a moment." After quite a few of those he said "Sorry, sir, no message."

"That can't be right. The message light's on."

"Someone must have tried to call you and rung off."

"Didn't you take the call, or whoever was doing your job? Can you tell me who was trying to get in touch?"

"We'll have noted the number if it wasn't withheld." I heard a faint sound just identifiable as the turning of a page. "The call was placed at ten past five this afternoon," he told me and read out my home number.

I thanked him and hung up but kept my hand on the receiver. Surely if Lesley's call had been important she would have left some message. Perhaps she'd simply wanted a quick chat when she would have assumed I'd just checked into the room, which I might have done except for the delayed train. Now it was well past midnight, and if I called back I was likely to disturb her and very possibly our son.

I let go of the phone at last and headed for the bathroom, where I reflected how unattainably luxurious en-suite facilities would have seemed to my parents in the years I'd gone on holiday with them. A shaving mirror on a metal arm magnified my doubts about the phone call until I pivoted it to face the ceiling. As soon as I switched off the bedside light I wondered if Lesley was lying awake, listening for sounds through the baby monitor that we'd kept by Toby's bed for most of the five years since his birth. I wakened several times in the hotel room, blinking to make sure the message light hadn't revived in the uncommunicative dark.

Sometime after four o'clock I fell thoroughly asleep, struggling into daylight to discover I'd been gone for almost five hours. I called Lesley at once, letting the phone ring longer than I hoped it would, until at last it brought her voice. "Lesley and Dominic Sheldrake," she said. "We must be busy just now but we want to hear from you if you aren't a cold call. Be sure and say who you are and leave us a message."

"It's Dominic. Just wondering why you called yesterday. I assume it wasn't anything crucial or you'd have said. If you were cut off you'd have called back, obviously, wouldn't you. If you're there now do pick up or I'll head for the train." I was saying all this at such length to give Lesley time to reach the phone, but she evidently wasn't there. "I'll be on my way, then," I said.

Rather than waste time breakfasting at the hotel – even using the bathroom felt like an undesirable delay – I caught a cab to Euston and sprinted to the Liverpool train. When the buffet car opened I bought a coffee and a sandwich, but not knowing what was happening at home pinched my appetite. I consigned half the sandwich to a bin, and as fields that shone with frost paraded past the carriage I did my best to occupy my mind with Bobby's book.

It developed the theme of economic addiction that she'd proposed in a notorious instalment of her column in the *Spectator*, where she'd compared people who demanded welfare to the children's character Burglar Bill, who declared "I'll have that" whenever he saw anything he wanted – Bills and Billettes, she called them. In *The Entitlement Trap* she argued that any positive effects of welfare were outweighed by the dependency it caused. From being grateful for a new or increased benefit recipients would progress to accepting and then expecting it, which led to feeling entitled to the support they hadn't previously enjoyed, followed by demanding it as a right because it had left them incapable of doing without it. Underlying Bobby's analysis was a sense that people had been tougher and readier to cope when we were growing up. She cited case after case as evidence of the contemporary trend, and despite my instincts I couldn't altogether disagree with her. I was more struck by how she'd changed since our schooldays. No doubt in my own way I had just as much. Of the three of us, Jim had come closest to living up to parental hopes.

A snowstorm met the train as it crossed the Mersey at Runcorn. Large loose flakes patted the windows, dwindling into delicate skeletons of ice. Along the cutting that led to the terminus, snow swooped through the gloom while moisture trickled darkly down the exposed rock that walled the train in. The platform at Lime Street was slippery with trodden snow, and so I couldn't even walk fast once I stepped down from the carriage. At least there were plenty of black taxis in the rank beneath the roof at the edge of the station. The driver of the foremost taxi raised his broad shaved head on not much of a neck to squint at me when I gave him my suburban address. The windscreen wipers started to repeat a squeak and a thump as the taxi veered out of the station, spraying the pavement with slush, and the driver said "Been somewhere?"

Presumably this was his way of asking where. "London," I said.

"Maggie's stronghold," he retorted, and with even more disfavour "She'll stay down there if she knows what's good for her, her and her mob. She may have beat the miners but she'll find out she can't mess with Liverpool."

Elsewhere hundreds of coal miners had gone back to work, ending a prolonged strike, but the city council was confronting Mrs Thatcher's government over local rates. "I wouldn't like to guess what may happen," I said.

The driver scowled at me in the mirror as if I meant to hold the future back. "Any twat like her, they'll learn."

Was he including me among those in need of education? Keeping quiet didn't end the dialogue. As we sped past the Adelphi, where a bedraggled wedding party was disappearing in instalments through the revolving doors of the hotel, the driver said "Pity more miners weren't from round here. We've got no time for scabs."

I wondered how Bobby might have responded, but said only "I suppose the men who went back had families to support."

"Your mates in the union's your family too. Let them down and you'll end up like your gardeners."

While I had an inkling what he meant, I said "I'm not sure how they're mine."

"They worked round where you live, didn't they? And people round there made out they were right." As he sent the taxi uphill past St Luke's roofless church, where the unglazed windows showed snow falling inside the ruin that commemorated the blitz, he said "Serve them right for caring more about their precious orchids than their comrades. I'd have sentenced them to worse than mowing grass."

When six men at Harthill botanical gardens refused to join a strike in case the famous collection of orchids suffered, the stridently left-wing council demoted them to mowing verges and demolished all the greenhouses. I imagine Bobby would have been reminded of Chairman Mao's way of educating intellectuals; I was myself. "Don't you think history matters?" I was provoked to ask. "That collection of plants was begun before Victoria was born."

The driver made a noise like a preamble to spitting. "You reckon plants are worth more than people."

This silenced me, but not as he would have wanted. I was recalling Christian Noble's subterranean garden, where the growths were more and worse than plants. As I gazed out of the taxi the snow seemed to flock into my mind, overwhelming my thoughts. I hoped Toby was enjoying it, wherever he might be. That drove Noble out of my head and reminded me how anxious I was to be home.

On Princes Avenue the spiky Christ on the wall of a church was amassing a plump white crown. On Smithdown Road a double-decker bus had skidded against a parked van, and brake lights reddened falling snowflakes while indicators lent the pallid storm an orange pulse. Further on a gang of boys shied snowballs at the taxi and then scampered into the Mystery park. Where a four-way junction of main roads curled around a pair of roundabouts, the storm assailed the taxi from every side, and I wouldn't have believed a mass of white could turn an interior so dark. Snow clung to the windows while the taxi sped beneath the laden trees on Menlove Avenue, so that I had to sit forward and peer through the windscreen when we turned along Druidstone Road. The snowfall had shrunk to a glitter in the air. "Here, thanks," I said and had to call the first word louder.

The driver plainly regarded a tip as an entitlement that barely warranted thanks. As soon as I clambered out onto the chilly padded pavement he drove off, spattering the snow beside the kerb with dingy pockmarks. A snowy crust froze my fingers as I opened the front gate, etching an arc in the snow on the path, beside which Lesley's flowers had mutated into fat white shapes. I hitched up my bag while I dug keys out of my pocket, and was aiming at the latch when the stout pine door swung inwards, bringing me face to face with my father. "Get yourself inside," he urged, stepping back so fast he almost lost his balance. "We don't want you catching your death."

Nobody else was to be seen or heard – not along the hall, where Lesley had renewed the bunch of winter flowers in the vase on the slim table draped with Greek embroidery, or up the stripped pine stairs. I might have asked my father what he was doing in the house, but found a gentler question. "Where is everyone?"

"Where do you think they'd be?"

"I really don't know. That's why I'm asking."

"I thought you had more imagination, Dominic. Where would you be at Toby's age? He's out at the back with his mother in the snow."

I should have known, and only concern for Toby had led me towards imagining some unspecified disaster. I wiped my feet on the shaggy Welcome mat and hung my coat in the cloakroom. Having zipped myself into a hooded waterproof more suited to the weather, I was heading down the hall when I saw another reason to be worried. "Dad, what have you done to yourself?"

"It's nothing at all. Don't give it a thought." As he fingered the bruise on his forehead I glimpsed how he restrained a wince. "You've got your boy to care about," he said. "God looks after us old folk."

"You still need to take care. Will you tell me what happened?"

His thick lips grew wry while his eyes tried to look even sleepier.

"Came down a ladder too fast, that's all. Serve me right for working on a Sunday."

"Dad, if work needs doing at the house, pay someone or at least let me know and I'll help."

"I'm not incapable or you'd be putting me in a home." His resentment subsided at once. "I'm just trying to do jobs I should have done when your mother was alive," he said. "I knew she'd have liked them seen to, but she never was a one to nag."

"All the more reason for me to help if it's in her memory."

"You're a good lad," my father said, which made me feel absurdly young and threatened to revive memories I thought I'd left well behind. "Anyway," he said and stopped short of the kitchen as if we might want to keep the conversation private, "how was your friend?"

"I didn't just see Bobby. Jim was there as well." My father was making me feel defensive, unnecessary though it was. "She's changed a lot. I think you'd like her more in some ways," I said.

I meant her politics rather than her sexuality, but he gave me no time to explain. "I wasn't trying to pry, son," he said. "You told me to open your invite when it came to the house in case it was important."

"I didn't think you were prying." Just the same, I was quick to add "You can rely on Jim, though. He's a police inspector."

My father looked ready to be sad. "You mean you can't rely on her."

"To end up the way you'd expect, I was meaning. I trust them both. Let's see what Toby's making of the snow."

A snowy glow was turning the pine panels in the kitchen even paler. I rested my elbows on the aluminium sink below the extensive window and gazed down the long white garden at my wife and son. Toby had built a snowman or at any rate a snow figure, half a dozen large snowballs piled as high as his head, and now he was poking multicoloured lengths of Lego into the column, a pair of them into each ball like the legs of a caterpillar. "He's picked that up from you," my father said.

While I sensed he meant this as a compliment, I had to ask "What's that?"

"Your imagination, son. He's an original, though. Odds on some of that's from his mother."

I had time to read her expression before she noticed me. Her round humorous face, still a little plumper like the rest of her ever since she'd had our son, had regained the look I was so fond of, the start of a smile that encouraged students to speak up in her lectures but often conveyed a sexier meaning to me. I very much hoped her reason for it wasn't just the sight of Toby's activity, heartening though it was. I was heading for the back door when she saw me. A word to Toby made him swing around, kicking up snow with his bright green rubber boots. "Daddy," he cried. "Come and see what I've done."

I used to say he was composed of the best of us, which largely meant his mother – roundish face, high forehead, wide dark eyes, small slightly upturned nose, generous lips presently broadened by a smile. Just the dimple in his chin showed I'd been involved. "What is it, Toby?" I called as I tramped across the squeaky lawn. "It's an insect, yes?"

He looked a little hurt. "It's a thing that grows."

I gave Lesley a quick hug and kissed her nose, the bridge of which was slightly dented – a flaw I'd always loved, left by a childhood collision with a swing. "How does it do that, Toby?"

"It grows and comes out and flies away."

"You mean it turns into a butterfly," Lesley said.

He was apparently too preoccupied to agree. "Now I've got to make its face," he said, but as he stooped to his plastic box of Lego a wind brought a renewed snowfall swooping across the garden. It felt like icy knives, and Toby flinched. "It doesn't want me to," he protested.

"There's too much of it just now, son," my father called from the kitchen doorway. "You come in till it settles down. It'll still be there for you to play with." As we all took refuge in the house he said "You get changed right now, Toby. Maybe he should have a bath as well."

"It isn't bedtime, grandad."

"You could always try and have a nap," my father said and glanced at Lesley. "Don't let me interfere if you think I'm not being any help."

"Would you like a nap, Toby?" When he shook his head she told him "Just get changed as grandad says, then. Shall I come and dry your wet bits?"

Toby looked sufficiently insulted for someone twice his age. "I can."

"Hot chocolate when you come down, and is it coffee for everyone else?"

I felt as if too much of this was delaying my question. As soon as Toby left his boots by the back door and padded upstairs I asked Lesley "Why did you phone me and not leave a message?"

"I had a little bit of news, but then I thought I'd leave it for when you came home and I had more. I'd have told you if you'd been there, only if I'd left a message you'd have wanted to speak to me."

"I was stuck on a train for hours. So what's the news?"

"I think we've found somewhere they know what's wrong with Toby and can help him."

"Well, that's..." I was afraid to enthuse until I knew more. I hastened to leave Toby's boots and my shoes and coat in the cloakroom, returning to the kitchen almost faster than my breath. "Tell me all about it," I said.

"I was talking to a different paediatrician at the hospital. I only wish we'd met her sooner. She says his condition is beginning to be recognised but most doctors don't know anything about it or won't commit themselves. Well, we didn't need her to tell us about them."

"So you're saying she'll take him and do what?"

"Not Chris herself. She sent me to the only place that's dealing with it anywhere near us. There are dozens of children like Toby, Dominic, and this place has been helping them for years."

My enthusiasm had started to fall short of hers. "You're saying it takes that long."

"No, that's how long she says the syndrome has been recognised. Even now it's only alternative medicine that's found an answer."

"What alternative?"

"One to all the drugs they've been trying on him. I shouldn't have said medicine. They use therapy at Safe To Sleep, a kind of meditation."

"They're not Buddhists, are they?" my father said.

"I don't think they're any kind of religious organisation, Desmond."

"I was only going to say that if the little feller needs religion, we've got one of our own."

Did he mean the country or just the family? If it was the latter, he couldn't even include me. Rather than revive old arguments I asked Lesley "So when are we going to look at this place?"

"I did today, Dominic. Toby did too. We're both very much in favour."

"You couldn't have waited for me."

"They only see people in the mornings." With the faintest suggestion of a rebuke she said "Usually you'd have been here."

"Let's be fair," my father said. "He did say the trains let him down."

I could only wonder if he realised how little his intervention helped. "Do you think I should have a look too?" I said.

"Of course you should. We can go tomorrow if you like."

"That's Sunday," my father said.

"It won't be a problem. They're open at weekends, otherwise they couldn't take children who are at school."

Of course my father's veiled objection had concerned the Sabbath. I thought Lesley was trying to leave it behind as she said "Only, Dominic..." She glanced towards the hall as we heard Toby padding down the stairs, a sound not much less soft than snow. "Yes, what?" I said.

"You mustn't feel left out, but we've already enrolled Toby at Safe To Sleep."

"Who's we?" my father said.

"I'm certain it would have been both of us." This looked like an appeal addressed to me. "Chris's little boy goes there," Lesley said. "Chris says it's the only place she trusts to do what he needs."

Toby trotted into the kitchen. "Can I tell daddy where we went?"

"You tell it like you saw it, Toby," my father said. "Show the grownups how it's done."

Rather than acknowledge any reproach this contained, Lesley told our son "Here's your chocolate."

He took a hearty mouthful from his mug – it bore constellations from *The Sky at Night*, his favourite television programme – and wiped away a tan moustache before anyone could tell him. "Daddy," he said with equal vigour, "it's a great big house with lots of children in, and they all sleep in a giant room."

"A dormitory, would that be?" I asked Lesley. "Or a ward?"

"Not really either. Those weren't what it felt like."

"Mummy, I know how it felt. I could feel all the children being asleep."

"Just like I was saying, Dominic," my father said. "He's got your imagination."

"Toby," Lesley said, "I think I felt it too."

While I didn't know if this was a riposte to my father, he seemed to think so. "Do you say any prayers when you go to bed, son?" he said.

"I don't know any, grandad."

"I'll teach you some. That's if I'm allowed."

"Perhaps we oughtn't to confuse him," Lesley said, "when he's about to start a treatment."

"You think God would confuse him." When she gave him a saddened look in lieu of an argument in front of Toby, my father said "You just ask God to let you sleep in peace at night, Toby. Keep asking if you have to while you go to sleep."

As Lesley looked ready to abandon her reticence I risked saying "I shouldn't think that can do any harm."

"Harm, I should say not," my father said. "If you want to know what I think, maybe he's not getting the peace a child deserves because you haven't brought him up in the faith."

Our silence must have told my father that he'd gone too far. "Anyway, I'd better take myself off," he said. "I only came to see him playing in the snow."

I thought Lesley couldn't very well not say "Won't you stay for dinner, Desmond?"

He sniffed the air. "You mustn't think I'm being rude, but what are you having?"

"I've made Indian. There'll be plenty for everyone."

"I better hadn't or I'll never get a proper sleep." My father let his mouth fall open, signifying inspiration before he said "Do you think it could be anything the boy eats that's messing up his nights?"

"They've looked into his diet and it isn't that," Lesley said.

"Well, so long as he likes what you give him. I know you like that sort of thing, and films as well." My father seemed unable to stop talking, unless he was demonstrating his right to carry on. "One of the ones you rate was on telly this week," he said. "Sorry if I'm thick, but I didn't get it. Just a lot of sweaty characters wailing and jigging about and only talking English when it suited them."

"*The Music Room*," Lesley said before I could. "It's pretty contemplative even for the director."

"That's what you call meditation, is it?" my father said and turned to Toby. "You try doing what I told you, son."

The three of us followed him to the front door. For the moment the snow had stopped again, though not before it came close to filling in my footprints on the path. I saw my father stumble as he reached the gate, and I was lurching after him when he swung around, knocking lumps of snow onto the pavement. "Stay in the warm, Dominic," he said. "I'll be taking care."

"Can we drive you somewhere, Desmond?" Lesley called.

"Don't you go risking the roads, love. That's what the buses are for." Having managed to shut the gate despite all the snow it heaped up, my father said "I hope I'll see you soon."

"You don't need us to tell you you're welcome," Lesley said but went back to the kitchen while Toby and I watched my father make his painstaking way towards the main road, patting the soft helmets of parked cars. When a bend muffled the shrill crunch of snow beneath his feet, we withdrew into the house. "Is grandad all right on his own?" Toby said.

"He isn't really, is he?" I felt as if my words had laid a trap for me. "On his own," I said hastily. "He's got us and his friends."

I thought Toby was about to bring up his grandmother, but he made for the kitchen to retrieve his mug and gaze out of the window. "Let's make sure the snow is staying off," Lesley said, "and then you can finish your creation if you like."

"I won't today, mummy. I'll stay in like grandad said."

"That's sensible of you," Lesley said and glanced out at the unfinished figure. "Or have you had enough of building him?"

"It needs a face but I don't know what to put. I'll dream of one," Toby said, and now I realise I was so desperate for him to outgrow his condition that his willingness to dream sounded like a hint of hope.

CHAPTER THREE
The Sleeping Room

Overnight the snow ceased, and by Sunday morning the main roads had been cleared. "Lamp," Toby said as I drove through Liverpool. "Shops. Bus." He hadn't been so monosyllabic for years, but we were playing I Spy with him. The sights his little eye spied were more sophisticated, though little was hardly the word for his eyes. On the outskirts of the city the land grew flat, and by the time we'd passed through Maghull and Ormskirk fields of unbroken snow stretched to the horizon from both sides of the road. Except for the occasional trees as white and fat as clouds the utterly flat land matched its own silence for featurelessness, and I let myself think it felt like a promise of peace. The promise was for Toby, not for me.

I hadn't prayed for decades, but if I had then it would have been for our destination to be what he needed. We'd exhausted all the ways that ordinary medicine had tried to help him. I still remember Lesley's panic and mine when at just a few weeks old he'd suffered his first seizure. We'd found him lying face up in his cot, limbs limply splayed, eyes not quite closed but blank. As Lesley picked him up I couldn't even see him breathing, and when at last she felt his tiny chest move she could only struggle not to hug him too hard. Neither of us had the least idea what to do next, which we were admitting in voices that sounded stiff with distress when Toby gave a cry and came back to us.

Nocturnal seizures were a form of epilepsy, they told us at the hospital. While it was unusual for them to begin at such an early age, most children grew out of them within a few years, or they could be treated with various drugs. All of those were tried on Toby over the years, offering new hope that never lasted long. We grew to dread finding him in yet another seizure, flat on his back in the middle of the night, limbs outstretched as though they were reaching for familiarity, eyes slightly open but unaware of us. I couldn't count the nights we lost sleep waiting for the baby monitor to bring the sound that meant he'd gone, a prolonged gasp as if he was giving up his breath. How much of his sleep might these episodes have stolen? The possibility that he'd been misdiagnosed until now and could be cured was my and Lesley's most heartfelt wish.

I must have been thinking some of this as I drove through the simplified monochrome landscape. I was waiting for Lesley to tell me where to turn off the wide deserted road when Toby called "Mummy, aren't we there?"

A line of trees had only just appeared to our left ahead. In a couple of minutes I saw they marked one side of an avenue that led to a large sandstone building several hundred yards from the road. "I think you're right," Lesley said.

I wasn't sure until we reached the gateway, where the left-hand granite gatepost bore a discreet silver plaque etched with the words SAFE TO SLEEP. As the high iron gates swung inwards I noticed a camera perched on the right-hand post, its lens peering through a crust of snow. The drive between the trees was a stretch of slushy mud, which hissed beneath the wheels as the gates crept shut behind us. At the end of the drive, tyres had drawn a blurred gibbous circle in front of the extensive two-storey house, which was topped with extravagant chimneys. As I parked the Volvo alongside three cars and as many minibuses, a large woman in a dark suit opened the front door and stepped out beneath a pointed arch. "There's Doctor Phoebe," Toby cried.

She strode to the car as Lesley opened Toby's door. "Dr Sweet, this is Toby's father Dominic," Lesley said.

The woman took my hand and then closed her other hand around it. Everything about her was considerable – not just her buxom figure and big face framed by reddish curls but the personality she conveyed without saying a word. She seemed so maternal she might have been embracing all three of us, emotionally at any rate. "Dominic," she said, keeping hold of my hand as if she wanted to protect it from the chill that whitened her breath. "I've so looked forward to meeting you."

I felt a little overwhelmed. "At least I haven't kept you waiting long. Till yesterday you didn't know I existed."

"We want to get Toby's treatment started, don't we?" As I made to respond she said "And of course you want to learn about it for yourself before you say yes. Come with me and ask anything you like."

She let go with one hand so that Toby could take it, and then ushered us and Lesley up the steps to the stone porch. Beyond it a wide lobby was illuminated by a pair of windows full of sky above a massive oak staircase, which split in two at a half-landing and led up to a gallery over the entrance. Somewhere on the ground floor I heard a murmur that might have been several voices speaking in unison. "Will you see what we do here or talk to me first?" Phoebe Sweet said. "Ask me anything at all you want to know."

There was at least one question I needed to ask, and she let go of our hands as she led the way past the stairs to her office at the back of the house. Diplomas in psychology and medical certificates graced the walls on both sides of an ample desk, behind which French windows overlooked expansive grounds where the occasional bush was reshaped by snow. As Lesley and I sat opposite the doctor she said "What will you do while we're talking, Toby?"

He sent the view a hopeful look. "Can I make something in the snow?"

"Our other children might be sad if we let you while they're sleeping, do you think?"

"Would you like to go in the playroom again?" Lesley said.

"Can I read?"

"Certainly you can," the doctor said. "We've books in there for whatever age you are."

"I'm nearly five," Toby said with all the pride his years conferred.

He made for the next room as though he was perfectly at home, and Dr Sweet murmured "I meant whatever reading age."

"He's years ahead," Lesley said. "We've always read to him."

I still had to raise my question. "Dr Sweet, is this a private facility?"

"It's independent of the health service, if that's what you mean."

"I was wondering about the cost of the treatment."

"You were referred to us by the hospital, weren't you? In that case it's nothing at all."

"I could have told you that, Dominic."

I was feeling doubly apologetic when the doctor said "Am I sensing reservations, Mr Sheldrake?"

"I'm just surprised you can afford a place like this."

"It's owned by the parents of one of our children."

I was moved to observe "You mean that's how grateful they are."

"Rest assured we don't expect that kind of gratitude. Knowing we're doing what we set out to do is enough."

"But you've got to make a living like the rest of us," Lesley said.

"Some people make donations, but let me say again we don't expect them. We're provided for."

"So can I ask what the treatment is?" I said.

"I'll show you shortly. Let me tell you at the outset we don't believe in drugs, not to treat nocturnal absence."

"I haven't heard it called that before."

"I think you will if the condition becomes more widespread. Don't ask me why it has developed so recently, unless it went unobserved before, but I can assure you it's far more psychological than physiological."

"Lesley was saying you go in for meditation."

"There are elements of that, or similarities. I can assure you it's a fully developed technique that produces the results you're hoping for."

"You were telling me it's had peer approval," Lesley said.

"It has," the doctor said and stood up. "Shall we see how it's progressing?"

As we made for the lobby, Lesley told Toby "We're just going to show daddy the sleeping room."

He joined us so eagerly that he didn't even leave his book behind, a copy of *Peter Pan*. "I was reading about the boy who flies," he said.

"What kind of boy would you like to be?" Dr Sweet said.

"One who sleeps all night."

I felt urged to promise that he would, but I still wanted to see how the treatment worked. We followed Dr Sweet past the stairs and along a hall, where I didn't immediately understand why I was doing my best to mute my footsteps, as she appeared to be muting hers. The voices I'd heard earlier were quiet now, but there was more to the silence – I felt as though I was approaching a hush more profound than simple noiselessness. When Dr Sweet halted in front of a door I thought it looked heavy enough to break the silence, but she inched it open without a sound.

Beyond it was a room in which at least thirty children lay face up on mattresses, three ranks along the room with space for more. A tall man stood at the window at the far end, gazing out at the blanketed landscape. Dr Sweet gestured me forward without a word, and I tried to stay as quiet while I ventured over the threshold. The hush that closed around me felt like an absence of breath, and I found I couldn't take one until I saw that the children were breathing. Their chests rose and fell so nearly in unison that I thought they must be conscious of it, and then I saw that despite lying in a posture that was entirely too familiar, arms and legs splayed as if they were reaching for companionship, every child had their eyes closed. I took the oldest children to be at least eight years old, while the youngest was a toddler on a mattress by the window. At that distance I was just able to see the tiny regular movements of his chest, and I felt my own breaths start to fall in with their rhythm. I might have grown as peaceful as all the children looked if I hadn't been distracted by whispers in the corridor.

I turned to see Toby grimacing with the effort to keep his voice down. As Dr Sweet eased the door shut I made for him. "What is it, Toby?" I murmured.

"He was wanting to join the others," Lesley said.

"I wish you could have, Toby," Dr Sweet said and ushered us out of the corridor. "Only everyone has to start together, do you understand? Otherwise you might wake someone up, and that wouldn't be fair, would it?"

"I don't want to wake the baby," Toby said almost too low to be heard.

The idea kept him quiet all the way to the room full of toys and books. Once Lesley and I were in the office Dr Sweet said "What's your verdict, Mr Sheldrake?"

"Can you tell me why the children were lying like that?"

"They weren't having seizures, let me say at once. Part of the process is to train the body to associate that posture with sleep instead of seizures."

"And I don't know if we've asked you how long the treatment takes."

"Maybe a year, but it should taper off to one session a week. Don't worry," she said as I tried to conceal some disappointment, "I think you may find he likes coming back."

"The others do, you mean." When she agreed without speaking I said "Except the one who's too young to say."

"I believe he does as well. He's Chris's little one, the lady who sent you to us."

I think that convinced me – the idea that the paediatrician believed that her child could be helped at such a young age. "We can start Toby on Monday if you're agreeable," Dr Sweet said. "We'll just need to put you on the route for the bus to pick him up."

As soon as I looked into the next room Toby shut his book on a picture of a boy among the stars. "Am I coming for a sleep?"

I found myself wondering if he might have eavesdropped, with his ear against the wall, perhaps. I couldn't blame him if he had, since I'd listened in to conversations when I was more than twice his age. "You'll be starting next week," I said, and his face brightened so much that I had to share his gladness.

He replaced the book between Hans Andersen and the Grimms and looked out of the window, where the shadow of a vast cloud was gliding through the grounds, snagging on fattened bushes and odd humps in the snow. By now Lesley and the doctor had joined me. "Sorry you couldn't make a snowman, Toby," Dr Sweet said.

"Never mind, you haven't finished your creature at home," Lesley said. "Have you dreamed up a face for him?"

"I don't want to any more."

I couldn't tell whether he meant completing the snow figure or dreaming of its face. I'd forgotten his remark by the time I drove away from Safe To Sleep, but I remembered it that night as I shut his bedroom curtains. The day had brought a partial thaw to Liverpool, and the figure's pairs of plastic legs had drooped and slanted outwards, so that it looked poised to crawl towards the house and to deliver a many-limbed embrace. The head had partially melted before a freeze fixed it in a new shape, a concave lump with icicles hanging from the forehead, a mass of translucent tendrils that veiled the hollow where a face should be. I remember feeling disconcerted that the weather should reshape it so oddly, and I had to make myself concentrate on reading Toby the tale of the emperor's new clothes, which made him laugh and look wise. Soon he was asleep, and that night he slept as a young child should. I was able to believe that all might soon be well.

CHAPTER FOUR

A Face in the Dark

"Truly this was the son of Gawd."

Most of my students laughed at this, though I suspected some of them were simply indulging my impression of John Wayne, but Alisha said "Why is that funny, Dr Sheldrake?"

I had a sense that she was trying not to be offended. "Maybe just my imitation was."

"It's funny in the film," Jojo said. "He's about as good an actor as a rock."

"I think he shows some range in Ford and Hawks," I said. "Take a look at *She Wore a Yellow Ribbon* and *Red River*."

Jojo's dreadlocks wagged as he shook his head. "Do we have to for your course?"

"I'm just suggesting you might enjoy broadening your view of his work." When Jojo rolled his eyes I said "To return to *The Greatest Story Ever Told*, I've seen it suggested that shot is a gag."

"A joke about Jesus dying on the cross," Alisha said as if she hoped the suggestion was the joke.

"In the sense that Wayne gets just that shot and just that line. The director started out in comedy, I ought to mention. He worked with Laurel and Hardy to begin with."

"That's not the same as poking fun at Christ."

"I don't think George Stevens was doing that. Comedy needn't preclude seriousness, do you think? Think of the porter in *Macbeth*." When Alisha looked unpersuaded I said "I'm not saying Stevens had to be aware of the comic element. We saw how Melville made a Christian film he thought was atheistic."

In *Leon Morin, Prêtre* Emmanuelle Riva seeks instruction from Belmondo's priest because she lusts for him. Alisha had agreed with the general view that the film was inadvertently religious, but now she said "They're not the same at all."

I was about to talk about unintended themes in fiction when Katy said "Who says you can't send up religion?"

This provoked Brendan, who didn't usually contribute much to discussions. "Maybe the law should," he said while his face grew as red as mine used to in my youth.

"They've tried, but most people won't be told what they're allowed to think. Look how some places banned *Life of Brian* and everyone just went to see it in the next town."

"Dr Sheldrake," Jojo said, "are you going to say that's another religious film that wasn't meant to be one?"

"I think you could make that case if you tried."

Brendan's face turned redder still. "More like the most blasphemous film ever made."

"You can't have seen much Buñuel." Before I could interrupt Katy, having seen contention in her eyes, she said "At the end of *L'Age d'Or* Christ comes out of an orgy and then goes back to do something to a girl."

"I'll be steering clear of his stuff, then."

"Aren't we seeing one of his films, Dr Sheldrake?"

"Yes, *The Milky Way*." I thought it best to assure Brendan "The director himself said it was a religious film."

"That's the one where Christ heals the blind men," Katy said, "but they act as if they still can't see, so it's no use."

"Let's not spoil the film for anyone who hasn't seen it." This sounded feeble even to me, but I was hastening to head off any further provocation. "Let's get back to the film we've watched," I said. "I want to suggest that Nicholas Ray's life of Christ is in its way as radical as Pasolini's..."

I reminded them how naturalistically Ray filmed the Sermon on the Mount, tracking with Christ through the crowd. I directed their attention to the use of architectural space, and the portrayal of Judas as a revolutionary determined to persuade Christ to take political action, but the most that any of the students would concede was that *King of Kings* was relatively radical in terms of Hollywood. Perhaps Toby's bad night had drained my arguments of strength, along with me.

This was months before Lesley and I heard of Safe To Sleep, and we'd felt utterly helpless as we'd watched him in his seizure, his outstretched limbs so stiff that they reminded me of rigor mortis, his chest barely stirring, his eyes so nearly shut that we couldn't see into their darkness. Perhaps the lack of sleep had left me inattentive to my words as well, because later that week the vice-chancellor came to find me for a talk.

I'd been discussing Christ figures with my students: Brando in *On the Waterfront*, Michael Rennie in *The Day the Earth Stood Still*, Leonard Nimoy in *The Wrath of Khan*, though he wasn't resurrected until the next *Star Trek* film... In every case I'd had to argue against skepticism, even over Rennie's character, who descends to Earth and calls himself Carpenter, dying for the sake of humanity before being raised from the dead. By the end of the tutorial I'd begun to feel my convictions were a kind of faith. As I made for lunch I saw colleagues approaching across the campus. They caught sight of me only to veer away, and one turned her wave of greeting into a gesture of farewell. I'd observed such behaviour often enough at university functions – lecturers abruptly abandoning their colleagues – to know why. I hardly needed to look around to confirm that I'd been singled out by the vice-chancellor.

He looked vague yet determined, reminiscent of an oncoming cloud that heralded a storm. His hair was as grey as his expensive suit, but turning white above his lofty forehead. Mentally I always cast him as a minor Roman senator, one of those who utter just a line or two while major players dominate the scene. "Dominic," he said. "A word, if I may."

This was far less of a request than it insisted it was. "Of course, vice-chancellor."

"I find myself a little discomforted by the news from your department."

Nothing recent came to mind. The Tierney tragedy was years old: Rose had drowned in the river when she was about to have a child, and Bill – her fellow lecturer and husband – had left the faculty. "Which news might that be?" I said and felt as if the vice-chancellor's style were affecting my speech.

"Tiresome as students can be, and I appreciate they are..."

He appeared to be leaving the sentence for me to complete, which only made me parody his language. "Ah," I agreed, "students."

"Imagine my surprise upon learning that some of them feel discriminated against. That's really not the done thing these days, you know."

"Dear me." This sounded too much like him as well, and I did my best to revert to my own voice. "Where has that been happening?"

"It grieves me to have to cite your film course, Dominic."

I wasn't ready to admit I'd known it must be. "Who's supposed to have been discriminated against?"

"According to my information, some of the more religious of your students."

Another bout of watching over Toby until he returned to us in the middle of the night had left me irritably brittle. "Are you saying they're saying I did it?" I said.

"Such is my intelligence, I'm pained to say."

"I'd like to hear how. I'd like to hear it from them."

"I should prefer to avoid confrontation. You understand you would be required to answer to a committee in that case."

I saw that he wanted to forestall any further damage to the university's reputation. I might have insisted on vindicating my name, but Toby's condition was sapping my energy. "Perhaps you can tell me who made the allegations," I said.

"I regret they were made in the strictest confidence, otherwise they would not have been made at all."

"Am I at least allowed to know what was said?"

"I'm saddened that you feel the need to ask."

A pause let me grasp that he was awaiting my response. "Well," I said, "I have."

"I'm led to understand you mean to show a lampoon of Christ made by these Monty Bison people."

Despite the accusation, I had to spend time stifling mirth. "It isn't about Christ, vice-chancellor, and in any case I won't be showing it. It just came up in discussion."

"But you propose to show a film that equates Christ with the Marquis de Sade."

"I'm afraid someone was confused if they weren't deliberately misrepresenting what happened. I just wish I'd been there when all this was alleged." As a hint of distaste wrinkled his lips I said "That was another film that was mentioned in the discussion. I'll be using a different film by that director, a critique of religion."

"One might question whether his attitude qualifies him to criticise. And you'll forgive me, but if the students are confused I have to question what that says about communication." Before I could speak – the response felt like a jagged object I had to expel from my skull – he said "I believe you were also mocking a sentence associated with the Crucifixion."

"No, I was examining how one film represents it."

"And how would you say that benefits your students?"

"I'm encouraging them to look again at things they may have taken for granted. That's what criticism should do, make us take another look."

"I assume you're speaking of the Bible."

That made me sound like Christian Noble, and it resurrected memories I'd thought were safely buried. "No, I'm talking about films," I said. "We've just been looking at Christ figures in the cinema."

"Portrayals of the messiah, I assume you mean."

"Characters who share some of his qualities or his experience." When the vice-chancellor only gazed at me I said "Take Brando on the waterfront. Karl Malden's priest explicitly compares the treatment of the dockers to a crucifixion, and he insists Brando has to lead them unaided at the end even though he's injured and nearly falls more than once."

"I have seen the film." Apparently this conveyed his view of it. "You're offering a course that studies how films portray religion," he said and held up a hand to fend off any objection I might make. "That's how I interpret the description, and I fancy students and their parents would. May I urge you to adhere more closely to it? I shouldn't care to have to deal with any further complaints or to need to make it more official, Dominic."

My rage at being so curtly dismissed began to lessen as I crossed the campus, and by the time I made for home I'd started to rethink my choice of films. While I could certainly have argued the case for everything I'd planned to show, our trouble at home was exhausting enough. I even tried not to wonder which of my students had complained, since I couldn't be sure Brendan had. At the next session I did watch for any sign of a blush, but he and Alisha and the rest of them might almost have been auditioning to play saints in a film. By the time Toby started at Safe To Sleep I'd almost forgotten the incident, since whoever was responsible seemed to be satisfied. As long as the students found the substituted films and the way I taught them rewarding, I did as well.

I owed most of my optimism to Toby's progress. From the outset he looked forward to being collected by bus, which plainly made him feel grown up. The nursery school had agreed to release him two days a week, so that he spent three at Safe To Sleep and every Sunday with us. Phoebe Sweet said they might reduce his visits soon, since in the first month of his treatment he'd suffered just two seizures. Each of those felt like an interruption of our hopes, and when I came home one day in March – later than usual, because the students had so much to say about *The Seventh Seal* – I was afraid he'd had another. I could tell from Lesley's face that she had news I mightn't like. "Is it Toby?" I said.

"It's about him. Apparently he's been scaring some of the children at school."

"By doing what?"

"Telling them what they may see when they go to sleep."

I might have felt relieved, but found a question I didn't want to ask. "How long has he been doing that?"

"Supposedly for months, but they've only just told their parents."

This time I did give in to some relief. At least the situation had begun well before we'd enrolled him in Safe To Sleep, which meant the treatment wasn't to blame. "Do we know what he's been saying?"

"Something about a giant face that lives in the dark."

"Mummy, that's not what I said."

The protest came from beyond the kitchen door, which wasn't quite shut. I couldn't rebuke Toby when this reminded me how as a child I'd left my bedroom door ajar to eavesdrop. Lesley and I had been keeping our voices down, but now we went into the kitchen, where Toby was crayoning a picture on the top sheet of a pad – an image of a large house above which an elongated cloud was hovering. "What are you drawing, Toby?" I said.

"Me at Doctor Phoebe's house."

"You put yourself in later and just listen to us. What's all this about a face in the dark?"

"It wakes up when you go to sleep."

"I don't understand what you mean."

"It's like it's waiting for you to go to sleep so it can have your dreams to make a bit more of itself. It's made of millions of them and it's like those spiders we saw hatching out of a ball, all running over each other. It's all right," he said as if he was determined to reassure us, "I'm never scared."

"Well," Lesley said, "some of your friends at school are, so you mustn't make up things like that to tell them."

"Mummy, I didn't make it up."

"In that case," Lesley said as though she needed to hold someone responsible, "who did?"

"Maybe the face did. It must be able to do lots of things in your dreams. It's ever so much bigger than the sky."

"Toby, that doesn't make sense."

"You dreamed that, did you?" I suggested. "Dreams needn't make sense. They're only dreams."

"There's lots of things in mine. You saw one."

"You dreamed about something we all saw, you mean," Lesley said.

"No, mummy, I saw it in my sleep and then I tried to make it in the snow for you to see."

"Your snowman. It wasn't a man, though, was it? What would you call it, Toby?"

"I don't think they have names. They hatch inside stars and eat them up, and that's why stars go black. The creatures want to make it all dark because that's where they like to live."

"That's very imaginative, Toby. Have you told Doctor Phoebe about it?"

For the first time since the discussion had begun he looked uncertain. "Shouldn't I?"

"I'm saying you should. Tell her all about your dreams and see what she thinks, and ask her to let us know. Do you think you may be getting some of these ideas from the astronomy programme you watch? The gentleman on there was talking about black holes, wasn't he?"

"I don't think he knows about the creatures inside stars or he'd have said. They're lots bigger than our planet, so he'd have to notice."

"Then I wonder where you're getting all this from," Lesley said and stared at me.

I felt accused until I realised that she didn't quite intend that. Like my father, she assumed I'd passed my imagination down to our son. Toby's dreams weren't much like any I'd ever had, and so I didn't see why I should be blamed for them – and then, in a moment that seemed to bring a good deal into focus, I knew what they were like. "Toby," I said, "I won't be angry if you say yes, but have you been in my desk?"

CHAPTER FIVE

The Voice of the Book

"I hope Toby didn't read these," Lesley said.

"So long as they still make you laugh."

"I expect they always will," she said, demonstrating with a token chuckle at a verse.

"You needn't force it so long as they did."

This earned me a smile less studied than the laugh. "You know they did, Dominic," she said and returned the student magazine to the drawer of my desk.

It had brought us together when we were students. I'd seen her reading it in the campus bar and laughing so hard that I couldn't help hoping my contribution was responsible. When I told her I'd written the verses – *Little Memoranda for Churchgoers* – she'd had to catch her breath and wipe her eyes before she could inform me how reprehensible my doggerel was and how eager it made her to read more of my irreverence. I would never write any more, but just then I no longer minded having been summoned to the dean's office for a stern lecture about offending the sensibilities of the faithful. When I told Lesley about the interview she had to overcome her mirth again to let me know she thought the couplets offered perfectly sound advice that anybody visiting a church would do well to heed:

> *If in a church you cough or sneeze,*
> *Say "Thank you, God, for this disease."*
> *If in a church you need to pee,*
> *Just contemplate eternity.*
> *And if your bladder aches with piss,*
> *Say "Jesus suffered worse than this."*
> *If while at church you bulge with dung,*

Pray "Holy Ghost, provide a bung."
In church a trait you'll need to ditch
Is scratching any kind of itch.
If in a church you chance to fart,
You pierce your saviour through the heart.
Even the highest form of mass
Can't sanctify release of gas.
Communion needs you to squelch
The slightest tendency to belch.
Before the altar, eructation
Will simply hinder your salvation...

I suppose I was celebrating how my time at university had liberated me from the last of my religious indoctrination. All the same, although my parents often asked me when I was going to write something for publication, I never showed that to them. I hadn't even expected it to see print – I'd only shown it to one of the editors to learn if it amused anyone other than me. If it hadn't appeared I might never have met Lesley, or would a different future have achieved this somehow? I doubt that we were so important to any scheme of things. I still have the magazine and the memories it embodies, but now I recall Lesley frowning over my transcription of Christian Noble's journal once we were sure that Toby was asleep. "You did read this, didn't you?" I'd had to prompt him.

"You promised you wouldn't be angry."

"Toby, I'm not. Just don't go in my desk without asking, all right? There might be things in there you really shouldn't read until you're older."

"I won't do what I did again, daddy."

"That's a good boy," I'd said, rousing a memory I sent back into the dark.

I'd kept the exercise book shut while showing it to him. I might almost have been trying to trap the ideas it contained to ensure no more of them reached him. Now Lesley was leafing through it as she sat at her desk opposite mine in our workroom. "I think I've had enough of this," she said, having turned just a few pages. "I can't see how you knew Toby had been looking at it."

"You will." I hugged her shoulders while I found the first pages. "There," I said.

Once I glimpsed the face behind the sky, while the noonday sun blinded everyone about me to its galactic vastness... Lesley's shoulders moved as though she was inclined to shrug. "I suppose that's something like his dream."

"The other one he told us about is closer." I had to search through the book to find the passage, by which time I felt as if any number of phrases and occult references I'd glimpsed were massing inside my skull. "Don't you think?" I said.

Perhaps our future bides its time in that darkness where no light may exist; where worms composed of darkness span the vast black stars they consume, battening on the stellar substance to impel their awful transformation... "I see what you mean," Lesley said, "and I wish he hadn't read it. I almost wish he weren't so literate so young. I wonder how much more of it he may have read."

"We could always ask him."

"I'd rather he put it right out of his head. We certainly don't need to remind him." She closed her fingers around mine in order to shut the book. "Make sure it's hidden well away," she said.

As I replaced it in my desk and covered it with other items I remembered hiding the original in the classroom. Lesley's gaze told me that she wished I could lock the drawer. "When did you write that?" she said.

For a moment I was silenced by the prospect of having to explain so much. "I was thirteen, but—"

"How did you think all that up? Who were you trying to sound like?"

"It wasn't like that. It's something I copied down," I said and glanced towards Toby's room overhead. "Let's talk where we're sure he can't hear us."

In the kitchen I poured us each a large glass of Rioja and took a good deal more than a sip from mine. "You were saying you copied it," Lesley said as if she couldn't quite believe I had.

"Yes, from someone's journal. His name was Christian Noble. He taught at the school Jim and I went to, Holy Ghost Grammar."

"You copied a teacher's journal? How on earth—"

"Let me just tell you it was a Catholic school, but he became some kind of spiritualist and then took it a lot further. Some of that got him fired from our school."

"You sound as if you were in favour. I didn't think we went in for religious intolerance."

"I'm sure you wouldn't tolerate anyone who exploited vulnerable people and believe me, Christian Noble did. He set up his own church eventually, but someone must have seen through it, because they destroyed the entire place."

Lesley looked more concerned than I found appropriate. "Didn't you think that was going too far?"

"Someone with a column in the paper didn't think it was. I've still got the clipping in my desk."

"No need to show me. I thought that kind of thing was why we teach our students to scrutinise media. Uncritical consumption, you used to say that was a good name for a disease."

"I still say so, but you didn't much like what you read of Noble's journal, did you? You may have noticed he kept addressing it to Tina. She was his daughter, and back then she was just three years old."

"That hardly means she was likely to have read it, though."

"Maybe not, but I think she may have, or else he brought her up with those beliefs. I'm certain she knew about them from the way she used to talk."

"How do you know about his family, Dominic?"

"Because even though he'd been fired from our school I knew he'd still be up to his tricks. It wasn't only me who thought so. Jim and Bobby helped me keep an eye on him."

"And do they both still think the same?"

"Bobby wishes we'd done more at the time. And they'd both like to know what's become of Noble and his daughter."

"Your friend wishes you'd done more than destroy a church."

For a moment I felt found out and accused. "No," I said forcefully enough that Lesley blinked her eyes wider, "she'd have liked us to do more about the little girl."

"You couldn't have done much as children, could you?"

"That's why we told our parents, but they didn't want to interfere. I'd say that was the wrong sort of tolerance."

Lesley parted her lips sharply enough to mean it as a retort, but said "I still don't understand how you acquired the teacher's journal."

"His father hid it at the school. I copied it all down and then I handed it in, but they behaved as if I was in the wrong instead of Christian Noble and gave it back to him."

"His father." In case this wasn't enough of a question Lesley said "Why would his father do that?"

"I'm sure it was to protect his granddaughter. He brought the book to show the head but then he panicked in case he was caught doing it. He still did his best to persuade the head to deal with his son, though, especially that church of his."

"You're saying he did that in public even though he hid the book."

"No, they talked in the head's office." Now I couldn't very well not say "I listened in the corridor."

"You do seem to have been obsessed with your teacher, Dominic."

"You might have been if you'd seen how his father acted. He got himself run over while he was trying to find someone who'd stop his son."

"How do you know he was doing that?"

"Because he was chasing me and Jim and Bobby to find out where we lived so he could talk to our parents, and we saw him fall under a tram."

"Oh, Dominic," Lesley said, reaching across the table to clasp my hand.

"How did that affect you all at that age?"

"I dreamt I saw him come back." The memory drove me to add "In bits."

"I'm not surprised." She squeezed my hand before withdrawing hers as if the memory might be contagious. "You don't still think about it, do you?" she murmured.

"Not for a long time. No reason now."

"That's right, so don't." While I could tell she would have liked this to be her final comment on the subject, Lesley said "There's one thing I think needs explaining. Why would your teacher use that kind of language in his journal? Surely it can't have been how he spoke."

"Nothing like. I think it was meant to sound like an ancestor."

"Why would he want that?"

"He was into calling up the dead. I told you he went beyond spiritualism. I think that was part of it, the voice of the book."

"You're saying that's what he believed. You aren't saying you do." When I shook my head, which went some way towards expelling any secret thoughts I had, Lesley said "So long as we've stopped Toby believing in that nonsense."

"I think I did, don't you? It's not as if he believes in Peter Pan or anything like that. I'm sure I convinced him the journal is the same kind of thing made up for adults." At that moment Christian Noble seemed as remote as the past, with any threat of his influence shut safely in my desk. "And he's promised not to scare his schoolmates any more," I said, but just for a moment I wondered if I was too anxious to reassure myself.

CHAPTER SIX

A Visit and a Game

That night I saw a man in rags fleeing through an urban wasteland. The miles of derelict houses looked not simply ruined but drained of colour and substance, as though the world had grown thin. Despite the devastation, the city was surrounded by trees that rose from the horizon, towering so high that their tops were lost in a pallid fleshy overcast too thick to be composed of clouds. Then the lanky crooked trunks stirred, revealing themselves to be quite unlike trees as a dozen of them raised their tips around the dead city to range across the roofs in search of their prey. The fugitive dodged into an empty church, where the vacant windows might have been arching their eyebrows to mock his desperation. Soon the limbs of the presence that had replaced the sky closed around the church and grew thinner with eagerness as they groped through the windows for their quarry. As he dashed shrieking out of the church, several filaments fastened on his skull and elevated him like an offering above the church until he withered, relinquishing all colour while his cries grew inhumanly shrill. The husk that the spidery clutch let fall was unable to die, and staggered twitching and emitting a pinched giggle through the lifeless streets as the fattened filaments withdrew to the horizon and the pallid mass that loured over the world quivered with some momentary form of repletion. It wasn't the first time I'd seen a victim perform such an involuntary mindless dance, and I had the dismaying idea that the spectacle was just a euphemism. In that case I was desperate not to experience the reality it veiled, and my plea came out as heartfelt as any prayer. It had less success at finding consonants, but I managed to utter enough of a noise to waken Lesley. "Don't wake Toby," she whispered in my ear. "What's wrong?"

"Juster dree." This was close to the thought I was struggling to have, but I needed the right words to convince myself. "Just a dream," I said with all the force I could summon up.

"Not so loud, Dominic. What were you dreaming, for heaven's sake?"

If I'd been more alert I might not have said "Something like Toby did."

"I hope you aren't starting as well. One's enough for us to deal with."

"I'm fine now I know where I am." Her dim face on the pillow next to mine looked less than wholly reassured by this, and so I kissed her forehead. "Don't even think of worrying about me," I said. "Let's catch up on our sleep."

I watched until her eyes closed, and once I was sure they were staying that way I shut mine. I managed not to open them while I did my utmost to drive the vision of the unnaturally inhabited sky and its prey back into the dark. I was able to tell myself it had been just a dream brought on by encountering Noble's journal once again, and couldn't the similar vision I'd had as a teenager have been a dream too, along with the malformed face I'd glimpsed on my pillow and the monstrous body it possessed? That memory left me too uneasy not to reassure myself that the face beside mine was Lesley's. The sight helped me regain sleep, and so did the thought that the derelict streets had been a version of the ones that used to surround Christian Noble's church.

In the morning I woke with a sense of a task left undone. It felt like a remnant of my dream, and nagged at my mind throughout the discussion I had with the students about Bergman's *Through a Glass Darkly*, a subject Katy raised. The vision of God as a spider seemed too reminiscent of my dream, even if it was just schizophrenic Harriet Andersson's delusion, eventually repudiated by her father's faith in God as love incarnate. Brendan and Alisha were determined not to see this coda as ambiguous. I did, but I let Katy argue the point, because I'd realised what the dream had left me anxious to learn. I wanted to know what occupied the site where the Trinity Church of the Spirit had been.

Ten minutes' drive from the university brought me to Edge Lane, the main road leading to the motorway out of Liverpool. In my teens Edge Lane and Kensington had bordered two sides of the blitzed district around the church. When I turned the car off Edge Lane I couldn't see a single ruined house, and might almost have imagined that my memories were false. Every few hundred yards the roads with shops embedded between houses were crossed by even narrower streets, terraces of dwellings that looked compressed by their neighbours, every one boasting a railed yard no wider than a coffin in front of a single-storey bay under a pair of windows each less than half its breadth. I could easily have fancied that the houses were huddling together to conceal a secret they mightn't even acknowledge, an impression that intensified as I saw the sign for Joseph Street ahead.

It was high on the side of a corner house that might have been designed to stay inconspicuous – a white pebble-dashed two-storey block with a window beside the sign. The front was featureless apart from a pair of meagre windows and a door that a plastic number rendered only slightly less anonymous. All three windows were obscured by cheap white plastic blinds shut tight, and I was reminded of the city drained of colour in my dream.

Terraces of cloned houses led both ways from the corner. No house had even a token front yard. The massed anonymity felt like a denial of the site the houses occupied, where the Trinity Church of the Spirit once stood. A dead cat lay beside the kerb in front of the corner house – run over, no doubt, but it put me in mind of a sacrifice. I halted opposite, because its condition looked worse than an accident could quite account for. I was climbing reluctantly out of the car when the front door of the corner house swung inwards and a woman squinted at me, blinking as if daylight were as unfamiliar as I was. "Are you from the council?" she called across the road.

She was a dumpy unkempt woman with a face dulled by pugnaciousness and framed by greyish curls that appeared to be unravelling. When she folded her arms hard to underline her purposeful expression it looked like a bid to do away with her already flattened breasts. I was about to claim to be a disinterested passer-by until I saw she might have given me a way to obtain information. "Why, madam?" I said.

"Are you here about the vermin?"

The word seemed too imprecise to let me risk saying more than "Vermin."

"That's what my man always called them." Some aspect of this made her angrier. "He's gone but they've not," she said.

By now I was on the pavement, and glimpsed moisture in her eyes before she rescinded it with a fierce blink. "I'm sorry, have you lost your husband?"

"Last year, and I'm blaming them. He wore his heart out trying to find them, and we got no help from the council." Even more defiantly she said "We were never wed, and I don't care who knows it now."

"I'm sorry," I said, only to realise that it came at least two of her remarks too late. I'd run out of useful ambiguities, and had to ask "By vermin, do you mean criminals?"

"I'm talking about the rats we've got under the house."

I found I'd wanted to hear nothing like that. "You've seen them," I hoped aloud.

"My man did, I'm sure of it. I think he was trying to tell me, but he'd had a stroke. Couldn't talk till he died or even write. Maybe he will." Before I could enquire into this, not that I was anxious to, she said "I'm still hearing them."

I was even less eager to learn "What do you hear?"

"Them crawling round down there and scuttling about and God knows what else you'd call it. I don't know how they've got the space to get up to all that. It isn't like there's a cellar," she said, and then her face grew duller with suspicion. "If you're from the council, where's your badge? You're asking a lot and not telling me a thing."

"I didn't say I was. With the council, I mean." I needed to discover more, and desperation suggested a ruse. "My relatives live up the road," I said. "You aren't alone with your problem."

"Have they seen the vermin?"

"I'm afraid not." I'd begun to feel as I used to when slyly deluding my parents. "I'm sure everyone who's heard them will be on your side," I said.

"Have they had the pest control in?" When I shook my head as vaguely as possible the woman said "We've had them twice. They're as much use as a nun in a brothel."

I saw that I wasn't expected to laugh. "Then I think you should all get in touch with your councillor."

"We've done that too. They're all too busy taking on the government, and they say we should be glad we've got a house."

"I'd keep after them and make sure everybody who's affected is involved. Are there many who are?"

She stretched her arms wide as if she were mimicking a crucifixion, indicating the terraces that adjoined her house. "Everyone along there," she said, "and down the side as well."

I was afraid she might ask the names of my imaginary relatives. In some haste I said "Perhaps you could get your councillor to find out what used to be under the houses."

Suppose this made someone dig too deep, historically or physically? I could hardly take back my advice, and so I turned away, to be confronted by the dead cat in the gutter. It looked worse than it had from across the road – eyes bulging nearly clear of the sockets, teeth bared in an agonised grimace, body twisted and legs drawn up in a convulsion that put me in mind of the death throes of a spider. "Has someone been using rat poison?" I said.

I had to look around when the woman didn't speak, though I found her silence rather more than ominous. "We never," she declared, and I was making to apologise when she said "That's how my man looked when he had his stroke."

My unease must have been obvious, because she held out her hands as though offering an invisible gift. "He's not like that now."

Despite my lack of faith, I very much hoped she would confirm "You mean he's gone to a better place."

"No, he's here with me. I feel he is."

I wouldn't have dared to ask how. I wanted to think her defiance was a means of fending off the threat of disbelief, not denying or ignoring any aspect of her experience. I profoundly hoped she wouldn't encounter any transformation of the sort that had driven Mrs Norris out of her mind. "So long as it's a comfort," I mumbled, retreating to the car.

Before I was halfway home I'd managed to rationalise everything I'd heard and seen. I preferred to think the woman's sense that her partner had returned was just a consolatory fantasy, not least because I hadn't heard her start to talk when she'd withdrawn into the house. Why shouldn't the streets be infested with rats as she and her neighbours believed? Surely the state of the dead cat suggested they were right; it didn't prove anything else. I thought of telling Lesley that I'd visited Joseph Street, but even though I would have said I'd found nothing to worry about, I suspected that she would have felt I was still too obsessed. Since she didn't ask why I was a little later home than usual, I put the whole incident out of my mind.

I'd brought home an afternoon's worth of essays to mark – not a great many, but I liked to take my time. I would have dealt with them while Toby was at Safe To Sleep so that I had Sunday free for the family, but that Sunday he'd invited a friend round: Claudine, another of Phoebe Sweet's patients, who lived just a few miles away in Woolton. She was a slim long-legged redhead with large eyes in an otherwise small face that conveyed an impression of drowsy alertness. As I read the essays, where I was always happiest to find surprises – Katy thought the donkey Balthazar in Bresson's film was meant to show that all creatures had souls, Alisha suggested that its name evoked the member of the magi who became ruler of Damascus after visiting Christ in the manger and defeated Herod in battle, Brendan maintained that the animal was supposed to recall the donkey Christ rode into Jerusalem and to embody Christ's humility in its purest state – I heard the children playing in the garden. Their voices seemed as bright as the clear blue April sky and the birdsong that ornamented tree after tree in the suburb. I heard cries of "No peeking" and "You're it" and "Can't catch me" like childish annotations of the material I was reading. They fell short of distracting me until a new game led to a minor argument, and Toby's protest was odd enough that I glanced up. "You bit off," I thought he'd said.

In a moment I grasped that he'd told Claudine "You be toff." Though I couldn't interpret this either, it reminded me how Bobby used to direct games with Jim and me, dictating our roles and actions. I turned my head towards the window in time to hear Claudine say "You're missed a blown, then."

This didn't seem to make much sense, even if I interpreted it as "You're Mr Blown." Were they borrowing characters from a children's book I didn't know? I eased my chair away from the desk and made for the window between Lesley's work area, where her analysis of *Under the Volcano* kept company with copies of the book she'd annotated, and mine. As I peered around one of the floor-length curtains I felt like a child in a game myself.

I almost made an inadvertent sound, because at first I thought Claudine had suffered a seizure. She was supine on the lawn with her limbs outstretched in the position I knew all too well. Toby stood about a foot behind her head, and I thought he was murmuring under his breath – in fact, both children were. As Toby began making an odd slow gesture that suggested he was raising a virtually weightless burden off his friend, Claudine widened her eyes. "You don't do that to toff."

"So you can't be him."

"I can if you'll be you."

I expected this to lead to further disagreement, but my son lay down readily enough, splaying all his limbs. He looked close to holding hands with Claudine, and I was unnerved by fancies their position brought to mind – that they were about to rise hand in hand into the sky, perhaps, though they could equally have been participating in a séance. I was trying to find the sight as peaceful as it surely ought to be, the children lying on the grass framed by rockeries and flowerbeds and shaded at the far corners by a pair of apple trees, when Claudine spoke. "Now we're going in the big dark."

She sounded younger than her age, and I could tell this was intentional. Toby closed his eyes as he said "Where the dead people grow."

"We won't turn funny cos we're still alive."

"We can just look and come back."

This time I didn't quite manage to stifle a noise, whatever word it might have aimed to be. The children rolled over in unison and raised their heads to gaze at me as though I'd wakened them from an afternoon nap. I unlatched the central pane and leaned out of the window. "What was all that about? What made you say those things?"

"I was talking how the baby talks," Claudine said.

"The baby in our game," Toby said. "We were only playing."

His eyes were as wide as Claudine's, and I wanted to think they were as uncomplicated as the cloudless sky, but I'd heard too much. "What game?"

"It hasn't got a name," Claudine said. "We were making it up."

I was distressed to feel they were competing to sound innocent. "Making what up, Claudine?"

"It's a story like you've got in your desk, daddy," Toby said.

"Then how does your friend know it?"

"I'm sorry," my son said and gazed towards the kitchen, which was next to the workroom. "I know I promised I wouldn't tell any more stories, mummy, but I told Claudine before I said."

I gripped the windowsill and leaned out to see Lesley at the kitchen window. "Lesley," I called, "have you been hearing all this?"

She was turning to me when the phone rang. I saw her prompting me to answer the one in the hall, though she was closer to the extension in the kitchen. When I kept hold of the sill she sent me a faint reproachful frown before stepping back. I waited until the phone finished ringing, and then I said "What did Toby tell you, Claudine?"

"His story like he said."

"I heard that, but which story? Can you tell me what it was about?" In a bid to hide the urgency of my concern I said "I'm just interested, that's all."

Both children opened their mouths. I could have thought they meant to answer in chorus, but they hadn't made a sound when behind me Lesley said "Dominic."

"In a moment," I said without turning. "I just want—"

"Dominic, it's your father."

"Ask him to wait. I shouldn't be too long." The children closed their mouths as if they'd been spared the interrogation, but I said "No, tell him I'll call him back."

"He isn't on the phone. It's about him." Lesley had lowered her voice, which made me turn at last to meet her anxious look. "He's had a fall," she said. "They've taken him to hospital."

CHAPTER SEVEN
Subterfuges

"There's some right miseries in here," my father told me. "And I don't just mean the ones in bed."

He looked determined not to be one of them. His right arm and leg were both hoisted up in plaster casts, like a supine mime of striding, but his broad big-nosed face seemed set on ignoring his condition, at least to the extent of maintaining a loose thick-lipped grin. His eyes were sleepier than ever, which I took for the effect of painkillers. "Dad," I said, "how did you do that to yourself?"

"Playing at Laurel and Hardy, son. Both of them rolled into one."

The best I could do by way of a smile was more like a wince, and he raised his free hand in a feeble sign of reassurance before letting it flop on the blanket. "Caught my leg in the ladder coming down," he said, "and did the arm trying to break my fall. Just them and a couple of cracked ribs. Like the medico says, it could have been a lot worse."

"Dad, I asked you to let me know if you needed help with jobs around the house."

"I wasn't having you come all that way just to help me change a damned lightbulb. When I end up that helpless, God forbid I ever will, you can stick me in a home."

"Surely you don't want to end up like this either."

"I'll be fine once I can have a fag. Maybe they'll let me have an ashtray till I can get to the smoking room."

His head wobbled up from the pillow as we heard an eruption of coughing somewhere along the corridor outside the ward. I hoped he might take this as a warning against cigarettes, but apparently this didn't occur to him. "Just so he doesn't keep that up all night," he muttered. "I've enough of a job getting off to sleep."

His head fell back as if he meant to give sleep an immediate try, and when he kept his vague gaze on me he might have been clinging to consciousness. "Anyway, never mind me," he said. "How's our little man been sleeping? How are they treating him at his new place?"

I had to pick my way among my thoughts before I could risk answering. "We've had fewer incidents since he started going there, in fact weeks with none."

"You don't look as pleased as you ought to, son."

I'd imagined my doubts were hidden. My mother might have sensed them, but I hadn't expected it of him. "I wouldn't mind knowing more about the treatment," I said.

"Is that all? Don't try fibbing to your old dad. I know my son too well."

I felt not just guilty but childish, especially when he winked at the horizontal audience in the nearby beds. Having searched for a truth I could tell him, I said "I'd just like to watch a session."

"Then you go and do it, son. You're the boy's dad."

"They say having parents there distracts the children from the treatment."

"Can't you watch without them seeing? The powers that run things ought to be able to fix that." He levered up his head with his free hand to scrutinise my face. "Are you having second thoughts," he said, "about this Buddhist thing of theirs?"

"Lesley told you they weren't Buddhists." For a moment I was on the brink of saying more than "I'm not sure what they do."

"You don't think they're Christian, I'm betting."

"I've no reason to believe it."

This might have sounded like a sly admission, but my father's head sank back. "Better see they haven't brought it from abroad," he mumbled. "I know you and Lesley like the flicks and the food, but just don't go like the Beatles did, getting brainwashed with foreign beliefs."

"I'm sure that won't happen."

"I know I can trust you after me and Mary brought you up right. You'd never betray your mother's memory." As I nodded, not least to hide my face from him, he said "Just don't go letting your wife talk you round."

"I've absolutely no reason to think she would."

"I'm telling you, it's like a foreign country round here." He seemed scarcely to have heard me, and I thought drugs were involved in his speech. "It's nothing like it was when you were born," he complained. "I swear to God, I've seen more coloureds since they brought me in here than you ever see in town."

"Dad, I don't think you should—"

"Don't worry." Since he was unable to lift his head, he raised his voice. "Everyone along here agrees about the blackies," he said. "They're doing a good job for us, but they shouldn't be here when we've got millions out of work."

I felt as though he was driving me away from any observations I might have wanted to make about Safe To Sleep. I don't know how I would have enticed him away from his subject if a woman hadn't said behind me "Mr Sheldrake."

I heard she was Jamaican before I turned around, and blushed on my father's behalf. "The patient needs his rest now," the nurse said.

"Come again when you can. Bring the family if they want to visit an old cripple. It'll do me good to see some familiar faces." A car with its radio turned up to thunderous sped past outside the windows at the far end of the ward, and as the bass thumps moved on my father said "Sounds like the natives are restless."

I felt my face grow hotter as I held the door out of the ward open for the nurse. Once we reached the corridor I murmured "Truly sorry about that."

"Not your fault, Mr Sheldrake. We shouldn't argue with a parent." As I left her a sympathetic look she said "He's not the worst in here by a mile."

I might have stayed to express more regrets – even though I wasn't implicated, I felt pitifully apologetic – but I had matters to resolve elsewhere. I drove home as fast as I could, trying not to be distracted by thoughts of my father or concerns I hadn't yet dared to define. I was in sight of the house when I saw Claudine's mother's car emerging from the drive. I hit the horn and waved and put on speed, all of which Judith appeared to take as a greeting followed by a farewell. She swung her car away from mine before she returned the wave without looking back, and I saw Claudine watch me dwindle in the mirror.

As I parked the Volvo next to Lesley's Victor on the gravel in front of the house, Toby ran to me. "Has grandad gone to grandma?" he cried.

"Of course not, Toby." I climbed out before adding "He fell and hurt himself, that's all. It just shows you have to be careful however old you are. You'll see him again soon."

"I know, daddy." As he dodged past Lesley into the house Toby said "Maybe we always will."

I might have asked how he meant that, but Lesley was waiting to speak. "It isn't too serious, then."

"Any fall like that is at his age," I said for only her to hear. "He won't be going anywhere for a while."

"So long as he's in good hands," Lesley said and stroked my arm. "I thought you seemed a bit distraught. You looked as if you were about to run into Judith's car."

"I just wanted a few words with her about Safe To Sleep." I heard the kitchen door shut as Toby went into the garden. "I'd have asked if she's seen them carry out the treatments," I said.

"But we have." Lesley looked as though she hoped to be no worse than puzzled as she said "I have twice."

"We've just seen the children asleep, haven't we? We don't know how it's done."

"We know Phoebe Sweet and her people don't use drugs. What do you actually want to find out, Dominic? Aren't you happy with the results? I am."

"You know I want whatever's best for Toby. Why should anyone mind if we watch? As my father says, we're the parents."

"You've been discussing Toby's treatment with him."

"He asked after Toby. I couldn't very well not talk about it, could I? I did try not to let him realise I had doubts."

"I hope he won't try to put us off the treatment." When I failed to offer more than the space between my hands, Lesley said "What doubts?"

"I've already told you, Lesley. I'd like to watch a session and see exactly what goes on."

"Suppose your being there stops them from sleeping? Suppose it makes them associate sleeping with being watched?" Before I could question why it should, Lesley said "And what's made you so concerned all of a sudden? Has it something to do with the game Toby and Claudine were playing?"

I thought it unwise to risk a direct answer. "Did they say anything about it while I wasn't here?"

"No, and I didn't ask them. I think you quite upset them with all that interrogation, Dominic."

"But how much did you hear? Did you catch what they were saying about the dead?"

"I heard nothing of the kind. Are you really certain they were talking about that?" She gave me no chance to answer. "And if they were, Toby said he was sorry. He did say he'd told Claudine a story before he promised us he wouldn't tell any more."

"So you think no harm's done."

"I hope not, but I think keeping on at him might cause some."

"I wasn't planning to." However much I might have wanted to question Toby, I couldn't now – not even, as I realised might have been a possibility, about Safe To Sleep. "We'll forget about it and let him do the same," I said.

I didn't know how much of an untruth this might be. Much of the rest of the day felt like one, since I was pretending not to have a plan. Before dinner we watched Rolf Harris daub paint on canvas to reveal the shape he was sketching, and Toby gave a happy gasp as the subject of the painting grew identifiable. Now I realise Harris might already have made his film that warned against paedophiles – it was released later that year – and I wish this were the only reason why these memories feel treacherous as quicksand. It was my turn to read to Toby in bed, and he joined in the tale of Thumbelina, insisting I continue when I gave way to his voice. As we read aloud together I had a sense that he was secretly amused. I was more at ease with the pleasure he took in Thumbelina's flight that saved her from marrying her subterranean suitor, the mole, though I couldn't tell why Toby gave an odd laugh when her diminutive prince was daunted by the enormousness of her saviour, the sparrow. Once the tale was done, Lesley came upstairs to say goodnight, and I took the opportunity to sneak into our bedroom.

That night Lesley slept long before I did, and Toby had been asleep for hours. My thoughts were keeping me awake, especially the fear that Lesley mightn't need the alarm to rouse her. In fact both of us were asleep when Toby came into the room. "Mummy, daddy, they're outside."

His urgency sounded not too far from panic. I'd grown insensible enough to leave most of my memories behind. "Whatoby?" I mumbled. "The children. They're waiting for me."

As Lesley opened her eyes I regained my sense of the situation. "I'll go," I told her and struggled out of bed.

From the window I saw a large white minibus parked across the end of the drive. It was as silent as it was unmarked, and I thought the driver might not have sounded the horn. Surely this just meant he didn't want to disturb our neighbours, but the unannounced presence felt ominous, as though it represented an assumption that we had no choice over yielding Toby up. I put on my bathrobe and slippers, which left my feet aching from the gravel by the time I reached the bus. "I'm sorry, we've overslept," I said.

The long-haired burly driver met this with an uncommunicative blink. Behind him half a dozen children of various ages were strapped into their seats, looking eager for some kind of release. "Do you have many more pickups to make?" I said.

"Six with yours," he said and swept a greying lock of hair behind his right ear.

"You go on and collect the rest. I'll bring my son in the car."

Another blink erased any trace of an expression from the driver's eyes. "I'm paid to get them all."

"Don't worry, I'll explain if it's necessary. My son won't be ready for a while, but he'll be there by the time you are."

The driver twitched his eyebrows in the facial equivalent of a shrug. "They won't let him in if he's late," he said and started the bus.

Returning to the house, I heard Toby in the bathroom. As Lesley looked out of the kitchen with a packet of cereal in her hand she said "Why did you turn off the alarm?"

"I picked up the clock in the night. I must have done it then by mistake."

Just the last two words weren't true. When Lesley gazed at me I was afraid she'd found them guilty, but she said "So have you asked the bus to wait?"

"The driver's on a schedule. I told him I'll take Toby." Without a pause I said "Could you look in at my department and ask someone to run *Diary of a Country Priest*?"

I felt more ashamed of putting her to trouble than of all the subterfuge, especially when she gave me a resigned smile. "Toby," she called up the stairs, "daddy will make sure you aren't late."

As I showered and dressed I heard her keep telling him not to rush his breakfast. I was less than halfway down the stairs when I saw him stand on tiptoe to unlatch the front door. Whenever we were held up on the roads through Liverpool, by tailbacks or traffic lights or behind parked lorries or at roadworks, I sensed his yearning to be reassured that we wouldn't be out of time. Sometimes he clasped his hands together in a gesture like a sketch of praying, or else his leg began to jitter up and down beside the gear lever. His anxiety seemed to crowd out mine, until I was close to regretting the plan I'd contrived on his behalf.

He grew more nervously impatient, gripping his legs as though to still their restlessness, once we left the outer towns behind. Beneath a slow plump whitish sky the open countryside let us see for miles ahead, but there was no sign of the bus. He lurched forward against his safety belt when the gates at Safe To Sleep hesitated over admitting us, and I was about to lean out of the car to show my face until the gates swung inwards. We were just a few yards along the avenue when I saw them creep shut in the mirror.

A few cars were parked in front of the expansive sandstone house, but no buses. As I halted the Volvo beside the cars, Phoebe Sweet opened the front door to wait at the top of the steps. Her broad maternal face looked concerned even before Toby ran to her. "Mr Sheldrake," she called while she patted Toby's head, "is there a problem?"

"They never woke me up," Toby protested.

She turned him by his shoulders to gaze into his face. "Who didn't, Toby? Careful, now."

I saw her steady him as he almost lost his footing on the steps. "Mummy and daddy," he said. "Their clock didn't work and I haven't got one."

"Don't worry even a titchy bit. You're the very first to arrive, so you should thank your dad."

Toby turned his head while she kept hold of his shoulders. "Thanks, dad."

He'd never called me that before, and I couldn't help feeling he'd matured more swiftly than I'd noticed. "So long as I'm some use," I said, a bid at a joke.

"I can't imagine anyone saying you weren't. Now come along, come in." She steered Toby into the house and then glanced back. "Both of you," she said, "of course."

I'd set foot on the bottom step when she swung around. "Just a moment, Toby," she called.

I wondered if she'd changed her mind about letting me in, and what I could have done to cause it. As she stood in front of the doorway I wasn't far from fancying that she'd grown as weighty as a statue, and just as immovable. I was opening my mouth, though I wasn't sure whether to call Toby or ask what was wrong, when I heard a car approaching up the avenue. "We'll just see who this is," Dr Sweet said.

As Toby reappeared a green Volkswagen emerged from the drive. I always thought the humped carapace of those cars resembled a shell more than the insect they were named for. When the car drew up beside mine Toby said "Daddy, it's Chris."

"She's the lady who referred you to us," Dr Sweet let me know.

I took the tall newcomer to be in her thirties. Her long smooth plumpish somewhat oval face was fringed by short soft black hair. "Chris," Dr Sweet said, "here's Toby's father."

"Mr Sheldrake." The woman strode up to me and held out a hand, searching my face with her large dark eyes. "At last," she said. "I've already met your wife."

Her hand was so cool it came close to chilling mine. "I'm glad to meet you finally," I said.

"Don't say it's final." She appeared to consider smiling as she released my hand. "You'll be glad I sent Toby here," she said.

I thought it best to silence any doubts just now. "I don't need to ask if you're happy with the treatment for your own child."

"Indeed you don't," she said as she returned to the car. "It's all I could have hoped for."

I wanted to believe that she had no reason to feel otherwise – that I'd let my imagination get the better of me, taking my concern for Toby close to paranoia. I watched her stoop to remove her toddler from the child seat in the car. As she bumped the door shut with her hip and made for the house without bothering to lock the vehicle, he gazed up from her arms. His face took after hers so much that I could have imagined that his large dark eyes were keen to share all the knowledge hers contained. When she climbed the steps I kept pace with her, having thought of several issues to raise so that I could stay close. "How young was he when you diagnosed him, if you don't mind the question?"

"Ask anything you'd like to know, Mr Sheldrake. He was hardly born. That's how it is with all of them."

"It was with Toby. I only wish we'd known you then." As she favoured me with a sidelong smile I said "Does the cure take longer if they start it when they're older, do you think?"

Dr Sweet glanced back from ushering my son across the lobby. "It's the same for all of them, Mr Sheldrake. Once they start they all progress together. That's another reason why it's so important to treat them as a group."

When she turned away I murmured "I think I'm being told off for making Toby miss the bus."

Chris widened her eyes, which remained as dark. "How did you do that?"

"Lesley and I overslept, I'm afraid."

"I don't think anyone should blame you. I'm sure you've lost plenty of sleep over your son."

"And you over yours, I imagine." Since she appeared to feel this needed no response, I said "Have you diagnosed many cases?"

"Quite a few in my time. I believe you've seen them."

I thought I must have misunderstood. "You don't mean all the children who come here."

"Yes, all of them. You've experienced what happens when someone else diagnoses your case."

"I wasn't criticising, I assure you." I found I didn't quite know what I'd meant, and looked away from her challenging gaze only to meet a miniature version. "That's an alert little chap you have there," I said.

"He's eager for the world."

"That's how children should be." We'd halted at the foot of the stairs, midway between Phoebe Sweet's office and the sleeping room, and I had a sense that everyone was waiting for me to leave, though surely not the babe in arms. I tried not to feel unreasonably persistent for asking "Why do you think all these cases have been developing so recently?"

"Maybe it has to do with how the world's changing. Or maybe they've been with us in the past and just not recognised for what they were."

"So what would they have been taken to be?"

Chris gazed at me as the child in her arms did, and I had the impression that she was in no hurry to answer. She was parting her lips when Toby cried "Here's the rest of us."

I heard an exhalation loud enough for a substantial chorus of breaths. It came from the doors of the bus that was braking at the near end of the avenue. The bus halted by the steps, and as the children made for the house I saw them trooping towards sleep. They looked so calm I could have fancied they were sleepwalking although awake. Surely this wasn't just inaccurate but absurd, since their eyes were wide and eager. Dr Sweet moved to the doorway, and Toby joined her as if to help her welcome visitors. "That's my dad," he kept saying with what I hoped was pride, or "There's my dad."

"Is he with Doctor Chris and Doctor Phoebe?" one of the older girls asked.

"No, he's just my dad. He had to bring me this once."

That didn't sound much like pride, and I felt faintly abashed as I followed everyone towards the sleeping room. Chris had gone ahead as if she and her child were leading the procession. "You all know where the toilet is," Dr Sweet said, "and then you'll be ready for the rest."

As children queued outside a room off the corridor I felt prompted to ask "The rest of what?"

"Ready to go for the rest we bring them, Mr Sheldrake."

I watched Chris lay the toddler down on a mattress by the window at the far end of the sleeping room and straighten up to gaze at him. I supposed I ought to be impressed by how he adopted the seizure position without being arranged or even told, but I found this unsettling in such a young child. As I tried to think of questions to ask, both women turned their eyes on me. "I'll see to settling Toby down," I said, "since I'm here."

I had to wait for him to leave the toilet, by which time quite a few children had given me rather more than a glance on their way to the sleeping room. Toby emphasised his with a wincing frown, which he renewed when I took his arm to help him lie on a mattress. "I'll be all right now, dad," he muttered.

I was embarrassed to embarrass him at his age. As Chris rejoined Phoebe Sweet in the corridor I followed her to murmur "Could I have a word?"

I expected them to realise I preferred the children not to hear, but they stayed outside the sleeping room. "What is it, Mr Sheldrake?" Dr Sweet said without lowering her voice.

She looked as immovable as she had at the top of the steps, and I could only speak lower still. "As long as I'm here, do you think I could watch this session? I'd really like to see how it works. I'll be absolutely unobtrusive, I promise."

I imagined only the women could hear until a boy lying close to the corridor protested "Toby's dad isn't staying, is he? We won't sleep."

I might have wondered if this was a plea or a defiant statement of intention. "You won't even know I'm here," I tried to assure him.

"We will," another boy cried, and a girl contributed "It's got to be just Dr Phoebe and them."

"Well, Mr Sheldrake," Phoebe Sweet said, "do you think you have your answer?"

As I tried to come up with a way to justify lingering I saw that almost every child was waiting for my response. Only the toddler had kept his face turned up, away from me. When I saw that Toby was no less anxious for me to leave than the others were, I gave in. "I'll see you when they bring you home," I told him.

"I'm sorry you were disappointed," Dr Sweet said. "I'm sure you understand."

"I'll see Mr Sheldrake out, Phoebe," Chris said.

I kept my reaction to myself until we reached the steps. "Forgive me, but how is it that you're staying if I can't? Is it because your son's so young?"

"No, Mr Sheldrake," the paediatrician said and let me see how deeply dark her eyes were. "Dr Sweet and I will be having a professional conference."

I wouldn't have imagined that my face was capable of growing hotter than it had when I'd embarrassed my son in front of all of them. "Sorry," I mumbled and headed for my car. As I climbed in she gave me a bow I hoped wasn't meant to be ironic, and then she returned to the house. My head was a jumble of thoughts and emotions, and my feeling that there was a thought I should have didn't help me think.

I was back in Liverpool and driving to the university when what I'd overlooked caught up with me. My whole body convulsed, and a thoughtless reaction made me stamp on the brake, very nearly causing traffic to pile up behind me. As irate drivers sped past me, blaring their horns, the clamour felt like a succession of alarms that were sounding in my head far too late.

CHAPTER EIGHT

Secret Names

"Could I speak to one of your paediatricians?"

"What's it concerning, please?"

Having failed to anticipate the question, I fumbled for an answer. "I'd like to make an appointment," I said.

"Is it concerning a child?"

"It would be." In case the woman on the switchboard recognised the sarcasm, I scrambled to add "My wife's and mine."

"Did you want to speak to anyone in particular?"

"I believe she calls herself Chris."

"Do you have a last name?"

I was afraid so, but didn't want to risk making a mistake. "Are more than one of them called that?"

"I don't think so." After a pause that might have represented thought or consultation the woman said "I expect you mean Chris Blone."

"Now you say it, that sounds very much like her." I was glad nobody could see my face as I said "I only heard the name once, and I couldn't be sure."

"I'll put you through." A silence made me hold my breath, only for her to say "Putting you through."

I sucked in another breath to hold and clenched my teeth. I was grinding them hard enough to hear as well as feel by the time a voice spoke. "Chris Blone. Please leave your number and I'll call you back as soon—"

This was all I heard before cutting her off. I hadn't realised how much I had been hoping to be wrong, but I couldn't mistake the voice. I took time to calm my breathing down, though not my thoughts, and then I dialled again. "Did you just try to connect me with Chris Blone? She isn't there."

"I didn't think she would be. You can leave a message."

"I'd rather speak to her personally." I had to tell the lie so as to ask "Would you know where she might be?"

"She'll be at another facility. She's there quite a lot of the time, but I'm afraid I can't give out the number." The operator might have been offering me a tacit apology by saying "It's to do with her own child."

I already knew which place that was. I thanked the operator and let the phone drop on the cradle. I'd been right in recognising how Chris had stooped to place her child on the mattress and bowed to me from the top of the steps, that snakelike trait that I'd originally encountered in her father. There was worse to confront, not least how Claudine had directed Toby to be Mr Blone when they were playing in the garden, a game surely based on the treatment at Safe To Sleep. I was dismayed not to have identified Chris sooner – her face ought to have been familiar, even if motherhood had lent it plumpness – and unnerved to wonder if she had recognised me. I ought to find out all I could before I told Lesley what I'd learned. I left my office so fast that I almost forgot my briefcase.

I did my best to look unstoppable, but as I came in sight of the car park I saw the vice-chancellor approaching along a transverse path. I stared straight ahead as though I'd located my car and put on speed as well, but he called "Dominic, a brief word if I may."

"Could it wait until tomorrow if it isn't urgent?" I was tempted to stride past before he reached the intersection. "I'm rather in a hurry to get home," I said.

"As I say, I'll be brief." He paused as if he'd finished, and stared at me until I came to a reluctant halt. "I assume," he said, "that you were amused by my gaffe."

Bewilderment made me wonder if I should be wary. "I don't think I knew you'd made one, vice-chancellor."

"It would tax me to believe that, Dominic. Imagine my surprise when I caused great hilarity by referring to the picture we discussed."

"I'm sorry, which picture was that?"

"Not a painting," he declared, though I hadn't meant to suggest it was. "Your specialty, Dominic. A film. It required some effort on my part to establish that the troupe who were responsible for it call themselves Monty Python."

I recalled his mistake now, and had to clench my face to keep it mirthless. "Isn't that what you called them?"

"I rather think you know the name I had for them."

"Vice-chancellor, I wasn't sure what you said and I didn't like to make an issue of it."

"You might have known that others would." The reprimand sounded almost wistful, and I was about to take it for a dismissal when he said "I gather you were elsewhere today when your students watched your film."

"I had to take my son to, to a place where they're supposed to be helping him." This roused all my ill-defined fears for him, which made me angry enough to demand "Who told you I wasn't there?"

"His mother."

"Then surely she'd have told you why."

"That was the case, yes. I simply wondered what was taking her to your department." As I attempted to decide whether he meant to defend Lesley or himself he said "She summarised the film for me. I gather it concerns a priest who achieves nothing of significance and then dies of cancer."

"Is that really how she put it?" When he gave the question a weary wordless look I said "It's a film about suffering and grace. Most accounts of it find it deeply religious."

"So long as you do." Apparently my nod was insufficient, because he said "Challenge your students and stimulate their thoughts by all means, but I don't believe we're here to undermine their faith."

My fears and my impatience to be home provoked me to speak before I had time to consider. "That depends what they have faith in."

"I hardly think that's up to us to judge. I rather suspect the student body might raise a protest if we did." Having weighted this with a stern look, he said "I see you're anxious to toddle off home, but I trust you'll keep my observations in mind."

I left all this behind as I hurried to my car. I was far more concerned about talking to Toby – so concerned that I was scarcely aware of driving home. I'd just about decided on a question to ask by the time I parked next to Lesley's car. I was letting myself into the house when the question deserted me as I heard Toby's voice.

He was telling somebody about a fall – as far as I could tell, about falling into infinite darkness. He was saying all of us at home would think he was brave – I had to assume this included my father – but wondered whether something would ever end. I didn't know if he meant the fall or some other reason for disquiet, because I could hear just enough to make me nervous. I eased the front door shut and stole across the hall to listen, but Toby had grown silent. I inched the door of the front room open without hearing any more, and couldn't keep quiet any longer. "Toby, what were you saying?"

"How long have you been listening out there, Dominic?" Lesley said with a sketchy laugh. "Don't you remember it from your childhood?"

For a moment I thought she was reminding me how I used to eavesdrop as a child, not least on Christian Noble's father and the headmaster. "Remember what?" I said and advanced into the room.

Lesley looked puzzled if not concerned, and I saw why. Toby had been reading to her the first of Alice's adventures, the fall down the rabbit hole. Was I so obsessed that I hadn't even realised he was talking about someone other than himself? I couldn't let this bother me when there was so much else that I needed to establish. "Well done, Toby. You were making it sound as if you weren't even reading," I said in the hope of placating them both.

"Shall I read to you as well now, daddy?"

"Let's leave it until later. I'd like to have a little talk."

Toby shut the book but held it on his lap, where it looked like impatience embodied. Lesley's reproachful blink made it clear that he wasn't alone in willing me to be concise. "Toby," I said, "what's the baby's name?"

"Which baby, daddy?"

"The one Chris brings to sleep with you all," I said and belatedly thought to ask Lesley "Do you know?"

"I've no idea. I don't believe I've ever heard his name."

"You mean you've never heard her call him anything."

"She says her little one, I think. Does it really matter?" As she saw I would say that it did Lesley shook her head at me or at herself. "No," she said as if she hoped to close the subject, "she calls him her little toff."

"Like the baby in your game with Claudine, Toby." I was finding it hard both to speak and to be careful of my words. "Toph short for Christopher."

"Is it, dad? We didn't know."

"No, but you knew what you were playing at, didn't you?" I had an unhappy sense that he was no less devious than dealing with Christian Noble had made me as a child. "Just tell your mother," I said.

"Why don't you tell me, Dominic, instead of—" Lesley suppressed whatever she preferred our son not to hear. "You tell me," she said.

"Your game was about the sleeping room, Toby, wasn't it?" When not even his silence denied it I said "What exactly do they do to you there? You haven't really told us."

"They help us have a sleep. Isn't that what you and mummy want?"

"You know we do. We're glad you can. I'm asking how they help."

"They say things like mummy used to sing when she was trying to get me to sleep."

"A lullaby, you mean. They say them or they sing them?"

"It's like both."

"What are they? Can you tell us some of them?"

"I don't know what kind of words they are. They're not like ones we say. They get inside your head and help you, like Dr Phoebe says."

"It sounds like a mantra to me, Dominic. I hope you don't object to that, even if your father would."

I might have retorted that she'd stopped taking care what our son heard, but I needed to keep up the questioning. "Who says them, Toby? Does Chris?"

"Dr Phoebe and the others do. You've seen them and mummy has."

This struck me as less than an answer, but before I could pursue it Lesley said "Dominic, I think that ought to be enough."

"Just bear with me a moment." As her gaze weighed on me I said "Toby, what do you dream when they put you to sleep?"

"We don't, daddy."

"You're saying you don't dream there at all."

"That's what he said, Dominic."

"How can you say the other children don't?" When he only added his gaze to his mother's I said "Then where did you get the things you and Claudine were saying in your game?"

"He's already admitted that, Dominic. From the book in your desk."

"Is that what you said, Toby?"

"I'm sorry," he said and turned his eyes from me to his mother. "I promised I wouldn't do it again."

Once more I felt cheated out of an answer, a trick in which Lesley was unwittingly complicit. "Now I'm certain that's enough," she said before I could speak. "Come and set the table for me, Toby." She followed him to the hall and then glanced back to say low but urgently "We need to talk."

I was at least as anxious to have a discussion, and so Toby's presence felt like a barrier between us at dinner and until he went to bed, where he insisted on reading Lewis Carroll to us. I couldn't help feeling uneasy when Alice changed size in her dream, even though she retained her shape. I heard how Toby relished the episode, but at last he nodded over the book. Once Lesley had eased it out of his hands we each left him a kiss on his smooth forehead. When we reached the downstairs hall I murmured "Shall we have a drink?"

"I just want a talk." Lesley carried the baby monitor into the front room and shut the door as soon as I was past it. "What do you think you're trying to do to Toby?" she demanded.

"I'm trying to establish the truth. I'm sure we both want that for him."

"What truth are you talking about, Dominic?"

I tried to ease her towards realising what I knew. "Have you noticed anything about Chris's name?"

"Just that it's a very common one, so I can't imagine what you—"

"Her last name."

"It's Blone," Lesley said and sat in the nearest armchair as if fatigue had overtaken her. "What do you think you can make of that, Dominic? Why are you bringing it up now?"

"I've only just discovered what it is. I didn't know until I rang the hospital."

"Don't hover over me like that. Sit down." When I did so opposite her Lesley said "You're telling me you called the hospital about her."

"Only to confirm her name. I didn't say anything about her."

"I'm glad of that at least, and I hope you won't even think of it." Lesley's gaze grew sadder as she said "Is this more of your obsession? I can't even see how it fits. Please just tell me what on earth you have in mind."

"Think about that name and I believe you'll understand."

"I'm thinking." Lesley tried to add a smile but couldn't keep it up. "I've thought," she said, "and I still have no idea."

I was unable to hold back any longer. "Lesley, she's Christian Noble's daughter."

On the far side of a pause that felt as though we were both holding our breath Lesley said "What makes you say that, Dominic?"

"I ought to have known her as soon as I saw her. She's put on weight since she's grown up, but I should have spotted the family trait."

"Which do you mean?"

"The way they come at you like snakes. Her father always did, and she used to when she wasn't even Toby's age."

"I still don't know what you could mean."

"Like this." I inclined my top half at her from the edge of the armchair, hoping that I didn't sense her determination not to flinch. "Maybe she doesn't do it as much as him," I said, "but believe me, it's there."

"And that was your excuse for interrogating Toby?"

"It was my reason for trying to get at the truth, but it wasn't the only one. Can't you see how she and I don't doubt her father have done their best to hide their names? Only at the same time they've tried to be clever. It's as if they're mocking the rest of us, challenging us to notice what they've done, except they think we can't because they believe they're superior to everybody else."

Lesley gazed at me as if willing me to finish. "Which names?"

"Her own for a start. I wouldn't have realised when I used to know her, but of course it has to be Christina. Her father always called her Tina. You might think he was trying to hide how much the name he gave her is like his."

"I wouldn't, no." Lesley held out a hand towards me, though not far enough to touch. "Dominic..."

"Not just her name, her son's. It must be Christopher, and yet they've done their best to make it sound nothing like." At once I had an insight too disturbing to keep to myself. "Didn't you read what Noble wrote about them?" I said. "She was his second person and there'd be a third. Now we can see he meant her child."

Lesley let her hand fall on her lap as though it had proved useless. "What are you trying to say he meant?"

"I'm not entirely sure, but it must be connected with that church of his. I need to find out where that's operating."

Her fingers on her lap drew inwards but stopped short of clenching. "Dominic, have you any reason whatsoever to believe he's involved in our lives?"

"We both have. You heard Claudine, remember."

"Heard her doing what?"

"Telling Toby who he had to be when they were playing." Since this only made her frown I had to say "He told her to be Toph and she wanted him to be Mr Blone."

"Are you absolutely certain?" Before I could answer she said "And I don't mean you should ask them."

"Aren't you? What do you think you heard if it wasn't that?"

"Nothing at all like it. I didn't hear anything until you started shouting at them."

I felt as if language was no longer to be trusted. "I promise you that's what they said."

"Can you honestly say you couldn't have misheard them?"

I thought this was a desperate suggestion, not least because desperate was how it made me feel. "Misheard what?"

"Couldn't Claudine have said Chris Blone?" When I didn't answer instantly Lesley said "But I'm telling you again, don't you dare to ask them."

If she'd shaken my confidence, it mostly held firm. "Just supposing she said that, it doesn't explain much, does it? How closely are you saying Chris is involved in Safe To Sleep?"

"As closely as she needs to be, I should think. She referred all their patients."

"More closely than that if she takes part in the treatment."

"Who's to say she does, Dominic? All we know is that Claudine may have put her in their little game, which I think you're making altogether too much of."

"We've seen Chris has something to hide. We need to know what she's hiding."

"You mustn't tell me what I've seen, and I think you're making too much of this business about names as well."

"How much do you think we should make of it when it's actually Noble?"

Lesley parted her lips without immediately speaking. "It isn't, Dominic."

"You know what I mean. The letters spell the name."

"But they don't. I suppose I can see where you got the idea." As if I required sympathy she said "You heard it on the phone but you haven't seen it written down, have you? It's bee ell oh ay en."

I was dismayed to think I'd tricked myself until I saw I had been. "That just proves how devious they are, don't you see? It's their old name twisted round but they can pretend it isn't."

Lesley looked as if she wished she needn't speak. "Dominic, I really think you need to do something about this obsession. Maybe you should start by destroying that book in your desk."

"It's evidence, and so's everything else that I've kept." Although I saw this left her less than happy, I had to go on. "I need to find out what the Nobles are up to," I said and tried to placate her. "If it turns out Chris isn't involved in anything we should know about, surely you'd like me to establish that."

"I don't believe you need to. If she really is who you say, maybe it isn't surprising that she changed her name when she grew up. Maybe it shows she doesn't want to be associated with her father or his beliefs."

"What about the things Claudine and Toby were saying in their game? Doesn't that show he's had some kind of influence?"

"That's already been explained. Toby found them in that wretched book of yours."

I was dismayed to realise that he hadn't quite said so — that perhaps he'd inherited deceitfulness rather than imagination from me. Before I could risk hinting at any of this, Lesley said "If you do anything that makes him worse I'll never forgive you, Dominic."

"I hope you wouldn't think I could."

"I hope I'll never have a reason." As she stood up she might have been leaning her gaze on me. "Now I will have that drink," she said.

I wanted to think she was right about me, even in her doubts — to think I was just obsessed with aspects of my past that were too remote to threaten us. In the kitchen I took a bottle of Chablis out of the refrigerator while Lesley planted a pair of wineglasses on the table with a solitary brittle clink, and then I tried not to scrutinise Toby's crayon drawings that were taped to the metal door. One showed a yellow crescent moon that resembled a claw poised to close on a star, and another depicted a comet with a rudimentary grin approaching a dwarfed planet Earth. Perhaps these derived from his favourite television programme, but the drawing that concerned me most was his view of the Safe To Sleep house. At the time he'd said he was putting himself in the picture, but I thought I'd interrupted him before he could. Now I didn't want to look too closely at the shape floating above the roof. Of course it was meant for a cloud, and Toby had done his best to draw the kind of vague shape it would take. Only someone obsessed would imagine it was supposed to have embryonic arms and, at the broader end of the pale elongated form, the beginnings of a face.

CHAPTER NINE

The Treatment

"Would you have a few minutes for a chat, Mr Sheldrake?"

"You be good for your teacher and I'll see you when you get home. Look for mummy when you come out of school." As Toby ran across the playground to Claudine, apparently the only other pupil who also went to Safe To Sleep, I said "What is it, Mrs Dixon?"

"Just about Toby. I suppose it can wait if you're in a rush."

She was a large-boned knobbly woman who always looked so earnestly concerned with the children that she had no time for taming her tousled hair. "I'm afraid I'm rather behind schedule," I said, "but if you can give me some idea of what it is..."

"Don't let me keep you if I'll make you late for work."

As patiently as I could manage I said "I'd like to hear."

"It's just about his stories, Mr Sheldrake."

"I'm sorry, I thought he'd stopped telling them." I glanced in his direction in case I could catch his eye, but he and Claudine were surrounded by children and had their backs to me. "What has he been saying now?" I said.

"Let me just assure you that as far as the school knows he's kept his promise. We've had no more complaints from parents." As I closed a hand around my sleeve to prevent myself from looking at my watch, Mrs Dixon said "I was meaning the stories he writes."

"I haven't seen those. I don't believe he's brought them home."

"That's what I was afraid of. I'm sure you must know he's an imaginative boy, a literate one as well. It's no wonder he's so far ahead in his writing."

"I'm happy to hear that, but you were saying you were afraid."

"Yes, that if he isn't taking his work home to show you and Mrs Sheldrake he may be destroying it."

I wasn't sure I wanted to learn "Why would he do that?"

"I suppose because he's been made to feel guilty about his imagination." If this was any kind of accusation, the truth was too complicated to address. "What are the stories about?" I said.

"Other worlds and that sort of thing. I expect it has to do with all these *Star Wars* films and the rest of them. They're not my taste, but I know children like them."

"Toby hasn't seen any. Mrs Dixon, are you saying his stories are like the ones he was telling the other children?"

"I should think so. I don't really know enough about sci-fi, isn't that what they call it, to judge. It's always dark, and it goes on for ever, and there are creatures living in it that you can't even measure. Not my sort of cup of tea at all."

I wanted to be gone, but I had to ask "Do any of his friends write stories like his?"

"I think he's one on his own, Mr Sheldrake."

No doubt this was intended as a compliment. "Not Claudine, for instance," I persisted.

"Certainly not her." Mrs Dixon glanced around and lowered her voice, so that I expected to hear worse than "She's years behind your Toby in her writing."

"I'll talk to him later. Thank you for alerting me," I said and hurried out of the shrilly clamorous schoolyard.

I couldn't delay any longer. I was already worried that I mightn't have enough time. This was one of the days when Lesley was the mother who collected Toby and Claudine from school and took them to her home, and my first chance to do what I was sure had to be done. As I drove out of the city I could have fancied that every hindrance I'd encountered while driving Toby to Safe To Sleep had grown worse – a set of traffic lights that scarcely turned green before reverting to red, a parked lorry the length of a block of shops, twice as many roadworks holding traffic up with temporary signals – and I fell to muttering if not snarling words that weren't yet in everyday use. I was on edge until I reached the open countryside, where the buses that picked the children up were nowhere to be seen. I was almost in sight of the Safe To Sleep house when I turned along a side road.

Spiky hedges several yards tall hid my car at once. I'd located the road on a map in the university library, and it would take me behind the house. I drove as fast as I dared, braking hard at bends, which were far more numerous and sharper than the map had shown. When the hedge on my right gave way to a stretch of aspen trees I drove onto the grass verge alongside and lowered the window. Between the silvery trunks I could see splinters of amber – sections of the distant sandstone house.

I climbed out onto the slippery unyielding verge to retrieve the binoculars I'd hidden in the boot. I almost hadn't realised I needed to buy a set yesterday on the way home. I tried not to make much noise in shutting the boot, despite how far away Safe To Sleep was, but the thud sounded no more muted than my pulse. I strapped the binoculars around my neck as I moved into the copse, and had the unwelcome irrelevant thought that the first time I'd read the word in my childhood I had taken it as saying corpse.

The grounds of Safe To Sleep were on the far side of a field beyond the trees. At least the grass in the field was almost as tall as me. It was less than a hundred yards away, and I hadn't expected it to be so hard to reach. Most of the gaps between trees were too narrow for me to squeeze through, and as I searched for a route to the field I could easily have fancied that the hindrance was deliberate. It didn't help that almost as soon as I entered the copse I'd begun to feel as if there were more trees at my back than I'd passed. Perhaps this was an effect of the gloom that the close growth produced, a closeness that seemed to have trapped a marshy chill among the clenched skeletal roots. By the time I'd struggled halfway through the copse I was wishing I had tried to breach the hedge instead. I felt not much better than lost in a maze, and so desperate to be out of it that I tried to force some of the thinner trees apart, which only dislodged chunks of bark undermined by lichen. I soon gave that up, because I didn't want to touch the pallid objects that squirmed out of the exposed timber. I was almost ready to turn back when I saw that the nearest the copse had to a path led away from the direction I was following and ended at the edge of the field. I dodged along it, almost tripping over roots that I hadn't thought were raised so high, and lurched out of the copse.

A chill breeze pursued me out of the trees, where leaves whispered in chorus and pallid catkins writhed like the parasites I'd uncovered beneath the bark. The house was in clear sight beyond the hedge across the field, and as I ducked it felt like being forced to imitate the Noble mannerism. Pale grass fat with seeds swayed around my face as I peered towards Safe To Sleep. I would have to cross the field with my head bowed if I didn't want to risk being seen.

In just a few paces I saw what lay under the grass: molehills everywhere I looked. I could only think the wind that made the heavy grass-blades grope at me was also causing the mounds to emit a noise I wasn't even certain I was hearing – a faint deep murmur that appeared to range here and there before closing around me once again. I hadn't realised moles left the tops of their mounds open, but presumably the wind across the holes was producing the phenomenon. I was more troubled by a sense that although I was out beneath the pale May sky, the gloom of the copse had stayed close at my back. No doubt keeping my head down helped cut off the already muffled sunlight. Every so often I strained my eyes up without lifting my head, hoping I hadn't much further to tramp through the oppressive vegetation – the swollen stalks that kept nodding closer, the smell that reminded me more of mould than grass, the omnipresent barely greenish pallor that made the field look like a faded representation of itself. I wasn't far beyond the middle of the field when I heard a distant but familiar noise – the engine of a minibus.

Despite the underlying murmur of the field I could tell that the bus was approaching Safe To Sleep. I did my best to sprint across the field, snapping grass-blades and dodging around mounds, while the binoculars dealt me thump upon insistent thump until I clutched them to my chest. Once I nearly tripped over a mound, which felt firmer than loose earth – more like a hummock in a marsh – and yet quivered with the impact. I thought I must have widened the hole in the mound, since the indistinct murmur seemed to converge, lending an unnatural voice to the grass that had grown restless all around me. For some moments the low ominous sound and the agitation of the grass kept pace with me as I made for Safe To Sleep.

The hedge bordering the grounds stood several feet higher than the grass. Well before reaching it I was able to raise my head. The twigs were even spikier than the hedges on the side road, and so black and glossy that they put me in mind of insects. They didn't bear a single leaf or any fruit or blossom, as if they were so thickly entangled that nothing other than the polished black claws could emerge. I heard the bus draw up beyond the house, and I was searching for a gap through which to spy on the proceedings when the doors of the bus opened with a gasp like an expression of relief.

That was all. I should have been hearing the chatter of children as they piled out of the vehicle, but I wasn't even sure I could hear feet on gravel. I was dismayed by how glad I felt that Toby wasn't among the abnormally muted children. As a distant gravelly whisper ceased I found a gap between the twigs, just large enough to make it worth pressing the binoculars against the hedge. While one lens showed me only a blurred spiky tangle of blackness, the other let me focus on the sleeping room.

Open curtains fringed the high wide windows. I was afraid someone might draw them, but perhaps leaving the room unconcealed meant nobody thought the activity could be seen. Children had begun to gather in the room, and I was twisting the screw to bring their faces into sharper focus when I glimpsed movement on the floor above. A man had stood up, and I saw his back as he left the upstairs room.

Whether he was the owner of the house or just a tenant, I wanted to know who he was. I concentrated on the upstairs window in case he returned, and was peripherally aware of how the children in the sleeping room disappeared as they lay down. The man hadn't reappeared by the time the last child took her place on a mattress, and I was waiting for him to show up when he came into the sleeping room.

He was tall and thin and greying, but I couldn't see his face. He had his back to me while he talked to Phoebe Sweet at the door. She closed it as he moved along the room, leaning down to speak to each of the hidden children. He was growing more recognisable as he advanced; his stoop was – that swift fluid stoop. He inclined his upper body towards the mattress by the window where I guessed the youngest child lay, and I remembered how he'd stooped to his daughter in her pram in the graveyard, exactly as he was bending towards his grandson.

I didn't realise how close I was pressing to the hedge until I saw and heard and felt thorns scrape the lenses of the binoculars. As I recoiled, Christian Noble straightened up. I was about to lower the binoculars in case any gleam on the glass alerted him to my presence when he moved down the room and sank out of sight with a deft lithe motion that looked positively reptilian. I guessed he'd lain down on a mattress, and now I saw Phoebe Sweet cross the room to lie down opposite him. They must be about to begin the Safe To Sleep treatment, and I wouldn't be able to see what they did unless I ventured closer to the house.

I'd already seen there was no way through the hedge I was at. Had I time to return to my car and search further? I'd no idea how long the session might last or how likely it was that anyone could trespass unobserved. I was straining my eyes in a last look through the binoculars, willing some activity to become visible, when I heard a new sound.

At first I wasn't sure if it was separate from the murmur that the wind was raising from the mounds of earth. Once I recognised that it was beyond the hedge I peered through the binoculars, but the sleeping room might have been deserted for all I could see. I let the binoculars drop and was disconcerted to find I hadn't noticed molehills lying low among the bushes that stood sentry in the grounds of Safe To Sleep. I thought they might be producing the unidentifiable sound until I realised I was hearing words, however faintly. I cupped my ears, leaning as close to the hedge as I could risk, and made out Christian Noble's voice.

It wasn't by itself. A woman was intoning words with him, and there was a third voice, higher but no smaller. I knew it must belong to Toph, which I found doubly unnerving – although the infant was audible, none of the other children were. He was speaking in absolute unison with the adults, repeating at least a dozen words over and over. I felt the repetition ought to let me make them out, especially the one the voices chanted loudest. I strained my ears until they ached and cupped my hands closer around them, and the word seemed to swell towards me out of the hypnotic repetitions. All at once it was far too familiar, because I'd heard Christian Noble shout it in the Trinity Church of the Spirit more than thirty years ago: Daoloth.

So he was teaching his grandson the faith just as he'd taught his daughter, and involving the other children as well – involving my son. The notion appalled me so much that it seemed to have left me unable to move. Now that I'd identified the name I heard it more clearly each time it recurred. It sounded as though it was rising out of the otherwise incomprehensible chant, and I could easily have fancied that it was reaching for me.

I found myself lifting the binoculars, which brought me the impression that the sleeping room had grown as uninhabited as a void. Of course I could see nothing of the sort, though I might have imagined the room had grown darker. I was trying to decide when I heard and felt thorns clawing at glass.

As I let the binoculars fall on my chest and retreated a step I was confused by thinking I hadn't been sufficiently close to the hedge for the thorns to reach. Or had I momentarily lost my balance? Certainly the ground felt as if it had shifted stealthily underfoot. No doubt this was vertigo brought on by straining my eyes too hard, and the writhing of the grass-blades all around me didn't help. They appeared to be groping for patterns at least as elaborate as the tangle of the hedge that bordered Safe To Sleep, and I was further distracted by the murmur of the mounds, a chorus that I could have thought was growing increasingly rhythmic. Surely the chant from the house was confusing me, since this was the rhythm that the murmur seemed to have adopted. I felt uneasy for more reasons than I cared to define, and thought I'd seen and heard enough.

I'd hardly set off across the field when the murmur ceased, isolating the chant at my back. The stillness around me felt unpleasantly watchful, as though I was observed not just from every side but from beneath. I couldn't avoid brushing against the swollen grass-blades, which made me feel as if seeds were gathering on my skin. The sensation suggested insects too, but I could see nothing there at all. As I struggled through the clinging grass the chant fell silent, and I wondered nervously what might be taking place at Safe To Sleep. The chant had lodged in my skull, and the unknown syllables together with the name I knew too well were still resounding in my mind when at last I reached the copse.

Perhaps the chant befuddled me, because I couldn't see the way back. I could almost have imagined that the trees had rearranged themselves since I'd used the path. I had to turn away from the direction I'd been certain was the right one, and even once I managed to slip between the trees I felt as if I were trapped in a maze far larger than the copse. The sight of my car parked beside the road only maddened me by looking close but feeling increasingly remote. A wind that I couldn't sense was enlivening the foliage, which responded with a whisper unnecessarily reminiscent of the kind of hush you might address to a child who was unable to sleep. As the dangling catkins writhed they might almost have been striving to imitate the insects I saw everywhere I looked, squirming out of the trees but remaining embedded as if rather than nesting in the timber they might be extensions of the material. I was desperate not to touch them, especially those that reared up towards me, revealing how transparently gelatinous they were, as I tried to sidle past the trees. When a bloated tendril found my cheek it felt like a cold dead tongue, somehow animated. The touch unbalanced me, and I fought my way through the trees, grabbing sections of the trunks where no activity was visible, hauling them apart so furiously that I felt them splinter. When I reached my car I spent minutes tearing grass out of the verge to wipe my hands, by which time all movements in the copse had ceased; even the grubs had withdrawn inside the trees. At last I was ready to drive, and had to remind myself where I was going – to visit my father in hospital and then to the university for my afternoon tutorial, not yet home. Just the same, the thought of Lesley made me realise that however much I'd learned today, it mightn't be enough to persuade her. I had to do something that would.

CHAPTER TEN

A Consultation

As Lesley came into the hall I said "I'm afraid my father's not so good."

She was only starting to respond when Toby followed her out of the kitchen with a crayon in his hand. "How bad is he, daddy?"

It wasn't just the question that dismayed me, it was my son's grin. I had the appalled notion that he might welcome my father's death for the same reason Christian Noble would. "How bad would you like him to be?"

His grin collapsed as if pierced by my sharpness. "I only meant has he been naughty."

"What else do you think he could mean, Dominic?"

"I'm sorry, Toby. I'm a bit worried, that's all." This was certainly true, though not the understatement. "You don't need to be," I assured him.

"Shall we talk about it later, then? Toby's got something to show you." Lesley steered me towards the kitchen without quite touching my arm. The table was arrayed with crayons, lined up in the order of the spectrum, though I couldn't recall when Toby had started arranging his crayons that way. He'd been filling in an enormous yellow full moon that hung above a row of spiky black trees. "He's illustrating his story," Lesley said.

A sheet of paper next to the picture was covered with his small handwriting, which had already earned him Mrs Dixon's praise for neatness. I read the first words and felt as though the breath I'd taken had lodged like an obstruction in my chest. *Once upon a time there lived a boy called To who could fly. Every night he flew past the moon and all our planets to play with the stars.* Before I could restrain myself I demanded "Why is he called that?"

"Why would he be, Dominic? What do you think it could be short for?"

Of course Lesley meant Toby. No doubt this was likelier than Toph, but I wished she had let Toby answer for himself. I read to the end – the boy To rode away on a comet, which carried him through galaxies and eventually into a black hole from which he emerged earlier than he'd begun his voyage across the universe, letting him return home for a full night's sleep to be ready for his parents when they came to waken him. "Very imaginative, Toby," I said, trying to mean no more than that. "It's better than I could have written at your age."

"Just finish off your moon," Lesley said, "and then we'll have dinner."

Both activities felt like postponements, and so did Toby's hour of approved television, not to mention his bath. I did my best not to wish away the book he read to us at bedtime, though I grew uneasy when Alice wondered if she'd been changed in the night and found herself compelled to recite mutated words: "How cheerfully he seems to grin, how neatly spreads his claws..." I had to grin as well, since Toby did. Lesley eased the book out of his hands once his eyes stayed closed, and we tiptoed down to the front room. "So how is Desmond?" Lesley said.

"He's caught a cough of some kind. I don't need to tell you he's blaming foreign bugs that he thinks immigrants have brought into the hospital." I sank into a chair as Lesley did. "I shouldn't mock him," I said. "It isn't helping his ribs."

"Have you been to see him?"

"Yes, of course. how else do you think I—" In a bid to save myself from the verbal stumble I said "I went this morning. That's why I wasn't there to run the film if anybody asks."

"Who's going to?"

"Well, the vee cee rather seems to think you're my keeper." Her disconcertingly searching look had provoked the comment, which I wished I'd kept to myself. "I expect my father will be fine," I said. "They've got him on antibiotics."

"That's one person cared for, then."

"Are you saying someone hasn't been?"

I hoped her question wasn't meant to incorporate an answer. "What did you think of Toby's story?"

"Just what I told him. I wouldn't like to think you don't trust what I say."

"I gather Mrs Dixon mentioned he'd destroyed his other work."

I hardly thought this was an answer, but said only "Let's try and see he doesn't destroy any more."

"I don't think I was responsible, Dominic. I think the way you kept on at him might have been." As I strove not to respond she said "If he has anything we don't like in his head, writing it down may help get rid of it."

"I'm all for that. The more he puts on paper the better."

"Perhaps we should ask Phoebe Sweet what she thinks."

"When do you want to go and see her?"

"No need for that. One of us can phone her."

I saw Lesley snatching back the chance to visit Safe To Sleep she'd inadvertently given us. "We can both talk to her on the phone," I said.

"She won't be at the house now, and I haven't got her number."

"Then we'll have to when she is and we're both free."

The delay aggravated my impatience, not least with myself. How could I have panicked when I ought to have continued watching Safe To Sleep? Had I really let myself be scared off by a few molehills or even a good many, and some rotten trees with insects in them? Perhaps the sight of Christian Noble had made me feel like the nervous child I'd once been, but that was no excuse. That night I could hardly sleep for guilt, not just about the pathetic trepidation that had cut my observations short but over using my father for a subterfuge. Though I'd visited him in hospital, it had mostly been to give me a reason not to have been present while today's film was shown, and I hadn't known in advance that he'd contracted an infection. I felt guiltiest for deluding Lesley – as reprehensible as I had when I'd started lying to my parents. Even hugging her in her sleep felt close to dishonest, especially since her body was so stiff I could have thought she didn't welcome my touch.

The call I made in the morning from the university was dishonest too. "Can you tell me when Chris Bloan will be at the hospital?"

"She isn't here yet, but she'll be in all day."

My deviousness was growing defter. Brother Treanor and quite a few of his staff would have called it devilish, and I suspected my father might have as well. "Remind me," I said, "her room is near one of the maternity units, yes?"

"It's just along the bottom corridor. Would you like to leave a message?"

"I'll need to check my schedule. I'll call back."

I meant to call, but not by phone. I was so anxious to be there that I had to struggle not to curtail that morning's discussion. Our theme was resurrection, and I was incautious enough to suggest that the miracle Joel McCrea's priest performed in *Stars in My Crown* – apparently raising his beloved from the dead – was handled with exactly the same sensitivity the director brought to voodoo in his earlier film I *Walked with a Zombie*. Alisha seemed not much less offended than Brendan, and when even Katy looked bemused I could only recommend them to track the other film down. "Never take for granted. Look for yourselves," I said. "You can't judge what you haven't seen."

Somebody who wasn't there might have retorted that I'd done so at Safe To Sleep, but I'd seen Christian Noble, which was enough. As soon as I'd dismissed the students I hurried to my car. While the hospital was close enough to walk to, I wanted to save all the time I could. I regretted the decision well before I found space in the visitors' car park, and once I had I sprinted into the hospital.

I'd readied an excuse in case anybody asked where I was going or why, but all the receptionists were busy with enquiries. As I strode along the ground-floor corridor I did my best to look purposeful rather than determined or worse, especially when I came face to face with a security officer. "First child," I told him, "a son," which apparently convinced him, perhaps because there was a room full of the newborn just ahead. He watched me come abreast of it, and I had to reassure myself that he might simply enjoy seeing my reaction to my supposedly new child. I was about to mime delight as I turned to the inner window of the room, but instead I lurched forward so abruptly that my forehead almost thumped the glass. Tina Noble was in the room.

She was pacing between two rows of cots with tiny infants in them. Although she had her back to me, I couldn't mistake that sinuous darting swoop she made towards each child. I didn't realise I'd clenched my fists until my hands began to ache. I managed to relax my fingers, and was wondering if I should dodge out of sight so as to catch her off guard when she bent more decisively towards a cot in the middle of the room. Her hands were clasped behind her, which I found suggestive of reptilian limblessness, but now she extended them above the cot and began to gesture in the air.

It could almost have been some form of blessing, at least to begin with, though I was put in mind of actions a magician might perform. Having passed her hands back and forth across each other in an increasingly rapid repetition that appeared to set her fingers quivering with eagerness, she cupped them gradually upwards as though pointing at if not beyond the sky. They could have represented flames or the tendrils of a carnivorous plant; they might have signified the energy they were drawing from a source, unless they were demonstrating their voraciousness. I found I couldn't move until I knew where I'd seen some coaxing gesture of the kind, and then I remembered how Toby had raised his hands over Claudine on the lawn. Was I hearing Tina Noble's voice, faintly through the glass or in my head? It felt as though her actions were rousing syllables in my skull, just three of them. If I opened the door of the room I should be able to hear anything she said. I'd managed to wrench myself out of my paralysis, which her gestures had produced somehow, when I noticed that the security man was still watching me along the corridor. "What's she doing in there?" I blurted. "Quick, look."

His slowness might have been rebuking my impatience or representing officialdom. "Quick," I pleaded as Tina Noble mimed twisting or tying up an invisible item, if not both. "Did you see?"

He didn't answer until I looked at him. His impassive flattened face might have been counselling calm. "That's Dr Bloan," he said.

"I know exactly who she is. I want to know what she was up to."

"She looks after the young ones. She'll be checking up on them."

I followed his gaze and saw Tina Noble moving down a row of cots, consulting the chart at the foot of each one. "She wasn't doing that before. Didn't you see anything she did?"

"What are you asking about, sir?"

Though the last word sounded like a gentle warning, I wasn't about to be daunted. "It looked as if she was performing some kind of ritual. You must have seen what she was doing with her hands."

"I think I did," he said and stared at me as if I ought to know what was coming. "I believe she was saying a prayer. Don't you have any time for it yourself?"

"It depends what you mean by religion." I might have added more if not too much, but just then Tina Noble turned and saw me at once. Her eyes widened, and so did her mouth in a gradual smile. However much this looked like pleased surprise and a greeting, I took it for a challenge. I kept my eyes on her as she crossed the room and eased the door shut without a sound. "Mr Sheldrake," she said, "or is it Dr like your wife? What brings you here today?"

"Is he saying he's a doctor, Dr Bloan?"

"He teaches at the university, Otis. I didn't mean he's claiming to be one of us."

"He wanted to know why you were in there. I tried to tell him."

"I expect you said I was attending to the children's welfare."

"Maybe praying for them too."

"Why, Otis, I thought I'd kept that to myself." She gave him the smile she'd used on me. "I hope it didn't make you uncomfortable," she said.

"Not when I teach it to my own kids. It's a shame more of us don't. Maybe it'll come back."

"I'm sure we'll see more faith in the future," Tina Noble said and turned to me. "I shouldn't think you're here to talk about religion, are you? Let's chat in my office."

I was tempted to confront her in front of Otis, but afraid that he would intervene too soon. Perhaps my savage indecision was apparent, because he said "Will you need me, Dr Bloan?"

"I can't think of any reason, can you, Dominic? You don't mind if I call you that. Don't worry, Otis," she said, since he was lingering. "We're professionals, me and the Sheldrakes."

I managed to swallow my words until she ushered me into her office, a clinically white room where diplomas and certificates came near to covering a wall. They failed to lend the austere place much personality, and I thought they were as much of a disguise as the name they displayed. I sat on one of a pair of plump leather seats in front of the white metal desk, and as Tina Noble took the solitary place behind it I couldn't keep my words back. "So what shall I call you?"

"If we're using our first names it's Chris."

"Not Tina." When she widened her dark eyes I thought I'd taken her unawares. "Tina Noble, to be absolutely accurate," I said.

"Dr Sheldrake." She sat forward, clasping her hands on a blotter like a flattened rectangular section of moss, a posture that put me in mind of a priest about to deliver a sermon – at least, a parody of both. "What is that supposed to achieve?" she said.

"Just letting you know I haven't been deceived."

"Is that how you see it?" She looked absurdly sympathetic, close to wistful. "What do you think you know?"

She sounded as if she were addressing a child, which enraged me almost beyond thinking. "I know your father brought you up to believe you could play with the dead."

"What an odd way to put it, Dominic. How do you think it would sound to anyone who heard?"

"Like the truth. Don't try to play with me." I wondered if she meant to aggravate my rage, though her eyes looked as empty of guile as the blue sky beyond the window. "Don't bother trying to persuade me it didn't happen," I said as calmly as I could. "I heard you and Christian calling up your grandfather."

"When might that have been, Dominic?"

"Don't you know? How often have you done it, for God's sake?"

"I thought you said you didn't want to play. If you're fishing you need better bait than that."

"I'm talking about when you weren't even as old as my son. I'd like to hope you didn't really know what you were doing."

"I was never like that. We aren't any more." As I made to ask what she meant, despite suspecting that I wouldn't like the answer, Tina said "It was you outside the house that night, was it? My father always thought so."

"And what did he do about it?"

"Have you forgotten, Dominic? Did it bother you so much you can't bear to remember?"

At once I recalled the cold clinging touch of the fog, which had solidified into the insufficiently insubstantial grasp of a misshapen pursuer. I had to dismiss all that from my mind so as to steady my voice. "That's all, is it?"

"Wasn't it enough? My father thought it seemed to be. If you don't mind hearing the truth, he didn't care that much."

"Care about what?"

Her sympathetic look was back and more unbearable than ever. "He didn't find you terribly important," she said.

This came close to making me reveal why her father ought to care – because I'd destroyed the contents of the vault beneath his church. I managed to restrain myself enough to grasp how she'd admitted who she was. Had she abandoned the deception because nobody else could hear? Just as carelessly she said "What happened to your friends?"

"Happened in what sense?"

"Weren't they involved in the old man's death as well?"

The way she referred to her grandfather disconcerted me so much that I had to curb my answer. "Nothing happened to them. They said they didn't even dream."

"Who was the girl who tried to push me as high as I liked? Roberta, that was her name. Do you know what became of her?"

"Of course I do. She's a journalist. I shouldn't think your family's overfond of them."

"It depends what they write and what they make happen. They don't matter as much as they think, but that's most people." As I thought of Eric Wharton, Tina said "Maybe she does. I still remember the rapport we had."

"Jim's with the police, and he never liked what your father was doing."

"We've no problem with the police."

I had a sudden sense of how grotesque the conversation had become. I'd mentioned Jim's profession as a warning, but Tina's acknowledgement of her own identity seemed almost to have reduced me to reminiscing about the past. "Forget my friends," I said. "Just tell me what you were doing in the babies' room."

"The neonatal unit, you mean." She might have been correcting my immature usage. "My work," she said.

"Even your friend Otis didn't think that was all, but he isn't here for you to lie to. Don't tell me you're still afraid to own up."

"That isn't why I'd be afraid." For a moment her eyes grew so dark and deep that I could have thought I was gazing into a void. "I told you but you don't seem to hear," she said. "My work."

I found I was nervous of learning "What work?"

"Preparing the children."

It was harder still for me to ask "Preparing them for what?"

"The future." With a hint of pride that I found worse than inappropriate she said "Making them more like me."

I tried to laugh, though I wasn't sure how much I should. "You think wiggling your fingers at them is going to make them believe all the stuff you believe."

"There's no need for belief when it's the truth."

If I'd been on the way to any kind of mirth, I wasn't now. "You and the rest of you at Safe To Sleep try to put it into their heads, don't you? I'm only glad Toby's at school today and not there."

"It won't make any difference. When do we have him next?"

"Never if I've anything to do with it." Realising how difficult it might be to persuade his mother provoked me to demand "How involved are you? Don't you know who's there when?"

"We don't see them as individuals." As I made to protest, having bared my teeth, Tina Noble said "All of us are less than atoms of the future."

I heard myself descending into banality as I retorted "Speak for yourself."

"I am, and my father and son."

"I think your father may rate himself a lot more highly."

"Not as we see further." She revived her sadly sympathetic look while she said "So you're proposing to take your son from us."

"More than proposing, believe me."

"And what do you think that will achieve?"

"Getting him out of your hands and your father's for a start."

"You think that will help him. You think that will bring him back now." Her sympathy was yielding to disappointment. "Why wouldn't you want him to have an inkling of what's to come?" she said. "I've told you, it's preparing him and the rest of them. I can promise it makes you stronger."

I could hardly speak for my mounting dismay. "That's what Safe To Sleep is really all about, is it?"

"I suppose it's a bit of a shock, but do you think you need to make quite so much of an issue of it? You saw a few hints of the way things are when I first knew you. You were young and you seem to have survived."

I had a sense of listening to a mind utterly remote from mine or else deranged, or both. It took some effort for me to say "You mean Phoebe Sweet and the rest of you make them see that kind of thing."

"They're already seeing it. We're helping them be at their ease with it." Having revived the sympathetic look that I'd started to detest beyond words, Tina Noble said "Let me just say you wouldn't have seen much when you were younger. Those were hardly even hints of hints. Once you see what they symbolise there's no point in being terrified. However terrified you are, it can't contain the truth. If you're equal to it, it enlarges you till you won't know yourself."

I felt as though I was recoiling from some kind of brink as I said "You won't be doing that to my son."

"I'm sorry you've ended up like this, Dominic. My father used to say you had an enquiring mind. You almost make me wish I hadn't gone to any trouble in the first place."

I was about to ignore this as not meriting an answer, and then it nagged at my mind. "What trouble? When?"

"I said almost. Please forget I mentioned it at all."

I might have if she hadn't grown so abruptly unforthcoming. "What have you ever done that involved me?"

I glimpsed the flicker of a frown on her smooth forehead. She was searching for an answer, and at once I was appalled to grasp what she didn't want to say. "You were talking about Toby, weren't you? What have you done to him?"

The rest of the truth caught up with me, and I might have lurched across the desk at her if I hadn't assaulted her with just my raised voice. "My God, you gave him the seizures in the first place. That's what you were doing just now in the babies' room."

Her face had barely started to own up to an expression when somebody knocked at the door behind me and immediately came in. "Is everything all right, Dr Bloan?" Otis said.

"It's very far from all right," I protested, twisting to face him. "Didn't you hear?"

"I heard you shouting." He kept his heavy stare on me while he said "What do you say, Dr Bloan?"

"I'll leave it to Dr Sheldrake. Do you want to tell Otis anything, Dr Sheldrake?"

I didn't know whether this was a taunt or just an assertion that speaking out would be pointless. "No, I'll tell you," I said and shoved myself out of the chair. "You and your people will never see my son again."

"I wonder." As I struggled not to lose control in front of Otis, Tina Noble said "I should discuss that with your wife."

"I'll be more than discussing it," I declared and stalked out of the office, not looking back to see if Otis followed. I would have called Lesley from the nearest phone if I hadn't been due to teach. I ran to my car and drove to the university, already knowing the afternoon session would feel as though it might never end.

CHAPTER ELEVEN
Voices of Reason

I was in sight of home when I saw a car parked next to Lesley's. Had Tina Noble reached her before I could? I swerved through the gateway so fast that the tyres screeched on the gravel, and then I realised that the car belonged to Claudine's mother. The Mazda wasn't even the same shade of green as Tina Noble's Volkswagen. As I let myself into the house Lesley emerged from the kitchen, and her guarded reluctant look revived my apprehension. "What is it, Lesley?" I said as quietly as I could.

"Shall we leave it for later?"

"Let's have it out now." I could hear Toby and Claudine in the back garden, which meant they wouldn't hear us. "Have you been talking to someone?" I said and saw she had. "What did she say?"

"Just that she thinks I'm right about Toby and his stories."

"Who does?"

"Phoebe Sweet. I know we said we'd talk to her together but I'm sorry, I wanted to hear what she thought. She says we should encourage him to write them down so he knows they're only stories."

"I'm sure she'd like to persuade somebody they are."

"Please don't, Dominic. I can't believe this is you. It needn't be."

"Has she been saying that as well?" I was instantly ashamed of the retort, but then I glimpsed a look that wasn't quite denial. "Has anyone?"

"Dominic, I wish you'd wait until—"

"Who?"

"If you must know right now, I've been speaking to your writer friend."

At first I didn't know who she meant, and then I could hardly believe it. "Bobby Parkin? How did you get in touch with her?"

"Your address book was on your desk. I didn't think you'd mind."

"I don't know if I do yet. Why did you call her?"

"I wanted to hear what she thinks about—" Lesley glanced towards the kitchen and lowered her voice. "About the business you were all concerned with when you were at school."

"I already told you, she wishes we'd done more to save Tina Noble from her father. If we had, perhaps there wouldn't be a situation now."

I was far from ready to leave it at that, but Lesley looked over her shoulder again before murmuring "That isn't what she said to me."

"Don't worry about Judith if she's there. I want her to hear what I say." All the same, I might have been less eager for Claudine's mother to learn "What's Bobby been saying?"

"I believe she prefers to be called Bob these days, or Roberta if you aren't her friend." This might almost have been a rebuke for not alerting Lesley to the preference. "I'm afraid she agrees with me," Lesley said.

"About what?" As Lesley hesitated I demanded "About me?"

"She thinks you're too obsessed with these people from your past. You're better concentrating on your family, she says."

"She wouldn't say that if she knew what's going on." Not far from rage I said "She certainly didn't tell me I was obsessed when I met her. I wouldn't be surprised if the woman she's with has been working on her mind."

"Don't you like to be judged by us women, Dominic?"

Judith had come to the kitchen doorway with a mug of coffee in her hand, which might have been displaying how severely clipped her unpainted nails were. Her face was nearly as rectangular as Claudine's, a shape emphasised by its frame of black turfy hair. Her substantial eyebrows always seemed to be raised in a challenge, and now she pursed her lips, driving out their meagre colour and letting them admit just a hint of wryness. "That isn't what I meant at all," I said.

"Am I being scatterbrained or does he sound the eentiest bit defensive?" When Lesley didn't speak Judith said "Don't say if you'd rather not for any reason. Only I'd have thought your family would have been top of your list of priorities, Dominic."

"They most emphatically are. I'm sorry if you thought you heard anything different. They mean as much to me as I presume Claudine does to you."

"No call to presume. That's what her father did too much of."

"I wasn't, and I need to talk to you about her." I saw Lesley make to intervene, but I slipped past Judith and headed for the garden. Toby and Claudine were swooping past each other on the lawn, arms stretched wide. I could have fancied they resembled figures flying off a pair of crosses, a notion Lesley would have taken to confirm how obsessed I was. "We'll just be talking for a few minutes," I told the children and shut the door.

I turned to find both women in the kitchen, watching me more closely than I thought was required. "Shall we all sit down?" I said.

Lesley hesitated before sitting next to her friend, opposite me across the table. "Judith," I said, "will Claudine have told you about any strange dreams she's had?"

"She tells me everything. We're best friends."

"So forgive me, are you saying yes?"

"If you insist on bringing it up, then yes."

Since I didn't understand her reaction, I could only persist. "What kind of dreams?"

"The kind Toby gave her by telling her stories." As I let out a syllable more like a grunt Judith said "Lesley knows I wasn't one of the parents who complained. They don't seem to bother Claudine, so I'd no reason to."

"I hate to say it, but that's why you should be concerned."

Judith lowered her head like a boxer and peered hard into my eyes. "Lesley, what's he saying about me?"

"I'm sure he doesn't mean it that way. Dominic—"

"That's right, it isn't about Judith. I'm saying Toby didn't cause the dreams."

"I think he did, even if he is your son. Lesley told me he picked it all up from some book you wrote. Please don't try to say he didn't give those children dreams. I can well understand you may feel guilty yourself."

"I'm only talking about Claudine." I was frustrated not to have time to deal with all Judith's remarks, but I needed to address the crucial issue. "Try and think back," I said. "Could she have started having her dreams before she met Toby at Safe To Sleep?"

"I've no reason to think so. She would have shared them with me if she had."

I was nervously certain that Judith was wrong. "I'd like to ask her, or you can."

"I don't need anyone's permission to talk to my own daughter, Dominic."

"You surely can't think I meant it that way, but we need to establish the truth for the children's sake."

"For your son's, you mean. I'm afraid I can't see how—"

"For all of them. Will you ask her, please?"

"You're rather fond of shouting women down, aren't you?" Once her stare had kept me quiet for several seconds Judith said "I've heard no reason why I should."

"Because I know you'll find the dreams started as soon as she had her first seizure."

Lesley made to speak, but Judith was faster. "I'm glad if you've seen how bright she is, but do you honestly imagine she can remember that far back?"

"Maybe not, but I've a feeling I know somebody who can." Barely in time I saw it would be unwise to say so. "The first one she remembers, then," I urged instead.

"I'm not going to remind her of her problem. I won't risk undoing all the good they've done at Safe To Sleep."

"Then we'll get the truth from Toby. Leave Claudine outside if you like, but I want you and Lesley to hear."

"No, you mustn't," Lesley said. "You heard Judith. I won't have Toby disturbed either."

She looked as concerned as Judith did in her own way, and it felt like confronting a monolith. "Doesn't anybody want to hear the truth?"

"What are you calling the truth?" Judith said.

"The whole thing is a front for Christian Noble," I said and kept my eyes on Lesley. "It isn't just his daughter. He's involved as well."

"I've no idea what any of that means," Judith said.

"Yes, you have." It was plain that Lesley preferred not to say any more, but as Judith produced a grimace like the start of a remark, my wife said "It's the business we were talking about earlier. He means Chris Bloan."

Judith's understanding look provoked me to demand "Is there anyone you haven't discussed me with, Lesley?"

"Maybe there's someone she ought to," Judith said.

For the sake of the children I suppressed a retort. "Are you in touch with any of the other parents who use Safe To Sleep?"

"A few of us know each other." At once Judith added "Why?"

"I'd like to speak to as many people as I can."

"If it's the kind of thing Lesley was telling me about, I should think the fewer who hear it the better."

"She doesn't know anything like everything." Desperation had started to make off with my control. "I've found out more since."

"Frankly, Dominic, I don't want to hear if it's anything like what Lesley was telling me."

"Not even if it protects your daughter?"

"I don't see how you could believe undermining Dr Bloan and her reputation can do anything of the sort." Before I could respond Judith said "I really wonder if you've got some problem with empowered women. Lesley was saying you believe you know who Dr Bloan's father is and you think he's been putting some unscientific nonsense in her head. You must be thinking of two other people, because I don't know many women who are as sure of themselves as she is. I wish I did."

"That's how the Nobles work. Whatever they need to seem to be, they convince everyone that's what they are."

"Everyone except you, Dominic?" Judith said and stood up. "I hope you can keep a rein on this, Lesley. If you need any help—"

"You aren't leaving already."

I'd meant only to hope that she wasn't, but Judith gave me a piercing look. "You're interrupting again, and I really don't care to hear any more."

"Won't you at least let me tell you why you should take Claudine away from Safe To Sleep?"

"Especially not that," Judith said as she opened the back door. "Claudine, we're going home now."

Frustration and dismay let my words loose. "Well, Toby won't be there tomorrow."

Lesley cleared her throat so hard it sounded painful. "He most certainly will."

"That's the spirit, Lesley. Don't let yourself be bullied." Twice as loud Judith said "Claudine, we're leaving right now."

Having raised a token protest, the children came in readily enough. As the two of them made for the front door Judith lingered to murmur "If you need to get in touch for any reason, Lesley, you know where I am."

Judith was following the children when Lesley sent me a whisper as sharp as her glance. "None of this in front of Toby, Dominic. Not a word."

I said none while we saw Claudine and her mother off, but when Claudine called "See you tomorrow, Toby" I sensed how tense both women grew. The impression persisted once I was alone with my wife and son, and it revived whenever silence fell. It joined us for dinner and for Toby's favourite television programme, which showed stars apparently fleeing into the depths of space. It loitered in his room while he read to us about Wonderland, giggling at the mouse's tail that described a tail on the page, though I couldn't find much amusement in the sight of words trying to embody a physical shape. When he fell asleep Lesley reached for the book as I did, and I had the dismaying suspicion that she might prefer me not to touch him. I eased *Alice* out of his small limp hands and returned it to the shelf full of books beside his bedroom window. Lesley led the way down to the front room, and I'd barely closed the door when she said "So what have you been up to now, Dominic?"

She might have been addressing a delinquent child and despairing of him. "I saw Tina Noble," I said, "and she didn't bother hiding who she is."

"What do you mean, you saw her?"

"I confronted her at the hospital. She was—"

"Confronted her how? Was anyone else there? Have you made any trouble for her?"

"There was just a security man, and he couldn't see she was up to no good." Lesley's concern for the woman had thrown me. "Believe me," I said, "she was."

"You're saying you made her call security."

"No, he was there when I found her. She sent him off before she owned up. Does that sound like someone with nothing to hide?"

"I think it might, yes. You already said she wasn't bothered by it." Before I could argue, Lesley demanded "Did she say anything about Toby?"

"Not in so many words, but—"

"You haven't made it awkward for him to go to Safe To Sleep, because if you have—"

"I'm sure they'll still want him, but that isn't the point. Tina Noble and the rest of them aren't the cure, they're the cause."

Lesley sat back in her armchair. Perhaps she was simply bracing herself, but I could have thought she was recoiling from me. "What do you mean, Dominic?"

"I caught her in the neonatal unit. She was performing one of their rituals over the newborn."

"I thought you said security was there."

"She managed to convince him she was praying. I told you and Judith, that's how the Nobles operate."

"Oh, Dominic." While Lesley looked as though she might want to take my hands, she stayed where she was. "It's his job to be observant," she said. "Don't you think it's more likely he was right?"

"Not where the Nobles are concerned. Lesley, I think they're using the children the same way they tried to use the dead."

"That means less than nothing to me, Dominic."

"You read what Christian Noble wrote. They try and send them places they wouldn't dare to go themselves."

"You can't be saying that's what they do at Safe To Sleep."

"I wish I didn't have to but I'm sorry, I'm not wrong. I saw Christian Noble there. I think he's living in that house."

Lesley seemed increasingly reluctant to speak. "When do you think you saw him?"

"Yesterday, when my students were watching the film. Don't worry, I made sure it was shown."

As I grasped this might be the least of her anxieties Lesley said "How could you have seen him?"

"I bought some binoculars. They're in the car. I got into the field behind Safe To Sleep, and I saw him with the children in the sleeping room. I'm sure he was performing another of his rituals. I'll swear I heard him."

Well before I finished I could see that Lesley wished I would. "You think Phoebe Sweet would be involved in anything like that," she said.

"She has to be. She must be in his cult."

"I wondered if you'd get round to using that word." As I made to respond Lesley said "I'd give anything not to have to say this, but it feels to me as if you care less about Toby than all this nonsense from your childhood."

"I only wish it were nothing but nonsense. I care about it because I care so much about him."

"Then just let him carry on with the treatment that's helping him."

"Haven't you understood anything I've said? We don't know what they may be doing to him, and we need to ask him. Not now, when he wakes up."

"Not then either. We know exactly what they've done to him. He's told us and we've seen. It's you who doesn't understand, Dominic, and let me tell you—"

"Don't you believe anything I've said?" When Lesley didn't answer I pleaded "How can we let him go there if there's even the slightest risk that he could be involved with a cult?"

"Maybe we shouldn't care what they believe so long as they're helping him." As I struggled to tone down my response to this Lesley said "I'm starting to think you're more like your father than you'd want to be."

This silenced me, because I felt it might be as accurate as it seemed unfair. "I'm sorry," Lesley said at once. "I shouldn't be saying that while he's in hospital."

"Say the truth, whatever it is. That's what I've been doing. Can't you believe that?"

"What have you really told me, Dominic? You saw Chris Bloan with the newborn and someone who I think you must agree would have been objective said she was praying. You thought you heard the man from your past saying the sort of thing you've written in your book, but could you really be sure at that distance? And since you were so far away I wonder if you could have mistaken someone else for him."

"You'd rather think all that than make sure Toby's safe."

"No, that's exactly what I'm doing for him." Lesley took a breath so deep I heard it shake. "And I'll warn you now," she said, "if you undermine his treatment I'll be taking him away."

No doubt she took my silence for defeat, although it was simply frustration so painful that I clenched my fists. I opened them when she stared at them, because I was dismayed to think they resembled a threat of violence. There seemed to be no further point in speaking, since I couldn't own up to my thoughts. It looked as if I needed to protect Toby on my own, which left me feeling worse than isolated. However misunderstood and solitary I'd sometimes felt as a child, I would never have expected growing up to bring that back.

CHAPTER TWELVE

The Three

That night I hardly slept, even when I thought Lesley was asleep. Too often I wondered if she was pretending in case I tried to sneak Toby away to protect him, besides which I was afraid of sleeping past the time I needed to be up. All this felt worse than staying alert for the sound that heralded one of Toby's seizures. That the only noise the monitor picked up was his even breathing didn't reassure me, since I knew why he was so thoroughly asleep. Every so often I drifted into unawareness, which felt fruitlessly brief and infested with thoughts. As soon as I saw a hint of the dawn I crept out of bed and shut myself in the bathroom for a muted shower. I was dressing in the bedroom for fear of waking Toby when Lesley stirred and groped in search of me. I hoped she would revert to sleep, but she blinked until she located me. "Whatime sit?" she mumbled.

"It's early yet. You go back to sleep for a while."

She struggled across the bed to fumble for the alarm clock. "Where are you going at this hour?"

"Don't worry, just to work."

Depending on interpretation, this wasn't quite a lie, but it fell short of satisfying her. "You can't need to do anything this early."

"I'll be being prepared. I may as well get to it since I'm awake."

I sensed that she was only gradually recollecting last night's argument. "Don't let me drive you out, Dominic."

"It isn't that at all. I know you wouldn't," I said and hoped that notwithstanding her threat last night it was the truth. "Tell Toby I'll see him when we're home."

"Aren't you having some breakfast at least? Give me five minutes and I'll come down."

"It's all right, I'll grab something. You stay in bed."

I stooped to leave her a kiss, and her lips shifted a little on mine while her hands clasped the back of my neck. It felt as if she wanted to delay me, but I'd misled her long enough. Perhaps I did need sustenance – I was somewhat unsteady with lack of sleep – and I found a muesli bar in the kitchen. At least I had it to show Lesley when I saw her watching from the top of the stairs. I couldn't think of anything to say, and only waved the item before making for my car.

Milk floats were droning through the suburbs, and early postmen were at large with their bags, prompting the occasional dog on a lead to bark. There weren't too many vehicles on the roads for traffic lights or delivery lorries to hinder. By the time a reddened sun rose, swollen like a leech by mist that lay above the fields, I was in the open country beyond Ormskirk. The only vehicle in sight was mine. I drove to the entrance to Safe To Sleep, and was wondering how to reach the house if the gates didn't let me in when they swung wide. If I'd had my window open I might have been able to hear them, but just then they seemed stealthy as fog.

Through the trees on both sides of the avenue I glimpsed mounds of earth in the grass. Condensation lent them an unappealingly gelatinous look. I could have thought I saw more than one of them grow restless, but took it for an effect of the mist that lingered on the grass, unless moles were peering out and retreating underground before I was remotely sure I'd seen them. The gravel in front of the house grated under my wheels, and I was parking next to a solitary Viva when I saw movement in the porch.

The front door had opened, but the low sunlight from behind the house only darkened the interior. I could barely see the figure in the doorway until it moved forward, gaining definition so gradually that I might have fancied it was regaining its shape. Then it bowed towards me, and I recognised Christian Noble even before I made out his face. The long smooth oval seemed hardly to have aged, and together with that purposeful darting movement it reminded me more than ever of a snake – a cobra without a hood. It put on a noncommittal smile as I climbed out of the car. "Aren't you a parent of one of our children?" Noble said from the top of the steps. "I'm afraid you're here before the lady who takes care of them."

His smile wasn't admitting whether he'd recognised me. If this was a game I could play it as well, and I said "What would you like me to do?"

"Let me offer you the hospitality of my house."

"That's very thoughtful." In case this betrayed my wariness I said "Thank you" as well.

Noble didn't turn his back until I was on the steps, and he shut the door as soon as I ventured into the house. Although light had started to creep down the stairs from the windows that overlooked them, the corridors stayed dim. "So this is all yours," I said, not entirely conversationally.

"I've benefited from the generosity of admirers."

I could tell this was a boast rather than a confession of dependence. "Have you always lived like that?" I couldn't resist enquiring.

"Dear me, some people might think that was quite a personal question. It's up to individuals to decide what they think is worth supporting."

I might have retorted that he hadn't left Mrs Norris to decide for herself, or many like her at his church or even hers. Instead I asked "Do you live here all by yourself?"

"Not remotely. I've companions to spare. Some of them come and go," he said, turning away before I could read his face.

When he opened a door, light that looked drained of energy sprawled into the left-hand corridor. I followed him into the room, which had a view between the trees all the way to the gates. The panelled walls were unadorned, and the room contained very little besides several thickset armchairs even darker than the panels. A black dresser displayed indistinct figurines in the dimmest corner, but I saw nothing more human, not even a book. As Noble sat facing the avenue, his chair uttered a leathery breath. "Please do find yourself a place," he said.

I sat diagonally opposite him, where I could watch his face and have a peripheral sight of the drive. "So what brings you to us at this hour?" Noble said.

"I wanted to speak to someone before the children get here."

"Ah, then your child will still be coming on the bus."

I almost couldn't speak for loathing and dismay. "That's the plan."

"Dr Sweet will be here by then, but may I help you in some way?"

I fought down emotions in order to ask "Are you involved in the operations here?"

"Why, of course." As I did my best to brace myself for his admission Noble said "One of the children is ours. I don't know how we could be more involved."

My words were growing harder to control. "You don't participate yourself."

Noble stretched out his hands in a crucified pose before lifting them to gesture backwards. "Would you not class this as participation?"

For a nervous moment I thought he was sketching if not commencing a ritual. I didn't realise that he meant to signify the building until he said "I would hardly house something I didn't believe in."

I had to swallow as an aid to saying "So what do you believe?"

"In the future, if you want to use that term. It's all you can see if you've learned how to look."

"I thought we were talking about the children."

"What are they except our future? Surely you'll agree they ought to be prepared for it in every way that's open to us."

"Is that—" I struggled not to clench my fists while I tried again. "Is that what you're doing here?"

Noble turned his head to present me with a smile that looked almost regretful. "What do you think we're doing, Mr Sheldrake?"

It wasn't just my name that took me off guard. He sounded too much as he used to in the classroom; he might have been catching out a pupil who thought himself clever. All my years only just let me regain calm as I said "So you knew who I was."

"I make a point of knowing who visits my house. You were about to tell me what you think of Phoebe Sweet's methods."

So he hadn't abandoned the game he was playing. Perhaps he was finding out how far he could deceive me, in which case joining in might gain me information despite his guile. "You're saying she's responsible," I said.

"She's the doctor in charge, yes."

"I know that, but did she come up with the treatment?"

"How much do you know about alternative medicine, Mr Sheldrake?"

"Perhaps not as much as I should. What would you like me to know?"

"Most of it has been rediscovered, not invented. It's stood what you might call the test of time. It's been waiting for the world to find it, or catch up with it if you like."

"It's generally Oriental, isn't it? Is that where Phoebe Sweet's technique comes from?"

"No indeed, an older source." With an unreadable variation on his smile Noble added "If you want to think in historical terms."

"How else would you like me to think about it?" I nearly asked him when he'd abandoned the historical view he'd taught at school. "What other way is there?" I said.

"The way of the worm, Mr Sheldrake."

I felt dangerously close to learning too much, and wondered why he would take the risk. "I don't think I know what that is."

"Everybody will in time," Noble said and laughed as though he'd made a joke. "Count yourself among the first to know. I expect you've heard of Ouroboros."

"The legend of the snake eating its own tail."

"All legends are symbols, like most of the universe."

This provoked me to retort "Including us?"

"Very much so, but we're speaking of the worm." With a look he might have turned upon an excessively talkative schoolboy Noble said "It's the oldest legend insofar as those words have any meaning. It appears in many cultures, and it's older than the world."

"You'd wonder who thought it up, then."

"Perhaps you may learn." While his pause wasn't long, it felt ominous. "Time is the worm," he said. "The future has the past between its teeth, and at the same time the opposite is true. They eternally consume each other and are constantly reborn. That's the first of the many truths the Bible was designed to conceal."

"You're saying that's all the tempter in the garden really was."

"Not even fractionally." I wondered if he might repeat the name I'd first heard him pronounce at the Trinity Church of the Spirit, but he said "Time is a symbol too. It's a way of reducing the universe to a level the unenlightened mind can cope with."

"We've moved a long way from Phoebe Sweet and her methods."

His silence let me dread that I was wrong before he said "Have you found anything to say about them?"

"I still don't know what principles they're based on."

"Principles," he said in a voice like a stifled laugh, and was plainly about to continue when he peered towards the corridor.

At first I wasn't sure what he could hear, even once I started hearing it myself. The sound was soft and rapid, though not entirely regular, and as it grew louder I realised that it was approaching. I'd just grasped that it was descending the stairs when it left them to enter the corridor. It was faster now, and seemed to have spread into a determined shuffling. When it arrived at the door I heard the newcomer start to fumble at the panels, reaching upwards for the heavy doorknob. The knob twisted a slow inch and subsided, and I heard Tina Noble say "You can't quite do it yet. Your body's not as ready as your mind."

The doorknob turned so gradually that I might have been watching a demonstration of how it worked or else an assisted bid to use it. The door swung open to reveal Tina Noble and in front of her the youngest member of the family. He was dressed in a pale blue one-piece suit that left his hands free but covered his feet, which gave his legs an oddly uncompleted look. He trotted with increasing confidence to an empty armchair and hoisted himself onto the seat by digging his fingers into the leather, where he immediately squirmed around to face me. As the infant pushed himself back so that his spine was supported, Christian Noble said "And this is only his first year."

A doting grandparent might have made the remark, but here it sounded threatening at best. I was trying to decide how to respond when Tina Noble said "Christian, that's—"

"A face from the past, as they say. We know exactly who he is and where he comes from. Don't we, Dominic?"

I did my best not to feel menaced, though being watched by three versions of the same long smooth oval face didn't help, especially when the smallest gaze seemed just as searching as the others. "We've stopped pretending, have we?" I said.

"So long as you have." As his daughter took the seat between him and the child, who was nearest to the window, Noble said "It can be useful to observe how men behave."

"Why are you here?" Tina Noble said to me.

"I'm sure you know that as well. I want to hear what you think you're doing with the children."

"You've already been told that," Noble said as if he had done so himself. "They're being prepared for the world to come."

"The world you'd like to create, you mean." When three unblinking gazes greeted this I demanded "Weren't the dead enough for you? Have you got to destroy children's lives as well?"

"Mr Sheldrake, I would have expected better of you." He might have been correcting a pupil again. "Destruction is creation," he said. "That's another lesson you might learn from the Ouroboros."

"Just what do you imagine you're creating?"

"What the future calls for." His daughter was answering now. "Try not to worry so much," she said, reviving her intolerably sympathetic look. "The newborn are much stronger than you might think. They can accept more than the dead because they're only starting to be formed."

"More than you dare to, you mean." I could hardly speak for abhorrence. "You're using them because you're afraid to go where you send them," I managed to add. "You're worse than cowards, both of you. I can't think of a word."

"Mr Sheldrake, you disappoint me more and more." Noble clasped his hands on his chest, a gesture that might have been parodying prayer or even the stance of a corpse. "Let me urge you to enlarge your thinking," he said. "Here's a text for you to ponder: a little child shall lead them. I expect you know it from your book."

"That's not my book." However true, this struck me as woefully feeble, provoking me to add "But I've got yours."

I couldn't help flinching, if only internally, as the listeners sat forward in that same swift reptilian movement – all three of them. "Got what?" came the response.

I found this more daunting still, because little Toph had asked it, in a voice distinctly clearer than I'd ever heard from anyone so young. I almost spoke directly to him, but by the time I turned to Christian Noble I'd quelled the answer I had been about to give. "It's all here in my head."

I was afraid he might sense I was being protective – I didn't want to put my family at risk – but he was preoccupied with telling Toph "Mr Sheldrake found a journal of mine that somebody had taken into his school, Christopher."

I remembered the screech of the wheels of a tram, and the aftermath. "Not just somebody," I said. "Your father."

"Only in name," Noble said and sent me a look that hardly even bothered to express weariness. "I might as well have been left by the kind folk. He was never involved in our lineage."

"Was that why he hated what you did and what you were?"

"He had a mind as small as most. We enlarged it for him a little, didn't we, Tina?"

By now my detestation tasted like bile. "Was that your revenge on him?"

"Mr Sheldrake, why should I have been as petty as you're trying to suggest?"

"I thought you might have been punishing him for trying to save his granddaughter."

"No, we simply wanted him to be of use." Before I could react, Noble said "Mr Sheldrake means your mother, Christopher. We know none of us need saving, don't we? We could say we're the ones who are saved."

"Tina's mother didn't think so, did she?" I retorted. "I wonder what happened to her."

"Hospital, Mr Sheldrake, and death."

Although I might have predicted his indifference, it left me without words. "Have you any further questions," he said, "or shall we deal with why you're actually here?"

"You think you know."

"Think."

Whatever this meant, it unnerved me, because it came from the baby seated upright in the armchair. In any case my rejoinder had been weak, and Tina Noble said "We more than think."

"You're still determined to prevent what has to happen, are you, Mr Sheldrake?" her father said. "Your energy would be better spent in trying to understand."

"I've understood enough." This sounded so pitifully inadequate that it drove me to declare "I've already stopped you once."

"Mr Sheldrake showed my musings to the headmaster at the school, Christopher." As the child's eyes appeared to deepen and grow even darker Noble said "Can you really still believe that could have hindered me in any way, Mr Sheldrake?"

I'd said too much, and I attempted to make flinging my hands wide the whole of my answer. I saw three pairs of eyes find it insufficient before Noble said "I don't think he does. What else can he mean?"

I was appalled to fancy that I glimpsed a hint of a response in the baby's eyes, but it was his mother who answered. "Could it be the church?"

"Well, Mr Sheldrake? Do demonstrate the courage of your convictions."

"Yes." Having been provoked to say that much, I had no reason not to admit "I didn't destroy everything. Just what needed it."

I had an uneasy sense that, like all the watching eyes, the room was somehow growing darker. "Your friends were involved, were they?" Noble said.

"They weren't even there, and I don't know who was. I expect someone who'd read Eric Wharton's column smashed up your church."

"Ah, Mr Wharton, that devious fellow. I think he may have been surprised by what he found he'd invited. I suspect that may be your case as well, Mr Sheldrake." Once his lips and Tina's and the baby's had twisted into faint simultaneous smiles Noble said "So are you owning up to nothing?"

"I broke into the vault. I'll let you guess the rest."

For a moment, unless it was far longer, I couldn't separate the silence from the darkness that seemed to have crept indefinably closer. "Well, Mr Sheldrake," Noble said, "you've earned yourself some attention. Do acquaint us with your plans."

I didn't know how intimidated he meant me to feel, and I hadn't time to care. "I told your daughter, you've seen the last of my son."

"Is he all you care about?" Before I could risk admitting that I wouldn't be satisfied until I'd lost the Nobles all their young victims, Noble said "I'm afraid you've exhausted our hospitality. We won't allow you to disturb the children who have been entrusted to us."

This almost left me incapable of speech, but I managed to ask "How do you propose to get rid of me?"

"Shall we call the police?"

Tina gave this a tentative nod, but the child looked disappointed, as though he'd been robbed of a treat. Though I had a dreadful sense of knowing why, I said "You don't mind the police hearing what I have to tell them."

"Mr Sheldrake, the police we would call know more than you do."

I thought I grasped why he hadn't bothered threatening me with worse. I was tempted to make the Nobles summon the police so that I could learn who else was implicated in their operation, but suppose this prevented me from rescuing Toby? "You haven't won," I said as I rose not entirely steadily to my feet. "I won't be going away."

"You'll leave our property, Mr Sheldrake. You have five minutes to be gone and then we'll be making sure you are."

I was disconcerted when none of them followed me, simply turning their heads in unison to watch me leave the room. I could well have imagined I was being trailed on their behalf. I hurried along the dim corridor and glanced up the deserted stairs before letting myself out of the house. As I made for my car I saw all three Nobles watching from their seats beyond the window. I'd climbed into my car when they began to speak.

Though I couldn't hear a word, I saw they were chanting together, emphasising a trinity of syllables that they repeated more than once. While I felt worse than childish for letting this unsettle me, I drove away at speed. Was a wind causing trees to stoop towards the avenue and shifting the earth of some of the mounds in the grass? It seemed odd that the trees were leaning towards the car from both sides, and I hadn't time to judge how restless the mounds might be. Surely the Nobles wanted me off the property, and so it made no sense for anything to hinder me. I reached the gates in well under five minutes of leaving the room, and as soon as they opened I drove onto the road.

I saw the bus at once, turning a bend on the far side of several fields. I sped out of sight of the camera by the gates and waited with my engine running. When the bus swung around a bend a few hundred yards ahead I flashed my headlights. The bus began to slow down, and I glanced in the mirror, which showed me only the empty road. I was about to switch off the engine and step in front of the bus when a hand closed over my face.

I might not have known it was a hand, given how the swollen fingers squirmed. Although I couldn't see it, I felt the cold bloated fingertips grope everywhere on my face as if they were searching for a way in. Panic left me only remotely aware that I could still see the road and the bus. At least, I could until the fingers found my eyes and slithered into them. I felt the filaments of which the fingers were composed swarm deeper, and in a moment I was blind, or else my brain was no longer able to process my sight. My whole body convulsed, and the car lurched forward at speed as my foot slammed the accelerator down. I was terrified of colliding with the bus, and had just enough presence of mind to wrench the steering wheel to the left. I felt the car tilt into a ditch, and thought at least this much was safe. Then an impact flung me sideways, and my head struck the window so hard that the glass shattered, or my skull did. That last moment of consciousness felt as if the sky had collapsed to let in the dark.

CHAPTER THIRTEEN
Hard Words

When I awoke I heard Lesley and our son in the room. This seemed more reassuring than I understood, and I didn't need to open my eyes. It had to be the weekend, or Lesley would be telling me that it was time to go to work. The day must be well advanced, given how bright it was, and it felt muggy too. Which aspect of this was a relief? Of course, it had to be past the time when Toby would have left for Safe To Sleep, and so either it was Sunday or we were keeping him at home. The oppressive heat was less welcome, even though Lesley had put a thinner quilt on the bed. In fact, the bed itself felt oddly thin, both the mattress and the equally ungenerous pillow. This bothered me enough that I reached out an arm to recapture how the mattress ought to feel. The bed was scarcely half the width it should be, and my fingers bruised themselves against a wall.

At once I remembered the car crash, and I was afraid to open my eyes. It wasn't only that the driver of the bus must have brought me back to Safe To Sleep. The memory had revived the sensation that had caused the accident – the swarms of filaments writhing deep into my eyes. I was terrified that some remnants might be buried in there, lying dormant until I roused them. Yet I had to look, because Toby was at Safe To Sleep despite all my efforts, and had the Nobles lured my wife here too? I took a breath that made my chest ache and seemed to cleave my skull with pain, and then I forced my eyes wide.

The white wall in front of me was as blank as amnesia. At least I was able to see it, and so far as my headache let me judge, my eyes were undamaged. I heard voices at my back, too low for me to recognise or understand them, and I turned hastily over. One of the fluorescent tubes I'd mistaken for sunlight sailed past overhead, and then the long room full of supine figures started to plunge downwards so uncontrollably that

I squeezed my eyes shut and grabbed my mouth. While this just about saved me from puking, it didn't quell the savage pain in my head. I kept my eyes closed tight until the sensation of plummeting began to subside, and then I risked slitting them to look for my wife and our son.

I was at the end of a row of beds on the left side of a hospital ward. Although all the beds were occupied, no visitors were to be seen. I was turning my head towards the doors to the entrance lobby, which were beyond the foot of the bed — I felt as though moving even a fraction faster would set the room spinning once more — when my immediate neighbour raised his voice. "Nurse, this one's woke up."

He was a stocky red-faced man with almost as much stubble on his chubby jowls as on his broad flat scalp. The reverberations of his shout had scarcely died away when he sat up in bed to deliver another, but the doors swung back to let a small muscular wide-hipped nurse into the ward. She gave my neighbour an admonitory look before trotting to my bedside. "How are you feeling, Dominic?" she said. "Or should we call you Mr Sheldrake?"

"Ominous willed ooh."

I heard myself say that, though perhaps it wasn't even so distinct. The nurse gave me a sympathetic look that revived unwelcome memories of Tina Noble, and I had to remind myself that I couldn't be in the hospital where she worked. "Whereof Myfanwy?" I was anxious to learn.

The nurse looked as confused as the antics of my speech made me feel, and I tried again. "Myth Amelie," I said more fiercely than the words that came out warranted.

My jowly neighbour tapped his temple with a finger and pointed at me. "He's asking where his family's gone."

"Visiting's over for today, Dominic. They'll be here again tomorrow."

"Bow rhythm."

"Both of them, yes, I think so."

"Lucerne swat cheese head."

When the nurse cocked hers as though an oblique view of my words might clarify them, my neighbour wagged his finger. "I reckon he's asking if you're certain that's what his lady said."

"Dad's wry."

"I believe she did, Dominic." The nurse peered into my eyes. "Now can you tell me how you're feeling?"

I raised my fingers to my forehead but flinched from touching the section that had hit the window of the car. "Bah heady. Verbid," I did my best to emphasise. "Ann dinners."

"I'll give you painkillers for your head and I'm sorry, what was the rest of it?"

"Dinners. Dinners," I said with increasing desperation.

"If you ask me he's saying he's dizzy," my neighbour said.

I began to nod a confirmation and instantly regretted it. "Soy. Cunts peak brolly." Having heard myself apparently say this, I thought it best to add an apology that emerged as "My apocalypse."

"Don't worry your head over that, Dominic. It's quite a common symptom."

"Howl on we ill ass?"

"We can't predict that. Generally a few days. I'll get you those killers, and doctor will be round soon."

I rather wished she'd used some less informal term for the medication. As she made for the lobby my neighbour said "If you've got any more to say for yourself, remember you've got an interpreter."

"Ankh hoover image," I mumbled, not even knowing how much I meant the thanks I'd struggled to pronounce.

I let my head sink back on the meagre support of the pillow and closed my eyes. I was drifting close to unconsciousness when the nurse murmured in my ear "Here it is now for you, Dominic." I parted my lips while she tilted a dinky plastic cup, and then I tried to regain unawareness. The medicine took its time over assuaging the vicious pain in my skull, but perhaps my thoughts helped. If Toby had visited me he couldn't be at Safe To Sleep, and the nurse had reassured me that he wouldn't be there tomorrow. Whatever harm I'd done myself, it had to be worthwhile if it had saved my son.

I saw no urgency to think beyond that, and quite soon I was so thoroughly asleep that I resented being roused. A surgeon's attentions wakened me, and more than one offer of meals that I incoherently refused did. As night fell, not that I was aware of it while my eyes were shut, the uninvited heat turned me sweaty and restless and prone to being woken by various hospital sounds – groans, coughing fits that played at coming to an end much sooner than they did, muted discussions that might have been professional but annoyed me with the suspicion that they weren't, the squeak and bump one lobby door produced every time it closed, just not faint enough for me to be able to ignore. Eventually waiting for the next repetition of the noises kept me awake, and I had to call for pay colours – the medicine, I meant. Daybreak multiplied the noises, and I was still subsiding into a vague version of sleep only to keep resurfacing when Lesley murmured my name.

She was speaking so quietly that I could have thought she preferred to leave me asleep. Opening my eyes wide opened up a headache too. It felt as if the fluorescent glare had penetrated my softened skull, and my eyes winced shut. I'd had time to see Lesley sitting by the bed – her face looked as if she was trying to balance determination and concern – but that was all, and not enough. "Ways to be?" I heard myself ask.

Her pause was almost an answer, and one I was dismayed to imagine, before she said "What did you say, Dominic?"

"Tow bee." I left such a gap between the syllables that I might have been mocking the question or the name, though I was simply ensuring it was clear. "Where?" I persisted.

"He's at school. It isn't Judith's day but she's picking them both up."

"So long he snow whereas." Frustration with my speech aggravated my headache and turned my voice harsh. "Nowhere else," I managed to articulate.

"I've said so once. Can't you look at me?"

"Pain. Canoe corn hers?" I squeezed my eyes tighter in case this helped me pronounce "Nurse."

"I'll come back in a moment," Lesley said, and the door preceded its muffled bump with a squeak. For a change the sounds were welcome, and so was the kiss of the plastic cup. As I swallowed I heard Lesley murmur "How is he?"

"Doctor's satisfied, but we'll be keeping him in for at least a few days."

The door repeated its noises, and then I heard only a generalised mutter of patients. I had to slit my eyes to see that Lesley had returned to the skeletal metal chair. "Better?" she said.

"Will be." I sensed her gaze was prompting me to ask "How stow bee?"

"How on earth do you think he is? He saw his father smash up the car and have to be taken away in an ambulance. What did you think you were trying to do?"

"Ahead to stub Grenoble's." With a furious effort I brought out "Had to stop them."

"I can't understand you, Dominic."

My stubbly neighbour leaned towards her out of his bed. "Bet I can tell you what he's saying, love."

"I'm sorry," Lesley said, "this is a private conversation."

"Well, excuse me for having a heartbeat," the man said and returned to mumbling at his wife.

"I mean I can't understand your behaviour, or at least I hope I don't." Before I could find words and try to utter them Lesley said "Why do they say you're speaking like that?"

"Symptom." Heartened by pronouncing that, I added "Fewer wurzel bear."

"Don't try to explain if you can't."

I suspected that she didn't have just the indistinctness of my speech in mind. "Said few err words bet err," I took some time to articulate. "Short err too."

"Just say what you did."

"Saw no bull." This was a waste of effort, since she already knew. "Met him," I said. "Talked."

"When did you? Where?"

"At their house. Beef or docked or sweet came."

As my neighbour's wife smiled across his bed, presumably assuming she'd overheard an endearment, Lesley demanded "What was said?"

"There you sing chilled wren, like I toll dew."

Lesley gazed at me as if my syllables took even longer to arrive than to produce. "Someone told you that."

"No bull. Said much more. Tell you it all when I can."

"And why the crash?"

"Meant to stop bus. Not with crash. Meant to flag him down."

"Then do what?"

"Take tow bee home. Won't have them may king him inn too one of them."

Speaking at such length threatened to renew my headache. "But you crashed," Lesley said.

I thought bemusement had slowed her voice down until I grasped that she was trying to ensure I understood, and then I realised she'd been simplifying her language too. "No knee to tall kike sat," I protested and had to make it clearer. "Don't speak like I'm child. Mind's not gone, just pro nun see a shun."

"Then please tell me what caused the accident."

My headache felt more imminent, making me careless with my words. "Thing they put in car. Stop dyes were king."

"What sort of thing, Dominic?"

I shut my eyes in case this helped fend off the headache, and heard myself mutter "Hand."

When the headache shrank, subsiding into a dull throb, I saw Lesley waiting for me to reopen my eyes. "You're going to have to see someone," she said.

"See ying you."

"You know what I mean," Lesley said almost too low for me to hear. "We can't go on like this any more, especially where Toby's concerned. We need to get you some help."

"No body Mick's dup with the no bulls."

"I've no reason to suppose he has anything to do with anyone you might object to."

More than my condition hindered my speech now. "You've bin disgusting, disc cussing me wish woman, with someone."

"I had to talk to someone, Dominic. I couldn't be alone with all that any more."

"You warn tall own."

"You know I didn't mean that, but I couldn't talk to you, could I? Or I could have, but you wouldn't have known. The man I've been told about has worked with people like us. He was Rose Tierney's psychiatrist when she was in your department."

"Dint helper mush, diddy? Kill der sell."

"Her husband said Colin Hay wasn't to blame, if you remember. I believe she was the only patient he ever lost."

I was searching for words to pronounce when the ward sister bumped the door open. "Start saying your goodbyes to your visitors now, everyone."

"Not been here long," I concentrated on objecting.

"I have," Lesley said, "but you were asleep." Before I could try to retrieve the discussion, she stood up and bent to kiss my forehead. "You get some more rest. We'll both be here later, I promise."

At least she wasn't proposing to keep Toby away from me, and for the moment this was enough. Once she and my neighbour's wife had gone he winked at me. "Was your judy aching your ear like my ould girl? And they say it's men are all the same because they're men."

"She's doing her best when it must be hard for her," I made the effort to articulate before sinking warily back on the pillow.

Once the dizziness faded along with some of the headache I found I didn't want to think much. No doubt I could visit a psychiatrist if this reassured Lesley, because Toby was far more important than me. Although she hadn't said so, I had a sense that my intervention or the car crash if not both had ended his visits to Safe To Sleep. The thought let me wander into unconsciousness, and nothing wholly woke me after that until I heard his voice. "Do you think dad's come back again?"

I propped up the pillow behind my head and set about raising myself as the doors from the lobby swung back. The walls and beds began to sink like an unstable image on a screen, and then they grew steadier. I turned my eyes but not my head towards my family, to see that Toby was outdoing Lesley for concern. I could only hope this was as uncomplicated as it looked. "Dad," Toby called, "you're back."

"Hour shunt relic on." My words were as treacherous as ever. "Wars hunt real lee gone," I more or less repeated.

"Mum said you'd started talking funny." He giggled while he asked "Are you going to all the time?"

"Shoed stop soon."

"Maybe reading books will help you talk like it helped me." As though offering further encouragement he said "They've brought your car home. It wasn't very wrecked."

"It must be hard err than my nog in."

This authorised Toby to giggle again. "Your plaster's nearly as big as grandad's."

I hadn't realised I bore one. When I gingerly fingered my temple I found it owed some of its unfamiliar tightness to a dressing. The injury wasn't as tender as yesterday, though Lesley winced on my behalf, but my gesture roused Toby's concern. "Why did you wreck the car, dad? Were you trying to drive like people do in some of your films?"

I saw Lesley prepare to intervene if the look she sent me wasn't enough of a warning. I felt acutely frustrated, not just by the prohibition but because of my unwieldy speech. "Not a stunt," I said. "Just care less ness."

"But why were you there? I'd got the bus."

As Lesley's look grew yet more eloquent I said "Had a talk with some one. That Saul."

I wasn't sure what made him ask "Are you sleeping lots, dad?"

"Quite a lot. Why?"

"Because you've got a room with all these people. It isn't fair if they keep you awake when you and mum fixed it up for me to sleep."

I didn't need to glance at Lesley to know how little she wanted me to respond. I had to restrain myself so fiercely that my head began to pound. "They don't," I told him.

"Shall I tell you a story, then?"

My neighbour's wife gave this an appreciative sigh. I did my best not to sound ungrateful but felt childish for saying "Don't want to sleep yet."

"I can tell you one for you to remember when you do."

"That's kind of him, isn't it, Dominic?"

I heard Lesley willing me to indulge him, and I couldn't very well not say "Tell me, then."

"Once upon a time there was a boy who thought he was a comet." Toby's voice took on a rhythm not unlike an incantation. "Every night he flew past the sky and went round all the stars," he said. "And then he flew out where there aren't any stars and they're so far away you can't even see them. It's so big out there that things have to get giant to fill it, and it's so dark they can be anything they like. So the boy got longer and longer till he met himself, and he could go all the way back to when nothing was alive, except it's really a kind of life people don't know about yet. And because he could meet himself he came back every morning without anyone knowing he'd gone, and that's what he did till the things he met came to find everyone."

The noise my neighbour's wife made presumably expressed some version of approval, but I was more aware that Lesley was awaiting my response. "Thanks for may king that up for me," I said.

While this appeared to placate his mother, I thought Toby was about to argue, but he said "Shall I tell grandad as well?"

"You can when you see him next."

"I can now. He's in the other room."

"The ward along the corridor, Toby means," Lesley said.

"You me nobly toad—" I took a breath and tried again. "You didn't think to tell me we're in the same hoss spit tall."

"There wouldn't have been much point if you weren't able to get up, would there? He can't come to you just now. He still has his infection."

"Well, maybe I can go." I dug my fingertips into the mattress to lever myself up, only to sink back as the room slipped awry at once. "Maybe I will later," I conceded. "Tell him I will as soon as I can."

Toby undertook to, a promise he repeated at the end of visiting. He hugged me so hard that I could easily have fancied he was striving to encompass me, and Lesley gave me more of a kiss than she'd left me last time. "I'll bring him after work tomorrow," she murmured, and the thump of the door put a full stop to her sentence.

Once all the visitors had gone my neighbour turned to me, propping his prickly chin on a fist. "He's got some weird ideas in his head, your lad. Gets them off you, does he?"

"Not from me." The idea dismayed me so much that I demanded "Why me?"

"Seeing as how you make films I reckoned he might of been watching them."

"Don't make films. Teach them."

"How's that work? They wouldn't let me train up any lads if I didn't have my engineer's certificate."

Arguing would have required too many words, and I restrained myself to an open-handed shrug. "Weird films, are they?" my neighbour persisted.

"You might think some. Just now" – I assumed they were still being shown to my students –"they're re lid jus."

He peered at me as if I might be mocking him by splitting up the syllables. "So you're with the God brigade."

"No need."

Presumably he felt he'd made his views about qualifications plain, because he only shook his head. "I don't know where we're going, me. Where we'll all end up, like. Still hanging round for somebody that knows."

Did this prompt thoughts of Christian Noble? At first I was glad when my neighbour's ruminations turned to films. The recent *Scarface* was a favourite: Al was the man, and the judy was gear, and there was some good shooting in the film but (my neighbour lowered his voice to inform me) too much fucking language. I murmured noncommittally, feeling much as I did when a dentist's attentions blocked my speech. I seemed to have invited an account of most if not all the films the stubbly man had seen, and we'd regressed as far as *Gone with the Wind*, where he enthused about the scene in which Rhett Butler carried the protesting Scarlett to his bed, before I had an opportunity to interrupt by catching the attention of a nurse. Yes, they would keep me informed about my father's condition, and I could visit him as soon as I was able to walk along the corridor. This gave me an excuse to shut my eyes in a bid to recuperate faster, though my neighbour called as if quite a distance separated us "Missed Lee Marvin out. He was in a weird film I reckon you'd like. We can talk about it later."

The prospect of another monologue helped the heat to keep me restless, and so did the nocturnal noises of the ward. I was afraid that lack of sleep would exacerbate my dizziness, but when I risked a trip to the toilets I found that I could walk not too far from straight. After breakfast I felt safe to ask a nurse "Can I go and see my father down the core rid door?"

She examined me and told me to be sure I was up to the expedition. As I made my practically steady way past several trolleys and an impromptu conference of doctors I caught a tang of nicotine from a smoking room. When a nurse let me into Intensive Care I thought at first I couldn't see my father. Quite a few supine figures were tethered to monitors and bottles, but surely none of the wasted shapes belonged to him – except that the man in the third bed on the left bore a simplified variant of his face, less colourful and fleshy than last time I'd seen it. He caught sight of me and succeeded in lifting the arm that wasn't burdened with a tube. "What a family for getting in the wars," he said. "The blackie told me you were here as well."

His voice was as feeble as his gesture and the smile he tried to raise, but I made for him carelessly fast and had to grab the rail at the foot of his bed. "Don't keep using that word, dad," I murmured.

"There's a lot worse, son. I don't know how they expect us to keep up with what they want us calling them." As I tried again to hush him he said "Anyway, she's one of us, not like these Allah wallahs that we're getting now. At least she's got a cross round her neck."

I let this go in the hope he would as well. "How are you fee ling?" I said and tried to make my words less sluggish. "How are they saying you are?"

"They're still chasing my bug. They think they've got it on the run, and then I'm praying I can go home." His last word barely reached the surface before giving way to a clogged laborious breath. "I'm not as bad as that sounds," he wanted me to hear.

"You keep your en err gee for getting better and don't worry about me. Just a knock on the head, and I'm over the worst."

"They said you had a crash. How'd you leave the other feller?"

I had an unhappy sense that my father wanted anyone else involved to have come off worse. "There was only me," I said and tried to rein the truth in. "I was diss track ted."

"You shouldn't be like that at your age. Don't say I was taking your mind off the road."

I wasn't going to tell him what had done so – even the threat of memory revived a crawling inside my eyes – but I said "I'd been putting things right for Toby."

"What's the matter there, son? Is it mixed up at all with that thing the nurse let him tell me? Seemed like he thought I needed a bedtime story. I don't want anybody thinking I'm ungrateful, but it didn't sound quite right to me."

"Why do you say that?"

"I know you used to enjoy making stories up, but it wasn't like any of yours. He had a boy flying out past the edge of everything, and when I told him God must be there, do you know what he said to me?"

"No." I found this easier to say than "What?"

"He made out it was full of things that people used to think were gods when they got a hint of them. And he said we'll all find out what they really are, because they're coming back or coming here. He'd got some idea it was both, but he couldn't sort it out in his head, and no wonder."

Despite my unease I thought this could be useful. "What did Lesley make of all that?"

"She didn't hear it. She was talking to the nurse." As my flare of hope went out my father said "Where's he getting stuff like that from? Don't say from you or his mother."

"I promise it isn't." I felt as though my words were set free by saying "It's Christian Noble and his family. They're back."

"Christian." His thoughts seemed to snag on the name. "Who's he again?"

"He taught at Holy Ghost. He drove Mrs Norris out of her head. You and some of the other parents got him fired from the school."

"So we damned well did, and good riddance." My father's eyes had regained a gleam. "And didn't someone who wrote for the paper drive him out of town?"

"Eric Wharton, that's right. Only then he was drown din an accident, if you believe that's what it was." When my father showed no interest in this I said "But now Noble's back, and his daughter is. She has all his beliefs, and she's hell ping him feed them to chilled wren."

"Are you telling me he's doing that to Toby?"

"I only just found out they run the place we've been sending him for treatment. You thought it might be Buddhist, but it's their kind of spirit yule lissom."

"I hope to God you've got him out of there."

"Of course we have, but there are dozens of children."

"Was he why you had your crash, son?" When I risked a careful nod my father said "Just let me get better and you can count on me if you want someone by your side."

I couldn't help thinking of the Tremendous Three. "Dad, I wasn't trying to involve you. You don't want to cross them, believe me."

"Don't fret about me, Dominic." The mission seemed to have lent him strength, and he raised his voice. "I've dealt with your Mr Christian Noble once," he declared, "and I can dakh wakakh agh agakh."

This was just the start of a coughing fit, and as I mimed helpless sympathy a nurse hurried over. "We said you mustn't get excited, Desmond. Say bye-bye to your son now and you can see him later."

I couldn't judge whether he was parodying her instruction as he went to some trouble to articulate "Byakh bakakh."

"I'll come back soon, dad," I said, and the nurse gave me a look that sent me out of the ward before he'd finished coughing. I heard him all the way along the corridor and even after I sat on my bed. When my neighbour wondered whether Lee Marvin returned to Alcatraz in *Point Blank* only after he was dead I hushed him, which he took as a rebuff. Whenever anyone in another ward began to cough I did my best to hear that it wasn't my father. At last I felt sufficiently reassured to doze and let my latest headache drift away. Perhaps those were the final hours in which I was able to believe all could be well.

I was awake before any evening visitors arrived, and able to discuss John Wayne with my stubbly neighbour. We were recalling his last film, in which the role of a gunfighter dying of cancer prefigured the actor's own imminent death, when I heard Toby in the corridor. "Shall I give it to dad or grandad?"

"If you like I can photocopy it at work," Lesley said. "Then you can keep it and they'll each have one."

"Then there'll be three," Toby said.

He had to be restrained from running into the ward. "Do you want to see my picture, dad?" he urged. "It's my best one."

"Of course I do. Give me a good look."

As he opened the pad he'd been holding under his arm, Lesley sat on the chair by the bed. She was watching for my reaction, but I didn't grow tense until Toby turned the page towards me. For a moment I was afraid to identify the image, and then I saw what it portrayed: not Ouroboros but a comet whose tail vanished into its wide-eyed smiling face. The thin pale shape was almost circular, framing a yellow sun and a white moon and the earth, which was blue and green. "It's the boy who thought he was a comet," Toby said.

"I see that. It's very good, Toby." While I was nervous of saying too much, I found myself asking "If he only thinks it, why is it how he looks?"

"Because," Toby said as gravely as only a five-year-old could, "he isn't old enough yet to see what he is really."

My neighbour laughed and raised a thumb as if he'd stubbed it on the answer. "He's got you there, mate."

"I shouldn't show grandad just now," I said.

"Why not?" Lesley said with a hint of sharpness.

"The nurse told me not to get him excited, that's all." I was afraid the last two words might have been redundant if not suspicious, and so I said hastily "Did you do that at Judith's, Toby?"

He glanced at his mother, and I glimpsed her terse nod. "Claudine's, dad," he said.

I wanted to believe him, and very much wished I wasn't hearing myself say "What was that about?"

Lesley lowered her voice to indicate I should restrain mine. "What was what, Dominic?"

"That look just now. What don't you want Toby to say?"

"Nothing that we need to talk about right now." When I started to protest she said lower still "Shall we save it until you're home?"

"It started here and I'd like to finish it. Toby, what were you going to say?"

"I said it, dad."

I had to fight to keep my voice down. "What would you have said if you hadn't been told not to?"

"Nothing, dad. I really was at Claudine's."

"After you went home with her, yes? Where were you before that?"

"Stop harassing him, Dominic. If you're so eager for the truth you shall have it. He's been where he needs to go, whatever you may think."

My voice came out as a savage mutter. "You sent him back to Noble and his crew."

"I sent him to Dr Sweet, and you have to realise—"

"I told you who's behind her." I was additionally dismayed to realise "You're teaching him to lie to me."

"Toby, go and see grandad for a few minutes. You remember where he is."

"Stay where you are, Toby." My eyes might well have grown as fierce as my low voice as I said "You're too fond of sending him off by himself. Can't you understand he's in danger?"

"Do as I say, Toby, or we'll have to be on our way. See if grandad wants to hear another of your stories."

"No, wait," I cried and floundered across the bed as he took a hesitant step towards the corridor. I made a grab for his arm but missed, because a spike of agony had jabbed so deep behind my eyes that I might as well have gone blind. "Fuck," I snarled, a word I'd never previously used in public and had very seldom said. "Fuck."

"I'm sorry, Toby, but we're going home if your father's going to behave like this."

"Go." At once I was desperate to say more, though every word sharpened the pain in my head. "Take him home and keep him there. Don't let him anywhere near Noble and the rest of them."

"Come along now, Toby," Lesley murmured, and I was left with a kiss – just one, my son's – on my forehead. As I heard the door thump shut and tried to lie as still as assuaging the pain might require, my neighbour's voice came close. "I don't know what kind of bad way you're in, mate, but just keep an eye on the language."

"Sorry." By now each syllable increased the pain, no matter how terse I tried to make them. "Could you call nur," I said before I couldn't bear to speak.

"Go and get her for him, Marge."

I heard the door thump, and soon it did again. I thought this heralded some relief until my neighbour's wife said "She won't be long." At last a plastic cup nudged my lips, and some time after swallowing I was able to believe the pain had begun to shrink. I kept my eyes shut and did my best to hold my mind as blank as my vision. Thinking wouldn't help my state while it was all I could do. As the pain receded it drew me towards sleep, but I wasn't aware of having lost consciousness until a woman murmured "Mr Sheldrake."

I was dismayed to think that Tina Noble had tracked me down while I was helpless. My eyes jerked wide, reviving a threat of pain, and I saw she'd put out the lights. No, they were only dim, suggesting that it was the middle of the night. I had to narrow my eyes to make out a face I didn't recognise and to establish that it belonged to a nurse. "Mr Sheldrake," she whispered, "can you walk?"

"Where to?"

"Just along the corridor. Your father's asking for you and we think you'd better come."

I didn't want to ask why, because I was afraid I knew. When I raised my head it encountered no pain, but I took some care over finding the floor with my feet and standing up. The thump of the door as it shut behind me sounded like an isolated heartbeat, giving way to silence. Was the lighting in the corridor feebler than I would have expected it to be? I had a sense that too much was at a low ebb, and a glimpse of the nurse's wristwatch told me the time was almost four o'clock. I wasn't sure why this made me stumble faster towards the other ward.

My father lay face up with his arms extended to the sides of the bed. While this wasn't quite the posture I knew all too well from Safe To Sleep, it seemed unnecessarily similar. I hoped only the muted illumination made his eyes look far dimmer than normal as they turned towards me. "Sorry to get you out of bed, son," he said in very little of a voice. "Were you asleep?"

"I've had plenty of sleep, dad. Just now I'm not doing much else."

I sat by the bed and reached for his hand, but he made a weak fist and edged it away from me. "No need for holding hands, son," he said with the faintest hint of vigour. "We're grown men. We don't want anybody thinking we're something else."

I felt disconcertingly wistful for saying "I should think people could see I'm your son."

"Not when it's this dark. Let's not waste time arguing." He made a visible effort to lift his head from the pillow, but must have decided to save his energy for speaking. "Afraid I may not be as much use to you as I wanted," he said. "May have to leave that Noble character to you after all."

"I can deal with him, but don't start thinking you're out of the running just yet, dad."

"That's my boy. You carry on being positive." Before I could urge the attitude on him my father said "I want you to tell me one thing, and then you can make me a promise."

"Anything at all."

"About your Mr Noble, when you were at school." My father's

eyes flickered sideways as though to ensure he wasn't overheard. "That book you had of his," he muttered. "I know you always said not, but you pinched it, didn't you?"

I saw his eyes gleam in an ineffectual bid to peer into mine. I'd barely opened my mouth when he said "Tell me the truth and I can rest easy, Dominic."

His plea overrode my doubts. "I suppose you could say I did."

"We always knew, me and your mother. Thanks for that. I can trust you now."

"You mean you haven't all these years."

"I mean when you promise. I said let's not argue, son." He fumbled to clutch at his chest as trying to raise his voice dislodged a raw cough. "Will you do whatever you have to that'll keep your boy safe?" he said once he could.

"Dad, you don't need to ask."

"I know, but it'd help me rest if I heard you promise."

"I give you my word I'll go to any lengths to make sure Toby's safe."

"That's all I wanted to hear." When he lifted his shaky right hand in my general direction I took it despite his reluctance, and he gave mine a determined shake that let me feel how thin and light his hand had grown. "You go and catch up on your sleep now," he said. "The sooner you get better, the sooner you can look after your boy. And I don't know if you pray any more, but if you ever do, say some for me."

When I looked back from the door I saw he had already closed his eyes. I found I couldn't breathe until I was certain he was doing so. The nurse who'd fetched me tried to look encouraging as I made for the corridor. How long had my father suspected if not known that I'd left his religion behind? His acknowledgement that I might have almost made me want to rediscover prayer on his behalf.

As I lay awake in the dim ward I willed him to be wrong about his own state. Surely just his enervation had made the nurse think it was imperative for me to go to him, and once he was over the infection he would regain his strength. The thought let me doze, but another one jolted me awake – that I'd lied to him once more by pretending I'd stolen Noble's journal. Noble's father had, and he'd meant it to be read. I was tempted to go back to my father, though how would the truth help? Sleep overtook me before I came anywhere near a decision, but the ward was still keeping its lights low when someone murmured in my ear. "Mr Sheldrake," the nurse from the other ward said, "I'm afraid your father's gone."

CHAPTER FOURTEEN
Speaking of the Dead

As I paced behind my father's coffin towards the church I was troubled by how few mourners I could recognise. I saw Jim's parents and Bobby's next to them, but theirs were the only faces I knew in the sombre crowd. Lesley's parents weren't there, since they hadn't known my father, and in any case they lived and taught in Canada. She and Toby were at my back, the only other people following the coffin. I heard my son begin to whisper until his mother hushed him. I almost turned to intervene, because I should have liked to hear whatever he might have said. It was less a fear of impropriety than of losing my balance and staggering against the coffin that kept me faced towards the church.

I'd been out of hospital for just a few days, and life at home felt like a truce that would have to be broken soon. Organising the funeral had taken all my time and energy, which meant I'd had to nominate a colleague to assess my students. Toby was attending all his sessions at Safe To Sleep. Lesley hadn't brought up the situation any more than I had since our confrontation at the hospital, but we both knew the conflict wasn't resolved. Judith helped remind us by not letting Claudine visit now that I was home, instead entrusting her to another parent at the school, having apologised to Lesley while she knew I could hear. Once my father was buried and remembered I meant to protect Toby however I could. I'd promised my father as much, and perhaps that was the best way to commemorate him.

The church was a long concrete hall furnished with pale pine pews beneath arched beams of the same material. The pointed windows contained saints pieced together out of splinters of rainbow glass. Beyond a cut-price altar the largest window showed Mary with her infant in her arms under a spiky sun. As the undertaker's quartet lowered the coffin into place before the altar, an usher guided us towards the right-hand front row, where Toby ended up between Lesley and me. "We've got the best seats," he said.

"Toby," Lesley murmured.

"It's all right, Toby, you can talk. Just not that loud." I found I was anxious to hear any observations he might make about the funeral or in church. "What did you mean?" I said.

"Where we can see best from."

I wasn't sure I wanted to learn "What are you expecting to see?"

"I don't know, dad. I've never been to one of these before."

Lesley's look warned me not to question him further. I saw Jim's and Bobby's parents file into the pew opposite ours, and heard dozens of mourners shuffle to their seats. In the midst of the muted bustling Toby said "Why do they put people in boxes when they're dead?"

"It's a way of showing respect, Toby," Lesley said. "That's why we're here."

"I thought they mightn't want us to see them."

I saw she would have liked to let this go, but I had to ask "Who mightn't?"

"The men who carried grandad. It's like they want to lock him up."

"Nobody can do that any more," Lesley assured him.

"I know." Our son sounded impatient to establish "They can't stop him flying away now."

I suspected that I knew where this idea had come from, but couldn't make sure just now. "When do we have to cry?" he said.

Lesley glanced at me and seemed relieved to find I wasn't outraged. "Whenever you feel you have to," I said.

"I don't know if I'm going to. I don't think grandad's really gone."

I had no chance to ascertain what Toby meant by this, because the priest had come to stand beside my father's coffin. Father Harty was a round-faced wide-mouthed man who gave the impression of constantly restraining ebullience, just as his name appeared to have suppressed an appropriate vowel. He toned his voice down to express gentle reassurance as he said "We are gathered here today to celebrate the life of our departed relative and friend Desmond Sheldrake..."

Toby looked bemused by the description but didn't query it aloud. I felt distanced from the ceremony, not least since I'd had to leave so much of it to the priest. He'd told me which my father's favourite hymns were, for example, and soon everybody stood up to sing one. "Oh God, our help in ages past..."

I sang the words from the pamphlet that bore a smudged photograph of my parents, in which they were several years older than my wife and I were now. It brought back a memory of spying from my bedroom window on a man with a pram in the graveyard, and I did my best to concentrate on the hymn, though I felt unable to engage with the sentiments until a verse seemed to fasten on my mind:

"Time, like an ever-rolling stream,

Bears all its sons away;

They fly, forgotten, as a dream

Dies at the opening day..."

It wasn't just that I was anxious to determine whether these ideas had any special significance for Toby, though I could see no reaction when I tried to watch him without turning my head. It was more that I was certain someone in the church had raised her voice at the start of the verse. I thought she was near the back of the church, but once we reached the next verse I couldn't hear her any more. Soon we all knelt to recite the Lord's Prayer, though I confined myself to intoning the amen, which Toby echoed – the second syllable, at any rate. We sat while Father Harty read to us, though I would have preferred to hear about somebody other than Lazarus. At least the next hymn – *Abide with Me* – was one I'd liked in my childhood. I still did until a few words seemed to rise out of the body of the hymn. "Change and decay in all around I see..."

I was convinced that not only my mind had emphasised the line – that the woman's voice had. I glanced back, but at once the voice was lost in the amateur chorus, and Lesley gave me a quick frown. We sat down to be told about Christ and the thief – "Today thou shalt be with me in paradise"– and even this made me wish I hadn't let my father think I'd stolen Noble's journal. I was able to derive a little wry amusement from *All Things Bright and Beautiful*, since Bobby's father visibly resented the suggestion that God put the rich man in his castle and the poor man at his gate. More prayers brought us to communion, and most of the mourners joined the queue for the wafer, but I would have felt worse than hypocritical, even if my father would have liked me to participate. "What are they having to eat?" Toby whispered.

"They believe it's God," Lesley said barely loud enough for him and me to hear.

"That's too little," Toby said, stifling a giggle. "You don't eat gods, they eat you. I don't mean really eat. They're so big and special they can have millions of galaxies inside them."

I saw Lesley hoping I agreed he was merely being fanciful. I did my best to look unconcerned, because the prospect of facing the congregation while I spoke about my father had put me on edge despite all my years as a lecturer. Another hymn followed the communion, and within seconds I was listening so hard I felt in danger of a headache.

"Come, holy ghost, creator, come
From thy bright heav'nly throne.
Come take possession of our souls..."

I'd scarcely been reminded of the school where I'd encountered Noble and his beliefs when the woman's voice behind me rose to embrace the third line. I was convinced it swelled again at "teaching little ones to speak and understand" and "thrice-blessed three in one". Once the congregation took their seats again Father Harty paused, which I found unnecessarily dramatic. "And now," he said, "Desmond's son Dominic will share some personal memories of his father."

As I sidled past her Lesley squeezed my elbow, offering support of some kind, and Toby whispered "Can I as well?"

"Tell people about grandad, do you mean?" Lesley murmured. "You can afterwards if you like."

"He'll hear me better when everyone's quiet. I expect he'll hear dad."

At once I remembered how Christian Noble believed the dead were desperate to cling to any scraps of their personality they could salvage, which might explain some of the rudimentary messages mediums claimed to receive. I hoped Toby had nothing of the sort in mind, and did my best to think that nothing I might say could affect my father now. I took care over climbing the steps to the pulpit, gripping both the smooth slim handrails. I gazed across the lectern at the congregation and saw the woman at once.

She was sitting by herself on the furthest occupied pew. Her pointed oval sharp-featured face was tied up in a black headscarf and framed by faded bushy red hair that the scarf hadn't altogether managed to contain. While everybody was intent on me, I was sure her eyes were wider. I saw mourners willing me not to lose control, but I thought she was urging me to speak, and I vowed not to leave the pulpit until I'd made her betray that she was an intruder. Even if the Nobles hadn't sent her, I felt certain she followed their faith.

I took a breath and instantly forgot the entire speech I'd been working on for days. I'd wanted to ensure I didn't falter or end up babbling when my turn came to speak. Losing my prepared speech felt too much like a symptom of concussion and the threat of a vicious headache as well, and I could only snatch at memories and talk about them as they surfaced: times we'd spent together when I was at school and less often since, jokes he'd told, traits that made him unique, advice he'd given me when I was young and indeed significantly older, though I hadn't always followed it and in some cases regretted that now... These fragments hardly even started to piece a life together, especially if you gave any credence to Christian Noble's belief. Humpty Dumpty in the afterlife, I found myself thinking, an image that enraged me as much as the solitary woman did, not least because I was sure she believed the ideas I couldn't evict from my brain. Perhaps the way to combat them was to confront her, and I searched for thoughts that might mean more to her than she would like. My parents had brought me up in the faith he'd adopted, but this didn't seem to bother her. Neither of my parents had doubted at the end or sought solace elsewhere, but her wide-eyed face stayed uncommunicatively neutral. In his last hours he'd asked me to pray for him, and I was certain everybody here would, an observation I directed straight at her. When her gaze flickered aside from mine I didn't have to think what to say next. "I'm sure we all wish my parents will be together for eternity," I said, and the woman looked down at whatever her hands were doing, invisible to me. I stared hard at her on my way back to the front pew, but she didn't raise her eyes or her head.

"Thank you, Dominic," Father Harty said, "for gifting us those deeply personal insights into your father," which left me wondering how much of this was exaggeration meant to compensate for a lack. He led prayers for the departed and for those left behind, petitioning not just to be heard but to be graciously heard. He blessed the coffin and swung a censer at it, and I felt more remote than ever from the ceremony, though I couldn't help wishing with no conviction at all that his performance were able to fend off the likes of Christian Noble and his secret practices. Suppose, having learned that my father was dead, Noble used him as a warning to me?

Once the undertaker's men had plodded past us with the coffin, my family let me out of the pew. As we marched in slow motion along the aisle an organ played a thin tune, a hymn I couldn't name. The woman at the back of the congregation blinked at the coffin before lowering her eyes again, and didn't look at me when I stared at her. While the men loaded the hearse, the surviving Sheldrakes climbed into the limousine behind it. Toby strapped himself into one of the seats facing backwards and looked pensive. "I never cried."

"I expect you felt sad, though, didn't you?" Lesley said.

As he considered this I said "You shouldn't make yourself feel what you don't really feel. I'm sure grandad would want you to be true to yourself."

"Why do we need to be sad if he isn't really gone?"

I saw Lesley assume he had some notion of heaven in mind. Though I suspected he meant something else entirely, I couldn't question him now. As the limousine crept after the hearse he watched the procession of cars we were leading, and I could have thought his view bordered on the regal, as if he felt he was observing his inferiors. Surely this came from riding in such a luxurious car, and I told myself my son was just an ordinary boy, or at least only a precocious one – that he could be made ordinary, at any rate.

The hearse led us into Anfield Cemetery, where injured grey figures beneath the trees wore crowns of fallen leaves. As the limousine halted beside an expanse of grass on which new stones gleamed white or black, I caught sight of the window of my childhood bedroom. Nobody was there – the house was unoccupied, and I would have to put it up for sale – but for a moment I felt threatened by fancying that time had played a trick. I was recalling how I'd watched Noble and his daughter from my window, and the impression seemed more present than an ordinary memory. If I'd been watching now I would have seen a father and another child under Noble's influence.

Father Harty came to the family grave as the undertaker's quartet lowered the coffin onto a stand. He led the mourners in a farewell prayer, and when we all had the last word I thought Toby said "Our men" or else "Ah well." I was distracted by the woman whose voice I'd kept hearing at the church, who appeared to be trying to stay inconspicuous. The priest blessed the coffin before it sank into the earth, and then an undertaker's man who looked permanently stooped by the weight of a succession of coffins handed me a miniature spade with which to scatter earth on the wooden lid. Lesley followed me, and Toby copied us while looking puzzled. "Can grandad hear that?" he said.

I saw how his innocence charmed and touched the mourners. I tried not to think he was pretending to be naïve, unless he was referring to a notion Christian Noble had put into his head. "I'm sure it won't disturb your grandfather," the priest said.

Mourners started queuing for the ceremonial spade, and I watched the woman in the black headscarf advance towards the grave. She was almost the last to take the spade, and lingered over spilling earth. I was about to approach her when Toby said "Grandma isn't waiting down there, is she?"

The woman retreated into the crowd, and I told myself that he couldn't have meant to let her escape. "Of course not," Father Harty said. "They're both elsewhere and you'll see them again when it's time."

Even this conjured up Christian Noble's activities, though not in Toby's mind, I hoped. I saw gravediggers waiting for us to depart so that they could fill the grave in. As I headed for the limousine I tried to see which car the woman made for, but couldn't find her in the crowd. The limousine gained speed once we reached the road, and I remembered thinking as a child that people always drove away from funerals faster than they went to them, as if they'd jettisoned some ballast that had been weighing them down.

Soon we were back at St Gabriel's. The entrance lobby led both to the church and to an elongated windowless concrete extension, the church hall. I stood outside with my family to shake hands and accept the occasional respectful hug along with everyone's sympathetic comments. At first I didn't see the woman I was looking for, because her scarf had drooped around her wiry neck. As the queue ahead of her grew shorter my palms kept turning clammy, and I had to wipe the right one on my funereal jacket. Her approach left my throat dry, which reduced my voice to little more than a croak, and when she reached me I took an audible breath to compensate if not to brace myself. "You're the lady who put so much into the hymns," I said.

"Amy Hennessey. I'm one of the old souls."

Just in time not to show any unease I recollected that Old Souls was the club for the elderly that Father Harty organised. All the same, her handshake was so dry I might have called it reptilian, and so light it felt insinuating. "Truly sorry that you've lost your father," she said.

"You think I have, then."

"I imagine even Father Harty would," she said and made for the church hall.

I followed the last mourners into the long room, where a pair of trestle tables were covered with a buffet. Toby gave them a hungry look as Jim's and Bobby's parents joined us to be introduced to Lesley and my son. "You've been a credit to your parents," Mrs Parkin told him, "and I know your grandpa would have been proud of you too."

She and Mrs Bailey began discussing him with Lesley, and I turned to the men. "We heard you saw our Jim and Bill's daughter in London," Mr Bailey said.

"Yes, at Bobby's book launch, or I should say Bob's."

Mr Parkin made a face and then another. "Is she still with that woman?"

"Carole, do you mean?"

"I wouldn't know what it calls itself. The one that helped to make her into what she thinks she's got to be." As I searched for a response I would be comfortable with giving he said "At least Desmond saw your Toby, and Kevin here's seeing his Jim's kids. I don't reckon we'll be seeing any grandkids out of her."

"She and her partner could always adopt if they wanted."

Though I was taking Bobby's side, my retort seemed almost childishly unwise now it was out. While Mr Parkin didn't bother grimacing, his tone did the job. "You'd like to see a kid brought up in that kind of setup."

"There are worse ways to bring up a child." At once I saw my cue and realised Lesley wasn't listening. "Christian Noble's, for instance," I said.

"Not much wrong with being Christian if you do what the man really said. Him and Marx might have got on, I reckon."

"I'm talking about somebody called Christian. His name's a pretence like the rest of him." I was growing desperate, because I didn't know how long Lesley might be occupied elsewhere, and hardly sufficiently far away either. "You remember Mr Noble," I pleaded with Jim's father. "You and my dad organised getting him fired from Holy Ghost because of the things he was trying to teach us."

"That's not quite how I remember it." Before I could pursue this he said "You saw how he affected people, Bill. The lady who showed up at the coronation party with her dog, it was his ideas that drove her mad."

"I'm with you now. They got his dad run over by a tram as well."

"And now he's teaching them to children Toby's age and even younger," I said. "He has to be stopped, and I could use some help."

Both men gazed at me, and I was afraid I'd said too much too soon. "Still teaching, is he?" Mr Parkin said. "How old's the bugger now?"

"I don't think he's a teacher in that sense. He's involved in, in a children's care facility, and his daughter is as well."

"Involved how?" Mr Bailey said.

"He's feeding all the children his beliefs, and she's helping. You've seen what they can do to adults, so what do you think—"

"Are they doing anything illegal?"

"If it isn't," I said desperately, "it most certainly ought to be."

"A lot of things ought," Mr Parkin said. "What our Roberta's up to would be if it wasn't for a queen that was even more ignorant than most of her lot. Victoria, that was. Wouldn't believe there was such things as Roberta and that woman."

"Bill," his wife murmured behind me. "Please, not here."

I said no more until the women recommenced talking, and then I kept my voice low. "Even if it's technically legal you surely wouldn't want children to be indoctrinated with it. You wouldn't have wanted it for Bobby or Jim."

"There's a lot of things I don't want in her head," Mr Parkin retorted, "but I've found out I can't stop them. I've given up trying before it knocks any more years off my life."

"If this Noble fellow and his daughter aren't breaking the law," Mr Bailey said, "I can't see what's to be done."

He glanced past me, and I realised the women had fallen silent. When I looked around I saw Lesley watching me, and Toby was. Mrs Parkin read my wife's face and moved away. "Come and get something to eat, Bill."

"We will too," Mrs Bailey said and waited to make sure her husband followed.

It was plain that Lesley didn't know how much to say. I saw her decide and part her lips, just as Father Harty joined us. "Did you want to ask me a question, Toby?" he said.

Toby looked puzzled if not daunted. "Did I, mum?" he said.

"Not as far as I know either," I was provoked to tell him.

The priest dropped to one knee, an action meant to bring him closer to the boy rather than heralding a prayer. "Didn't you want to know what I was giving people at communion?"

"Little biscuits."

"Wafers, that's correct. A bit like the ones I expect you've had with ice cream."

When Toby didn't respond, never having had any such thing, Lesley said "Like a cornet, Toby."

"That's so, a cornet." Just the same, Father Harty seemed to feel his theme was making an escape. "Now this may be hard for you to understand," he said, "but God can change every one of those wafers into himself."

"I've seen things change like that." As the priest looked indulgent but skeptical Toby said "What does he taste like?"

"Just the same. The change takes place inside us, in our souls. Don't worry if all this is a bit too much for you to grasp just yet."

"I know things as big as that," Toby protested.

"Well then, would you like to tell me what you believe?"

"Shall I, mum?"

"You tell Father Harty," I urged before Lesley could speak. "Tell him some of your beliefs."

When Toby hesitated the priest said "What have you been thinking today? I'm sure they were good thoughts."

"Clouds are shapes dead people try and take," Toby said and

pointed at the ceiling in lieu of the sky. "Up there it's dark for ever and ever."

Father Harty gripped one knee to shove himself to his feet, and I could have thought he was recoiling until he patted Toby's head. "Your grandad used to say you were an imaginative little chap like your father," he said. "Just have a think about the things we were saying in church, though. They aren't stories like those, they're the truths God tells us."

I was on the edge of asking him where he thought Toby's notions came from, but he moved away to speak to some of his parishioners. "Shall we have our food now?" Toby said.

He sounded like a boy of his age, and I yearned to believe that this was still the core of him —that Christian Noble hadn't laid claim to his essence, changing it for good or very much the opposite before I was able to save it. "Let's," I said and ushered Lesley after him.

Several women who I guessed were widows watched appreciatively while he heaped a paper plate with sandwiches and sausage rolls and crisps and quiche. I was making a rather less ambitious selection when I saw Amy Hennessey retrieve her coat from a hook near the door, and I put my plate down. "Miss Hennessey," I called.

I wasn't sure whether she heard me through the mass of conversations. She didn't linger to put on her coat before heading for the exit, and I hurried across the room. "Mrs Hennessey," I tried calling. "Amy, do you have to leave so soon?"

When she turned I thought she'd taken time to render her expression blank. "What is it, Mr Sheldrake?"

"We haven't had a chance to talk."

"We did before," she said and shrugged her coat on. "I don't want to keep you from your friends."

"You won't be. By all means stay and talk."

She looked down at a button she was fitting through its hole. "What about, sorry?"

"Why are we all here? About my father."

"I thought you said it all. Will you excuse me?"

I was growing so tense that I blurted "For what?"

"For coming to the funeral, if you like." As she turned away she said "According to you he's with who he wanted to be with."

Before I could ask where she thought my father was, she hurried out of the church hall. I was making to pursue her when Lesley caught my arm. "For heaven's sake, Dominic," she said low. "What was all that about?"

I swung around to face the room, which involved pulling free of her grasp. "Does anyone here know Amy Hennessey?" I called. "What does she have to do with my father?"

"She's one of us widows," said a woman who had watched Toby at the buffet. "She's had her eye on him since she joined Old Souls."

"What do you mean, had her eye?"

"What on earth do you imagine, Dominic?" Lesley said, trying to conceal her distress. "No, never mind what you imagine. Just realise what this lady means."

When the woman's face confirmed she thought Amy Hennessey's intentions had been amorous, I said "When did she join you?"

"Not long after Christmas," my informant said.

"Not long before my father died," I muttered and saw I'd made Lesley feel worse. However irrational my comment might sound, I felt the woman could have thought it likely that my father hadn't long to live. "Let's not leave Toby on his own," I said, only to sense that Lesley couldn't be sure why I did.

My outburst had undermined the gathering. Once a few mourners began to make their exit the rest weren't slow in following. Jim's and Bobby's parents were the last to leave, saying in various ways that they hoped all would be well. By now the occasion felt like a postponement of whatever Lesley had in store to say to me. So did the rest of the day until Toby was asleep, having read to us how Alice wondered what would become of her when she succumbed to uncontrollable growth. Perhaps my unease with the idea was apparent, and a further reason why Lesley confronted me once we were downstairs. "Dominic, you can't keep on behaving how you did today. When are you going to see someone?"

I had to persuade her I was giving in while I tried to plan on Toby's behalf. "If you have Colin Hay's number," I said, "I'll see if I can make an appointment right now."

My fingers seemed to want to fumble as I dialled. Certainly they felt stiff and almost too swollen for my forefinger to fit into the holes.

If this was reluctance, I needn't have suffered it, because the number proved to be out of use. Directory Enquiries told me Dr Colin Hay was no longer to be found in Britain. At least I didn't have to convince Lesley of this, since she'd overheard. "You're going to have to speak to someone, all the same," she insisted, and at once I knew who it had to be.

CHAPTER FIFTEEN

Helpers

"I saw your parents yesterday, Jim."

"I haven't spoken to them yet this week. How were they? How's your dad?"

"They don't change any more than you do. My dad's gone. They were at his funeral."

"I'm so sorry, Dom. I wish I'd known. Your parents weren't any older than mine, were they? You don't expect them to be taken so soon."

"Taken." The word meant more and worse to me than I knew it did to him. "He had a fall," I said, "and then he caught pneumonia in hospital."

"I thought they were supposed to be able to cure that." Jim's protest vibrated the phone at my ear before he said more gently "May he rest in peace, and your mother."

"I hope that too."

"They'll be in my prayers, and I know my parents will say one. Do you still go in for that at all?"

"I haven't since before we left school. Speaking of which—"

"Maybe you should give it another chance. It's never really gone, and it might be a comfort to you." When I didn't answer he said "Will you have some family who are?"

"A wife and a son." As a response this felt close to dishonest. "Your parents mentioned you have children," I said.

"Robert and Dominic. They're quite a pair."

For the duration of a long breath I had no words. "Jim, thank you, really. I wish I'd known when he was christened." This sounded like a rebuke, and so did "Why didn't you say when we saw Bobby? Or did you tell her before I showed up?"

"Carole gave me the feeling she didn't care much for youngsters, so I kept mine to myself. Why didn't you say you had a family? Was there someone you didn't want to know about them?"

He'd begun to sound like the police officer he was, but then it was this side of him I needed. "It might have been because I was worried for my son," I said.

"They can keep you awake at night and no mistake. What's the worry with yours?"

I took a prolonged breath as an aid to taking care how much I said. "Toby's had a sleep disorder pretty well since he was born. Nocturnal absences, I've heard them called. Seizures in his sleep."

Jim was silent long enough to let me wonder if my son's name had disappointed him. "You'll be getting him some treatment, won't you?" he said.

"We thought we'd found the ideal one, only now I've discovered Christian Noble and his daughter are involved."

"Good God, him again?" Jim might have been disgusted with him or with me for bringing Noble up. "I thought he made himself scarce after his church was wrecked," he said. "What are you telling me he's up to now?"

"He's running a private facility where they claim they can treat children with Toby's condition. Tina Noble has been sending children there. She's, she's a paediatrician." I'd nearly said more than I thought Jim would believe, but I managed to add only "Her father's putting his ideas in all their heads."

"They didn't stick in ours, did they? Not mine, at any rate."

"He had to keep most of them quiet at school. He doesn't have to any more, and these children are a lot younger. Toby's only five."

"I see that could be serious. So what are you doing about it, Dom?"

"I've tried to take him away from the place, but his mother won't hear of it. She thinks it's helping him."

"Do you think she could be right? Women have an instinct for these things, and she sounds a reasonable lady."

"Yes, she called you about me, didn't she? What exactly did she say?"

"Just that you seemed a bit obsessed with Noble, and she wanted to know what I thought of him."

"Has she spoken to you since?"

"She hasn't, old friend. I don't know why she would."

So she couldn't have told Jim about my crash. "Well, now you know why I'm obsessed, and I hope you understand. Lesley doesn't even know as much about Noble as you do."

"How do you know he's mixed up with the treatment your son's getting?"

"I saw him there. They use his house near Ormskirk. It's paid for by his followers, apparently. I went and confronted him."

"Good for you, Dom. What happened?"

"He boasted about giving the children his ideas. I've heard some of them from Toby, and Toby's mother has, only she won't recognise them. They're more of the sort of thing he wrote in his journal. Would you want anybody feeding them to Dominic and Robert?"

"I wouldn't, but of course we're Catholics."

I hadn't time to wonder if Jim meant this was why he found Noble's beliefs anathematic or a defence against them. "Any more than I want it for Toby," I said. "I've done all I seem able to do, but I can't stop Noble by myself. Will you help?"

He paused, and then he sounded wary. "What do you think I can do?"

"Would you rather not talk about it just now? Shall I call you at home later?"

"Is there a reason you can't talk now?"

"Of course we can if nobody's listening in. We can if we won't be saying anything we'd rather people didn't hear."

"I hope I don't know what you mean by that, Dominic."

My full name made the warning even more official. "I mustn't have meant anything," I said.

"Then of course I don't care if anybody hears. So what are you asking me?"

"I know you must be busier than I am, but do you think you could find the time to investigate Noble and his operation?"

"Near Ormskirk, you said. I'm afraid that's well out of my jurisdiction, Dom. I can't really trespass on another force, even for a friend."

I felt absurdly childish for having failed to take this into account and for feeling hollowed out by disappointment now. "Couldn't you at least look into whatever he's been up to since the newspaper exposed him?"

"Would you like me to see if I can have a word with someone on your local force?"

"No, don't do that. Noble told me some of them were his people and if I called the police about him they'd deal with me on his behalf."

"That's a very serious accusation." As I wondered whether Jim was blaming me or Noble he said "All the same, it isn't necessarily against the law."

"What, using the police for your own private ends?"

"Who are you saying is doing that, Dom?" I'd grasped that he might have me in mind by the time he said "We don't know if he was telling the truth, do we? Did he mention any officers by name?"

"He didn't, but I have to tell you I believed him."

"Sorry to say no crime has been committed, though. There might be one if any members of the force targeted you on his behalf, but even then it could be hard to prove."

"Doesn't it matter if police are members of his cult? Is it allowed?"

"It isn't in our mandate to interfere with people's beliefs." Jim hesitated, though not long enough to let me think how to go on. "Do you mind if I ask you something?" he said.

"Why would I when you're a friend?"

"You know I've no time for the kind of thing Christian Noble believes, but is that as important as curing your lad?"

I had to swallow before I could speak. "What are you suggesting, Jim?"

"How long is the treatment supposed to go on?"

"No longer than I can help."

"What I mean is it won't be for ever, will it? Don't you think he may grow out of whatever Noble tries to feed him? You were brought up as a Catholic just like me, but you aren't one now."

"That isn't the same thing, not even remotely."

"I know that. One's the truth and the other one's tripe. That ought to make it easier to wean him off it, don't you think?"

"Not the way Noble works. Not when he's got Toby so young."

"Try not to despair, Dom. Remember how they used to say we

never should at school. Can't you separate the stuff Noble believes from the treatment your son's getting?"

"I can't. That's precisely the problem."

I could have said more, but I knew it wouldn't convince Jim; he would only think the problem was my mental state. "Maybe you should try and trust his mother's judgment," he said.

"I thought you were a policeman, not a marriage counsellor."

"I just thought I was your friend."

"Of course you are." I was embarrassed as only men could be with men in those days, and felt my face grow red. "I wouldn't have called you otherwise," I said.

"Then can I give you a bit more advice? They say once you've been a Catholic you're always one deep down. Do you think if you found it again it might be the best thing for your lad? If you want to stop him believing Noble's nonsense you ought to have some beliefs to give him. I wouldn't say this if I weren't your friend and you hadn't got in touch about the situation, but maybe your dad would have wanted you to come back to the church."

I gritted my teeth to trap retorting that he'd missed his way and should have joined the priesthood. All I could find to say instead was "He did ask me to pray the last time we spoke."

"As I say, I'm going to, but you might as well. After all, he was your dad."

"I'll leave it up to you," I said too low for Jim to hear, and louder "I promised him I'd do whatever it took to keep Toby safe."

"Don't get yourself into trouble with the law, Dom. Will you let me know how things work out?"

"I'll be in touch, and thanks." I hardly knew what I had to be grateful for, even when I said "Thanks for letting me talk."

As I let the receiver slump into its cradle I heard voices along the corridor outside my office, and strained my ears to make sure that I wasn't hearing Lesley – that she wasn't on her way to urge me once again to seek help. At least Toby was at school today, not at Safe To Sleep, but my conversation with Jim had left me even more uncertain how to save my son. It hardly seemed worth bothering to make another call, but I supposed I should while I had time before the afternoon session, and I dialled the second number I'd copied out of my address book. The third pair of trills was cut in half by a woman's voice. "Hello?"

It might have been a caution rather than a greeting. "Hello," I said. "It's Dominic."

"Who are you saying? This is Carole Ashcroft here."

"Hello, Carole. This is Dominic Sheldrake. We met at Bobby's, at Bob's launch."

"Bob calls you Dom. She can't cut me short, though."

Since I couldn't tell whether Carole was stating a fact or expressing defiance, I said "What have you two been up to?"

"By which you mean..."

I hadn't thought my choice of words was quite so unwise as she made it sound. "Your work," I said. "What have you been writing lately?"

"You won't have read my series, then."

"I don't see your partner's column usually either. I'm more of a television news man."

"That's you, isn't it? Films are your life. I wonder how much longer anyone will have any time for print."

"I've a good deal myself, and my students have as well."

"I'm glad to hear you're teaching them that at least." Before I could react to this Carole said "But the world's changing more than most people notice, or maybe they don't want to be aware. A lot of this country that you might like to think is public has gone private, or it's going."

"My son is being treated at a kind of private clinic, and I'd say—"

"Well," Carole said as if she had no time for my contribution, "that's what my current series is about, and more people ought to read it while they can still make a difference."

"That's what I'm trying to do for my son."

"I know if you have a family you can think they count more than everybody else." Without a pause Carole said "Were you phoning to speak to Bob?"

"I'd like to."

"I'll see how busy she is."

The phone left me a thud followed by a silence just as dull, which had begun to feel like an omen if not a definite answer by the time I heard a rattle of plastic. "Dom," Bobby said, "I should have rung you. My mother called last night. I was sorry to hear about your father."

"Don't worry, Bobby, I mean Bob. I suppose we could say one good thing has come out of it."

"Bobby's fine from you. What are you saying is good?"

"At least it put your parents back in touch with you."

"My mother wasn't out of it. My father still is." As I made to commiserate Bobby said "You never told me you had a son."

Rather than suggest this mightn't have appealed to Carole I said "If I'd started talking about him I might have said too much."

"What about, Dom? You can tell me now."

"He's got a sleep disorder, or at least that's what they call it. Lesley and I thought we'd found a cure, but it turns out the Nobles are involved."

The prospect of explaining yet again left me almost too weary to speak. What could Bobby offer besides sympathy, if even that? "You mean your old teacher," she said, "and his daughter who I met once."

"There's a grandson too." I pulled up short of saying any more about the toddler who'd sat like an adult to watch me from the armchair. "Tina's in maternity," I said. "She's sending children to the place her father runs. I think she runs it with him."

"She's keeping that secret, you're saying. Because the hospital might have a problem with it, do you mean?"

"They would if they knew what she and her father are doing to the children. All the things we heard them talking about at his church, they aren't just putting them in the children's heads. They're making the children take part in the rituals."

"How do you know all this, Dom? Did your son say?"

"He's said more than he might like us to realise, except Lesley can't believe that's what it means." Fearing Bobby mightn't either, I said "I confronted Noble but he doesn't care. He thinks nobody can touch them."

"Who do you think could?"

"I wish I knew. I can't stop them by myself, and I've a feeling that the other parents will have been warned off listening to me." In a bid to sound less paranoid I said "No doubt Noble thinks he can get away with anything because the place is private."

"It sounds like a candidate for investigation."

"You're saying someone should do that?" I didn't know how much hope I could feel for suggesting "You mean Carole?"

"No, Dom, I mean me."

"I didn't know that was the kind of thing you did."

"Anyone who reads me knows I'm for privatisation, but shouldn't journalists keep testing the evidence? Are the Nobles selling their treatment as a new technique?"

"That's their trick, yes."

"Then I could have heard about it, and I want to write a column about a good example of outsourcing. Do you think Mr Noble would go for that?"

"I fancy he might if you put it like that." I was starting to feel I could hope after all. "You wouldn't know he was involved, though," I realised. "You'd need to speak to Phoebe Sweet. They make it look as if she's in charge of Safe To Sleep."

As I gave Bobby the address and phone number I began to grow nervous on her behalf. "You'll be careful, won't you? You don't know what he may be capable of."

"Dom, we aren't the Tremendous Three any more. I'm a pretty well known writer if I do say so myself. I've dealt with a lot worse than the leader of a cult, believe me."

I seemed to feel a reminiscence of restlessness deep in my eyeballs. "Eric Wharton was a journalist too, remember."

"Let's not make too much out of him. I'll be as careful as I need to be. I'll let you know what's happening when I've decided how I got the information and spoken to them."

I was wishing that I hadn't made it impossible for me to accompany her to Safe To Sleep when she said "Have you kept that copy you made of his journal?"

"It's at home in my desk."

"Could you fax it to me as soon as you can? It may help me focus what I'm looking for." She gave me her fax number, and I promised to send her the material tomorrow. "Whatever I find out, that's the truth I'll be telling," she promised. "Remember what we said."

"Remind me."

"Dom." Just as reproachfully she said "We'll always be friends, and—"

"We'll always look out for each other."

"That's us, and I'm sure Jim will if he remembers."

I gave in to wishing we could still act as the Tremendous Three, an adult version far stronger than we'd been. In the auditorium along the corridor I found my students arguing about the film I'd most recently shown them. Brendan was insisting it was disrespectful to laugh at a character even if he only fancied he was Christ, while Katy surprised me by agreeing, at least to the extent that it was wrong to laugh at madness. Jojo complained about the miracle the character appeared to perform – that it was absurd if not blasphemous – and Alysha spoke up for the students who'd been moved by the climactic resurrection. I felt compelled to suggest that Carl Dreyer depicted innocence as an aspect of faith, since it was actually a child who raised the dead in the film, though as soon as I mentioned the image I wished I hadn't. "A little child shall lead them," Brendan declared, but it wasn't the Bible this brought to my mind.

The debate broke up without reaching a conclusion about *Ordet*, not least because I felt unable to provide one, and I told myself the variety of views proved the film was stimulating. I was making for my car when I saw that several of the students who'd disagreed most fiercely with one another were at large on the campus, tearing down posters for a concert by a punk band, the Finals – Al Auschwitz, Bill Belsen, Ted Treblinka, Dan Dachau. Some of the objectors didn't merely rip the posters off the walls but rubbed them against their buttocks before crumpling the paper. I might have argued that the names were meant to express horror at the Holocaust rather than endorse it, or at least to keep the memory alive, but I needed to be home.

All the way the sky shone blue, but I couldn't avoid thinking of the darkness Toby believed it hid. Driving home felt like preparing not to raise any issue of the sort with him, though this involved pretending that such notions weren't in his head. When I let myself into the house I was greeted by the aroma of the cassoulet I'd made, which Lesley had put in the oven. She was playing catch with Toby in the back garden, throwing a big colourful ball. It had been his favourite for years, and I tried not to find the wide-eyed grin of its moon face disconcerting, however much it spun and turned upside down in the air. I tapped on the workroom window, and Toby gave me a broad grin that might have been imitating the moony ball, while Lesley tried not to look tentative. "Don't let me spoil the game," I called and went to my desk to transfer the copy of Noble's journal to my briefcase. But the exercise books weren't in the drawer.

For a moment that felt like losing not just my physical balance I thought the concussion from the car accident wouldn't let me recall where I'd put the books, and then a worse suspicion overtook me. I rummaged through the drawer, finding tales of the Tremendous Three and items clipped from newspapers but no sign of my copy of the journal. I strode to the window and tried to calm down before I opened it. "Who's been in my desk?"

As Toby caught the ball with a double slap that amplified its hollowness, Lesley turned her gaze on me. "I'm sure nobody has, Dominic."

"You're saying you haven't."

"I'm saying nobody else either. What makes you think otherwise?"

"I think somebody knows." I was sure Toby's innocent expression was as manufactured as the one the ball wore. "Toby?" I said.

"I never was, dad."

"You told me and your mother you had been."

"I mean never now," he said, and I might have been distracted by wondering what idea of time he had in mind – it sounded too close to Noble's – if he hadn't added "I never took your books again."

I felt no less dismayed than triumphant to ask "Then how did you know they're missing?"

"Dominic." When I kept my eyes on our son Lesley said "Because we knew that's what you must have meant. I expect you've put them somewhere safe. I hope you have."

"Don't play for a moment, Toby," I said as he poised the ball for throwing to his mother. "You haven't answered my question."

"Mum did. You can come and play as well."

"I want you to answer. We both know how you knew what's gone."

"Then you can tell mum."

As he gave me an innocent smile over the fixed grin of the ball I struggled to control my voice. "Will you put that down while I'm talking to you."

He twirled the ball as though he meant to aim its grin at me, and then flung his hands wide in a gesture resembling one I'd seen attributed to saints. As the ball bounced across the grass with a series of thin empty thumps, Lesley moved to stand behind Toby, holding his shoulders. "Dominic, can you please—"

"You need to hear this, Lesley." I felt her gaze grow fiercer as I lowered mine to Toby's face. "I won't be angry so long as you tell me the truth," I said. "Did someone ask you to take those books?"

His relentlessly guiltless look was enough of an answer for me, but he said "Who, dad?"

"Mr Noble, or is he calling himself Bloan as well?" At once I realised "Of course he is. That's what you and Claudine called him in your game."

Though I didn't see Toby react, Lesley said "Dominic, you're upsetting him."

"If I am it's because he knows it's true. Are you going to speak, Toby? Then just listen to me," I told both of them. "I'm guessing Mr Bloan who's really Noble asked you to find a book I'd hidden somewhere. I've said I won't be angry, I'm blaming him and not you, but did you tell him you thought I had some in my desk? Maybe you said you thought they were about the kinds of things you see when you're at Safe To Sleep. What did he promise if you fetched them for him?"

"Nothing, dad. Nobody did."

"So what did he say?" When Toby retreated into a blank silence I said "I'm surprised he didn't send something else to fetch them."

"Dominic, that's more than—"

"You hid them in your schoolbag, didn't you." This angered me as nothing else had. "It was the day you took it there," I said, "when you told us you wanted to show Phoebe Sweet what you were reading," and the phone rang at my back.

I twisted around in a rage and stalked across the room to seize the receiver, mostly to silence the bell. "Hello?" I demanded.

"Dom, it's Bobby. Just to let you know Phoebe Sweet says they'll be happy for me to spend time with them."

"Then I'm afraid they'll be taking care what they let you see. Can I call you tomorrow? I'm just in the middle of sorting something out. I don't know if I'll be able to send you what I said I would."

She'd scarcely answered when I hung up and strode back to the window. The garden was deserted except for the ball, which loitered like a cartoonish moon on the grass, meeting my glare with its inane grin. I crossed the room just in time to find Lesley urging our son along the hall. "Toby," she said, "you stay with me and draw until we have dinner."

"Wait a moment, Toby." I lurched out of the room and caught his hand, only to let go and recoil. He'd raised his eyes without altering his innocent expression, and as I looked into them I felt as if I were falling into a void – into the blackness his eyes appeared to contain, reaching immeasurably deep. "What has he done to you, for God's sake?" I cried.

"Go where I told you, Toby." As he made for the kitchen without looking back, Lesley turned on me. "I said what would happen if you carried on like this," she told me almost too low to hear, "and now I'm afraid it will."

CHAPTER SIXTEEN
No Place Like Home

My father's house smelled of memories, although none that I wanted to share – stale clothes, a gathering of damp, a trace of cigarette smoke, a crumpled greasy newspaper preserving some remains of fish and chips, which I found beside the chair that faced the television in the front room, along with the videorecorder he'd never learned to programme. The house felt like a shrine to the unfinished: an incomplete crossword weeks old on the dining-table, where a ballpoint with a gnawed plastic barrel bled blue ink into an empty square on the grid; half a dozen bathroom tiles propped against the wall next to the bath, under a bare patch of insecure plaster; a stepladder standing defiantly upright beneath a flex on which the lampshade had been dragged awry, nearly wrenching it free of the socket. As I cleared away fragments of the smashed bulb from the faded threadbare carpet I felt neglectful for having left the house in such a state after my father's death, even though I'd had so much else on my mind. I binned the crossword and the remnants of my father's solitary meal, and trudged upstairs with a sagging cardigan I found on the back of a kitchen chair to leave it on a hanger in his bedroom wardrobe. I was thrown by finding my old golliwog money box on the bedside table, and wondered if my father had kept it there as a reminder of my childhood or of some other aspect of the past he missed. I shook it, and it gave a hollow rattle before yielding up a tarnished penny, worthless now.

While that room had the largest bed, I wasn't going to sleep where my parents had. I opened all the windows, enclosing the house in birdsong from the trees along the street and in the graveyard, and then I devoted the afternoon to clearing cobwebs from my old bedroom and wielding the vacuum cleaner. I lugged my suitcases of clothes upstairs, past the framed homilies crowned with dust, but left the cases on the landing once I'd transferred the contents of one into the chest of drawers and the equally creaky wardrobe. I felt like my father, though not in a positive sense, for fetching dinner from the Chinese takeaway near the old Norris house beyond the railway bridge and watching television while I ate. I was seeking distraction from my dull unhappy thoughts, but even though one channel was showing a Hitchcock film I couldn't engage with it. The images seemed cut off from me, not only by the dust on the screen. When Henry Fonda uttered an inaudible prayer his face was transformed into an unfamiliar one. While I found the spectacle unwelcome, it occurred to me that I could have included the film in my course, since the wrong man was a Christ figure. The thought let me feel more rational, and I went up to bed.

I slept so little that I might as well have stayed awake. Apart from wondering how long it would take Bobby to expose Safe To Sleep, and forcing myself to wait until this made it plain to Lesley that our son was horribly at risk, I was acutely aware that the family grave was visible from my room. Eventually I went to the window, to see that the headstone was shifting. No, I realised once I'd fumbled the window open, some other stealthy activity was in progress. Small dark tattered shapes were swarming up the memorial as though hatching from the grave, and I found it hard to breathe until I grasped they were shadows of leaves on a tree near a streetlamp, though I couldn't feel the breeze that made them restless. However mistaken I'd been, the sight convinced me that I ought to watch out for my father. I was afraid that now he was dead, Christian Noble might find a use for him.

I craned out of the window until I began to hear the thumping of percussion, the only audible element of music somebody was playing. It felt disrespectful when it could be heard all through the graveyard, not to mention inconsiderate towards the culprit's neighbours so late at night. Or was it a record? When I strained my ears I still couldn't hear even a hint of the music I'd thought was the source. Perhaps the insistent pounding was closer than I'd assumed, in which case it must be muffled. As I stared out at the Sheldrake grave I began to dread that I knew where the sound was coming from – the sound like fists thumping the underside of a lid. The idea sent me stumbling downstairs and into the back yard, where I pressed my ear against the fence alongside the cemetery. The thudding was louder, and I had a distinct sense that it involved a wooden surface. I was digging my nails into my palms when I managed to relax my fists, having realised at last that the noise was my own pulse, amplified by flattening my ear against the fence.

I still felt the need to be vigilant on my father's behalf. Each night I had to make myself leave the window and try to replenish my sleep. Once I was in bed I generally managed to stay there until morning – at least, I did until the night I heard the voice in the graveyard. To begin with I wasn't even sure it was one, that vague blurred moan that rose and fell as it seemed to endeavour to gain strength, but as it grew louder I couldn't deny that it was struggling to form words. I staggered to the window and saw that the family grave had acquired a new shadow, a dark patch in front of the headstone. No, it wasn't a shadow, because it was restless even though the tapestry of leafy silhouettes on the memorial was quite still. It was a hole, and it was gaping wider to emit more of a voice.

I had no idea which clothes I dragged on before dashing out to the graveyard. As I ran between dilapidated angels and inscriptions too dim to read I recognised the pleading voice. Misshapen and painfully strained though it was, it belonged to my father. "Don't let him take me," he was begging. I was nearly at the grave when I saw that the hole in the mound wasn't just a hollow. It was a mouth, and I could see its tongue coated with earth. It might have been miming its efforts to speak, because as the thick lips widened in a grimace they crumbled, spilling some of the soil of which they were composed into the throat and stifling the feeble plea. By now I was striving quite as hard to find my own voice, and when at last I rediscovered how to produce it I let out a cry even weaker than the entreaties of the mouth that had grown as wide as the mound. The cry took far too long to surface, which made me feel like the tenant of the grave. When at last it succeeded in wakening me, I found myself in my old bed. I felt like a child again, but now there was nobody to comfort me, just the dark that had gathered in the empty house.

I didn't sleep a great deal after that, but next day I managed to teach. It felt like a pretence, and my life did now – a pretence that all was well or would be. So long as Toby ultimately would, that had to be enough. Meanwhile I was doing my best to construct a life for myself in the house to which I'd returned if not reverted. I'd unpacked my suitcases and borrowed hangers from my parents' room to use in my wardrobe, and I'd succeeded in cleaning the kitchen sufficiently to feel comfortable about cooking meals there. I wondered how soon I might do that for Toby, but at present Lesley didn't want me seeing him, and I'd managed not to insist for fear that we would both upset him.

While her department wasn't far from mine, we seldom met by chance on the campus. I couldn't judge whether she was avoiding me until I saw her near the university library, when she turned away as soon as she noticed me and walked away at a speed close to a barely restrained run. The sight made me feel emptied of all the memories we shared, and I headed in the opposite direction with no sense of where I was bound.

Of course the situation couldn't stay so unresolved. I suppose I was hoping Lesley would relent, having decided Toby still needed a father. Next day he was at school, and as I drove to work I thought this might be a good time to approach his mother. By the time I reached Communication Studies I was planning to call her and suggest meeting for lunch. I thought she'd anticipated me when the solitary envelope in my pigeonhole proved to be addressed in her small neat handwriting. *Dominic Sheldrake*, it said.

The formality took me aback, but it was only a taste of the tone of her unsigned note. *Kindly inform me how soon you will be available to meet my lawyer.* I wanted to believe she had to write like this to control her emotions, but the impersonal remoteness almost made me crumple up the note. I had nearly half an hour to spare before I saw my students, and I made for the Department of English. As the building came in sight I saw her heading for it and realised I'd only just missed her delivering the note. "Lesley," I called loud enough to make several students look.

She hesitated without turning and then took another step. I thought she meant to take refuge in her department, but she visibly straightened her back to wait until I moved in front of her. "What is it, Dominic?"

Her dark eyes were withholding the gleam I'd grown so used to, and the shape of her generous lips made them look burdened. "You wanted me to get in touch," I said.

She might have been lowering her voice to set me an example. "You could have left me a message."

"Why slow communication down like that? I'd rather we were face to face."

"It isn't just about what you want, Dominic. It has been too much of the time. I'm not supposed to be in contact with you any more than absolutely necessary."

"Supposed by whom? By this lawyer you've hired?"

"That's right, by somebody who knows what should be done. Somebody who can make sure it's as civilised as possible."

"Lesley, how on earth have we come to this?"

"If you don't know, then that's your answer."

"I know we're having problems, nobody knows that better than I do, but can't we work them out between us?"

"What do you think I've been trying to do? But I can't any more by myself."

"You don't need to. You've still got me."

"You know perfectly well what I mean. Don't try to play on my emotions, Dominic." As my own came close to destroying my control she said "Colleen Johns warned me that might happen. That's one reason she told me to keep it in writing."

"She's your lawyer, is she? May I ask how you chose her?"

"Judith recommended her. She handled Judith's case."

"Which is to say her divorce." When Lesley's lips hinted at a grimace that might have been reproachful or regretful, I said "Do you honestly think we need to go that far? Are you really proposing to split us up for good?"

"It isn't just about us." Remorse glimmered in her eyes and seemed about to moisten them, and then it vanished. "Not even mostly," she said.

"I know that better than I think you realise. How is he?"

"My son is as calm as I expect a boy of his age can be under the circumstances. And I'm sorry if you'd rather not hear this, but I'm glad Phoebe Sweet is caring for him."

My guts had stiffened at her first words, and now my mouth did.

However my face looked, it made several passing students rather more than glance at me. "Let's end this now," Lesley said. "When are you free to meet Colleen?"

"Have you already forgotten my hours? My afternoon is clear tomorrow, just like yours."

"I'll have to check that it's convenient for her. Judith can collect Toby from school." With something like concern she added "You might want to find yourself a lawyer."

"That's one thing I won't be doing. Yours can take all the responsibility for whatever we're made to do."

At once I wanted to qualify my outburst, but Lesley's gaze had strayed beyond me, and she seemed not to know how to look. "Am I interrupting an interdepartmental conference?" the vice-chancellor said.

"No," I turned to say, since Lesley left the answering to me, "a private one."

"I feared as much."

I couldn't help demanding "Why do you say that?"

"It was apparent at some distance that your discussion was hardly professional."

"I'm sorry," I said but added "If we need to be."

"I would simply counsel keeping it less public. It's of paramount importance to present a united image to the students. I wonder if a private word or two in my office might be appropriate."

"No need. We're already meeting someone who'll apparently be taking charge."

"Please keep my offer in mind nonetheless," the vice-chancellor said, at which point I grasped that he hadn't meant it as an official warning. "May I assume the discussion is done?"

"I'll leave you a message with the arrangements," Lesley told me and made for her department at once.

I was about to head back to my own when the vice-chancellor murmured "Are we looking at a crisis of some ilk, Dominic?"

I saw it was pointless to say much, and that was how it felt to say anything at all. "We don't agree over bringing our son up."

"Have you reason to believe his mother is mistaken?"

"Any number of them."

"Then if you set them out calmly and rationally I'm sure she will give them due consideration. I shouldn't care to think that any member of the staff was less than reasonable."

I wondered how thoroughly his last remark was aimed at me, since his interrogative gaze was. "I've given her every reason I can," I said. "She's not convinced."

"Then perhaps you should consider shifting to her position." When I didn't risk a response he said "Or are both sides entrenched?"

"You can put it that way if you like."

"I never like to hear of conflict on the campus. Are you able to acquaint me with the likely resolution?"

"Just now it looks as if we may be splitting up."

"It distresses me to hear it. I very much trust it won't lead to any further public confrontations."

"We'll try and keep our feelings out of sight. Now if you could excuse me, I've a class to teach."

"You should have alerted me that you were late for it, Dominic."

"I'm not yet," I retorted and hurried to the auditorium, where some of my students proved to have watched the Hitchcock film on television. Usually I would have welcomed such a productive coincidence, but just then I could have felt the course I'd planned had been diverted, yet another of the frustrations that had invaded my life. An extended disagreement whether the wrong man's prayer summoned the culprit to justice only reminded me of the dispute my marriage had become, and I couldn't even decide which view to take. I offended more than one student by suggesting that it didn't matter, and had to explain at length that I meant ambiguity was fruitful, however much I yearned for certainty in my life.

When I returned to my desk I found Lesley had left me a voicemail, briskly confirming tomorrow afternoon's appointment and providing the address. That night attempting to plan what to say kept me awake once I managed to finish my vigil at the bedroom window. After lunch, or rather the time I would have had it except for lacking any appetite, I reached the car park nearest our departments just as Lesley's Victor left it for the road. My hand began to rise in an instinctive wave, and then the situation brought it down. She might have thought I was trying to hitch a ride, in which case I fancied she would have put on speed.

I drove downtown and parked in a multi-storey near the waterfront. Colleen Johns' offices were uphill in the business district, on a Victorian alley off a main road. They overlooked a sex shop with a window painted the black of a gap between stars. As a pink-faced man stole out of the shop, clutching an emaciated brown-paper packet that no doubt hid a magazine if not a wad of photographs, he had to dodge a young woman who looked steeped in orange paint – an artificial tan. I watched him flee while she shoved the door inwards with the pizza cartons she was carrying, and then I turned to see a woman staring at me from an upper window. As she stepped back I thought she gave her head a terse shake.

The lawyer's offices were on the first floor. Chipped stone stairs led around the iron cage of a vintage lift shaft to a mosaic landing, where a door named COLLEEN JOHNS AND PARTNER boasted a brass bellpush in a marble socket. Since the door wasn't locked I strode in, to be met with a reproving frown from a lanky long-haired blonde packed behind a desk. "Mr Sheldrake," she barely asked before announcing me through the switchboard. "You're to go in," she said, and surely not with concealed amusement "I think you're late."

The woman who had observed me from the window was indeed Lesley's lawyer. Her extensive face was pallid where it wasn't thoroughly freckled, and almost surrounded by curly russet hair. Her thick red eyebrows stood so high that they appeared to have tugged her eyes wide, flattening any expression out of them. Her long nose gave a faint succinct sniff, and her thin pale lips stayed straight as she granted my hand a token shake. "Colleen Johns, Mr Sheldrake," she said. "Did you find something of interest across the road?"

Lesley was already seated at one corner of the desk across which Colleen Johns was leaning. She might have resolved to hold her expression as neutral as the lawyer's, because it didn't change as I said "Just an embarrassed punter."

"More men should feel that way. Please do sit down." As I took the hard straight chair at the other forward corner of the desk, she said "You're determined to control the proceedings, I hear."

"I just want what's best for my son."

"He isn't your personal property, Mr Sheldrake. Is that how you regard your wife as well?"

"Of course not, and obviously I meant our son," I said and turned to Lesley. "If you recall, that's how you talked about him recently yourself."

"I hope we won't be playing tit for tat, Mr Sheldrake. I'm getting the impression that you don't care very much about the outcome."

"There's nothing I care more about just now. What on earth makes you say that about me?"

"I believe you were advised to instruct a lawyer of your own."

"I don't see the need. I'm still hoping we can work this out in a way that doesn't hurt anyone."

"Is that some kind of threat, Mr Sheldrake?"

"Lesley knows perfectly well it's nothing of the kind." I gazed at her, but her eyes stayed on the lawyer. "It's exactly the opposite," I said.

"Then I hope we can keep our language plain and clear. I'll set out the position as we see it and you'll have an opportunity to state your case. I have to tell you that we feel your treatment of your son amounts to child abuse."

For as long as it took me to breathe in as hard as I could I felt close to losing all control, but regained enough calm to say "I can't believe you think that, Lesley. Safe To Sleep, that's where he's being abused."

"Harassing Mrs Sheldrake isn't going to help your case. I take it you're referring to the religious cult you heard of as a child."

"Lesley's told you all about that, has she? Yes, they're behind the place our son was sent for treatment. Not just behind, involved in every aspect of it. Programming the children with everything the cult stands for, which I can't believe either of us really wants."

"I'm getting the impression that thinking you're right is more important to you than the welfare of your child." Without giving me time to reply the lawyer said "The court might conclude you're making these accusations to divert attention from your own behaviour. It might assume you've heard about Satanic child abuse in the news."

"This isn't Satanic. It's real and it's worse," I protested, and was about to dismantle her suggestion when she said "So in your mind that justifies harassing your son and his friends."

"Just one friend, and I haven't harassed anyone." Though the lawyer raised her eyebrows to emphasise her skepticism, I managed to say only "I tried to question them about the treatment they're receiving, that's all."

"I understand they were referred by a highly respected paediatrician."

"Dominic's convinced she's a member of the cult."

"Not just a member, and you know it, Lesley." I saw no point in keeping quiet about it now. "One of the family that's responsible for it," I said.

"You've talked to the doctor about it, have you, Mr Sheldrake?"

"I have, and I promise you I'm not mistaken."

"It seems to me you need to think you aren't mistaken about anything. So may I ask what happened? You questioned a respected doctor and she told you she helps to run a secret cult?"

"She didn't just admit it. She and her father boast about it."

"Only to you, it seems."

"That's because they don't think I can make a difference."

"Which is why you've taken out your frustration on your family, in particular your son."

"You know that's not true, don't you?" When Lesley didn't look at me I leaned towards her. "Lesley," I pleaded.

She didn't even glance away from Colleen Johns, and might not have wanted me to hear her say "I don't any more."

"Kindly keep your distance, Mr Sheldrake. It looks to me as if you're trying to bully your wife."

"That's not the case and Lesley knows it," I said, sitting up on my chair like an obedient child. "I simply want to establish the truth."

"Then perhaps you'll allow me to sum it up and refrain from interrupting."

"I haven't interrupted yet." I tried adding a laugh at having done so now, but it didn't work even for me. "I'm listening," I said.

"There's no doubt in my mind that the court will grant Mrs Sheldrake a divorce on the grounds of mental cruelty and unreasonable behaviour."

"Mental cruelty." When this failed to prompt an answer I demanded "What mental cruelty?"

"You've been displaying it here, Mr Sheldrake."

"That's—" I stopped short of the scatological in order to appeal to Lesley. "Are you going to let her do all your talking?"

"Do you prefer women not to have a voice?" Colleen Johns said.

"It strikes me you only like yourself to have one. Lesley's got plenty of one when she's allowed to use it."

"By whom, Mr Sheldrake?" Before I could reply the lawyer said "I'm giving her the voice she ought to have. Do you plan to interrupt throughout my submission?"

I hadn't looked away from Lesley any more than she'd looked at me. "I'm listening," I said, though my teeth kept some of it in.

"I'll cite just a few instances of your behaviour. I've no idea what you meant to do when you ran your car off the road, but I should think you were lucky not to be prosecuted for dangerous driving. You could have injured any number of children, including your son. You certainly distressed them at a time when it could hardly have done them more harm."

"You wanted to know what I meant to do." I was still gazing at Lesley's dogged profile in search of a response. "The car got out of control somehow," I said, "but I was there because I was so concerned about our son."

"You're interrupting again, Mr Sheldrake, and I trust you aren't trying to intimidate your wife." When I turned to face the lawyer she said "Glare as much as you like. You won't intimidate me."

"I haven't tried to intimidate anyone."

"I'm afraid your family would disagree. You tried to force your son to confess to a theft Mrs Sheldrake is certain he never committed, didn't you? I wonder if you were accusing him because you had to feel he was as guilty as you were. You couldn't bear admitting that you nearly ran him over."

Before I could start to refute this, Lesley twisted around on her chair. "And you made him feel you couldn't bear to touch him, Dominic. That's the end so far as I'm concerned. Explain it if you can."

I opened my mouth at once, only to realise that any explanation I could give would make her think worse of me. "I need to let him know I didn't mean that," I said.

Perhaps this sounded like a plea, because both women looked determined to remain unmoved. "May we know whether you intend to contest the divorce?" Colleen Johns said.

"I'll go along with whatever Lesley's sure she wants."

Though this felt like slyness posing as compromise, it was the best I could think of. The lawyer nodded as though I'd confirmed I didn't care much, which provoked me to add "So long as we agree about Toby."

"We'll be applying for full custody, allowing you supervised access. And we'll be seeking some financial recognition of Mrs Sheldrake's trouble."

Lesley blinked uncertainty into her eyes. "Is that necessary, Colleen?"

"The strain you're under can't have helped your work, Lesley. I wonder if it means you earned less than you should. And if childrearing duties haven't been evenly divided, we should look for compensation there as well. I trust you see that's fair, Mr Sheldrake."

"I'll do whatever Lesley thinks is right."

"Please don't respond to that now, Lesley. We need to discuss matters further." In case this dismissal was insufficient Colleen Johns said "You'll receive the appropriate forms within the next few days, Mr Sheldrake. Kindly complete and return them as soon as possible."

I was already looking at Lesley. "What about Toby in the meantime?"

"Lesley, I'm strongly advising against contact till the situation has been finalised."

"That's how it has to be then, Dominic."

"That's what you think he'd want, is it?"

"I know he won't want you making him feel he disgusts you somehow, and I'm not about to risk that. Nothing you can say will change my mind, so please don't try."

I saw the lawyer raise her hands from the desk and had a grotesque notion that she was going to applaud. They looked close to doing so when she pointed them at me, presumably indicating that the emptiness between them was all I could expect. I was heading for the door, burdened with a bid for dignity that felt sullen and dull, when Lesley said "Your friend rang, Dominic."

I swung around to find her still facing the lawyer. "Which friend?"

"The female one. Roberta."

"Is this something else I ought to know about, Lesley?" Colleen Johns said.

"Good God, you're eager for material, aren't you?" I protested. "She's a lesbian."

"Do you have some problem with that, Mr Sheldrake?"

"I haven't even if you are. You've just heard she's a friend." When the lawyer's face grew monumentally blank I said "What did she want, Lesley?"

"I wasn't let into the secret. I gave her your number and I assume she'll be in touch with you."

I saw she was aggravating the lawyer's suspicions, but it seemed to be yet another issue I couldn't address without worsening the situation even further. "Thank you for that, anyway," I said, which sounded like a reproach for everything else. As I let myself out of the room the receptionist looked primed to revive her frown. Flattened echoes of my footsteps toppled down the lift shaft, and I felt trapped in something like the metal cage, however insubstantial. I could only look forward to hearing from Bobby about Safe To Sleep. Just now she felt like my solitary hope.

CHAPTER SEVENTEEN
A Sign

"What's wrong with your family, Dom?"

"I don't know what you mean," I said and gripped the receiver so hard that it gave a thin creak that sounded near to splintering. "What's happened now?"

"You aren't together."

"Just that," I said and managed to relax my aching hand. "Why, what did Lesley say had happened?"

"Not much. That's to say she didn't say much. She didn't seem to want to, at least not to me. Only that you weren't there any more."

"For good, you mean."

"I don't think she quite said that," Bobby told me, and I wondered if she was simply trying to lift my spirits. "Don't you want to say what happened either?"

"Safe To Sleep did. Christian Noble did. Lesley won't believe they're any danger, or she thinks they're doing Toby more good than harm. Now she won't let me anywhere near him."

"Dom, that's bad. I hope I'll be helping you sort it all out. Where are you living now?"

"Where we all used to live. I'm in my old house."

"That must be," Bobby said before editing her comment. "What is it like?"

"It feels as if I'm living backwards and losing the future I thought I had."

"Dom." Having loaded the diminutive with sympathy, she said "I wanted to let you know I've talked my way into Safe To Sleep, and they know who I am."

"Who does?" When Bobby didn't answer at once I grew more nervous. "How much do they know?"

"My column and my books. I didn't mean they realise I'm involved with you. I'm sure they don't, Dom."

I couldn't feel too reassured until I learned "Who have you met?"

"Phoebe Sweet and the children. Your son's Toby, isn't he? I've seen him."

"How is he? Could you tell?"

"I'd have to say he was unsettled. Phoebe Sweet's taking special care of him."

I heard and felt the receiver creak again. "What kind of care?"

"Doing her best to help him have positive thoughts. He was telling her he has a friend's birthday party tomorrow."

"That's right, Claudine's." It seemed to me that I ought to find the reminder useful, but just now I had to learn "What's your view so far of Safe To Sleep?"

"I'm starting to have my suspicions, but do you mind if I don't discuss them yet? I don't like to talk about anything I'm going to write. That's how we writers are."

"I wouldn't know any more." Too late I realised that Bobby might have been thinking of her partner, and to leave my gaffe behind I said "How long do you think you'll be there?"

"At least a few days. Would you like to meet while I'm so close?"

"I'd love to, you know that, but I wonder if we ought to risk being seen together."

"Maybe that's not so wise, but let's try after I've finished my investigation. I can't promise yet, but I think I may be able to watch some of their treatment sessions."

The flare of hope I felt immediately gave way to apprehension. "Bobby, just be careful what that may involve."

"Dom, I've told you they know all about me. They wouldn't dare do much to anyone like that." As I thought uneasily of Eric Wharton she said "I'd better go and get some writing done."

She was gone as soon as we said our goodbyes. A click triggered the dialling tone, and I was about to hang up when I heard another sound. Perhaps it was static, but it suggested stealthy movement, and I could have imagined that someone who had been monitoring the call had tired of keeping still. "Hello?" I blurted, and silence fell at once.

I listened for some time without hearing anything further, and had to cut off the connection to make another call. After more rings than I thought were necessary for her to reach the phone anywhere in the house Lesley said "Hello, who is this?"

"It's Dominic." I felt as if she'd hoped for someone else, particularly since she didn't answer. "Will Toby be at Claudine's tomorrow?" I said.

"Why do you want to know?"

"Because I need to collect items from our house."

"We'll both be at Judith's. We'll be leaving about noon, so please don't be any earlier. When you've taken all you're taking, could you leave your keys? Colleen says I should ask you to."

I might have said more if the mention of the lawyer hadn't blocked the way. The call was hardly finished when I started to regret agreeing to the terms. How could I have been so ready to give up a chance of seeing my son? That night it was mostly my error that kept me awake, and I spent hours after breakfast trying to decide how soon to drive to Lesley's – only Lesley's now, except that it was Toby's too. About noon could mean a little earlier, or at least I could take it that way, and I left the house not much after eleven. The car door gave the harsh squeak it had developed since the accident, and then I was on the road.

I was in sight of the family house when Lesley's car nosed out of the drive. Glancing along the road in search of traffic, she met my eyes at once. Her face wavered and immediately stiffened into blankness, a reaction that disconcerted me so much that I could only flash my headlights to prompt her to move. Toby leaned forward and gazed past her at me, and I was trying to make out his expression when he sat back. Was he too distressed to look at me, or hiding for some other reason? Lesley's car swerved onto the road with a fierce screech of tyres, and I saw the backs of her and Toby's heads shrink into the distance as if they were eager to leave me far behind.

I parked on the drive and let myself into the house, where I felt like an intruder. All the items Lesley and I had bought together – furniture, kitchen equipment, souvenirs of holidays with Toby and before he was born – seemed no longer to belong to me. Presumably we would have to decide the ownership of some of them, but just now they made the memories they represented feel attenuated, not much better than erased. When I collected the clothes I'd had no room for in my suitcases last time, I could scarcely bear to look at the bed I'd shared with Lesley, which loomed at the edge of my vision like a silent rebuke. I'd previously taken my computer, but now I returned to our workroom, from which I saw Toby's ball on the lawn, grinning upside down at me like a clown's ambiguous mask. I bore armfuls of reference books and magazines out to the car, and then I opened the drawer of my desk.

However desperate this was, I couldn't help hoping to find my copy of Christian Noble's journal. Perhaps that would mean I'd somehow overlooked it after all, or might Toby have put it back to deceive his mother? Dismayed by the suspicion, I was almost glad there was no sign of the journal. All the newspaper cuttings were still in the drawer, and so were my tales of the Tremendous Three. I hardly knew why I was bothering with those, but I found space for them on the back seat of the car. I had a final look around the house but didn't feel encouraged to linger. I tugged the front door shut with the key I twisted in the mortice lock. For the duration of a long sigh that felt like giving up breath I wanted to keep hold of the keys, if only so as not to feel so cast out, and then I manoeuvred them off the ring and thrust them into the letterbox. I was rearranging books and magazines on the back seat when a car halted on the road, blocking the driveway. I was about to make my presence more apparent until I saw it was a police car.

The front doors opened in unison, and two brawny men in uniform rose up as though they'd practiced the routine. In another simultaneous movement they donned their peaked helmets, covering scalps that gleamed pale through their glossy black hair. One man's face was as unusually rounded as his eyes and nose and fat-lipped mouth, while his colleague's eyes and mouth were so small they looked squeezed, unlike his nose, which the moist pink nostrils appeared to have enlarged. The men paced along either side of the drive as if they were preparing to close in on me. "Is this your house, sir?" the small-eyed fellow said.

"It was. No, as a matter of fact it still is. It will be for a while."

The round-faced man parted his thick lips with a moist pop. "Which?"

"As I say, it's mine and my wife's."

"Joint mortgage, is it, sir?" his colleague said.

I had the grotesque notion that he was about to offer financial advice. "That's the arrangement, yes."

"Just show us, can you?" the round-faced man said.

I was in danger of yielding to some form of mirth. "You want me to show you our mortgage."

His lips popped again, a sound like a breath breaking a surface. "Show us how you got in and we'll check the house."

"Why should that be necessary?" More than embarrassment was making me defensive, but I had to say "Unfortunately I no longer have the keys."

His partner's gaping nostrils flared as if they'd scented an offence. "How is that, sir?"

"My wife and I are estranged at the moment."

"Then may we ask how you gained entry?"

"How do you know she didn't let me in?" When they met this with an identical look as lacking in depth as expression I said "She wanted me to leave the keys once I'd finished with them, so I posted them into the house."

"So what proof can you show us you live here?" the round-faced man said.

I tried to feel this was a request, not a challenge or an accusation, as I took out my wallet and extracted my driving licence. "I should think this covers it."

He peered at it while his colleague opened the boot of the car. "Got something with your picture on?"

"Luckily for, as it happens I have." At least I'd stopped short of saying he was lucky, and I found the passport I'd retrieved from my desk. "As a rule I wouldn't have this with me," I said.

"Not thinking of leaving the country, are you?"

"I've no such plan at the moment, but is there any reason why I shouldn't?"

"Depends if you're taking anybody with you, maybe."

All at once I felt even more suspicious than he appeared to be. As he handed back the passport I said "Now you've established who I am, may I know your names?"

His mouth puckered inwards, acquiring a resemblance to a navel, and then popped wide. "Black," he said no means unlike a warning.

"Far," his colleague said.

It must have a final consonant that I couldn't hear, but I had to fend off the idea that the combination of names came close to invoking a void. As I pocketed my wallet Farr said "Can I ask what's in these cases, Mr Sheldrake?"

"Clothes. My togs. Do have a look if you need to."

"If you wouldn't mind, sir."

"To tell you the truth, I'm minding a hell of a lot." While I didn't say this or use even stronger language, I'd assumed he would turn down my suggestion. "Investigate them, then," I said. "They aren't locked."

"We'd prefer you to open them, sir."

I stalked around the car and unzipped the suitcases. "My secrets are revealed," I said. "Rummage all you like."

"Pack them yourself, did you?" Black said.

He sounded like a customs officer, a similarity I did my best to shrug off. "Can't you tell?" I retorted. "I'm the man responsible."

"Right enough, it's still a woman's job."

Before I could insist I hadn't meant that, he set about pawing through a case while Farr performed a fastidious search of the other. I glanced about to see if anyone was watching, but nobody else was in sight. I'd rather hoped someone I knew might have come out of their house to witness the situation – indeed, so that I could appeal to them. Eventually Farr eased the zip shut, and as Black gave his a few rough tugs the small-eyed officer opened one rear door. He leaned in to examine the spines of the reference volumes and the covers of the topmost magazines, and then he rested a hand on the exercise books. "What are these, Mr Sheldrake?"

At once I realised what I'd overlooked, and found it hard to speak. "What do you think they might be?"

"I really couldn't say, sir."

"Or do you mean you'd rather not? Was anyone wondering how many copies I had?"

Farr straightened up with an exercise book in his hands, a movement that looked threatening and ominously reminiscent too. "I don't understand what you mean."

"Then find out what you've got there. Go on, have a good look."

The policeman opened the book of my childish tales and frowned at the faded handwriting. Eventually he said "Someone's copied those old children's books, have they? The Famous Five."

"Yes, that's what I meant by copies." I didn't know whether my sarcasm was apparent or what it might achieve. "I wrote them a long time ago," I said. "Do check that's all the other books are too."

By the time he had I was more than ready with a question, but it didn't bother being one. "Now that you're satisfied, perhaps you can tell me what all this has been about."

"Just routine, sir. There won't be any need to take it further."

"You just happened to be passing, did you? I'd like to know what you saw that you thought was in any way suspicious."

"Maybe someone saw you taking stuff out of the house," Black said.

"And called you, are you saying? All the neighbours know me," I said and couldn't restrain myself any longer. "But how did you know my name?" I challenged Farr. "You didn't see my licence or the passport either."

"Must have seen it on your case," Black said and slammed the boot so hard it shook the car.

I was belatedly aware that I might be exacerbating any danger I was in, a sense that left me feeling isolated, cut off from the familiar suburban houses and the cloudless sky. I'd managed to stifle my answer when Black tramped around the car and stared at the back seat. "What are those?"

"Just old newspaper clippings."

"We don't need you to tell us that. What's so interesting you've kept it all this time?"

Farr moved aside to let his colleague duck into the car and leaf through the cuttings about Eric Wharton and written by him. "Remember him," Black said, perhaps to convey that he did, and reared up to face me. "Some folk thought he was a bit too fond of poking his nose in."

This time I was unable to control myself. "Are you saying I am?"

"We wouldn't do that, sir," Farr said, returning the book of my tales to the back seat. "Thank you for your time, and please drive safely."

I couldn't be sure that his last words were a gibe, but as the policemen made for their vehicle Black turned his head. "Maybe watch out who you're saying what to, Mr Sheldrake."

I was provoked not just to reply but to follow them. "What am I supposed to think he means by that?" I demanded.

Both men swung around and held up their hands to halt me, one hand each. "Nothing happened here today, sir," Farr said. "I'm sure you'll agree you have no cause to mention it to anyone."

Their gesture looked close to ritualistic, but it didn't deter me as much as their gaze did. I wanted to believe that the sun had suddenly but instantly clouded over, blackening the day and the men's eyes. Otherwise I could have been staring too far into the sockets, into a darkness that might have been using the faces as masks – a darkness so deep that I felt drawn into it, robbed of any balance. I couldn't even tell if the sensation was physical or mental or both. I was unable to look away or to see anything besides those eyes, but I had the impression that Farr's nostrils had yawned eagerly wider while Black's mouth had grown as circular as any worm's. As I struggled to take a breath the policemen turned away, and I couldn't be sure that I'd glimpsed their faces reverting to the ones they showed the world.

I leaned against my car until I heard them drive into the distance, and when I tried doing without its support I found I hadn't finished shaking. The bright day and the familiar street felt like a shell that hid emptiness if not something worse. At last I drove to my old house, so carefully that I might have been following Farr's advice. It didn't help that I'd looked into the boot to see that neither suitcase was labelled with my name.

CHAPTER EIGHTEEN

Communications

When I answered the phone Lesley wasn't speaking to me. "Toby, I asked you to stay in the garden," she said, and then closer and lower "Hold on a moment, Dominic."

"Is that dad? Can I talk to him?"

"Toby, what did I just say?"

"You said hold on a moment, Dominic." As I wondered what expression – innocent or crafty – accompanied his response he said "Can't I just say hello?"

I was about to make myself heard in the silence he'd elicited when Lesley said "Just be quick."

I heard the receiver change hands and then "Hello, dad. How are you?"

The question seemed too formal for a five-year-old. "Hi there, Toby. How's everyone?"

"We're good. Mum made lots of dinners at the weekend so she doesn't have to make them every night, so we can spend more time together."

"I'm sure that must be good for both of you."

"I've read her nearly all of *Alice* now, and there's another book where she goes in a mirror. Does that turn you inside out, dad? Going some places does."

"You haven't been anywhere like that."

This was more of a question than I wished it had to be. "Only watched," he said.

As I searched for a reply Lesley said "Toby, you were meant to be quick."

"Just another minute, mum," he pleaded and went on at once. "Dad, Mrs Dixon liked a story I wrote and said I should read it to the class."

"Well done, Toby." All the same, I hesitated before saying "What is it about?"

"There's a place past all the stars that's so dark you have to make your eyes light up to see. And a spaceship gets lost in it but To, he's the boy they have to ask if he'll help them, he can make his eyes so bright he takes them back where they came from."

I couldn't very well not comment. "I'm glad your teacher likes your stories, Toby."

"She said it was poetic, didn't she, mum? Only I left out the part I didn't think they'd like."

If Lesley hadn't been listening to him I might not have asked "Which part is that?"

"The spaceship wouldn't really have got out, because there's a creature that lives in the dark, only maybe the dark's what he is. Or maybe the dark is his mouth that's like a black hole or what black holes are trying to be. Maybe they're just thoughts he has, bits of the universe he's thinking about. And he's so big and hungry, if you even think about him too much he'll get hold of you with one of them and carry you off into the dark."

"Well, don't," I blurted. "Don't think about it at all."

"Toby, say goodbye now," Lesley said before he had a chance to speak.

"Goodbye, dad. Will you talk to me again soon?"

"That's the least I'll be doing," I declared, but only for myself to hear.

"Goodbye, Toby. Be good for mummy. And yes, we'll speak soon."

I heard the back door shut – it sounded very far away – before Lesley picked up the receiver. "Is he as cheerful as he seems?" I said.

"As much as I can help him to be."

I did my best not to take this personally. "Then I'm glad."

"He's strong for a boy of his age." Lesley took a breath that might have included a sigh. "I'm sure you're responsible," she said, "to some extent."

No doubt she aimed to make me feel a little less excluded, but I had an awful inkling that Toby's experiences at Safe To Sleep might be the real source of his strength. The notion of the kind of fortitude he must have needed to develop appalled me, but what was the alternative just now? "I'm sure we both are," I said, and with the faintest surge of hope "Why were you calling me?"

"Why were the police here before?"

"Because they saw me playing the removal man and supposedly they were checking I wasn't up to no good." I couldn't risk straying any closer to the truth, since she would only take it as more evidence of mental disturbance, but I said "Who told you about them?"

"Wouldn't you have wanted me to know?"

"Why wouldn't I?" I'd begun to feel we might never reach the end of the series of questions. "I just want to know who was watching," I said.

"The Booths across the road."

"They must have been careful to stay out of sight. I wonder why they didn't venture over."

"You know they've grown cautious since they retired. They said they don't expect to see police round here." She cleared her throat as if she needed to dislodge her next question. "Have you had the court documents yet?"

I felt as if I'd nearly reached the Lesley I knew, only for her to recoil. "Not yet," I said.

"Then please deal with them as soon as they arrive. I shouldn't think we'll have any reason to be in contact until they're in the system."

I was about to tell her that we might, in the hope of regaining some closeness, when it became plain that she meant this as a goodbye. As I dropped the empty phone into its cradle I couldn't help wishing that the call had been from Bobby instead. I hadn't heard from her for days – not since she'd talked her way into Safe To Sleep.

She still hadn't called by Monday morning, which was the start of graduation week. For me it was always the highlight of the academic year – watching my students in their gowns and mortarboards stride across the stage to be presented with their scrolls – but now I kept wishing I could see Toby's achievements at school instead. Each day began with the staff parading in our ceremonial outfits through the Philharmonic Hall. Thick carpets toned our footfalls down to a muffled shuffling, while the auditorium several storeys high seemed to dwarf the ritual into insignificance. No doubt this was only how it felt to me, but I was oppressed by reflecting that Toby was involved in a wholly other kind of rite.

Each evening as soon as I was back at my old house I checked the phone, but the last number to have called was always Lesley's, and always another day older. On Wednesday I found a sombre brown envelope waiting for me in the hall. It contained the divorce papers, and I felt irrational for being most dismayed to find I had to complete an acknowledgment of services form. As I filled in my details and my intentions, the spaces I was given made me feel hemmed in by officialdom, reduced to penning letters as painstakingly as a child, all of which kept the emotions I ought to have experienced out of reach. Dull resignation almost wiped out any hope. Once I'd signed away my marriage I tramped to the post office on the main road before I could be overwhelmed by second thoughts. I'd sent the papers on their way when I heard a screech of brakes amplified by the bridge that spanned the road. The place hadn't seen a tram in decades, but the noise brought to mind a scream of metal and a human one, and a fear of what may happen to the dead.

During the lunch break at Thursday's graduation ceremony I found Lesley in the crowd. When she saw me she glanced around in search of support if not of concealment, and I felt compelled to wave a hand, however reassuring that looked. "I just wanted you to know I've sent your forms back," I murmured.

"Have you done as we agreed?"

"You've never known me to break my word, have you? Don't tell me your opinion's sunk even lower."

"Please don't make a scene here, Dominic," she whispered, though I'd kept my voice down. "I take it the answer is yes."

"That's what it is," I said, feeling stupidly clever, and retreated down the long room. The vice-chancellor joined her, and after some conversation he headed for me. Staff moved aside for him and then away from me, but I wondered how many of them heard him say "So the process is in motion, Dominic."

"If you mean between me and Lesley, then the wheels are turning, yes."

"May we trust they're well oiled?"

I wished I hadn't used the metaphor, since I seemed to be trapped in it now. "I don't think anybody's going to need a can."

"You're assuring me the process will be smooth."

I'd begun to lose patience with being translated. "I won't be sticking a tool in the works."

When he frowned I thought he meant to rephrase this as well, but he said "Can you guarantee a cessation of hostilities?"

"I don't think I can say. Which do you have in mind?"

"The sort that was apparent just now. Imagine my surprise upon observing such a spectacle at an official function."

"I wouldn't have said there was much to observe."

"Really quite enough." Before I could judge whether this was an observation or a directive, he said "We can't have open conflict on our campus, I'm sure you'll agree, or indeed the covert kind. May I trust that matters will have been resolved to the satisfaction of all concerned by the autumn term?"

"I think that's up to Lesley too. What did she say when you asked?"

His eyes might have been telling me that he hadn't done so or that I had no business questioning him. "I'm quite certain she is seeking closure," he said and leaned towards me, lowering his voice. "If one thought oneself liable to cause conflict in one's workplace, one might profitably consider moving on."

He left me at once, but the suggestion lingered in my head throughout the afternoon ceremony and as I drove to my old house. I wasn't about to consider moving away from Toby, but was there an alternative I oughtn't to dream of? The undefined thought dogged me as I parked on the grass verge outside the house, and then I heard a phone ringing. It was mine, and I almost snapped the key in the lock as I hastened to open the front door. Dashing into the hall, I snatched up the receiver. "Hello?"

"Dom, are you free?"

While I was delighted and relieved to hear Bobby's voice, her words were too open to interpretation. "Free how?"

"To meet, of course."

"That's what I hoped you meant. When?"

"As soon as you like. Can we now?" She sounded eager and excited, as I hadn't heard her since our childhood. "I've got plenty to tell you," she said.

CHAPTER NINTEEN

The Result of an Investigation

By the time I found the Harvest Moon I was afraid of being visible from Safe To Sleep. The pub backed onto a field that stretched to the trees alongside which I'd left the car while I spied on the house. Once I'd parked in front of the pub, a broad building as black and white as the moon and capped with shaggy thatch, I could still see the copse. Perhaps the trees were catching a wind and stopping it short of the field behind the pub, because although the long grass didn't stir, the trees looked restless. I could have thought the contorted trunks were squirming – certainly swaying across one another to form patterns too intricate to grasp, which gave me fitful distant glimpses of red brick. As I peered at the trees, a man who was drinking at a table outside the pub said "Are you lost?"

"Just wondering what that place in the trees might be."

He tapped ash from his cigarette into an ashtray embedded in the middle of the table and yanked at the lead of the golden retriever lying beside him, though the dog had barely raised its head. "Wouldn't get lost round here if I was you," he said.

"I wasn't planning to, but why in particular?"

"Don't be fooled by how open it looks. Could be you can't see as far as you think," he said and devoted himself to a mouthful of beer.

As I made for the pub the dog gave a muted growl, which earned it another tug at its neck. Beyond the small thatched porch I found a large room full of tables, with booths along three of the walls. A few booths were occupied by couples, but there were no solitary drinkers, and Bobby wasn't to be seen. A man who I guessed was the landlord stood twirling a towel in a pint glass behind the bar opposite the door. His long greying hair was trammelled by a rubber band, and a piebald moustache drooped at the sides of his wide loose mouth. The handles in front of him displayed names of real ales: Parson's Fart, Witches Secret, Beater's Reward, Poacher's Bag..."Which do you recommend for a beginner?" I thought it best to ask.

He put down the glass and flapped the towel, and a shape like a bird's wing imitated it in a mirror behind a rank of bottles hanging their heads. "Depends how real you want to get," he said.

"Nothing too strong when I'm driving."

He gave me a look that might have been rebuking me for cautiousness if not for being in charge of a car. "Try a pint of Hunt's End."

He hauled on a pump and handed me a foaming pint, in which I tried not to see too much of a resemblance to cloudy urine. The first mouthful assailed me with yeast that eventually made way for bitter hops. "How's that for your taste?" the landlord said.

I swallowed the mouthful and a grimace. "I should say it's authentic."

"It's that and no mistake. Folk come from miles around."

"They'd have to, wouldn't they? There's nowhere very near except the big place across the field."

The landlord fixed his gaze on the glass he was wiping. "I don't fancy we get any trade from there."

"Why's that? What is it, a hotel?"

"Some kind of institution where they send kids."

"How do you know that? What have you seen?"

When he met my eyes I thought the questions had betrayed my concern until he said "I was driving by the other morning to the farm we get our produce from. Saw somebody delivering a crowd of youngsters in a bus."

I felt my face blaze with guilt but couldn't see that in the mirror. I was grateful no lights were on, despite the lowness of the sun. "Have you any idea why they're there?" I said.

"Getting treatment is my guess, but don't ask me for what. Someone's using a deal of electricity over there, though."

I was unsure how much I wanted to learn "Why do you think that?"

"You can feel it in the air when you go past. And sometimes you can see it on that field across there, like the haze you get on roads in the summer. So long as they keep it over there we'll let it be their business."

Since I'd experienced nothing of the sort on my visits to Safe To

Sleep, I could only think that the situation had grown worse – that the Nobles had caused more to happen than I knew. Since the landlord seemed to have no further information or opinions, I sat down to face the door across a table near the bar. Now I noticed that each of the five massive beams above the room was carved with a phase of the moon, crescents and semicircles flanking a full moon on the central rafter. Some of the yeast in the beer had subsided, and I took the occasional token sip as I watched the door. It opened often enough, but never to admit Bobby, and each time the twilight had given up more of its glow. Well after I should have I thought to ask the landlord "Was there a lady in here before I came? Could she have been looking for someone?"

"A lady." Just in time to suggest he mightn't mean this as an insult the landlord said "Is that the one that's outside?"

"If she was she's gone."

"Out at the back," he said, pointing to an unmarked door beside the bar. "Most folk don't sit out there any more."

I didn't like to ask why. I nearly left my drink, and not only out of haste. As I hauled the door open the elbow of its metal arm emitted an arthritic squeak. Bobby had her back to me at a bench attached to a table, one of several in a small beer garden that was otherwise deserted. Her table was the closest to the view of the copse across the field and the house that the trees virtually hid. Despite the noise the door had made she didn't look at me, and I wondered if she was entranced by the stealthy twilit antics of the trees. "Bobby," I said, and when she didn't respond "Bob."

"Dom." She left her hands upturned on either side of a tankard on the table and turned just her head. "I told you," she said, "from you Bobby is fine."

"Why are you out here? I nearly missed you."

Before I'd finished speaking she turned to the field. "Watching," she said.

I peered in that direction, but even the trees appeared to have been stilled by the gathering dusk. "What can you see?"

"Plenty when you know how to look."

I sat at the next table, on the end of the bench beside hers, not least because I didn't care to have my back to the Noble house. I was about to ask whether she wanted to point anything out to me when she said "I thought you'd let me down again, Dom."

I felt my face grow hot once more, because I'd been ambushed by the memory of catching her in the cinema with Jim when we were children. Altogether too defensively I said "When did I ever do that?"

"I really wanted you to be at my book launch as well as Jim," she said and swallowed a mouthful of pale yellow liquid from her tankard. "Never mind, don't worry about it or anything else."

Rather than ask how she could expect me to have no worries at the moment I said "How's your drink?"

"Not as pissy as it looks."

At least we could laugh, and did, which immediately felt like delaying the discussion we needed to have. As if my thought had triggered them, lamps in antique lanterns lit up at all four corners of the beer garden. "Do you think we'd better go inside?" I said.

"You aren't cold, are you? I think it's quite close."

I could have found her turn of phrase ominous, but I only said "In case anyone sees you with me."

"I'm happy out here. Going in wouldn't make any difference."

She was gazing towards the surreptitiously restless trees, and I told myself I was being too cautious. The fields were deserted so far as I could see, and even with binoculars anybody at the house would find it hard to make us out through the trees. "So tell me what you've found out," I said.

"Let me ask you a question first, Dom." She turned eyes full of twilight to me as she said "What do you want most in the world?"

"To have my family back."

"I was sure you'd say that. I believe I can help."

I'd had too many of my hopes collapse to seize this one. "You're the friend you've always been, Bobby, but how do you think you can?"

"If I bring you and your son back together, don't you think the rest should follow?"

"It might." Though I disliked sounding ungrateful, especially given Bobby's eagerness, I said "I'm still not sure how—"

"Let me tell you everything I have to tell you and you'll see."

Perhaps after all it was best to stay outside where nobody else could hear. For a moment Bobby seemed uncertain how to start, and then she said "I think we can forget what it was like to be a child."

"I suppose that's part of growing up. What do you have in mind?"

"We forget how much we could cope with. You especially, Dom. Coping, I mean, though maybe forgetting as well. You had to deal with a lot more than Jim and I did. There was that night in the fog, and then you went under the church."

"You mean you believe me now."

"I always should have." Before I could ask, however nervously, what had changed her mind she said "I can imagine how you may worry when you've a child of your own, but that's another reason to remember what children are actually like deep down."

"Are you trying to tell me I shouldn't be concerned for my son?"

"Don't let me trespass if you think it's inappropriate."

"Bobby, I don't understand what you want me to think, that's all."

"I just don't want you feeling bad when there's no need, so let me try again." She turned her whole body towards me, straddling the bench. "Believe me, Tina Noble's doing everything she can for the children," she said. "After all, that's her job."

I felt as if the gloom had lurched towards us out of the trees near Safe To Sleep. "Have you met her?"

"I've met the whole family, and I'll tell you one thing, Dominic. She's not the sort to be swayed by anyone."

"None of them are." While I had no idea why we were discussing this, I said "You mean you tried."

"No, I mean she's committed to doing whatever's best. I could see she knew her own mind the first time I met her."

"Bobby, the first time was in the playground at the park."

"That was when. Don't laugh at me, Dom, but I felt close to her then, and now I've found I still do."

"I'm not laughing." I managed to relax my hand, which had clutched at my glass in an instinctive bid to find the drink. "I couldn't tell you what I'm doing," I said.

"I hope you're not thinking I've been taken in, because you must know I'm not like that any more than she is."

"Bobby, whatever she's told you, she isn't looking after the children at Safe To Sleep. She's causing them to be the way they are."

"That's one way she's looking after them." As my mouth opened, feeling emptied of all sense, Bobby said "I trust her, Dom. I should think you'd agree that bonds you make when you're a child can last."

"And some never should."

Bobby gazed at me as if she wondered whether I had ours in mind, and I felt almost too betrayed to reassure her. Before I would have had time she said "You need to realise she isn't trying to make them worse. What she's doing is meant to prepare them."

"I've heard that line already," I said and was overtaken by rage. "What she's doing where?"

"At the hospital."

"She told you about that and you believe her version."

"Dom, do remember I'm a journalist. Just because I trust someone doesn't mean I don't investigate their claims, and that goes for you as well."

"I wouldn't expect you to, Bobby. That's why I thought you were there, investigating what I said."

"I was. I still am, in the best possible way," she said and raised her face as though inviting me to look deep into her eyes, where the light of the lamps didn't reach. "I've joined in."

At first I couldn't speak. I made to reach for her hand without knowing which of us I intended to comfort, and then I found I didn't dare to touch her. I'd remembered how the last time I touched my son it seemed to bring me closer to a void. I could only say "Joined in how?"

"I've experienced the treatment. I've been in the sleep."

I felt as though the darkness beyond the lamps had closed around us. "What have you seen?"

"There's no point in trying to describe it to anybody, Dom. You need to see it for yourself." As I searched for words in the dark place my mind had become, Bobby said "It isn't new, you know. Lots of people have survived it in the past. It just had a different name."

"I don't know what you mean."

"Nocturnal absences, they used to be called astral projection. That's the rudiments of it, at any rate. As Christian says, nothing's really new. There are truths behind everything if you know how to look."

"Whatever you call it, the children are being forced to participate."

"Dom, they aren't. I give you my word they look forward to it. It helps them grow as people, honestly."

"That's why the Nobles have to keep it quiet, is it?" I said in a rage that felt like despair.

"The world isn't ready for the truth yet, but the children will be. Anybody who's involved will. We can't stop what's coming, we can only prepare, and they'll be more prepared than most." An emotion that I couldn't place glimmered in her eyes as she told me "Tina says they will be even if they're dead."

I was appalled to realise that Bobby wouldn't believe any of this if I hadn't sent her to Safe To Sleep. I was close to apologising, because I had no idea what else to say, when she said "You shouldn't take my word for it. You ought to see for yourself."

"How are you proposing I should do that?"

"Come and take part in a sleep."

I was afraid that her experiences had undermined her reason. "Bobby, they know me. I couldn't do that without being recognised."

"Don't worry, Dom. I found out they knew me as well, but they don't care. Tina's known all along, from that time in the playground. She knew you and I are friends, I mean."

I couldn't help glancing across the field, having seemed to glimpse a spidery movement, as if the trees had sneaked forward or some presence they'd concealed had. Perhaps that was only the dark, but I felt spied upon, and had to force myself to speak. "What did she say about it?"

"That you should come and experience the sleep yourself, and her father agreed with her."

"Bobby, why do you think they would invite me after everything I've tried to do to them and the things they stand for?"

"I expect that now they've seen how I responded they're prepared to take a chance with you. And obviously they'd rather have you on their side, since you know something about their beliefs." Bobby leaned towards me, and I had the awful thought that she'd become so much a puppet of the Nobles that she was borrowing their trait, if not manipulated into imitation. "Will you give it a try?" she said.

"What in Christ's name do you think that could achieve?"

"I told you, Dom. Bonding with your son more than you ever have. And if your wife sees all the conflict is over, she ought to have you back. I would." Bobby straightened up to scrutinise my face, and I felt as if the night were gazing at me. "Aren't you still game for an adventure?" she said. "Remember how we used to be, us and Jim."

Dismayed by her eagerness, I looked away to be confronted by the trees on the far side of the field. The landscape was so drained of light that I could have fancied the trees had drawn some of the void beyond the stars down to the earth. Behind the trees I sensed the Noble house. No lights showed, and I couldn't help feeling that the dark was concentrated there, lying in wait for the children, impatient to invade them. The notion made me speak before I knew I would. "All right," I said. "Tell them I'm in."

CHAPTER TWENTY

Welcomes

As I switched on the hall light, the phone rang. My mind was so overloaded with thoughts that for an instant I imagined I'd somehow triggered the bell. Slamming the front door, I lunged at the rickety table beside the stairs to grab the receiver. Reasons why I might be called so late were crowding into my head. "Yes," I urged and thought it best to add "Dominic Sheldrake."

"Dom, I'm sorry. Had you gone to bed?"

"I've only just got home, Bobby." I squeezed my eyes shut as a preamble to asking "What's wrong?"

"Nothing whatsoever. They wanted me to let you know they're ready for you here whenever you want to participate."

I could tell she meant this to sound encouraging, and I did my best to feel it was. "Would tomorrow be too soon? I'm free then."

"It can be as soon as you like."

"I'll see you then, shall I?" When she confirmed it I wondered what else I could risk saying. "In the meantime," I said, "look after yourself."

"Honestly, Dom, I don't need to here. You get some sleep so you'll be ready for their kind. Oh, there is one thing I've been told I should tell you."

I found I didn't have much breath to say "What's that, Bobby?"

"Could you make sure you get here before the children do? Then there'll be plenty of time to explain why you're here and for them to get used to it before we start the session."

"I'll be in good time." I thought of wishing her a sound sleep or words to that effect, but it reminded me of how unaware she already was of her situation. "See you then," I was reduced to repeating.

That night I slept hardly at all. I couldn't help wondering whether the Nobles had some trick in mind, as I had. I was going to need to seem gullible, but would they believe I was? Since Bobby had succumbed to their persuasiveness, perhaps they could accept I was just as susceptible. The thought of Bobby revived my guilt over having put her at the mercy of the Nobles, even if I couldn't have foreseen that she of all people would be. "I'll get her back as well," I vowed, though I wasn't sure I'd spoken, and tried not to think I sounded like a character in a tale for children, or a childish tale, or both.

I left the house soon after dawn. I'd loitered in the shower, hoping it would help to wake me up, but the deserted roads felt like dreams – insubstantial, temporary, distorted by my mind. Set after set of traffic lights appeared to rouse themselves at my approach, toying with amber before rearing up red. From a side street I heard a violent argument, inside a house or otherwise out of sight, but couldn't tell how many participants it involved: perhaps just a solitary combatant, haranguing himself more fiercely after each pause for breath. As I drove along Walton Vale out of the city, one of the shop windows flared blue – no, a television screen as big as any of the windows – and then the pane went dark as a police car swung out of the street opposite, roof light flashing. Hundreds of yards ahead along an empty pavement I saw a balloon-seller trudging home with samples of his wares on strings, dragging them over the flagstones around him. I was alongside him before I realised he had a pair of leads in each hand and a dog at the end of every lead. Even then I had to peer in the mirror to convince myself.

As I'd driven through the streets daylight climbed the sky, but I had the impression that it was simply coating the vast dark. In the open countryside I was even more aware of the hidden darkness resting on the sky like an oppressive weight supported by a flimsy shell. Lying low in the midst of the land that stretched flat to the horizon was Safe To Sleep, which put me in mind of a spider poised at the centre of a web that had drawn me in. "Stay awake," I muttered at myself as I reached the gates. "Stay awake."

The gates swung inwards and then met behind me with as little noise as their image in the mirror. As I drove along the avenue I was conscious of the mounds that infested the grass on either side, because I couldn't quell a fancy that they shifted almost imperceptibly whenever trees blocked them from view. I tried to concentrate on the house, which felt as though it was growing ever more aware of me, even though I saw not a single face. I was parking near the wide steps when Bobby opened the front door and blinked at the sunlight. "Here he is," she called over her shoulder.

She sounded far too much like a member of the Noble family, or at the very least an old friend. This made me falter as I headed for the steps, and she held out her hands. "Don't be nervous, Dominic. There's honestly no need."

I wanted to believe that her behaviour was meant to help me trick her hosts, but she would have let me know last night if it were a pretence. I was about to respond, however little I could trust myself to say, when Tina Noble said "That's the way, Bobby. Bring our guest in."

She appeared at Bobby's back as though she was forming out of the gloom beyond the doorway. Her long smooth oval face leaned out to gaze at me, and I was put more than ever in mind of a snake, but she was deadlier still. She looked so much like a threat to my friend that I was provoked to demand "She's Bobby to you too, is she?"

Tina laid a hand on Bobby's shoulder, a move I found worse than manipulative. "That's what she called herself when we first met," she said.

I remembered the toddler on the swing, who had wanted to be sent past the sky. "Your mother didn't call her that," I said in case it made a point somehow.

"I don't think she liked me to have friends. You'd wonder why as a parent yourself."

I didn't need to wonder. I was sure Mrs Noble would have been afraid of how her daughter might affect other children if not infect them. I was trying not to feel the same about my son – surely soon enough I wouldn't need to – when Tina said "She called you Sheldrake, didn't she? Not even Mr Sheldrake, the way my father did. You didn't like that very much."

This revived the encounter so vividly that I could have thought she meant to undermine my sense of time. "And your other friend was Jim," she said. "She called him James, of course. Will we be seeing him as well?"

"I shouldn't think so. He's moved away, and he's with the police."

I might have brought up Farr and Black, but there was something else I wanted Bobby to know. "Just remind me," I said to Tina Noble, "what happened to your mother."

"She wasn't strong enough to deal with all the truth. She had a whole series of breakdowns, and they must have been too much for her as well. She took her own life." As I looked for even a trace of regret in her eyes Tina said "You can see the truth doesn't affect everyone that way, though."

When Bobby gave a gentle nod I realised Tina meant her. She still had a hand on Bobby's shoulder, and I had a sense that she'd reduced my friend to little more than a puppet. In the hope of breaking the tableau I said "You wanted me to come in."

"Decidedly so. We've been waiting for you, Dominic."

As I climbed the steps she let go of Bobby at last, and Bobby followed her into the house. "Close the door when you're ready, Dominic," Tina said.

I shut it behind me, which left the lobby darker than I thought it should be. Although indirect sunlight filled the windows above the half-landing, the lower staircase was little better than twilit, as if a remnant of the night had lingered or been drawn into the house. I found it hard to distinguish Tina's face as she said "So you've decided to give us a chance after all."

"For the sake of my son."

"That's a reason." I could have taken this for a sly question until she said "You'll be more equipped to relate to him. You'll be closer than you ever have been."

I struggled to pretend that I appreciated her concern. "Like your family," I said.

She emitted a sound like the beginning of a giggle. "Not that close."

I hadn't time to interpret this, having realised I should learn "Does Toby know I'm here?"

"None of us will have told him. Why do you ask?"

"In case it might put him off."

In fact I was establishing that Lesley didn't know, which left me feeling more complicit with Tina Noble than I cared to be until she said "I can't imagine you'll present a problem. He's coped with bigger things."

Rather than answer I swallowed, feeling nauseous with rage. As I searched for some remark that might disguise my thoughts, I heard movement upstairs – footsteps accompanied by scurrying. "Let's greet the novice," Christian Noble said.

The source of the scurrying appeared before he did. His infant grandson scuttled out of the left-hand corridor on all fours and immediately reared up, grabbing the banister. His miniature version of the Noble face looked so triumphant that I couldn't think he was proud just of his antics. While he had to plant both feet on every stair, he came towards me at such a speed that he barely had time to pat each upright of the banister. "Dominic Sheldrake," he piped, by no means only once.

I could easily have fancied that the repetitions of my name were a summons or a charm, and I found myself making an effort to resist both. His small but wide eyes were intent on me, and as he came closer their gaze seemed to strengthen, as if they were gathering the gloom into their depths. I had to force myself to look away to find Christian Noble, who was following him at such a stately pace that it suggested a ritual. "Well, Mr Sheldrake," he said from halfway down the stairs, "have you come to make amends?"

"As I've told your daughter, I'm here for my son."

When he paused I was afraid my words had inadvertently hinted at my plan. "That's all that will be necessary, then," he said.

"Can I ask how you mean that?"

As Toph rested a hand on the lowest newel of the banister and gazed up into my face, Noble said "We won't insist on any compensation for the past. Nothing you can do matters much, Mr Sheldrake."

"Not big enough," Toph piped with a giggle very much like the one his mother had curtailed. "Too little in the dark."

"I still can't get over how bright he is," Bobby said to Tina. "Do you think he's even brighter than you were at his age?"

"He would be."

"Because he's had you and his grandfather to help him develop, you mean."

"You can put it that way if you like."

I wondered how else you would put it, and felt provoked to ask "How about his father? Doesn't he come into it at all?"

At once three pairs of eyes were fixed on me. Not just the faces but the intense stares were so similar that I felt as though a single consciousness was observing me from three positions in the dimness. Perhaps the light from the windows over the stairs was interfering with my vision, because the lobby seemed to have grown abruptly darker. As far as I could make her out, Bobby looked bemused by the silence. The lack of any answer to my question had begun to feel oppressive, even threatening, by the time she said with audible relief "Here's someone else."

When she moved to open the front door I could have thought she was anxious to let more light in. The sun above the avenue drove the darkness back to loiter in the corners beyond the stairs. A Mini as blue as the cloudless sky was lining up beside my car, and when Phoebe Sweet climbed out she was plainly expecting me. "So you're joining us like your friend, Mr Sheldrake," she said as she trotted up the steps.

The succession of guarded greetings had begun to feel like a ritual in which I was trapped. "She's shown me the error of my ways," I said.

"And can I ask what you're hoping for?"

"To be together with my son again."

"Yes, we heard your family had been split up."

This felt far too much like an accusation. "Who told you that?"

"Why, Toby did. Who else would you think?"

"What did he say?" I had to ask.

"He'd like you all to be together as you were."

"Well, that's direct." I meant her words, not his. "I'd like nothing better," I said, "than for us to be a normal family as well."

Toph giggled as though at a private joke, and I struggled not to clench my fists, having been reminded that Tina Noble had ensured my family was far from normal almost as soon as Toby was born. Phoebe Sweet peered at Toph and then along the avenue. "Is that the children?"

In a moment I heard the bus on the road, and she waved a finger at me. I could have taken this for an admonition if she hadn't said "How are we going to present Mr Sheldrake?"

For the first time Bobby seemed a little nervous. "Present?" she said.

"Yes, to the children. How do we make sure they aren't troubled by having him here? You were a stranger they could get used to, but he's Toby's father."

"Make him small like me," Toph said.

He was sitting on the stairs now. While many toddlers might have done that, his back was so straight and his head so high that he resembled a prince on a throne if not a king issuing a decree. "How would you do that?" Bobby said with a hint of wariness.

"Sit him down like me. Put him out on the steps so they see him."

"That's a splendid idea," Phoebe Sweet said, and I saw Bobby regain her admiration for the youngest Noble. "You won't mind, Mr Sheldrake, will you?"

"Not if it makes life easier."

Toph giggled and rose to his feet in a single fluid movement. As Bobby looked no less impressed than Phoebe Sweet did he said "I'll sit by him so they see I'm with him."

Both the proposal and the way it was expressed struck me as worse than precocious, but I couldn't demur when so much was at stake, and I sat to the right of the front door. Though the top step was still chilled by the night, I didn't shiver until Toph perched beside me, splaying out his legs in a pose more childish than I'd come to expect of him. I'd braced myself against flinching in case he used me for support as he sat down, and so I managed to stay poised when he squirmed to lean towards me and gaze up into my face. "Not small enough. Go down two," he said.

"I should be on your level, should I, Christopher?"

He didn't speak, but his unblinking gaze appeared to darken and gain depth. As I shifted to the third step down I took the opportunity to inch sideways, away from him. My head was next to his now, and his scrutiny hadn't faltered. "Aren't I meant to call you Christopher?" I felt driven to ask.

"That's me now."

"So you don't mind if I use it." I couldn't help addressing him like someone significantly older. "There isn't a name you'd prefer me to use," I said.

"You'll know soon."

Christian Noble hurried out onto the steps, and I had an odd sense that he wanted to terminate the conversation. Perhaps he was simply preparing to greet the children, since the bus was through the gates. "Here are your companions, Christopher," he said.

The bus swung out of the avenue and halted parallel to the steps. More than a dozen small heads turned towards me, and an open window let me hear Claudine say "Toby, there's your dad."

"It must be all right. He's with Toph."

I was appalled to be grateful for the infant's presence and dismayed by how much trust my son placed in him. I made myself stay seated next to Toph while the children left the bus, though I felt not much better than pinned down by an unspoken command. Toby dodged around several children and ran to the steps. "Dad, why are you here?"

I did my best to think he wasn't wishing me elsewhere. "So we're together, Toby."

"Is mum as well?"

"Perhaps we'll talk to her about it. You've just got me today."

Claudine advanced to stand beside him. "Doctor Phoebe, can I bring my mum?"

The women had emerged onto the steps. I saw the question take Phoebe Sweet off guard, and it was Tina Noble who answered. "All in good time, Claudine."

A chorus of murmurs signified the excitement that an older girl put into words. "When can our parents come?"

"We said not yet, Debbie. They'll learn what you know soon enough. Toby's father is joining us today because he's Bobby's friend as well."

As I worked on manufacturing an appreciative smile, the children made another kind of murmur. "Don't say that's disappointment I hear," Christian Noble said. "You ought to be glad you're the chosen."

"And do remember being chosen means you have to keep our secret," Tina Noble said. "Some people wouldn't understand what it's like for us to go into the sleep, and by the time you found out who they are it would be too late."

"There are even people who would want to stop it," her father said.

I felt as if the entire Noble family had focused on me, a sensation like the closing of a cold yet insubstantial grasp. I was keeping my eyes on Toby as I did my utmost to retain my smile when Phoebe Sweet said "So are we all ready for our sleep?"

"Yes," quite a few children cried, and I told myself the chorus sounded only coincidentally like a hiss. As it subsided Toph said "What are we going to show Dominic Sheldrake?"

"He means my dad," Toby said. "Where'll they take us when we're asleep?"

A boy some years older than Toby spoke at once. "To listen to the head with moons for all its eyes."

The chorus of assent sounded more sibilant than ever, not least because Toph had joined in. "Don't expect too much of Toby's father when it's only his first time," Phoebe Sweet said, though she appeared not to be directing this at Toph. "Remember how that was for you, and he has more getting used to it to do. Line up like good children now, and when you've been you can wait in the sleeping room."

She might have been trying to reclaim the mundane on my behalf if not her own. As the children headed for the toilets, Toph took hold of my shoulder. He could have been supporting himself while he stood up, except that he'd had no need to do so on the stairs. I thought he was treating me like an acquisition, and I had to make an effort not to move out of reach, especially since the small fingers felt as if they were palpating my shoulder. Before they let go at last I'd begun to have the unwelcome idea that the fingers weren't moving – that their flesh was pulsing like a heart. The toddler rose to his feet and turned to the house in a single apparently effortless movement, and as he sauntered inside I made to follow him. "You may as well stay where you are, Dominic," Christian Noble said. "You'll be fetched."

I felt absurdly like a beggar told to wait outside a palatial residence. I heard children chattering beyond the lobby but couldn't distinguish my son's voice. A second minibus arrived, closely followed by a third, and the variously youthful passengers stared at me on their way into the house. I was gazing so hard at the mounds beside the avenue that more than one of them appeared to shift wakefully when Bobby came to sit beside me. "Don't start getting nervous, Dom," she murmured. "And don't try and force anything when you're in the sleep. You have to let go and then it'll come to you."

"I won't be forcing anything," I said, because I didn't mean to sleep at all. I thought the most demanding task might be to keep my eyes shut. Before I could grow too afraid of learning how her hand might feel, I reached to squeeze it. It was firm, not like Toph's had felt. This was such a relief that I might have kept hold, but for fear of embarrassing her if not myself I let go. We were sitting in a silence that felt like rediscovering friendship at its calmest when Christian Noble leaned out of the entrance in his reptilian way. "We're ready for you, Dominic," he said.

CHAPTER TWENTY-ONE

Beyond Sleep

I'd only just crossed the threshold when I realised I'd been so preoccupied with rousing nobody's suspicions that I'd failed to arrange the situation as I should. "Mr Noble," I said as neutrally as possible.

"Please." As he looked back at me Bobby shut the front door, and I could have thought Noble's face had attracted darkness. "I'm sure we know each other well enough by now," he said. "Christian, by all means."

"I wanted to ask if I can be close to Toby."

"Isn't that your mission here?" His eyes gleamed, though I could have imagined very little light was involved. "You're proposing to lie beside him," he said.

"I think that might be best."

"Best for whom?" The gleam sank into his eyes, but the darkness in them stayed alert. "Do come and see," he said, sounding not far from playful. "Everything is as it needs to be."

He led the way into the right-hand corridor. Though the door at the far end was open, I couldn't see my son. Children lay face up on the middle row of mattresses, but the mattress closest to the door was unoccupied. Now I realised Christian Noble was bound to take that place, blocking anyone's escape. If I'd anticipated this sooner, what could I have done? I strove to think as I followed him into the sleeping room with Bobby at my back.

Children were reclining on all three ranks of mattresses in the splayed pose I'd begun to find dreadful. If they still looked as though they were stretching out their arms in search of companionship, I couldn't have said whether they were seeking one another's comfort or inviting some experience I might prefer not to imagine. Toph lay on a mattress at the far end of the room with his eyes shut, but as I ventured into the room he called out "Welcome Dominic Sheldrake."

All the children opened their eyes wide as he did and turned them towards me. "Welcome Dominic Sheldrake," they said, so much in unison it sounded like a prayer.

I didn't want to fancy they were somehow interceding on my behalf. Surely this was how they greeted any newcomer. While I was acutely disconcerted to hear my son join in, at least it let me locate him at the near end of the left-hand row. I tried not to be dismayed by how pleased he looked that I was there – how eager to involve me. Christian Noble had halted beside him, and swung around to clasp my shoulder. "There's your place," he said. "I trust it will suit your purposes."

He used the hand to point before I could decide how firm it felt, though the touch had come close to making me shudder. He was indicating the mattress nearest to the door, between Toby's and the one where Phoebe Sweet sat up, sending me an earnest smile. "I'm here if you need me, Mr Sheldrake."

"Phoebe deals with any medical issues that may arise," Noble said. "They haven't for a long time, have they, children?"

"No," they said in chorus – Toby as well, and Claudine next to him.

Noble paced to a mattress halfway down the left-hand row. Perhaps his speed was designed not to disturb the children, but it looked as ritualistic as a priest's walk down the aisle of a church. His place was opposite Tina's across the room, while Toph lay at the other end of my row, the four of us marking out the corners of a parallelogram. As this started to remind me of Christian Noble's rite in the moonlit field more than thirty years ago, Toph raised his head so nearly vertical that I wondered how his neck could bear it. "Go like us, Dominic Sheldrake," he said.

"Like me, Dom," Bobby said and shut the door behind me as a prelude to tiptoeing between two ranks of supine children to the nearest empty mattress, some way along the left-hand wall. As she sank onto it she had to support herself with one arm, and I found her clumsiness unexpectedly reassuring. At least she hadn't acquired that unnatural gracefulness the Nobles displayed, Toph in particular. Once she was seated she raised a fist towards me and shook it slowly twice, our old code for the Tremendous Three. I remembered our adolescent vow and Jim's — that we'd always be friends and look out for one another — and was dismayed to think that while she'd looked out for me, I was failing her. Though my son had to come first, I felt worse than guilty. She gazed so steadily at me that I thought she'd sensed my doubts until she said "We have to lie down."

The sight of Toph had made me loath to do so — the sight of his face almost as pale and smooth as a new memorial, raised towards me like a stone at the end of the mound of the rest of him. I couldn't delay any longer in case I attracted more scrutiny, and I fell to my knees on the mattress before lowering myself onto my side and then turning on my back. I stretched my limbs wide in the approved pose, wishing I could touch Toby's hand, but all the mattresses were too far apart for any contact of the kind. "We have to close our eyes, Dom," Bobby said.

If everyone's but mine were shut, how would anybody know if mine were? Surely keeping them open would help me resist whatever the Nobles might do. Perhaps if I kept them practically shut, nobody who looked to make sure I'd obeyed would notice. I'd left them open just enough to capture a sliver of sunlight, which appeared to be flickering with nervousness, when Toph said "All eyes."

"All eyes," Tina Noble and her father said in unison, and I felt as if they were confirming a command. From their voices I could tell that all three Nobles were wholly supine, and might have concluded that none of them could be aware of my ruse, but I had an uneasy sense that one or more of them had found me out. I let my eyelids sag shut, and Toph spoke at once. "Our lullaby," he said.

I heard a faint but widespread noise that I wasn't sure I understood. Quite a number of the children had shifted on their mattresses, but I couldn't judge whether they were preparing to sleep or betraying some other form of anticipation. When I risked a sideways glance at Toby, he appeared not to have moved. I was so wary that I shut my eyes tight at once, and Toph said "The words."

At first I didn't know if I was hearing a response, and then I made out a whisper. It seemed to be rising all over the room, though I couldn't judge how many voices were involved. The harder I strained my ears, the more elusive it grew. It might almost have been just a succession of slow deliberate unanimous breaths, and my own took on its rhythm. Now I began to distinguish syllables, though I couldn't identify a single word. Here came a trinity of sounds I'd already heard, which might have been controlling the rhythm of the whisper. They commenced with a consonant almost too softened to function as one, which led to a syllable that seemed to be reaching for another, only to find an extended sound as emptily hollow as space. This brought the whisper to a final syllable in which the consonants dissolved so as to be subsumed into the exhalation. I knew I was hearing the name I'd read in Christian Noble's journal and heard him speak in the Trinity Church of the Spirit, but each time it was repeated I had the impression that it had grown less defined, as if to help it infiltrate the whole of me. It was intensifying my awareness of my posture – of my outflung limbs that made my body feel as though it was yearning for the sky or for a dream. I fancied that the whisper was growing more remote, and perhaps this meant I'd entered a dream, because I saw the cloudless sky overhead. How could I see it except in a dream when I was still in the sleeping room? In fact it was darker than ever within my eyelids, and the last of the whispered chant merged with that darkness. It was so dark that I wanted to open my eyes to reassure myself with just a glimpse of the room, but I'd lost the ability to open them, unless I'd forgotten how to do so. No, I had no eyes to open. I'd left them along with the rest of my body far below me, and now I was out in the vast dark, beyond the sky I'd seen.

Even if I'd anticipated some experience of the kind, shouldn't I have felt considerably more terrified and helpless than I did? I had to assume that the chant had lulled if not hypnotised me as well as enticing me out of myself. Perhaps the spectacle of the infinite night between the worlds and stars inspired so much awe that it passed beyond terror. Above all I felt safe because I seemed to be merely an observer, as if I were sharing someone else's dream. Surely I can blame the ritual more than myself for robbing me of thoughts I should have had.

I was more than glad to find that it wasn't entirely dark. The shock of inhabiting the void must have limited my senses until they were ready to venture wider. I saw I was surrounded by distant lights, though the closest objects had no illumination of their own. For a moment, if time had any significance out here, a world as ruddy as a dying coal looked close enough to visit, and then it was left far behind. Further still across the black abyss I saw a planet I knew was colossal, although now it was less than a marble composed of storms, and another shrunken globe that was encircled by a prodigy like a faded rainbow made of stone. The outer worlds grew successively darker, and the last one resembled a ball of black ice too far removed from the nearest light even to glint. Then it was gone, and there was only the starry void.

Except for my sense of sharing a dream I might not have been equal to the experience. I could have fancied that the void was drawing me onwards much as a vacuum sucks in air, mindlessly determined to fill itself with whatever was available. Despite the distant presence of a multitude of stars, I felt surrounded by sterile emptiness. The fragments of dead worlds – omens of the crumbling of the universe – that wandered it at random brought no relief. The stars were so remote that they kept most of their light to themselves, and whenever my headlong progress brought me closer to one I saw how it blazed in absolute silence, which made the whole spectacle resemble a dream more than ever.

Galaxy succeeded galaxy, separating into hordes of stars, each star immensely distant from its neighbours. Occasionally I saw a pair of stars that might have drawn together in cosmic companionship, but even their doubled light looked like a vain attempt to fend off the infinite dark. By now I felt as though the void had swallowed time, and began to wonder if my journey was to be as endless as the universe, a prospect I found unexpectedly manageable, possibly even alluring. Helpless awe might have swept away most of my ability to think, though I suspect the ritual had, and I was content to feel both escorted and protected. I'd begun to succumb to a kind of attenuated calm when I saw movement ahead.

It was beyond one of the immense spaces that made up most of a cluster of stars. It wasn't a meteor swarm or a comet; it didn't move as they did. It was pale and globular, and appeared to be ranging here and there among the stars. I wondered if it could be an errant planet at the mercy of their gravity, however fanciful this was, and then I saw it veer towards the largest nearby star, too purposefully to be drifting. It put me in mind of a moth attracted by the light – more grotesquely, a moth's egg that had somehow grown mobile, since the spectacle was just as abnormal. Now I saw that the pallid globe was so thoroughly pitted, presumably by meteors, that it looked as decayed as an ancient skull. This had to mean its substance was solid, but it wasn't as firm as a planet ought to be. As the object several times the size of the world I'd left behind approached the star, that side of its circumference began to swell towards the light. It looked eager to borrow the glow. No, it was absorbing the brightness, and as it began to shine with a pallor reminiscent of a light above a marsh, it came dreadfully alive. All over the increasingly gibbous sector that was consuming the light of the star, great holes had begun to gape.

Quite a few contained eyes, although the bulging whitish orbs were as pitted as the rest of the deformed sphere. Other holes were mouths of various sizes and shapes, all of which began to work and then to speak, by no means in unison. I couldn't have been hearing them in any ordinary sense, which made the elaborate chorus of whispers all the more insidious, as though the mass of simultaneous words in an utterly alien language was penetrating my essence. I had the unnerving notion that I might grasp them before I consciously understood them, or else they would grasp me. The colossal pallid sphere had started to rotate with a terrible deliberation as though to bathe its entire surface in the starlight it was feasting upon, and my unnatural composure faltered. All at once I dreaded being seen.

Surely I needn't panic. How could I be noticed when I was unable to distinguish even a trace of myself? The ponderous rotation of the relentlessly vociferous mass was about to confront me with a number of its sluggish pockmarked whitish eyes, which might mean I would glimpse the kind of consciousness that lived in them. Surely if anyone caught their attention, my escorts would instead of me – and at once I was appalled by realising who that had to include: Toby and the other children. The lurch of recognition was so violent that it wrenched me back into myself, where I was lying on the mattress.

So I hadn't ventured as far as I'd imagined, if my return was so instantaneous. The insight let the vision I'd just had feel no worse than an especially bad dream. For a moment this was pitifully reassuring, and then I understood that I'd shared the children's experience – that I'd been lured into using them as a kind of proxy, just as the Nobles used them. The idea dismayed and infuriated me so much that I barely succeeded in stifling a cry of disgust, not least at myself. I needed to postpone my feelings if I was to carry out my plan, and I focused on opening my eyes, only to find the task far harder than it ought to be. It felt as though my mind was no longer fully synchronised with the rest of me – as though I had to relearn how my body worked. Even when I managed to raise my cumbersome head and blink my reluctant eyes wide, I couldn't immediately make out the room, and I was terrified that someone might have seen me move.

Everyone was lying face up in the trance pose. Every eye was shut, but I couldn't tell how long I might have before someone noticed I'd stopped participating in the ritual. I sprawled on my side and thrust myself to my feet with one wavering arm. I still felt less than perfectly aligned with my body, and as I wobbled away from the mattress I stumbled against the door. The thump my elbow dealt it sounded loud enough to waken the entire room.

Nobody stirred. Not a single eyelid flickered, and I told myself that nobody was pretending they hadn't heard – not Christian Noble or Tina, not even Toph. I fumbled behind me for the doorknob and turned it almost gradually enough to prevent it from emitting a muted squeak. I edged forward while easing the door open and then leaned against the frame as I inched the door wide, by which time I was close to regaining my balance. I was afraid to delay any longer, and I supported myself with one hand on the wall as I stepped over my mattress to reach my son.

Stooping to lift him revived a dizziness that felt too close to a threat of leaving my body behind. I had to rest my clammy forehead against the wall as I slipped my hands beneath Toby's shoulders and behind his knees. When I straightened up I was afraid his weight might prove too much for me in my unwelcome condition, but he felt distressingly hollow, as if his body had lost substance or was yearning to abandon gravity. His unforeseen lightness made me stagger backwards, and my heel caught the mattress I'd vacated. I blundered across it towards Phoebe Sweet, and my foot struck the floor beside her with a resounding thud that shook the boards. I was so sure I must have roused her that I couldn't move for several seconds, and then I floundered out of the room.

Nobody followed us along the corridor, and I heard no sounds except my own all the way to the front door. The massive doorknob needed both my hands to twist it, and I laid Toby down on the stair I could most conveniently reach. He still hadn't moved when I returned to him, having hauled the door wide, and I didn't know whether to feel concerned about his quiescence or grateful that he wasn't causing any problem. I picked him up and tramped down the steps to my car, where I had to lower him onto the hood in order to unlock the doors. At least the metal wasn't hot enough to trouble him – in fact, I had the impression that the sun was scarcely higher than it had been when I'd closed my eyes in the sleeping room. I carried Toby to the back seat and strapped him in, and peered at his unresponsive face before ducking out of the car, slowly enough not to revive my giddiness. "Do you think that's advisable, Mr Sheldrake?" Christian Noble said.

He was leaning out of the doorway, splaying his fingers on both sides of the frame. He looked poised to launch himself at me, and perhaps that was what his faint amusement signified as well. Further stealth would have been pointless, and I slammed the passenger door as if this could keep Toby safe. "What?" I said as steadily as I could.

"You've just done it again." With a smile so faint it looked drained of meaning Noble said "Do you think you should risk waking anyone from our sort of sleep? They used to think it was dangerous even to waken a sleepwalker."

His apparent concern inflamed my rage. "A lot less dangerous than leaving anyone with you."

"Why, Mr Sheldrake, there's safety in numbers, you know. I must say I'm disappointed you're so unreceptive. I remember when you had more of a mind."

I was appalled to be reminded how the ritual had reduced the children to a single undifferentiated consciousness, a human buffer shielding the perpetrators of the rite from directly encountering its effects. Worse still, I'd failed to recognise my own son within that composite intelligence – even to remember he was there. Before my fury could find words Noble said "You shared so little of our vision I'm surprised it proved too much for you. You'll have gathered it wasn't too much for the children."

I felt dizzy again, mostly with nausea. "I was never here for that, but I'm glad I've seen exactly what you're up to."

"It's a pity you weren't taken further. You'd have been better prepared."

"I just want my son back."

"Why, Mr Sheldrake, I think you have him."

Noble's gaze had strayed to my car. In a moment I heard Toby voice a protest that fell short of words. As I snatched the door open I saw him struggling within the confinement of the seat belt as if he had no idea what it was. "It's all right, Toby," I murmured, gripping his shoulder. "I'm here."

He blinked at me and then at his surroundings. I'd begun to fear he had yet to return to himself when he said "Are we going home, dad?"

Before I could respond, Christian Noble was beside me. He'd descended the steps so rapidly and silently that I was reminded more than ever of a snake. "Is that what you want, Toby?" he said.

"I want us all to be together."

"Us, do you mean? My family and you and all the other children?"

I let go of Toby's shoulder in case my grasp hurt him. As I straightened up to confront Noble my son said "You left Doctor Phoebe out."

"Her too, of course," Noble said, "and anybody else who's with us."

Toby took a breath that dragged at the seat belt, and I saw he was working on a decision. I couldn't make my aching lungs function until he said "I was going home with dad."

"Just as you wish." Noble had already fixed his gaze on me. "It isn't important," he said.

I had to clarify the situation, however much this might provoke him. "You mean you're letting him go."

"You can't see me trying to hinder you, can you? Believe me, it matters much less than you imagine."

I was dismayed to think he meant one child made little difference. "Now if you'll excuse me," he said, "I must rejoin the faithful."

I hoped the gibe the last word seemed to hide didn't trouble my son. As I climbed into the driver's seat I realised Noble was loitering at the foot of the steps. He watched me drive away, and I saw him shrink in the mirror until he resembled a doll, not least in his stillness. It felt like a threat – a reminder that he didn't need to move. I remembered what had followed me last time I'd visited Safe To Sleep, and felt a reminiscent hint of writhing inside my eyeballs. Beside the avenue the mounds looked surreptitiously restless, another reason why all the way to the gates I felt almost too apprehensive to breathe. They took their time over letting me out, and even on the road I felt vulnerable, far too isolated beneath the wide thin sky. Safe To Sleep was well over the horizon before I felt even slightly safe, by which time Toby's silence had begun to bother me. I was uncertain what to say to him, but kept glancing in the mirror to make sure he was conscious. He seemed content to watch the passing scenery until he caught me watching him. "Did you see it, dad?" he said.

Despite the empty landscape all around us, I found the question ominous. "See what, Toby?"

"The head that feeds on stars." Before I could think how to answer he said "I liked taking you to see."

Dealing with this was harder still. I felt devious for meaning more than he might grasp as I said "I'm glad you did."

"We've been to see lots better than that. Lots bigger than it too."

"Toby, we're going to leave all that behind now."

He looked pensive, but he hadn't spoken by the time I glanced back at the road. "I suppose I can," he said, "if we're all together."

"Us and mummy, you mean," I was distressed to have to establish.

"Mum as well, dad." The words included a surprised laugh that sounded hearteningly childlike. He might have been waiting for me to meet his eyes before he said "I wanted you to come and fetch me."

I felt as if we'd rediscovered the bond we ought to share, and perhaps Toby had given me more of a reason to hope. I must proceed carefully, but surely anything I might have to do was worthwhile if it protected him, not to mention putting his life back together. I checked that the straight road ahead was clear for hundreds of yards, and then I met his eyes again. "Will you say that to your mother, Toby?" I said.

CHAPTER TWENTY-TWO

Something Like the Truth

"Lesley." Anyone but I might have been unaware of how she paused before adding "Sheldrake."

Apparently it made our son giggle to say "Toby Sheldrake."

"Toby." His mother had no time to be amused. "What's wrong?" she said.

"Nothing, mum."

"Then why aren't you asleep with the other children? Aren't they still asleep?"

"I expect they will be, but I don't need to go any more. Mum, can dad bring me home?"

I hadn't suggested the proposal, which threw me as much as it plainly threw his mother. Her silence seemed to loose a mass of static, amplified by the loudspeaker. The phone hissed like a snake until Lesley said "Who says you don't need to go?"

"They do, mum."

"You're at Safe To Sleep, are you? Who's there for me to speak to?"

Toby glanced at me but gave me no time to respond. "They'll all be with the children."

"Are you saying they've left you on your own? You stay right there and I'll come and take you home."

"No, mum," Toby said urgently enough to keep her on the line. "I'm not at Doctor Phoebe's."

I heard a fierce breath and a surge of static. "Where are you, then?"

"At dad's old house."

"Your father's there, is he? Let me talk to him."

As I opened my mouth Toby said "I wanted him to get me."

At last he'd reached the point I'd encouraged him to make to his mother. "Why, Toby?" she said.

"Because I want him with us like we were. That'll let me sleep."

I'd prompted none of this, which made it feel all the more hopeful. "Can you hear me, Dominic?" Lesley said.

"I've been listening."

"Then please bring Toby home at once."

"I was meaning to. I just needed to be sure you'd be there to let us in."

"Well, now you know. We'll talk when you're here."

I wasn't going to allow this to sound ominous. At least it meant I wouldn't be turned away at once. Before I could speak Toby replaced the receiver, so vigorously that the table opposite the stairs wobbled on its scrawny legs. Perhaps he was eager to be home with both his parents or trying to ensure his mother didn't change her mind. He hurried to open the front door and glanced along the faded musty hall. "It's a sad house, isn't it, dad?" he said.

"What makes you say that?"

"It hasn't got enough people in."

He sounded younger than he often did, which I couldn't help taking as a sign that he'd left Christian Noble's influence behind. I still imagined I could reconstruct the world as it had been – our world, at any rate. As I shut the front door I saw sunlight catch dust on framed glass, almost blotting out "Keep The Home Fires Burning" and "Thou God See All". Toby strapped himself into the back seat while I was on my way to the car. As I drove along the wide main roads I fancied that the cloudless sky was as straightforwardly blue as it should be on a summer afternoon. The sky shrank to a suburban size when I turned along our road, and I was only just in sight of the house when I saw Lesley at the gate.

Her face wasn't owning up to her thoughts. She stepped aside to let me onto the drive, where I parked beside her Victor. By the time I climbed out she was standing in the hall as though to reconfirm her ownership. "Come in now, Toby," she said as soon as he left the car.

I could have thought this was meant to exclude me, and I moved towards the house when he did. "You said we were going to talk."

"And we will." Lesley retreated a step, which could have been making room for me or ensuring that we didn't touch. "When I've had a word with somebody," she said and turned to our son. "What time do the children usually wake up?"

"They'll be awake now," he said with a hint of wistfulness. "They'll be having their drinks."

"How are you feeling, Toby? Just tell me the truth."

"I always do. I'm happy, mum."

Lesley looked away from him, though not at me. "Be a good boy and play outside until I call you."

"You won't send dad away again, will you?"

"I'll be doing what's best." As he made to speak Lesley said "Your father and I want to talk now. The sooner you're playing, the sooner we can."

Toby left us with a hopeful look not far short of a plea. Lesley didn't move until we heard the back door shut behind him, and then she led the way into the workroom, where I couldn't help thinking my empty desk looked vacated by someone who'd lost their job. Once she'd checked that Toby was out of earshot — he was pacing from corner to corner of the lawn while he murmured to himself, perhaps measuring the area in some fashion — Lesley sat at her desk. "You won't object if I call Safe To Sleep," she said.

"Why should I?" I felt as if Toby's scheme to reunite the family had superseded mine or at the very least subsumed it, so that my only option was to play it out, however much bravado this took. "Can I hear?" I said.

"I want you to, Dominic."

Her tone was as inexpressive as her face was determined to be. Both of us were silent while she keyed the number. The speaker filled the room with the repetitions of a bell, and I thought Toby must be able to hear, although his pacing didn't falter. He was at the far end of the lawn when the bell gave way to a voice. "Dr Phoebe Sweet."

"Phoebe, this is Toby's mother Lesley."

"Mrs Sheldrake." Almost as neutrally Phoebe Sweet said "Yes."

"Can you tell me why my son has come home early?"

"He said that was where he wanted to be."

"How is that going to help his treatment?"

"That's completed, Mrs Sheldrake. He needn't attend any more."

"May I ask how you reached that decision and when?"

"Just today. Let me assure you it's the right one."

"Shouldn't you have discussed it with his parents first?"

I wanted to feel encouraged by Lesley's reference to both of us, however brisk it sounded. "He just seemed very eager to go home," Phoebe Sweet said.

Lesley glanced at me, but her eyes conveyed no sense of how she meant to proceed. "His father took him," she said.

"I believe so."

"How did that come about?"

I found I was holding my breath while my ears began to ache. "That's what Toby wanted," Phoebe Sweet said.

"Perhaps, but how did you contact my husband? I assume he was at his old house." As she spoke Lesley turned her gaze on me, and I had to nod. "Toby doesn't know his number there," she said.

Now I couldn't exhale, and my ears were throbbing. Phoebe Sweet's voice sounded a good deal more remote as she said "The name will be in the phone book, won't it? I didn't call Mr Sheldrake myself."

She was playing a game even more devious than mine. She must have grasped that my version of events at Safe To Sleep had been cautiously partial, and was trying to say nothing that might contradict my account. Even if she was concerned only to protect the Nobles and their secrets, I couldn't very well reject her help. "So are you saying our son's cured?" Lesley said.

"As I say, there's no need for us to see him again."

"Then thank you, Phoebe. Thank you very much from all of us for everything you've done, and please thank anyone who was involved."

"I'll do that, and remember me to Toby." With a pause terse enough to betray haste Phoebe Sweet said "Goodbye, Mrs Sheldrake."

I didn't know if I would have achieved anything by speaking to her, and before I could think of a remark she'd gone. Lesley planted the receiver on its cradle, silencing its hollow drone, and rested her hand on it as she gazed at me. "Is it over, Dominic?"

I had a sense that misinterpreting the question would put an end to my hopes. "Is what over?"

"Have we heard the last of your Mr Noble and all the rest of it?"

Keeping quiet about the Noble family and their activities needn't mean ignoring them or letting them flourish unhindered, I told myself as I said "Will that give Toby what he wants?"

Lesley glanced towards the window to make sure he was still preoccupied with his game, and then she trained her gaze on me. "Are you really going to do that to me, Dominic?"

"I don't know what else I can do. Anything that brings all of us back together."

"I won't bargain with you. Have we heard the last? The answer's yes or no."

"Then of course it's yes. The biggest yes I've said since we got married."

I felt like a child with his fingers crossed behind his back, not least since her scrutiny didn't abate. "No more interrogating Toby and his friends," she said.

"None of that and no car accidents either. Believe me, I've been driving twice as carefully since then."

Was I overstating too much? Lesley looked determined not to blink until she'd extracted every answer she wanted to hear, and even then they would be subject to examination. As I searched for truths she would find acceptable, she closed her eyes. "All right," she said and opened them, though only to gaze at the phone. "I'll make one more call."

I opened my mouth before realising that I mightn't want to learn who she meant to phone any sooner than I would. It would certainly be unwise to betray I was nervous. The clacking of the plastic keys beneath her fingernails put me in mind of a typewriter – of a stenographer recording a confession. A bell started to trill close to her ear, and she glanced at me as a preamble to switching the phone to speaker mode. The amplified shrilling sounded harsh, and static added a rough edge to the voice that did away with the bell. "Colleen Johns and partner."

Lesley turned away to speak, and I couldn't see her face. "May I have a word with Colleen? It's Lesley Sheldrake."

"Of course, Mrs Sheldrake." With more concern than I found applicable the receptionist said "Is everything all right?"

"It will be."

Some inaudible communication must have taken place, but it wasn't between us. Even the static had hushed by the time Colleen Johns said "Lesley, how are you? You were on my list to call."

More hopefully than I could interpret Lesley said "Why was that?"

"Just to update you on our progress. We'll be bringing you all you're entitled to very soon."

"It would have to be that, of course." Planting her fists on either side of the receiver, Lesley leaned down to say "Please excuse me, Colleen, but I've decided not to proceed."

The receiver emitted a sharp breath like a sniff in reverse. "I thought we had an understanding."

"Certainly we have. You must charge me for all the work you've done on my behalf. I'm only sorry to have taken up your time."

"I wasn't thinking about money. We discussed second thoughts syndrome, if you remember. I told you how common it is and how much of a trap. Can I ask what's undermined all the resolve you had?"

"I was too hasty, that's all. I let my emotions get the better of me when I should have taken more time to consider the future."

"Lesley, those are classic second thoughts, and just remember we're allowed our feelings. We've finished letting ourselves be told they make us inferior to men. It sounds to me as if we need a proper talk. When are you free to come in?"

"There'd be no point, Colleen. I've made up my mind."

"I thought you had before. I must say I'm very disappointed, Lesley. I wouldn't have expected this of somebody like you. I'd have thought you would have wanted to set an example to victims who aren't as educated as you are."

"Excuse me, but I don't consider myself to be a victim."

"Then that proves you are one. Surely you can see that's another of the traps the dominant culture keeps us in." As Lesley began to retort, having sat back to put some distance between her and the phone, Colleen Johns demanded "Why are you on a speaker?"

"Just for convenience."

"Whose convenience?" When Lesley didn't speak the lawyer said "Is he there with you?"

"Colleen, everybody I know has a name."

"Your husband." Without apparent irony Colleen Johns lowered her voice to ask "Can't you speak as freely as you'd like?"

"Nobody stops me doing that, I assure you."

"I want to believe you, but do remember what you said to me yourself."

I saw Lesley hesitate. "What are you saying I said?"

"You agreed intimidation needn't be physical or even verbal," Colleen Johns said, and more loudly "If you can hear me, Mr Sheldrake, just remember that means I can hear you."

Perhaps I shouldn't have protested "I haven't said anything for you to hear."

"Thank you for proving the point I just made. Lesley, at least tell me you aren't at home."

"That's where we are."

"I specifically advised you not to allow him access. If you've yielded that much I'm really not sure how I can help you any more."

"Just send me your bill, Colleen. That's all you need to do, but please do realise that I'm grateful for all the trouble you've gone to."

"I wish you were grateful enough to follow through on your commitment. Every successful case is a blow struck for all of us. I'm afraid I'll have to leave you to it now. I've a client waiting who I think will make my work worthwhile."

Lesley laid the phone to rest and spun her chair to face me. "Let's put all that behind us," she said at once.

"There's not much I'd like better."

When she gazed at me I thought I'd been too eager to assume everything was well until she said "Don't ever make me feel like you did again, Dominic."

"I wish I hadn't, believe me. I don't know what I've done in all my life that could be worse."

"I hope there's been nothing and never will be." She shook her head at her own mangled grammar and gave it a wry smile that I dared to hope was meant for me as well, since she held out a hand. "Let's put Toby out of his misery," she said.

He still looked intent on his game, pacing the diagonals of the lawn now, but I wondered if he'd resolved to preoccupy himself so as to keep his mind off his parents. Lesley kept hold of my hand once I'd helped her up, and then put an arm around me as she opened the window. "Toby," she called.

He swung around and took in the sight of us. "Is dad staying now?" he pleaded.

"We're back together. Forget we ever weren't," Lesley said. "How do you think we should celebrate?"

A shine widened his eyes, which let me think he could still become an ordinary boy – one free of Christian Noble's influence, at any rate. "Can we go to Disney World like Claudine and her mum did?" he said.

CHAPTER TWENTY-THREE

Flights

"It's like somebody's put a lid on the world."

"You're right, Toby, a marble lid."

He leaned close to the window of the airliner, and his shoulder rose as if he was shrugging off Lesley's remark. "Only we came through it, and it's got shapes in."

I remembered how he'd told the priest at my father's funeral about shapes in the clouds. I was about to steer the conversation to a safer subject when Lesley said "What shapes can you see?"

"You aren't supposed to give them names. Things that change aren't meant to have any."

A woman standing in the aisle beside me while she flexed her legs sent him an admiring smile he didn't notice. I was afraid that Lesley might be more troubled than impressed by Toby's answer, but she said "What did you think the first time you were above the clouds, Dominic?"

I hoped this didn't remind Toby of my experience at Safe To Sleep. "They looked like sculptures to me."

"Sculptures in space," Lesley said, an image I'd been trying to avoid. "I'm the uninspired member of the family. I've always thought they looked like snow that nobody has walked on."

"Maybe someone does." As I willed him not to go into any detail Toby said "We're up near space now. Maybe you can see if you look."

He lowered his head to peer through the window and then leaned back while Lesley ducked towards the view. "I don't think I can quite," she said.

I was about to intervene to prevent Toby admitting he had when the woman in the aisle broke off talking to her friend behind me. "Maybe you'll be able to fly there when you're older, little fellow," she said.

"Some people can now."

I was desperate to head off any further comment he might make, but the woman said "Who would they be?"

With a five-year-old's disdain Toby said "Astronauts."

"Those, of course, silly me. I just thought you looked as if you meant someone else."

"You write about space travel, don't you, Toby?" Lesley said and told the woman "That's how he goes there, in his head."

"So long as he doesn't go out of it."

Presumably this was a bid for wit, but it came too close to the truth, which I was nervous he might be prompted to tell. When he giggled I had to say "We've no reason to think he's in any danger of the kind."

"Pardon me, I'm sure." As she returned to her seat several rows ahead the woman muttered "I didn't mean anything bad."

"I knew she didn't," Toby said and turned to gaze at both of us. "Didn't you?"

"Of course we did," Lesley said, and I agreed at once, though I was glad he didn't look at me too long or hard. I was acutely aware of how he was leaving Safe To Sleep behind, not just my involvement but everything he'd experienced there and all that had led up to it, including Tina Noble's interference with his infant mind. He was pretending to have lived the life Lesley wanted to believe he had, and I could only play along to save the one we'd recreated. It threatened to make our stay in Florida feel like a deception that had to be sustained for a week.

"There ought to be dinosaurs," Toby said when we arrived at the hotel in Orlando, though the setting looked like a jungle to me, luxuriant with palm trees that dangled drops of moisture from the tips of leaves and as humid as the heat that had engulfed us the instant we'd stepped off the plane. Toby was so taken with our suite that he ran back and forth through the rooms before settling on the expansive tenth-floor balcony as his favourite place. Surely all this was spontaneous, and I could grant myself a holiday from nervousness. Having his own television in his room delighted him, and it took both his parents to persuade him to turn it off so that he could catch up on his sleep.

Lesley insisted on leaving the inner doors ajar, which made me feel I had a reason to be apprehensive. I lay listening for sounds from Toby's room, and their absence wasn't reassuring. Once Lesley was asleep I tiptoed to look at him. He was sleeping on his side with one small bare arm outstretched towards the television. I saw his eyelids flicker, which presumably meant he was dreaming, surely a positive sign. I crept back to bed, where Lesley mumbled "Error you" and slipped an arm around me without wakening further. Quite soon I managed to sleep, though I had to quell the notion that I might join Toby there, and as far as I knew I didn't even dream.

Toby was up with the sun and eager to be on his way to all the magic. Just the same, he made time for the prodigiously vigorous shower and for the breakfast buffet, where he expressed the hope that his mother might start cooking bacon as crisply as Americans did. A bus brought us to the Magic Kingdom as they were opening the gates, and soon we were among the vintage buildings of Main Street. "It's like going back before you were born," Toby said, an observation I had no cause to find ominous.

I tried to think none of his comments were. "They aren't real," he remarked about the cartoonish spectral holograms that roamed the graveyard of the Haunted Mansion, and I told myself he wasn't comparing them with the malformed shapes of the errant dead. "He's escaped," he said of the tattered windblown skeleton that greeted new arrivals on the pirate ride, and I assumed he meant the remains had strayed from the mansion – Disney's, not Christian Noble's. I was glad he kept quiet in Space Mountain, where the starry dark through which the roller coaster raced was uncomfortably reminiscent of another experience we'd shared. He laughed when everyone applauded the concert in the tiki cottage, though I'd found the performance – not just artificial birds that sang but idols and flowers too – somewhat disconcerting. I was troubled by the observation that he made in Small World, not least because I didn't understand it, and was glad Lesley didn't hear. As our boat sailed between the multitudes of puppets like an endless horde of clones, all of them piping their title song, he said to himself "That's what they are too."

We spent days in EPCOT and SeaWorld, and then our idyll was done. By the time we boarded our night flight home, Toby's happy exhaustion had started to give way to the irritable kind. When we reached our seats he surprised us by saying "Mum, do you want to sit by the window? Or dad can."

"It can be your treat both ways," Lesley told him. "You'll see cities all lit up."

"I don't want to now. I've seen them."

"When have you, Toby? It was daytime all the way here."

"Don't care. I'll want to sleep."

As we heard him growing fractious Lesley relented. "Dominic, let me have the aisle and you can have the window."

Toby's head was sinking well before the plane eventually moved off. He raised it to watch a flight attendant adopt a crucified pose to indicate the nearest exit, but was nodding by the time she mimed the fall of the oxygen masks. When she advised everyone to read the safety instructions he fumbled the card out of the seat pocket and stared at the drawings as if they made up a comic that was too young for him. Before he returned the card to the pocket he peered at the image of a passenger on the way to reverting to a foetal posture in preparation for an emergency. "They're being like a baby," he murmured to himself. "That's not how you go."

By the time the plane began to taxi he was fast asleep. I watched lit streets sink beneath us and wished I could show him, but didn't want to waken him. Soon we were sailing over distant cities, clusters of tiny orange lights that put me in mind of constellations no longer vital enough to shine white. That wasn't how the universe worked – the ghosts of stars didn't fade that way – and so I managed to take comfort from the spectacle, a reminder that we were closer to the earth than to the space beyond the atmosphere. A glance showed me Toby with his chin on his chest and his fingers losing their grip on the edge of the seat, while Lesley was rereading the collected works of Mary Shelley for the course she would teach next term. I went back to watching the stately parade of minimised cities far down in the night, until at some point my mind went dark.

Toby wakened me. I felt a small hand grope at my shoulder, and his foot gave my knee a gentle kick. I blinked my eyes open to find the cabin lights were dimmed. When I turned my head, which felt burdened by slumber, I made out that both Toby and his mother were asleep. Lesley had stuffed her book into the seat pocket and was clasping her hands in her lap. Toby's head was thrown back, and his legs were splayed wide. He'd raised his arms and stretched them out, resting them against the seat on either side of his head. Despite sitting up straight, he was doing his best to adopt the position I knew far too well.

I could only hope with all my soul that he hadn't been in it for long – that he hadn't gone too far to be rescued at once. I even wondered whether he'd been reaching for my help, consciously or otherwise. I was pitifully grateful to see that he wasn't quite touching his mother, and I willed her not to waken before Toby did. Might changing his position retrieve him from his trance? I took hold of his hand to lower his arm and leaned over to whisper in his ear.

Gripping his hand felt like trying to grasp the dark. I could have fancied that he was as empty as the entrance to a void. I mustn't recoil, and I gripped him harder. "Come back, son," I whispered urgently. "There's nothing you should see."

Perhaps this brought the memory of the experience I'd had at Safe To Sleep too much to life. I felt as if I was keeping hold of a link to a darkness far wider than the sky. Whatever was stirring wakefully in it was too vast for my mind to encompass, and undoubtedly too dreadful, but attracting its attention would be a great deal worse. "Come away from that, Toby," I urged, feeling grotesquely parental, reduced to using words that weren't remotely equal to the situation. His hand stayed unresponsive, and I lurched forward to look at his face. His eyes were open, but only darkness was alive in them.

I remembered how Christian Noble had warned me against wakening him. I felt guilty and terrified, and then I recalled more of Noble's words. "My God, that bastard," I muttered, hardly caring who heard. "He didn't mean you didn't matter. He meant it doesn't matter where you are, because he can still use you."

I imagined I felt Toby's fingers stir, and gave his hands a fierce squeeze. "He won't, though," I vowed. "I won't let him."

My son's vacated eyes were as blank as his face, and I was afraid the colossal presence in the boundless dark was about to gaze at me out of them. "Toby, come back to us," I hissed and seized his arms to shake him, assuring myself furiously that Noble's admonition had been one of his lies. "Come back before mummy can see how you are. I'll find a way to stop the Nobles taking you from us, I promise."

Perhaps some of this reached him, or else the shaking did. His fingers wriggled as if he was trying to grasp something solid, and then they found the edge of the seat and clung there. His mouth worked while his eyes widened and narrowed, which looked as though he had to rediscover how to focus them. "You're on the plane, Toby," I murmured. "You're back with us." I didn't glance away from him until I saw him recognise me, and then I realised Lesley was aware of us. I was about to speak when I met her gaze, which made it plain that she'd overheard far too much. "You'll be hearing from me, but not here," she said.

222 • RAMSEY CAMPBELL

CHAPTER TWENTY-FOUR

Overheard

"So now I can't trust either of you," Lesley said.

She was sitting in the middle of the sofa in the front room. Her fists were planted on either side of her, ensuring that I couldn't sit beside her. Though it was early afternoon Toby was in bed, having slept as little as we had on the rest of the flight home. Until she was certain he was asleep Lesley had said hardly a word to me, but I'd sensed she was saving up a host of them, which felt like a gathering storm. I might have let her speak uninterrupted if that wouldn't have made me seem guiltier still. "You can trust me to do whatever's best for our son," I said.

"Such as teaching him to lie to his own mother."

"He didn't want to worry you, that's all. Neither of us did."

"You're saying it was his plan, are you, Dominic? Have you any idea how pathetic that sounds?" She gave me a look too weary even to contain dislike. "Perhaps you'd care to sit down," she said. "You won't intimidate me by standing over me."

"Lesley, I'm not trying to. I don't know where you'd get that idea." At once I thought I did, and tried to put Colleen Johns out of my mind so that I wouldn't be tempted to mention her. Once I was seated in the armchair opposite Lesley I said "Is that better?"

"Nothing is, and I don't know what can be." As I searched for an answer she might find acceptable she said "Let's see if you're able to tell any truth at all. What really happened the day you brought Toby home from Safe To Sleep?"

"I told you, he wanted to come."

"That isn't even half an answer. And you wonder why I don't trust you, or perhaps you don't. What's worse, you've made me feel like that about my own son."

I couldn't help recalling how my parents had behaved on learning I'd taken Christian Noble's journal, but the thought of Colleen Johns provoked me to say "He's still mine as well."

"You'd like to split him, would you? I think you may have succeeded." Before I could respond Lesley said "I want a proper answer. Did Phoebe Sweet really say he was cured?"

"It was never a cure in the first place. Christian Noble and his people were simply exploiting the children for their own purposes, the ones he's always had."

"Can't you even tell the truth about that?" As I made to protest Lesley said "It's only been a week since you promised we'd heard the last of him."

"You had then. You're saying you want the truth."

"And all I'm hearing is the same obsession you've had since you were a child. I honestly believe some experience you had back then must have harmed your mind more than you'll admit."

"Not harmed, just showed me what needs to be done." I was inspired or else desperate enough to say "And I'm not alone any longer."

"I'd say you're doing your best to make sure you are. Who are you talking about, may I ask?"

"Bobby Parkin's investigated Safe To Sleep. Maybe you should talk to her."

"Your friend who you told me was gay." When I nodded Lesley said "Investigated what exactly?"

"She spent time there." I was dismayed to think she might still be doing so. "And she participated in their ritual," I said.

"Ritual." Having dropped the word like an unwelcome burden, Lesley said "Who involved her in all that?"

"The Nobles, and I imagine Phoebe Sweet was there as well."

"That's not what I meant, and I think you know it. Whose idea was it for her to investigate?"

"As a matter of fact it was hers."

"She just happened upon Safe To Sleep, did she? Nobody brought it to her attention."

"I don't mind telling you I did that, but—"

"So your obsession still means more to you than Toby does. Perhaps I really should have a few words with your friend."

"I wish you would if I can contact her. Only you have to understand she didn't just participate, she's been won over."

Lesley made a sound too terse for even a mirthless laugh. "You mean she disagrees with you."

"I mean the Nobles have infected her with their beliefs."

"You're saying she doesn't share your view of what you call their ritual. Perhaps you ought to listen to her if it isn't too late."

"I don't need to. I've been there myself."

Lesley parted her lips some moments before she spoke. "You've been where?"

"At the ritual they want everybody to believe is a treatment. I don't know whether Bobby was responsible, but they invited me to take part."

"I think we're coming to the truth at last." Lesley's pause suggested that she didn't want it much. "When did you?" she said.

"Last week, and—"

"The day you took Toby away from Safe To Sleep?"

"I'm afraid it was then, but—"

"So he didn't call you to collect him at all."

"I don't believe we ever said he did."

Lesley looked as though she didn't want to see me any longer. "Then you've taught him to be as devious as his father."

"Lesley, he just wants to keep us all together. We both do."

"And my views don't matter, apparently."

"They most certainly do, but they need to be based on the facts."

"Do enlighten me. What don't I know?"

"I didn't really either till I saw for myself. The ritual – it's as Bobby says, it used to have another name."

"Bobby says that, does she? What name?"

"Don't laugh, but some people would have called it astral projection."

"I'm a long way from laughing, Dominic. Are you going to tell me what you saw?"

"You've seen some of it yourself. You've seen Toby in his trances." When Lesley betrayed no response I had to say "Only this time he took me with him. He and the other children did. The Nobles have a chant that sends them off. I tried to fight it so I could protect him, but it caught me as well."

While I spoke her gaze seemed to retreat from me. "You found what you wanted to find," she said.

"How can you think I'd want that?"

"I wish I didn't, but don't try to tell me that isn't what happened. It sounds to me as if the way they put the children to sleep affected you as well, but you had your own agenda." Before I could attempt to refute this Lesley said "Did Phoebe Sweet actually say he needn't attend any more, or did you simply take him?"

"What they said was that it didn't matter. I'm sorry, Lesley, but they were never going to put right what they'd started in the first place."

"That's what you told him on the plane."

Although I might have expected this, it threw me. "You did hear."

"I heard a lot you didn't want me to." Her anger surfaced as she said "Well, now I know the truth."

"I hope you do."

"I know you're so obsessed you've robbed Toby of the only treatment that helped him."

"You can't believe that after all I've told you." When she fended this off with a stare I said "There's more I could tell."

"You won't be telling it to me. You can tell it in court if you like."

"Don't take my word, then." In desperation I said "Ask Toby where he goes at Safe To Sleep."

"I won't be asking him and you won't either. In fact—"

While the phone provided the shrill interruption, it might almost have been speaking up for my nerves. "Don't you wake him," Lesley said through her teeth as she lunged to pick up the receiver. "Yes, who is it, please?"

I hadn't heard an answer by the time she twisted around in her chair. "It's your friend."

However accusing this sounded, I had to take the chance to say "Why don't you speak to her? Ask her what goes on at Safe To Sleep."

I thought her gaze was dismissing the proposal, and I was about to urge Bobby to speak to her when she said "Not that friend."

She held out the receiver as though she hardly cared whether I took it, and withdrew her hand so swiftly that I almost dropped the phone. "Sorry," I said, rather on Lesley's behalf. "Who's this?"

"It's Jim. I'm here in town visiting my parents."

"Can I call you back, Jim? This isn't a very good time for a chat."

By now Lesley's back was turned, and I couldn't make out her reaction. The computer screen she faced was as blank as a void. "Can we get together in the next couple of days?" Jim said. "I wouldn't mind a word."

"I'm not sure what I may be doing," I said and saw Lesley's shoulders draw together as if to form a shield. "What did you want to talk about?"

"I've had Carole Ashcroft on the phone. She's complaining you've got Bobby mixed up with Christian Noble's mob and thinks I ought to intervene." Possibly in case I might feel threatened, Jim added "I'm only doing it as a friend."

For a moment this seemed woefully inopportune, and then I wondered if it could be exactly what I needed. "Lesley," I said and covered the mouthpiece. "Don't think for an instant this is more important than Toby and us, but I have to meet Jim."

"Do as you choose, but please don't come back here afterwards."

"We don't want Toby upset again, do we? Let me sort this out with Jim and maybe I'll have more to say that you ought to hear."

She didn't face me as her shoulders slumped. "Just go, Dominic."

I had to take this for agreement – resignation, at any rate. "Jim, where do you want to meet? Let's do it as soon as we can."

"You'll know the Crown on Lime Street, won't you? I'll see you there in half an hour."

Returning the phone to its cradle on my wife's desk brought me close enough to touch her if she hadn't edged her chair away. "Lesley, I wouldn't be going if I didn't think this may help us," I said.

She turned her head to pin my gaze with hers. "I wonder if anything can."

At least she hadn't said she doubted that anything could – not in those words. As I made for the front door I heard her lift the phone. I was easing the door shut, less in a bid to overhear than to ensure I didn't waken Toby, when she said "May I speak to Colleen, please."

I almost went back, but Jim might well be on his way by now, and I had to believe he could help. As I drove into town the streets felt distant and brittle with jet lag. I parked three floors up beside the railway station and walked through the concourse, where an enlarged voice was announcing delay upon delay. I'd forgotten that the pub opposite the station faced the Forum, where I'd caught Jim and Bobby in the dark. The memory felt close to false after so much that had happened since, and I tramped downhill to the Crown.

The pub had just opened for the evening. A few dedicated drinkers sat by themselves in the extensive Edwardian room, beneath a ceiling like a pale inverted garden, florid with excrescences tipped with gold. I tried not to think of unnatural vegetation, but the stained-glass windows reminded me of the Trinity Church of the Spirit, however secular the images might be. Jim was sitting beside one with a pint of lager, which he raised to me as he stood up. "Same for you, Dom?"

"At least that much."

Jim's concern looked official but turned friendlier at once. "What's the crisis?"

"Lesley and I may be splitting up."

He gripped my shoulder on his way to the bar, repeating the gesture when he brought my drink. "What's the trouble at home?" he said.

I reduced the pint by an inch before saying "Christian Noble and the rest of them."

"You're still pursuing that, then."

"More like they're pursuing me. Maybe it's coincidental, or maybe someone recognised our name. Tina Noble works where our son was born. She gives babies a condition so she can send them to the place her father runs."

"That's extremely serious. Do you have proof?"

"Jim, you know how sly the Nobles are. I caught her at it once, but I'm sure that will have made her more careful about covering herself."

"You caught her doing what exactly?"

"Performing one of their rites in the neonatal unit." As I realised how much I was asking my old friend to believe I said "Call it some kind of hypnosis if you like."

"Would it work on children at that age?"

"It worked on our son."

Jim hesitated long enough to be suppressing the question he'd first thought of. "The place you're saying Noble runs, is that where you sent Bobby?"

"I didn't send her. She decided herself, but yes, that's the place."

"And what's happened to her, do you know?"

"The Nobles have. They've turned her into one of them."

"That doesn't sound like the Bobby we know."

"Exactly, which shows you how much power the Nobles have."

"She did have a thing about Tina Noble, though. That could explain it, I suppose." When I made my disagreement plain Jim said "People don't always behave as you'd expect them to. Believe me, I see that in my line of work."

"But you saw how rational she was last time we met. Even if I don't agree with most of it, her writing is as well. Can you honestly imagine her being converted to the sort of thing we heard that time at Noble's church?"

"Seems unlikely, only remember what I just said about behaviour." Jim took a drink so measured it resembled a demonstration of sobriety. "So have you tried to snap her out of it?" he said.

"She's in too deep, Jim. I let her persuade me to go and join in the rite they perform with the children."

"You think she's deluded but you reinforced what she believes. I wouldn't have thought you'd do that to her."

"Don't you sometimes have to do things you really oughtn't to get your job done?" When Jim met this with a stare that was at the very least a warning I said "I had to see what they were doing so I could save our son from it, and I hoped I could save Bobby as well."

"So did you?"

"I'm afraid she's still with the Nobles, in spirit at any rate." I was distressed to be reminded that I had no idea what might have befallen her as a result of my visit, and could only hope her reputation would keep her relatively safe. "I didn't even manage to save our son," I said.

"You mean you left him with them."

"No, it was his last session, but then I found it doesn't make a difference. The treatment was never designed to stop the children having the seizures they have." All I could risk adding was "It reinforces them, and that's the state he's been left in. He could have one whenever he's asleep."

"Are you saying Tina Noble gave them to him in the first place?"

I was distracted by a murmured conversation somewhere behind me in the room. Perhaps a missionary was on the prowl, asking drinkers if they prayed a lot. "I'm certain she did, Jim," I said.

"I wonder if there's a case for the police to investigate."

"I was hoping you'd think there might be."

Perhaps another man behind me was complaining that he'd paid too much for some item, but my jet lag made the low voice even harder to grasp. "Let me see if I can have a word with someone on your force," Jim said.

"I don't know if that would be such a good idea. Some of them are Noble's people."

The glass Jim was lifting stopped short of his mouth. "Where did you get that idea?"

"Two of them searched my car for no reason at all. Jim, I give you my word they let me know they were connected with the Nobles, but of course they didn't leave me any proof."

In my mind I saw their eyes and the threat of boundless darkness they contained, but I could hardly describe that to Jim. Were the men behind me complaining about holidays – about places they'd stayed that were hot? "Did you get their names at least?" Jim said.

"Farr and Black. I wouldn't know what rank they were."

"I've got contacts on the force. I'll see what I can find out about your men. Maybe I can fix it so they aren't involved in looking into this situation of yours."

I had an unhappy sense that Jim was indulging me. Even his choice of words seemed carefully ambiguous. I took the men behind me to be putting the world to rights, since I heard one encouraging the other to say what was what. They and jet lag meant I had to concentrate so as to respond to Jim. "Do you mind if I ask you another favour?"

"You can more than ask, Dom. If it's legal and I'm able you've got it."

"Will you come with me to the place Christian Noble runs?"

Jim frowned, though I wasn't sure this was aimed just at me. "And do what?"

"Observe as much as you can. Maybe if someone besides me sees what's wrong there, people will have to take notice."

Jim brought his gaze to bear on me. "Are you thinking of your wife?"

Of course I was, but I said only "It could help."

His attention drifted past me, and I thought he was considering my proposal, but then I grew aware of the conversation at my back. The harder I strained to listen, the more secretive the voices seemed to grow. Perhaps it was less a conversation than a series of repetitions, since so many of the phrases I thought I was hearing sounded similar: say what's what, play a lot, say it's hot, lay a loss, weigh a moth... By now I could have imagined my jet lag had begun to render them as senseless as a dream, and Jim was saying "It couldn't be official. I'd just have to be with you as a friend."

"That would be enough for me." I had to drag my mind back to our discussion. "I hope it would be for Lesley too," I said.

I'd almost identified the syllables the men kept repeating – not quite day of goth, I thought, and was no longer so eager to hear, never mind look around – when Jim called "Are you interested in us for a reason?"

I heard two chairs scrape the floor in unison. I felt fixed in the attitude of eavesdropping, as if the syllables I'd recognised at last had robbed me of the ability to move. I rediscovered the mechanics of my body in time to see the street door closing a last inch. Two figures so blurred that they hardly appeared to have shapes loomed on a stained-glass window and vanished. "Who was there?" I was anxious to learn.

"Two types who came in just after you and had a half of ale each. Nosey couple, but they didn't like attention very much."

"What did they look like?"

Jim frowned and took a drink, neither of which seemed to aid his response. "I mustn't have been concentrating," he admitted. "First time that's happened since I put on the uniform, and it'll be the last as well."

His lapse made me nervous, and so did discovering "How much did you hear of what they said?"

"They didn't say a thing, Dom. They just sat there trying to pretend they weren't watching us." Jim's puzzlement subsided as he said "Anyway, I'm on for taking a look at Noble's operation."

"You don't think someone might warn him in advance. Those two could have followed me here, you know."

"No need to start imagining that sort of thing, Dom." As I wondered if he might dismiss any more of my fears Jim said "And I wouldn't care if they had. Can you take me where we have to go tomorrow? Then nothing's going to stop us," and I thought he sounded like we used to, not like a policeman at all.

CHAPTER TWENTY-FIVE

The Contents of the Rooms

As Jim came out of his gate the sun raised its brow between two houses beyond the far end of the road. I might have taken this for a good sign if the intensified glare hadn't blinded me while I parked outside his parents' house. I was blinking a blank patch out of my eyes when he leaned down to me, and I fumbled to lower the window. "Shall I follow in my car?" he said.

"Let's just use mine. One less to hide if we have to."

Before he could comply I heard the rumble of a sash. His parents were at their bedroom window. "Enjoy your memories," his father called down.

"Don't be too shocked when you see how much has changed," his mother told him, adding "And don't get into mischief."

As he made his way around the car I shut my window, which emitted the pinched squeak it had developed since the accident near Safe To Sleep. Once he'd strapped himself in I drove under the railway bridge beyond the junction with my old road. "What did you tell them we're doing?" I said.

"Just taking a day to revisit old haunts."

I saw one of those ahead – the Norris house. A recent coat of cream paint made it shine as bright as innocence, and new curtains outdid the sky for blueness, but none of this could quell the memories the sight had roused, the rudimentary fingerprints embedded in the photograph, the blurred voice that sounded as though it was struggling to shape a mouth. "Did they wonder why we were starting out so early?" I said.

"I don't need that much sleep. I'm always up by now. I had to tell them you were too. We're the sort who catch the worm."

I couldn't help recalling my first encounter with the infant Tina Noble in the graveyard. At least I'd managed a few hours' sleep until

it was time to fetch Jim. Yesterday I'd returned from meeting him at
the pub to learn that Colleen Johns had been busy with a client when
Lesley phoned, and had yet to call her back. I thought better of trying
to ascertain how this made Lesley feel, and she proved to be no less
reluctant to risk conversation than I was. Even on the subject of my
move into the spare bedroom we kept up a painfully eloquent silence.
I was hoping the lawyer's lack of a response might give Lesley time for
second thoughts about her when Jim said "So what's the plan?"

"They'll recognise my car if they see it, but that may be in our
favour. Christian Noble doesn't think I'm a threat, so he may well let
me in."

"How about me?"

"I imagine he won't think you're one either. I doubt he thinks
anybody is."

"All right, so we've got in. What are we doing about Bobby if
she's there?"

I did my best not to feel that, since he was a police officer, he should
be planning for us. Perhaps he needed to forget he was for the duration
of our mission, or simply thought our visit was my responsibility,
which I supposed it was. "Maybe we can take her with us," I said.
"Maybe seeing both of us will bring her back to her old self."

I more than hoped this could be the case. After all, we were adults
now, not merely the Tremendous Three – indeed, not that any
longer. Surely the three of us were equal to Christian Noble, especially
given how unconcerned he was about who stayed with him. Either
I'd forgotten what had happened to another journalist who'd stood up
against him and his beliefs or I didn't want to remember.

Shadows dwindled as I drove through streets lined with dark locked
shops, and then the empty sky widened ahead. Jim and I seemed to
have run out of comments we could usefully or even pointlessly make
to each other. Well before we came in sight of Noble's land I was
wondering how to proceed if he didn't let us through the gates. I
could only pray, or at least my version of it, that there might be a
way in that I hadn't noticed and that Noble hadn't bothered fixing.
In any case, surely Jim must know a few tricks about gaining access to
properties. I held off asking him – no need yet to remind him that we
weren't here by invitation – all the way to the spot where I'd crashed

the car. I wasn't far past it when my foot faltered on the accelerator. The gates that guarded Safe To Sleep were open wide.

I wondered if my approach had been observed, although why would anyone have been so eager to let me in? Perhaps somebody had just arrived, except the gates would have shut as soon as anyone had passed through them. Or was someone on their way out? When I came abreast of the gateway the avenue was deserted. "I don't know what's going on," I said. "I've never seen the gates left open."

"Then let's find out," Jim said, which as a schoolboy I'd once made him say in a tale.

As I drove along the avenue I kept glancing in the mirror. I was nervous of seeing the gates shut like a trap, but they stayed still. They weren't the only distraction. I had a persistent sense of restlessness on if not above the mounds in the grass on both sides of the avenue, though glancing at them showed me nothing of the sort. I dismissed it as an illusion, some kind of shutter effect produced by driving past the trees. I was more concerned with the sight at the end of the avenue, though I wasn't sure of it until the car left the trees behind. The front door of the house was ajar.

The strip of darkness seemed to gape to greet me as I drove to the steps, and I could have fancied that the gloom concealed a watcher. Only the car was moving, not the hefty door, and as far as I could make out, the darkness was just dark. Rather than leave the car by the steps I parked closer to the drive. Some confused instinct – certainly less than a thought – suggested that if a speedy getaway was needed, this might help. Or was I loath to leave the car too close to the house? I couldn't have articulated the feeling to myself, let alone to Jim. "At least it looks as if we won't have to break in," I said.

"I hope you weren't thinking we would."

Jim was reminding me of his official status, which I'd thought he meant to leave outside the gates. I wasn't sure how to respond until he said more like the friend I'd known "Let's see what's there."

He was out of the car ahead of me. As I locked it he waved a fierce hand at his face and wiped his brow hard. In a moment an unpleasant chilly tingling settled on my skin. "Something's breeding round here," Jim complained.

While it could have been a swarm of insects too minute to see, it felt like electricity in the air. It faded, though my skin wasn't entirely convinced that it had, as we crossed the gravel. The trees of the avenue blocked off the sun, and I couldn't see through any of the windows, which made me feel as though the darkness was looming towards us like a watchful occupant or a crowd of them. Jim was first up the steps, and eased the front door inwards. I was wondering whether we should announce ourselves so as not to be accused of trespassing when he stooped to pick up an envelope. "Who's this?" he said.

He sounded oddly wary, and scrutinised my face as he displayed the envelope. The item of mail was a gas bill, which I found so unexpectedly and inappropriately mundane that I didn't see at first it was addressed to C. Bloan. "That's the surname Noble uses now," I said. "His daughter does as well."

"You're sure about that, Dom."

"I've met them both here. I recognised them and they didn't care."

Jim stooped to finger the carpet where he'd found the bill and then tested an adjacent patch. When he held out the envelope for me to touch I found it was faintly damp. "That's been there for a day or more," he said.

I welcomed his detective skills, not least because his observation proved that whatever had occurred at Safe To Sleep couldn't have resulted from our having been overheard yesterday in the Crown. "I'd better do this all the same," he said and turned to shout "Hello?"

The house sent back an echo of the second syllable, which might almost have been proclaiming a revelation. "Is anybody here?" Jim called louder, and eventually turned back to me. "Any idea what can have happened?"

I wanted to believe my previous visit had put a stop to Safe To Sleep, even if I didn't know how much that could accomplish. "Maybe we'll find out if we look."

"Coming in," Jim shouted up the stairs, where the gloom seemed to diminish his voice and deaden his tone. "I'd say we've got the place to ourselves," he said.

I remembered assuming Noble's church was more deserted than it had proved to be. If Jim and I encountered anything like I had, at least that should convince him there was more to Noble and his beliefs than he might want to think. Just a hint of wrongness would suffice

236 • RAMSEY CAMPBELL

so long as Jim couldn't explain it away. He took a step into the house and shook his head. "Where's the switch for the lights, do you know?"

As he peered at the walls that framed the doorway I ventured into the gloom, which seemed less to gather on my eyes than to accumulate within them. When I strained my eyes in an attempt to dispel the darkness, I might have thought they were simply attracting more. I was reminded how the fogs of my childhood would build up like soot in my nostrils whenever I breathed in. "It's all right," I heard Jim say. "I've found it now."

A metallic click came next, and then a series of clicks did, none of which relieved the gloom. "Looks as if they've been cut off," Jim said. "Let's see if there's more light further in."

He meant from windows, but I wondered why the pair above the stairs weren't admitting more illumination. Granted that the sun was at the front of the house, they still looked darker than they should. "Come out a minute," I urged Jim. "I've got a flashlight in the car."

"I'll wait here. It's not that bad."

It was for me, and I disliked leaving him alone in that darkness. When I emerged into the sunlight I had to blink my eyes clear of the gloom before I could risk descending the steps, and then I hurried to my car. I'd begun to regret having parked so far from the house, but I hadn't time to move the vehicle now. I found the flashlight among the maps and guidebooks in the glove compartment, and once I'd switched it on I had to aim it at my face to establish that it was working. As I returned to the house I saw that the sky beyond the roof had clouded over, which surely went some way towards explaining why the windows above the stairs weren't lighter. At the top of the steps I switched on the flashlight again and directed it into the house. "Hey, that's dazzling enough," Jim said.

I hoped he meant it was sufficiently bright, though I had a sense that it was hemmed in by the gloom. When I lifted it towards the stairs, an enormous centipede scurried away up the wall towards the landing – the shadow of the banisters. By the time the beam reached halfway up it was virtually indistinguishable from the dark beneath and between the windows. "Do you want us to go upstairs first, then?" Jim said.

I was simply testing the beam, which I found unhappily feeble.

"Let me show you where they took the children," I said and swung it towards the right-hand corridor.

Even once the walls enclosed the light, they failed to concentrate it much. As I led the way along the passage, the beam shrank to a dull glare on the door of the sleeping room. The gloom closed in behind us, and I resisted an impulse to glance back to make sure nothing else had. Presumably the carpet was deadening our footsteps, but I felt as if stillness was lying in wait for us – as if a presence silent as a held breath was. I took hold of the doorknob, which was so cold that it might never have been touched by sunlight. I had to twist the knob with all the strength of one hand and then nudge the door open with my shoulder.

The flashlight beam spread into the sleeping room and was lost at once. A flat dull glow like an omen of dawn or a postponement of daylight lay in the room, which was empty apart from the ranks of abandoned mattresses. For an instant I thought one of them stirred as though something had burrowed into it, but before I could locate the movement the entire room was still. "Is that it?" Jim said.

I was hoping he'd caught sight of the activity. "Is what, Jim?"

"That's what I mean. I wouldn't say this proves much."

"It's where they used the children."

Jim frowned at the mattresses and then at me. "Used them how?"

"Gave them seizures, all of them at once." As I wondered how much closer I could venture to the truth I felt as though the boundless dark I'd voyaged through with them was eager to reach for my mind. "They indoctrinated Toby and the rest of them while they were helpless," I tried saying. "They fed the children their beliefs. I'd have intervened sooner, but they'd given me a seizure too."

"How could anyone do that, Dom?"

"Call it a form of hypnotism. It was a chant that didn't just put you to sleep."

I was afraid he found the concept too extreme until he said "Was Bobby involved?"

"She was in a seizure too. I wish I'd been able to take her out of here as well, but I had enough trouble taking my son."

"How did you manage that when you say you were in a seizure?"

I was uncomfortably aware that his questions were growing more official. "I came here determined that I wouldn't be susceptible. It took some doing, but I fought it off."

"Well, good for you, Dom." The interrogation wasn't done, however. "Do you remember where you were in here?" Jim said.

"I'm not likely to forget. I was here by the door, and Toby was in this corner."

"Do you happen to recall where Noble was?"

"I'll show you." I paced between the mattresses, stopping opposite the one precisely halfway down the row against the left-hand wall. "He was here," I said, only to feel as if the mattress covered with a crumpled sheet was drawing me towards it, compelling me to stoop in imitation of its vanished occupant. "Jim, look at this."

He came to stand next to me and peer where I was indicating. Close to either corner near the wall, four faint but unmistakeable indentations were visible in the edge of the mattress, and a further mark had been dug into the upper surface a few inches from each group. "Did you see how that happened?" Jim said.

"No, but I can guess. He must have held on like that every time to make sure he wasn't carried off himself." Afraid I'd used too strange a phrase, I said "I saw him doing it a long time ago."

"You've got to be talking about France."

"The night we followed him. That's how he held on to his bed till he got up."

I hoped Jim wouldn't ask for an explanation, because I wasn't sure I had one. Instead he enquired "Bobby, where was she?"

When I pointed at the mattress near the door he moved to examine it, hands clasped behind his back with one finger drumming on a knuckle. "She didn't hold on, then."

"I didn't see her doing it." Since the look Jim gave me wasn't far from reproachful, it drove me to protest "Honestly, if I could have got her out without rousing anybody else I would have. I didn't realise Noble had come after me till I'd put Toby in the car."

"All right, Dom, I believe you." As I started hoping this might extend to at least some of the truth about Safe To Sleep, Jim said "Was Tina Noble here as well?"

"She was over there." When I reached the mattress opposite her father's I was able to confirm "She must have been holding on too."

Two sets of faint depressions like the ones across the room remained at the edge of the mattress. As Jim inspected them I said "And Toph was in the middle by the window."

Jim made a face that might have been trying to clutch at the name. "Who?"

"Her son. Toph short for Christopher. You'd think they were running out of names." The weak gibe didn't lessen the undefined nervousness I began to feel as Jim headed for that end of the room. "He's a year old if even that," I said. "I shouldn't think there's anything to see."

Jim bent to examine the mattress, and his finger drummed on the knuckle more insistently. "I don't see how this can be possible, Dom."

As I joined him I saw that the outside of the windows was coated with grime – with some dark substance, at any rate. It blurred the view of the grounds that stretched to the hedge through which I'd observed Safe To Sleep. If there was movement on the mounds in the grass, I hadn't time to spare for it just now. The mattress Toph had occupied bore the imprints of two small sets of fingertips at the length of a pair of infant arms, but that wasn't all. Opposite these groups of prints were two more, about a yard away and dug equally deep. "How could any child do that?" Jim demanded as if he were the victim of a trick.

"It wasn't any child."

Jim stared at me so hard he might have thought I was the problem. "What on earth do you mean, Dom?"

I wasn't sure I knew or wanted to put much of it into words. "That's how they've made him, his mother and her father."

Jim's stare relented or at least returned to the marks on the mattress. "I'm starting to think this could be as serious as you say," he admitted. "Let's see what else we can find."

We left the door open so that the enervated daylight reached along the corridor, though not far. Jim found nothing of significance in the next room, an extensive white-tiled toilet with a mirror above a sink. As we entered the room I had a fleeting impression of movement in the mirror, as if a shape had dodged out of sight within the glass, but thought I'd glimpsed the reflection of the door. Further up the passage we found an extravagantly capacious cupboard where mops and brushes leaned their heads together like gossips, while a dining-room large enough for several generations of a family extended along the opposite side of the corridor. I couldn't tell which end of the long table was the head, and wondered who had sat in that position. Surely Christian Noble would have, but I had an uninvited vision of Toph clambering up to perch and play the adult, since there was no sign of a high chair. I pictured Bobby dining with the Nobles, isolated by the room and by their triple presence. I preferred not to imagine any conversation they might have had. Wherever the Nobles were now, I hoped Bobby wasn't with them.

Although the front door was wide open, the lobby was at least as dark as it had been. It felt as if darkness was taking up residence. As I lit the way to Phoebe Sweet's office, insectoid shadows fled towards the windows above the stairs as if seeking a means of escape. At first I couldn't see what had changed in the dim room, where the desk and chairs looked somehow ownerless, and then I realised the walls were bare. "She's taken her certificates," I told Jim. "She was the doctor they used as a front, Phoebe Sweet."

"Then if she sets up somewhere else she'll be traceable."

I made for the desk in case she'd left anything inside, and was reaching for the nearest drawer when I thought I heard movement within. My approach could have disturbed a rodent, but I had the unappealing fancy that whatever had stirred was waiting to take hold of my hand. I dragged the drawer out to see it contained just a few distorted paperclips, and heard a noise in the drawer beneath it. The restlessness was louder now, and rather too much like someone fumbling at the wood. When I tugged that drawer open it proved to be empty, but I'd mistaken where the noise was coming from – one of the drawers on the opposite side of the well of the desk. It sounded as though it was groping to push the top one out, and I did my best not to be put in mind of a wakeful occupant of another sort of box. As I made myself open the drawer, its contents lurched towards me – a splintered ballpoint almost drained of red ink. The furtive noise was in the last drawer, and growing clearer. It sounded less like the fumbling of fingers than lips mouthing at the inside of the drawer, because it seemed to include a wordless mutter. I had a nightmare sense that if I opened the drawer I would see it was full of a face. Taking a shaky breath, I grasped the clammy metal handle and wrenched the drawer open. It contained nothing at all, but I thought I heard a noise under the desk —the creak of a board, mixed with a viscid slither. At once it was gone, and so far as I could see the carpet was bare. I straightened up to find Jim watching me. "Anything?" he said.

I didn't want to think he was as unobservant as this suggested. "What would you say?"

He stared into the lower drawers, which I'd left open, and then pulled out the upper ones. "I'd say she was making sure she didn't leave anything that might identify her."

"You didn't hear something just now."

Jim turned the stare on me. "What was I supposed to hear?"

"It doesn't matter," I said and was disconcerted to find myself echoing Christian Noble. "Let's move on."

Even when we left the office door wide, the corridor stayed unnecessarily dark. Across it was the room where I'd first spoken to the Nobles – all of them. I took hold of the doorknob and then hastened to switch on the flashlight, because I thought the knob felt softened, as if the gloom had somehow diluted its substance. The sight of the metal object fended off the impression, and I shoved the door wide.

The room was much as I remembered: the four squat leather chairs even darker than the panelled walls, the black dresser in the darkest corner. Last time I'd had no chance to examine the figurines on the dresser, and just one remained. Presumably the Nobles had left it behind because it was broken in two. It was carved out of stone so black that trying to identify what it might represent made my eyes ache. By straining them I saw it depicted a snake with a smooth darkly gleaming face that was to some extent human. The enormous eyes were devoid of pupils, and the thin lips were curved in a smile as wide as the head, protruding a scrawny tongue divided into three at the splayed tip. I drew back my hand from reaching for that portion of the figure, because I felt as though the body was poised to writhe in response. Perhaps the other section would as well, like a worm chopped in half by a spade. As I retreated a pace Jim scowled at the carving. "What would you say that's meant to be?"

"Noble mentioned something like it at his church, if you remember. There were others on here, but I didn't see what they were. There were three including this one," I recalled and was inspired to suggest "Maybe the Nobles used them for some kind of meditation."

"Meditation," Jim said in a voice like a grimace made audible.

"Yes," I said and was dismayed by the realisation that overtook me, "because they would have had one each."

Jim stared at the fragments as if he was challenging them to have any effect on him, and my gaze strayed back to them. I could have fancied their blackness was taking control of my vision, darkening the room and the view the grimy windows gave of the avenue. I was about to suggest that it was time we explored further when Jim said "We'll take these with us when we go. Someone who knows about that kind of thing should have a look at them."

I was thrown by having failed to notice that the serpentine body was equipped with rudimentary limbs – hands, at any rate, or else bunches of tendrils that sprouted at irregular intervals along its length. "I wouldn't mind showing Lesley as well," I said.

I'd begun to think that my experience in the sleeping room had left me attuned to the wrongness of the house. If Jim was less susceptible, perhaps that mightn't be altogether negative, though I wondered how he would react when he laid a hand on the carving. "What's next?" was all he said as he left it on the dresser.

Darkness paced behind us as the flashlight beam closed around the knob on the door at the end of the corridor. At least the doorknob was as solid as it looked. The large kitchen recalled a bygone era – the sink composed of the same ponderous grey stone as the working surfaces supported by tiers of drawers, the massive oaken table scarred by knives, the imposing range and oven of black iron. Jim was following me into the room when something darted across the flagged floor to vanish into the furthest corner. "What was that?" I blurted. "Did you see?"

"Too big for a mouse. It must have been a rat or something like."

I would have said very little like. Perhaps it could have been a snake, though on the basis of my glimpse a decidedly deformed one, too variously swollen to fit through the small hole in the skirting-board. I was left with a disagreeable impression that it had thinned and elongated like a worm in order to pass through. "It didn't look anything like that to me, Jim."

"No need to keep trying to persuade me things aren't right." As I tried to think how I could do so less obtrusively he said "I can see they aren't, and I'll help you convince your wife if you like."

"I'd appreciate it." Just the same, I was starting to wonder if I'd been too ready to welcome his relative lack of perceptiveness – if it could endanger him. "Have we seen enough in here, then?" I said.

"I want to see it all," Jim said and set about opening drawers and cupboards. I didn't know whether I was more hopeful or afraid that he might disturb some occupant, but all of them were empty of significance. A door I'd taken to belong to the largest cupboard led to a pantry equipped with bare stone shelves and a towering refrigerator, which contained just a half-eaten rotten apple like a joke neither of us grasped. "Time we went upstairs," Jim said.

The darkness in the corridor fell back towards the lobby as I poked it with the flashlight beam, and I did my best to think it wasn't loitering more than it should. I was also trying not to wonder what might have driven the Nobles out of the house, but I was distracted by realising I'd overlooked a room I ought to have remembered – the room where Toby had spent time while Lesley and I talked to Phoebe Sweet. I found the door with the flashlight beam and shoved it wide.

All the toys and books and games I'd seen last time were gone, along with a child-sized desk and a table that had been covered with crayons and paints and paper. The grimy daylight made the room look abandoned, and by no means recently. I was about to turn away when I saw that the bookshelves in the dimmest corner weren't entirely bare. A book lay sprawled on the lowest shelf – a fractured copy of *Peter Pan* in a tattered jacket. It might well have been the copy Toby had been reading, which was why I leafed through it. Surely he couldn't have been responsible for altering the illustrations, but the eyes of every airborne child had been enlarged and filled in with black ink.

Somehow they didn't look as vacant as they should, and I was peering into the depths of a pair of voided eyes when Jim glanced over my shoulder. "Kids these days don't respect books the way we used to," he said.

I could see no point in trying to persuade him that the changes represented worse than vandalism. I shut up Peter Pan's expanded eyes and dropped the book on a shelf with a hollow clunk like the fall of a lid. Leaving the door wide didn't lighten the corridor much, and the lobby was so dim that I wondered if the front door had closed by itself. It was as open as we'd left it, and once we reached the stairs I switched off the flashlight to conserve the batteries. The nearest window lit the upper flights of stairs or at any rate made them dimly visible, but I had to use the flashlight in the left-hand corridor upstairs. Off the corridor we found room after room denuded of furniture, where the only decorations were cobwebs in the corners, inhabited by bloated leggy denizens I preferred to leave unscrutinised. Up here the windows seemed to welcome very little daylight, and I'd begun to think that they weren't darkened on the outside after all – that the panes looked infested with murk. Jim confronted the rooms with growing disfavour. "They had to live somewhere," he complained.

"They must have been on the other side of the house."

I could have added that whoever had given the Nobles the house might have been trying to leave no sign of themselves. Even the bathroom at the far end of the corridor was as bare as the white-tiled walls. Someone's footstep dislodged a dangling drop of water from a brass tap above the metal bath, and I had a sense that it was lingering to hover in the air, as though time had begun to congeal. As I made to draw Jim's attention to the phenomenon, the drop struck the bath and trickled down the plughole with a gurgle shrill enough for mirth. Did Jim notice anything untoward? He squinted at the bath before saying "Nothing here."

The windowless gallery over the front entrance connected the tops of the staircases and extended to the upper corridors. As we crossed it I could have fancied we were passing above an abyss. Certainly the light from the door we'd left open barely relieved the darkness; in fact, I wasn't sure I was seeing light down there at all. Although a bathroom was visible along the right-hand corridor, it left the passage stubbornly dark. The gloom below us troubled me enough that I dodged down the stairs. "Where are you going, Dom?" Jim said as if he was determined not to be concerned.

I gripped the banister while I craned over to be sure what I was seeing. "The door's shut. The front door."

"No point in bothering about it now. Let's finish up here and then go down."

"But we left it open all the way. I know we did."

"It's an old house, Dom. Doors can shut by themselves. It's most likely subsidence."

I was afraid he was being too rational – too resolved to overlook the ominous. His explanation left me with an unhappy fancy that the house had tilted, allowing the door to creep shut. It infected me with vertigo, and I kept hold of the banister while I took a long breath. When my head steadied – a sensation unpleasantly reminiscent of my return to myself in the sleeping room – I shoved myself away from the banister and made for the corridor.

I roused a shape that advanced to greet me and Jim – my image in the bathroom mirror. I didn't immediately recognise myself, because I appeared to be lost in the midst of a swarm that was hovering in the mirror. No doubt the mass of particles consisted of dust on the surface, multiplied by its reflection that made it seem to extend far into the glassy depths. I retrieved my mind from trying to distinguish patterns in the swarm, which I could easily have thought was restless, and lit up the nearest door with the flashlight. The doorknob stayed as solid as it looked while I opened the door.

It revealed a bedroom, if not much of one. A black wardrobe yawned the length of a wall opposite a bed with an unclothed mattress. Flanking the window were a chest of drawers and a dressing-table topped by a triple mirror. I didn't care much for the sight of myself multiplied by three – it put me in mind of Christian Noble's beliefs – but otherwise the room looked unthreatening enough, and I made for the chest of drawers. When I opened the first one it exuded a scent suggestive of decaying flowers, and I told myself the small discoloured misshapen bag squashed into a corner was an abandoned sachet, despite its toadlike appearance. I wasn't about to try picking it up – at second glance it resembled a fungus, not least in the way it had started to quiver – and I hastened to shut the drawer. All the rest were empty, and I looked around to find Jim at the window. "Insects," he said.

I had to lean close to the window, because the panes looked stained, and not even on the surface. By straining my eyes I was able to make out some activity above the mounds in the grass, surely the swarming of ants, though it reminded me of the patterns I'd imagined in the bathroom mirror. "I expect the heat's bringing them out," Jim said.

I wouldn't have called the day hot or especially sunlit either. I supposed that needn't mean the swarms weren't ants, however dark and solid the hectic masses had begun to look. In some ways I was glad to turn my back on them, so swiftly that it revived my vertigo, and I could have thought my surroundings tilted a fraction. Jim shook his head, but before I could ask why, he was heading for the corridor. "Nothing here either," he said.

I felt it wasn't wise to separate, and hurried after him to the next bedroom. I could almost have imagine that the house had started to play tricks, because the room resembled the one we'd just left far too much: stripped bed, black yawning wardrobe, chest of drawers shut tight, triptych of mirrors conjuring a trinity made up of me. As Jim began to pull out drawers, which creaked like a tree, I couldn't help searching for details to prove the room was its own self. I was reminded of puzzles where you had to spot the differences between a pair of apparently identical pictures printed side by side. The memory felt capable of reviving more of my childhood, and I was trying to ensure it didn't bring back any childish weakness when I saw something was wrong with the bed. As I stooped to examine the bare mattress the sight turned my mouth dry. "What have you found, Dom?" Jim said, having finished his unproductive search.

"I hope I'm wrong, but look."

He joined me in staring at the marks near the upper corners of the mattress, two sets of five scratches that had dug so deep they'd torn the fabric. "Say what you're thinking," he said low.

"Whoever slept here must have made those. I think Bobby might have."

"Those bastards. If I find out they did that to her..." More like a policeman he said "Or anyone else, for that matter."

"Are you going to be able to make it official?"

"We'll have to see about that, Dom."

I left the flashlight off as we made for a second bathroom, even though the grudging sunshine beyond the doorway was reluctant to illuminate the corridor. I was preoccupied with the mirror, which wasn't covered with dust after all. I would have liked to think some effect of the light had produced the illusion of swarming, but could this explain what I was seeing now? My reflection and Jim's at my back looked more distant than they ought to, and somehow less than wholly related to us. In fact, as we advanced I had the impression that they were inching surreptitiously backwards, as if the mirror was drawing them in while enticing us towards them. When Jim's face set in a grimace that looked like a bid to fend off confusion I risked asking "What are you seeing there, Jim?"

"Exactly what's there. The two of us."

"Do you think something's wrong with us?"

"No, just with this place." As I made to follow this up he said "We'll talk about it later."

I thought it best not to aggravate any unease he was experiencing. I led the way into the bathroom as our reflections edged stealthily back, a sight that seemed to threaten a loss of all sense of direction if not of how space worked. I could see no trace in the room of anyone who had lived in the house. One item caught my eye – a murky drop of water, which appeared to be suspended in the air between a tap and the extravagant stone sink. I'd begun to think I needed to remember how to breathe by the time it fell, exploding on the sink with an impact that looked as slowed down as the sluggish sound. The plughole downed the trickle with a shrill noise that I told myself sounded nothing like a giggle, however much it resembled the one I'd heard in the other bathroom. "Let's move on," Jim said.

I took him to be saying that the bathroom contained nothing to delay us. His tone suggested no more than that, and I had to hope the lethargy that appeared to have overtaken the room wouldn't infect us. As we turned towards the corridor I had a sense that our reflections took significantly longer to move than we did, and couldn't help fearing they might detain us somehow. I switched on the flashlight in case this could fend off the threat, and regretted glancing towards the bathroom. There was no sign of the beam in the mirror, which showed just our dim distant silhouettes rendered more insignificant by the dark frame of the corridor. I trained the beam on the doorknob Jim was reaching for, and wasn't certain if I saw him hesitate before he twisted it and flung the door wide.

It belonged to the largest bedroom, in which a pair of empty wardrobes gaped at an immense bed. Three figures moved in unison to confront me with their doubtful faces until I turned aside from the mirrors and let Jim search all the drawers while I scrutinised the mattress. I had plenty to show him by the time he admitted defeat, but I had to swallow in order to say "They were here."

The bed was sufficiently broad to accommodate several people, even at arms' length. I could see where two of them had planted their outstretched hands, digging their fingers into the mattress. It was equally clear that a smaller sleeper had lain between the adults, gripping the surface of the mattress, and not only with its little hands. "My God, how sick is that?" Jim said. "I ought to have believed you sooner, Dom. Whatever's gone on here, it's worse than wrong."

There was one more upstairs room. Despite being smaller and darker than any of the bedrooms, it was too large for its contents − just a sizeable desk and a chair. The chair faced away from the view of the grounds, which suggested to me that whoever used to sit at the desk had been indifferent to the world. Was condensation obscuring the view? It looked as if the murk that blurred the window was inside the glass, giving it an unpleasantly gelatinous appearance. The desk was bare except for three exercise books, and I was disconcerted to feel that I recognised them. As I made for the desk I didn't know if I wanted to be right or absurdly deluded. I threw back the cover of the topmost book, to be confronted by handwriting I couldn't mistake.

I was nowhere near dealing with the implications of the sight when Jim came over. He frowned at the page for some moments before saying "That looks like your writing used to when we were at school."

"That's because it is mine. It's the copy I made of Christian Noble's journal."

Jim turned his frown on me. "How did it get here, Dom?"

"Our son took it. I'm sure Noble made him." Admitting all this let me say "I can understand that, but I don't understand why Noble's left it now."

I hardly knew what explanation I was seeking as I leafed through the book, unless I had a vague idea that Christian Noble might have added to the text. Someone had. All those years ago I'd left the final pages blank, having transcribed his entire journal, but now the first of them bore words − just a single unfinished sentence written in a childish but painstaking script. *What we behold we s,* it said, and its conclusion put me in mind of a reptilian hiss.

As I wondered what might have driven the Nobles out of the house before the writer could complete the sentence, Jim said "That wasn't you, Dom, was it?"

"I think his grandson may have written it."

"You mean the swine dictated it to a child of how old?"

"Unless it's worse than that. I think Toph, that's his grandson, may have thought it himself."

Jim's dismay lingered in the look he gave me, but I wasn't sure if it applied to the notion or to me. He went through the drawers of the desk, and I found I couldn't breathe much until he'd finished, despite hearing no activity inside them. "I'll bring these," he said and picked up the exercise books. "I think we've seen everything that matters."

I remembered how my plan to bring evidence away from the Trinity Church of the Spirit had fallen out, but surely the books were no danger to us. I felt rather more threatened by realising that I couldn't recall much of the layout of the house, as if the relentless gloom had dimmed my mind too. Jim loitered long enough to rouse my nerves before he said "Fair enough, let's get out. I don't like it any more than you do."

Just now I didn't want him to be any more explicit. I was first out of the room, mostly to ensure the flashlight led the way. Despite the time of day, the space beyond the corridor appeared to have grown darker. As I hurried downstairs with Jim at my back, a colossal elongated shape rose from the floor of the lobby to pace us on its myriad limbs – the shadow of the banister, bigger and vaguer than before. It vanished as we turned the bend in the stairs, and then its leggy relative accompanied us, growing smaller and more solid to await us. I tried to ignore its stealthy activity while I concentrated on the front door.

Even when I trained the flashlight on it, the door was barely distinguishable from the panelled wall. Indeed, I could have thought the wall was doorless, not to say unrelieved black. I could locate the door only by knowing where it had to be, surely where I remembered it as being. I stumbled off the bottom stair to advance through the gloom while the flashlight beam shrank, growing reluctantly brighter. If I could just find the doorknob – The nervous light wavered over the panels and set about wandering across the wall until I brought it back, rousing an unsteady shadow. It was too vague or else too shaky to have much of a shape, but it had to belong to an object protruding from the door. I used both hands to direct the beam until the shadow merged with its source, and I could have imagined it was adding to the substance of the metal object – surely not undermining it, at any rate. As soon as it sent me a tentative gleam I hurried to grab the doorknob like a lifeline. It quivered visibly, surely because I was holding the flashlight in the wrong hand. I was about to give Jim the flashlight so that I could use both hands to turn the knob when it yielded, and I stumbled backwards as the door swung wide.

I couldn't see the sun. I might have fancied that I couldn't even see the sky, given the utter lack of colour it displayed and how the featureless overcast lay almost as low as the treetops. At that moment my car seemed considerably more important, and I was making for it when Jim spoke. I was in the doorway – I was nearly out of the house – when he said "Hold on, Dom."

CHAPTER TWENTY-SIX

The Way Into the Dark

Escaping the ominous gloom of the house appealed to me so much that I was tempted to pretend I hadn't heard. If I headed for the car, would Jim feel compelled to follow? Then it occurred to me what he must have remembered – that he'd meant to bring the serpentine carving we'd found – and I was unhappily sure it wasn't wise for him to go back by himself. I was turning away from my car and the promise of release when he said "Is that another door?"

I had to send the flashlight beam in the direction of his gaze to locate the door, which was almost indistinguishable from a section of the panelling that boxed in the stairs. How had Jim seen it in the gloom? Presumably he must have been straining his eyes to make certain we hadn't overlooked anything significant, but I could have thought the door had waited to be noticed until we were about to leave the house. "It'll be the cellar," I said.

"We ought to take a look."

Perhaps I was simply reminded of the crypt beneath the Trinity Church of the Spirit, but I didn't find the proposition too enticing. Unable to think of any objection Jim was likely to accept, I trudged across the lobby as he advanced to the cellar door. By the time the light closed around the doorknob he had already twisted it and pushed the door inwards. I couldn't help listening for the kind of sound I'd heard from the crypt under the church, but the space beyond the doorway was as silent as it was lightless. I ventured forward to stand beside Jim and sent the flashlight beam into the dark.

It illuminated nothing but itself until I shone it downwards. Stone steps caged by wooden banisters descended about twenty feet to a floor that looked black with grime. When I raised the beam it petered out before reaching any wall, and I had an unpleasant fancy that the limits of the cellar were recoiling from the light as a slug would shrink from salt. "I don't think it's worth going down," I said.

"I will, though. Hang on here if you'd rather, or you could wait outside."

Would any of the Tremendous Three have behaved so pathetically? Certainly not in my stories and probably not in real life. I didn't know which was more childish, my thinking or my nervousness. Since Jim was here at my behest, how could I even consider abandoning him? "Let's just be sure the batteries hold out," I said, which didn't ease my apprehension at all.

As soon as I set foot on the top step I felt close to losing my balance. Though the step looked level it felt warped, and I grabbed the banister. I kept my hand on it all the way down, because the steps persisted in feeling crooked, however straightforward the flashlight made them appear to be. I tried to think the sensation was illusory, not the sight, since Jim plainly had no problem with the steps. As I illuminated his way down he flourished the exercise books. "I could have left these up top," he said, "but I thought I'd keep them safe."

The idea that Christian Noble's thoughts would be down there with us didn't help my nerves, but I didn't want to risk losing the journal again. Once Jim left the steps I turned the beam away from him to find we were surrounded by darkness too large for the light to define. "Do you think there's any point in going on?" I said but didn't hope.

"Never leave a scene till you've investigated every inch of it, Dom."

While I wanted to think his official self had spoken, I couldn't avoid knowing that he might have said much the same in one of my old tales. "Let's go this way," he urged, pacing straight ahead.

Despite the beam he looked ready to challenge the dark, and I hastened to keep up with him. I nearly lurched against him, because the floor wasn't quite as horizontal as it looked, unless my vertigo was back. The flashlight wasn't capable of resolving the impression, and I sent the beam further ahead, to be consumed by the dark. "Brace yourself, Dom," Jim said and immediately shouted "Hello?"

The eager darkness swelled towards us, surely just because I'd let the flashlight waver. "Who are you talking to?" I wished I didn't need to learn.

"Nobody I know of. Only trying to hear how big this place is." Louder than before he yelled "Hello?"

The shout was dwarfed by a space too large to see. I was reminded – unnecessarily, I very much hoped – of the void into which I'd been drawn from the sleeping room. "It sounds empty to me," I tried saying.

"We'll find out," Jim said and kept on.

The slant of the floor helped send me after him. While the beam persisted in levelling it, I could have thought the floor had tilted a little to coax us into the dark. Or perhaps the pressure of the blackness was driving us onwards – the blackness that massed at my back and beneath the ceiling, which the light didn't reach. Underfoot the floor felt somewhat softer than the stone it was composed of, and I assumed it was darkened by fungus rather than grime. I couldn't judge how far we'd gone when Jim halted, planting his feet wide in a stance that looked defiant if not ready for a confrontation. "Something isn't right here," he said.

I might have laughed at the understatement if I hadn't been nervous of asking "What in particular?"

"We can't still be under the house. We've gone too far."

His dim face darkened as I swung the beam around us in a vain attempt to find a wall. Surely I needn't wonder if the extent of the cellar was a means of enticing victims away from the way out – a trap. "I don't understand why anyone would build a place like this," Jim said.

"I'm afraid Christian Noble might have found a use for it."

"That's not my point, Dom. He didn't build it, did he? You said someone gave him the house. I can't see what a cellar this size could have been for."

I had an uneasy sense that we mightn't care for the answer – that perhaps it wasn't even the right question. "We won't learn anything by standing here," Jim declared and stalked forward.

I was about to follow doggedly when I realised what I was seeing. Trying to make sense of it kept me silent for too long before I blurted "Wait, Jim. Wait."

"No need to say it twice." He turned just enough for his indistinct face to show me a frown. "What's the problem?"

"This place doesn't just go too far. It's going down."

Jim peered along the flashlight beam, which lit up a stretch of the floor until it was overwhelmed by the dark. "I don't see it, Dom."

"Look at me. Aren't I higher than you now?"

His frown became a squint until he tried to clear his face of both. "I wouldn't say so."

"You have to see it," I said in desperation. "You're lower down than I am."

In fact our faces were level, which wasn't as it should be, since Jim was half a head taller. Just the same, the floor appeared not to slope, a contradiction that felt worse than vertigo. In a moment I couldn't judge our relative positions, which was more dismaying still. "Come ahead and you'll see we aren't going down," Jim said.

"I honestly don't think we should go any further," I said and was inspired, however nervously, to swing the beam upwards. "You must be able to see that," I said, not far from pleading.

"I can't see a thing there, Dom."

"That's what I mean. Where's the ceiling? Why can't the light reach?"

"Maybe it's the batteries."

I brought the beam down. Raising it had let the darkness rush at us, and I had a decidedly unwelcome impression that lowering the beam failed to drive all the darkness back where it had been. "Then we shouldn't risk going on," I said.

Jim hesitated and came to me, and I saw his head rise higher than mine. I was about to draw his attention to this when he said "Let me have a look."

He turned the flashlight towards his face and then shook it at the floor. "I'm sure it's got a good few minutes in it yet. Come on, Dom," he said and, handing me my exercise books, tramped after the beam towards the dark.

I was suppressing a childish impulse to demand the return of my flashlight when I saw what he was being made to do – not simply to descend a slope, however it was disguised. "Jim," I said, but perhaps he didn't hear, because the sight had parched my mouth with panic. "Jim," I said so loud that my voice seemed to collide dully with the dark, "for Christ's sake stop."

"No need for that kind of language, Dom." My urgency hadn't

even slowed him down. "I'm not stopping just yet," he said. "Come on, catch up."

"Jim." Seeing him recede into the dark trapped too many of my words in my throat. "You aren't just going downwards," I forced out. "You're going skewed as well."

As though articulating the situation had brought it into focus, I saw with awful clarity what was taking place. Jim was following a spiral route that might have been forced on him by an immense shell, unless he was tracing the path of a kind of frozen vortex in the floor. The notion of a shell, however invisible, suggested the presence of some form of life that was nesting beneath the house like an insect under a stone, and I wondered if it was the reason why the house had been so suddenly abandoned. I saw Jim tramping unawares to meet it, perhaps to rouse it, unless we already had. "I'm not, Dom, I promise," he was saying. "You're letting the place get to you. Catch up and you'll see you're mistaken."

I no longer welcomed his unawareness. Indeed, I'd begun to suspect it was letting the place gain some hold over him. "Just stop," I begged. "Stop and look at me. Shine the light at me as well."

Perhaps he realised he was leaving me too far behind, and in the dark. As he swung around, the flashlight beam did, but not as it should. It appeared to snag on an insubstantial or at any rate unseen barrier – a wall far too close to Jim. Then it went out, and I was swallowing in preparation for calling out to Jim when it flared at me. Either Jim hadn't noticed its momentary absence or he was ignoring the anomaly. He poked the beam at me and then past me, and I saw it waver as his face stiffened. More than darkness seemed to mass at my back, and I was afraid to look. "What is it, Jim?" I had to say instead.

He didn't speak while he paced towards me. Once he reached me he was silent for some moments, during which I couldn't breathe. Gripping the flashlight with both hands, he ranged the beam about beyond me. At last he said "Where are the steps?"

I turned to face the way we'd come and saw the beam of light trailing into empty blackness. "They'll be where they were," I said, which felt like an act of faith, not least that I hadn't turned too far and lost my bearings. "Shall we go back now? We don't want to lose the way out, do we?"

Perhaps Jim paused because he didn't want to have to ask "Which way are you saying that is?"

I could only pray – at least, the closest I'd come to doing so for decades – that I was facing in the right direction. "Give me the flashlight and trust me, Jim."

"Are you saying you know?"

"I'm saying I think so." I might have been conveying hope or desperation as I said "Unless you've a better idea."

He handed me the flashlight and took the exercise books, and I felt as though he was abandoning the dependability I'd relied upon. He was prepared if not anxious to trust my instincts, but how much could I trust them myself? As I stepped forward, following the light into a blackness so oppressive that it seemed to gather not just on but within my eyes, I had to cling to the belief that I was retracing my progress. It didn't help that however level the floor persisted in looking, I had a sense that the slope was growing steeper, as if it meant to send us sliding helplessly backwards into the dark. I didn't care at all for how the floor had begun to feel: softer than a covering of lichen could account for. I could only pace doggedly forward, struggling to walk in a straight line. The sensations underfoot suggested I was doing quite the opposite, and the flashlight beam swayed from side to side as if it yearned to find the steps as much as I did. It found nothing solid except the floor, which looked ominously dormant, as if the blackened mass was about to stir. I was trying to steady the beam – surely it was causing the illusion –when Jim said "I don't want to put you off your stride, Dom—"

"Then don't." At once I felt worse than ashamed of the retort, but I dreaded learning "What were you going to say?"

"Haven't we come further now than we came in the first place?"

This gave me the nightmarish notion that the underside of Safe To Sleep was so vast that we would wander until the light gave out and our bodies did. "I don't believe so," I said and did my utmost not to. "Don't distract me."

I was afraid Jim might object to being sidelined – might insist on taking over, as a policeman surely would. When he didn't speak I could only assume he felt as disoriented as I was striving not to feel. I had a dismaying sense that the darkness we faced had grown solider while the floor became more treacherous, not merely tilted but capable of swarming like a mass of insects as wide as the dark. The impression brought me to the very edge of helpless panic, and I had to struggle not to run. Unless I controlled myself we risked becoming even more lost in the dark. All the same, I felt driven to pace faster, because I had a daunting fancy that any hesitation would let my feet sink into the floor. Was the thick swarming darkness able to hinder my progress somehow? Despite my efforts I'd failed to put on much speed, and I was dismayed to feel that the dark was clinging not just to my eyes but to the whole of me, gaining weight as well. The idea had begun to overwhelm my mind, leaving far too little space for thoughts, when Jim said "What's that?"

He wasn't quite beside me, and I didn't want to look back in case this left me yet more lost. His tone didn't make me eager to ask "Where?"

"Over there. To your left. Put the light on it." He was beside me now. "Is it..."

I swung the beam in the direction all his fingers were indicating, and a dim thin shape reared up from the dark. It was made of wood. It was a post – the lowest upright of a set of banisters – and when the beam jerked higher I made out the steps. "Thank Christ you're here," I said. "I might have missed them."

I thought it showed how relieved he was that he didn't protest at my profanity. I didn't quite run towards the steps, but I couldn't tramp fast enough to outdistance a sense that my feet were in danger of being engulfed, as if the twisted slope that I was desperate to cross in a straight line concealed a swamp. In my haste to reach the steps I almost sprawled headlong on them. They felt more skewed than ever, and indefinably unstable, as if they weren't as solid as they had been. I clutched at the banister all the way to the lobby and turned at once to light Jim's way up. I felt so concerned for him that at first I didn't realise why he needed my aid, since he seemed to have no problem with the steps themselves. As I stepped back to let him through the doorway he said "Why the hell is it so dark?"

I turned to see that the front door had shut again, but this couldn't altogether explain the gloom. Shouldn't it be lighter now that the day had advanced? I had a disconcerting notion that we'd lost all sense of time – that we'd been in the vast space under the house for so long that night had fallen. The darkness in the lobby was scarcely less oppressive than the blackness down below, and I had to fend off the notion that it might hinder our escape. "We've still got light," I assured Jim, flourishing the beam. "Let's hit the road."

I was urging myself as much as him. I disliked the dark as much as I thought he was trying not to admit he did, and I wasn't far from feeling like an insect trapped in amber. Perhaps insects came to mind because my skin had started to crawl, a sensation rather too reminiscent of the swarming that I'd thought was imminent in the cellar. I marched across the lobby, keeping the flashlight beam on the front door as steadily as I could, and glanced back to make sure Jim was following. How could the windows over the stairs have shrunk? A band of black cloud must be blotting out their lower halves, and it was crawling up the panes. I jammed the flashlight under my arm and closed both hands around the doorknob. It yielded with a harsh squeak, but the door didn't budge, even when I hauled at the knob with all my strength. "Jim," I said, "can you—"

"Leave it to me." As I moved aside, still training the beam on the door, he handed me the exercise books and seized the knob with both hands. He twisted it as far as it would turn, then tugged. The door creaked like a tree trunk but stayed wedged in the frame. "Don't play games with me," Jim muttered, planting his feet wide as an aid to heaving at the knob with all his strength. Perhaps he was driven to a fiercer effort because the lobby had grown darker still. I saw his shoulders quiver with exertion, and all at once the door gave in. It staggered towards us on its hinges with a soft sound I didn't understand or care for, letting darkness spill into the house.

The blackness wasn't merely dark. I heard some of it slump across the carpet, scattering around Jim's feet. As he recoiled he gasped "What in God's name." I had to overcome my fear of seeing what the open door revealed, and I clutched the exercise books under my arm and closed both hands around the flashlight before raising the shaky beam.

It confirmed what I'd hoped the material strewn across the carpet couldn't possibly mean. The entire doorway was clogged with black earth. I heard the mass of soil whispering against the doorframe, and saw that it wasn't just cutting off our escape – it was inching upwards.

Parts of it were restless, perhaps with worms or other insects, unless the earth itself was writhing eagerly. "We're buried, Jim," I blurted as though he needed to be told.

I saw not just his dim face but his whole body stiffen with resolve, and he swung around. "Up, quick."

His voice sounded somehow enfeebled, which was how the flashlight beam had begun to look. As we dashed to the stairs I thought the floor lurched, and tried to believe only the beam had. The stairs felt warped, so that except for holding the exercise books I would have grabbed the banister, and softer than they should, as if they were on the way to being consumed or transformed, perhaps both. An unseen transformation might have explained why I felt not simply trapped but in some sense encircled by the house. Very little of the windows over the stairs was clear now – just two blurred meagre strips of dull sky were visible – and I could have thought the mounting blackness was determined to outrun us. The bend in the stairs felt more like a steep curve of a spiral, however it continued to look. I floundered around it and up a higher flight, and had barely reached the top when the windows behind me grew utterly dark, overwhelmed by earth. "Nearest room," Jim shouted at my back.

I had to glance around to reassure myself that he was closer than he sounded, and very nearly lost my footing on the tilted edge of the stairs. The flashlight beam mimed my unsteadiness as I sprinted into the right-hand corridor. The light fumbled at a heavy doorknob, and I was afraid the door might be even more thoroughly wedged than the front door had been. I freed a hand to twist the knob and then used all my force to thump a panel with my shoulder, and was caught off guard by how readily the door let me into the room.

Three panicked figures rushed towards me, displaying my face. I did my best to ignore them as I ran across the crooked floor to the window. I was unprepared for how disconcerting the view would look, of the gravel in front of the house puckered like a senile mouth to help swallow the building, and far closer to the upper floor than it had any right to be. I might have tried to welcome how it brought my car nearer if I hadn't seen what had become of the mounds in the grass. Each one was indistinguishable from the blackness it was emitting – a filament composed of swarming particles that rose to arch over the house. The tendrils might have been legs or the mandibles of an unseen monstrous mouth, and the sight of them revived the crawling on my skin, a sensation that felt capable of invading my flesh. I knew they must surround the house, a situation I found so daunting that I was loath to open the window. The windows were our only escape route, and I stuffed the flashlight into my hip pocket and planted the exercise books on the floor in order to shove at the sash with both hands, having released the catch.

For a moment I thought the sash moved, but only the house had, together with the rising mass of gravel mixed with soil. No, not only them: my car had as well. I was afraid the handbrake had failed, and then I saw the disorienting truth. The car appeared to be creeping rightwards because the entire landscape was, or rather the house was being twisted into the earth. The sight drove me to a frenzy, and I was heaving at the sash to no avail when Jim urged "Make room."

Although he was beside me, I could barely hear him. Whatever was occurring in the air – the change that made my skin feel infested – seemed to be consuming sound. Jim planted his hands beside mine under the top of the sash, and we wrenched at it together. I thought I felt the pane begin to give, but the sash remained jammed in the frame. As he redoubled his efforts Jim leaned his head nearly into my face. "Get something to break the glass."

I might have suggested trying the next room, but why should any other window be more use? I had a desperate notion that we should try to kick the glass out, and then I realised that the room wasn't quite as empty of potential tools as it felt; it wasn't devoid of furniture. I ran to the dressing-table and saw my three selves stoop in obeisance – no, to pull out the top drawer.

The handle felt clammy and not quite like wood, unpleasantly suggestive of a knob of fungus. It stayed firm as I tugged at it, but my effort faltered as I wondered if the drawer could be hiding some occupant. Hesitating might put us even more at risk, but I had to haul the drawer all the way out before I was able to see it was empty. As I crossed the softened floor, gripping the heavy object with both hands, I couldn't hear my footsteps. "Mind out," I yelled and wasn't sure if I was hearing my own voice except inside my head.

Jim didn't move aside until he saw me ram one corner of the

drawer into the pane. It felt like hitting gelatin, and yet I couldn't see even a hint of a shiver. I swung the drawer again like a hopelessly unwieldy club and thumped the middle of the pane with every ounce of strength. I imagined I heard or at least felt a splintering, too faint for me to judge whether it was wood or glass. Another violent swing that nearly overbalanced me, and a thin diagonal crack no more than a few inches long glinted in the pane, only to shrink to half the length as I tried not to believe what I was seeing. "Let me try," Jim shouted or at any rate mouthed, and I was glad to relinquish the drawer, since my hands were shaking so much I could scarcely keep hold. He slammed it against the glass, aiming at the crack, and at his third ferocious attempt the pane gave way, shattering outwards without a sound and more slowly than it should have, like an explosion of some viscous liquid. Jim used the drawer to dislodge jagged fragments from the sash and then flung it through the window. He clambered after it and turned at once to help me out of the house.

The sight of him almost paralysed me, because he was sidling past the window despite standing absolutely still. It made me feel that the world had begun to come apart, which distracted me so much that I had no idea what to do except seize Jim's outstretched hands. I was halfway across the sill when my thoughtlessness caught up with me, and I stumbled backwards to retrieve the exercise books. Jim supported me with both hands while I ducked through the gap and knelt on the sill, then helped me to twist around so as to step down, all of which felt as though he was being dragged stealthily away from me. When my feet struck the gravel I might have lost my balance without his support, given the inexorable progress of the earth around the house.

My car was still where I'd parked it near the avenue. Beyond it a dozen hectic tendrils had risen from the mounds to close over Safe To Sleep. Whatever lurked beneath the ground must extend at least nearly to the gates, a realisation that brought me close to absolute despair. My sense that an enormous mouth had gaped under the house was overwhelming me, and I fancied that the tendrils were extending from it like incarnated shadows of the shape the mouth belonged to, an impression scarcely expressible in words. I could barely think, because I felt more infested than ever, as if some element of the change that had overtaken Safe To Sleep was about to make me its own – as if the invasion that had swarmed deep into my flesh presaged some form of hatching. The solitary thought I managed to grasp was that I wasn't safe with the car, and as we ran across the sluggish vortex of gravel I thrust my keys at Jim. "You drive," I shouted.

I didn't know if he heard me; I wasn't sure I did. Presumably my gesture was enough, and my expression might have helped persuade him. He took the keys and was opening the doors by the time I dashed to the passenger side. As I tugged my seat belt across me Jim twisted the key in the ignition, but I heard no response. Worse, I felt none, and I was afraid the transformation of Safe To Sleep might have rendered the engine useless, as perhaps it had drained the electricity from the house. Then the car jerked forward, but had it moved only because the ground under it had? Not until it sped into the avenue could I let myself believe it was travelling under its own power, though apparently without a sound, and I turned to look back at the house.

In the minute since our escape it had sunk a good deal. Just the roof was visible, turning with a dreadful stateliness that suggested a performance of a soundless waltz. All around it the tendrils towered out of the mounds, feeding the house into the whirlpool of earth that I knew was somehow related to the spiral we'd found beneath the mansion. The sight of the frenetic particles that formed the tendrils roused an answering sensation in my flesh. Were the tendrils hindering the car? No, Jim had slowed to watch the house in the mirror. I was about to exhort him to put on speed when the house sank beneath the earth, brandishing its chimneys in what I could almost have seen as a gesture of defiance. The multitude of tendrils descended with it, clinging to the roof, and I couldn't tell whether they were helping it to be consumed or guiding it to some unimaginable form of acceptance, if not both. I was terrified to think that Jim and I might have suffered the same fate – that the tendrils might have a similar effect on me now that they were lowering themselves around the avenue, because my body had begun to feel as they looked. It was plain that Jim was unaware of them, and I was ready to urge him to leave the place behind – I would have to communicate in any way that worked – when he trod hard on the accelerator. Though I saw him speak, I heard nothing at all.

The car sped through the gates and swerved fast onto the road. We were past the hedge that enclosed the grounds of Safe To Sleep when I started hearing the engine. The faint whir grew louder as the swarming in my flesh dwindled into restlessness and then shrank beyond perception, though a dismaying memory lingered like a symptom. I hoped with all my soul that I'd left the experience behind, and did my best not to think the process had only grown dormant, ready for revival if it encountered some cause. I had to concentrate on Jim, who was speaking again. "Sorry, what was that?" I said.

"I need to report this. There's no telling how far it might spread. Do you know where there's a phone box?"

His voice had grown more audible with each word. "We passed one close to here," I said.

"I see it," Jim said, and so did I – a bright red glimpse between trees a mile ahead. The sight seemed as unreal as the increasingly blue sky and the fields on both sides of the road, irrelevant to the monstrous undermining of the world that we'd just witnessed. I was striving to retrieve a sense of the mundane, a reassurance I felt desperate for, when Jim said "My God, though."

I had to learn why he felt provoked to profanity. "What, Jim?"

"That's what I call subsidence," he said with a sally at a laugh, and I saw that whatever he might have experienced at Christian Noble's house, it was far less than the truth.

CHAPTER TWENTY-SEVEN

The Recalling

"Thrills and spills. They're the word for the year, are they, Dominic?"

I might have retorted that they were three words, not just one, but I said "I'm not sure what you have in mind, vice-chancellor."

"Your choice of films. Imagine my surprise to learn that you were teaching Alfred Hitchcock."

"I don't think I could teach him much." This was another comment I kept to myself. "He's proving to be a popular choice," I said.

"I rather think that has always been his aim, entertainment for the masses. I'm told he's promoted as a trader in suspense."

"He's regarded a good deal more highly than that by quite a few critics. Some of the directors who created the new wave started the reappraisal."

"Ah, the French. I was amused to hear that they take Jerry Lewis seriously as well." Having made it plain that he was waiting for a laugh I wasn't disposed to produce, he said "I remember Graham Greene had little time for Hitchcock."

I was reminded of a confrontation about Greene in my adolescence. I could have thought my life was accumulating echoes and reappearances, by no means all welcome. "You'll appreciate I take a different view," I said.

"I did see a handful of his films while I was at school. One attempted Buchan, I recall, and another tried to make a fist of Joseph Conrad." With enough reproach to be directing some of it at me the vice-chancellor said "They weren't too fair to Buchan and decidedly unreasonable to Conrad."

"I'm concentrating on his mature work. It's been responsible for some lively discussions."

"I take you to be saying you have, Dominic. So long as minds are being stretched."

This served as an unwelcome reminder of how far mine had been. I had to pull back from a sense that the pale October sky above the campus was just a flimsy shield, a pretence of fending off the endless dark. I did my best to ground myself by remembering today's discussion, where I'd outraged several students by suggesting that we couldn't trust the happy end, since the vision that exonerated Cary Grant was what Joan Fontaine wanted to believe, and visually indistinguishable from the earlier vision showing him to be a murderer. I'd encouraged the students to consider why we should feel entitled to expect particular narrative developments and how we responded if they were withheld. I was about to convey some of this to the vice-chancellor, despite feeling I had no need to prove myself, when he said "May I conclude matters aren't too lively elsewhere?"

"Forgive me, you're asking what is where?"

He gave this – my response or the situation it referred to – a pitying look. "At home, Dominic."

"We've come to an agreement. I thought Lesley might have said when you've kept up with her news in the past."

"Is it anything the university should know about?"

"You already do. We call it marriage."

A pained frown nipped his brow above the nose. "Life has returned to normal, then."

I was far from saying that, however much I wished I could. I was about to offer him a neutral answer when I realised that his frown, having turned acute, was no longer aimed at me. As I wondered who he regretted letting overhear him he said "May I be of some assistance?"

"No, but he can."

I knew the voice too well, but at least this time I had a witness. I swung around to face not just moonfaced Black but his fellow policeman Farr, whose enlarged nostrils flared as if he scented me or my reaction. "Good afternoon, Mr Sheldrake," he said.

"And a good afternoon to you, gentlemen. Why don't you introduce yourselves to my vice-chancellor."

"No call for that. It's you we want," Black said.

"Dear me." With no decrease of regret the vice-chancellor said "Will this be a university matter?"

"Just routine, sir," Farr told him. "We have reason to believe Mr Sheldrake may be helpful."

"It's Doctor, actually." Having established this on behalf of the university, the vice-chancellor glanced at students who were passing. "Perhaps your interview would be better conducted in private."

"No need for that either," Black said. "We'll walk him to his car."

His stare grew more round-eyed while his mouth turned rounder, an expression that seemed to trouble its recipient. Nevertheless the vice-chancellor said "If I can be of any help, Dominic—"

"You aren't now," Black said and thrust his face towards him.

I never knew what the vice-chancellor saw, but I thought I glimpsed Black's eyes swelling to a size the sockets should never have been able to contain. "Let me know what transpires, Dominic," the vice-chancellor said and strode away as if an imperative appointment had occurred to him.

Farr and Black watched his retreat, and then they turned to me so much in unison that it looked rehearsed. "Shall we walk, Mr Sheldrake?" Farr said. "I should think you're wanting to be home."

Students were staying well clear of us, but I raised my voice for them to hear. "So this is just routine, you said."

"It's one of those all right," Black said half as loud.

"I shouldn't think you'd want to draw any more attention to yourself, Mr Sheldrake."

"Or anyone you're close to either."

My voice came out low, not least because my throat felt as if an assailant had clutched it. "Who are you threatening?"

"Why, nobody at all," Farr said. "Certainly not your loved ones, Mr Sheldrake."

"We don't have to do a thing to your family. It's been done."

As I stumbled to a halt I had an acute sense of how fragile reality was, how much of a disguise: the campus buildings felt as insubstantial and impermanent as the sky. Even my own body was untrustworthy, since it left me barely able to pronounce "What has?"

"Why, your child has been prepared." As I tried to find more of a voice Farr added "He was some years ago."

"Like ours," Black seemed at once to regret admitting.

Farr glanced at him with disfavour before turning it on me. "Do keep on, Mr Sheldrake. You're meant to be walking, you know. I shouldn't think you'd want your pupils to see you being escorted by the police."

"They already can." All the same, I was anxious to make for my car, and I'd regained my voice. "Just what do you want with me?"

"More like what you want with us," Black said. "You and your pal on the force."

"He's really quite inquisitive, your Inspector Bailey. I expect he must have been surprised where his enquiries led."

I found I was nervous of asking "Where did they?"

"No bloody where," Black said. "We've got friends that are higher up than him."

As Farr sent him another glance I risked saying "So you'll have no reason not to leave him alone."

"Unless he annoys us again," Farr said. "We'll say as much for you, Mr Sheldrake."

"Or have we got to call you doctor like your vice man said? I'll promise you we wouldn't want you looking after any of our kids."

I wondered if Black was trying to provoke me in public so that he could treat me worse. He'd only reminded me of Phoebe Sweet, which prompted me to ask "So where are the Nobles and their doctor?"

The policemen exchanged glances across me, and I thought they might pretend some kind of ignorance. "Who needs to know?" Black said.

"I'd like to. That's why I asked."

"Somewhere they can wait," Farr said. "That's all any of us have to know."

Belatedly I grasped that Black had meant they were as uninformed as me. We were in sight of my car now, and a police vehicle stood on the double yellow lines alongside the car park. Since my escorts had fallen silent, I said "You've finished with me, then."

"We already had," Farr said.

"There's worse than us on the way," Black said. "Just wanted to remind you nothing's over."

They stayed on either side of me until I reached my car. Although there were questions I might have asked, I was desperate to be rid of my captors. As I unlocked the car they sauntered away side by side, and I was letting myself breathe with relief when they turned to confront me again. Each of them held up his left hand, a gesture that might have been a warning or a parody of benediction. I tried not to look at their faces, because I had the impression that Black's eyes and lips had grown perfectly circular while Farr's nostrils were distended as wide as his mouth. "What's happened to you?" I couldn't help demanding. "What are you?"

Neither of them spoke until I met their eyes. While darkness lurked within their combined gaze, their faces were no more than mundanely grotesque. "What you'll be," Black said.

I sat behind the wheel of my car until they drove away, and then until my hands were sufficiently steady to let me turn the key in the ignition. Even then I didn't start the car at once. I'd planned to go downtown to watch *Body Double*, a film that enough of my students had seen to make it worth including in discussions about Hitchcock's influence, but now I'd been reminded of too much that was unresolved. At once I remembered pretending in my adolescence that I'd been to see films, having spied on Christian Noble and his activities instead. I could see *Body Double* another day, and I drove out of the city along a route that was all too familiar.

I had to tell myself that the sky wasn't growing thinner as it widened, though it looked almost too attenuated to retain any colour. As the landscape spread around me, extending fields relieved by just a scattering of trees to the horizon, I could have fancied that it was making way for the Safe To Sleep site and whatever infested the land, allowing it more access to the void beyond the sky. Now that the house had gone, I was disconcerted to find I wasn't sure where it used to be. I had to tramp on the brakes when I saw I was passing the gates.

I'd almost failed to recognise them because they were sagging inwards. Someone had closed them and secured them with a heavy padlocked chain, and they bore a notice warning the world to keep out because of dangerous subsidence. I parked across the entrance and climbed out of the car. Even the trees along the avenue had collapsed, pointing their trunks at the site of the house while they flourished roots clogged with soil at the road. I gripped two bars of the gates and stared along the gravel drive until I began to wonder why. I was close to forgetting where I was and what had brought me there, if I even knew. I was simply gazing at abandoned land, featureless except for a track that led between two flat expanses of grass bordered by fallen trees to a circular patch of earth several hundred yards wide. There seemed to be no reason why I shouldn't seek a way in – but perhaps my nerves were somehow more alert than my mind, because my fists closed harder around the bars of the gates, bruising my fingers, which helped restore my sense of the situation. My memories were being drained, a process that felt as if the space they'd occupied within my head was filling with blackness that had seeped up from beneath the camouflaged landscape. I seemed to feel its tendrils start to range about inside my skull, as though a less than wholly insubstantial intruder was performing a kind of sluggish spiral dance to embed itself. I fled to the car, and when I trod on the accelerator I was terrified that blindness might hatch inside my eyes as it once had.

I didn't feel remotely safe until I'd driven for miles, well beyond outdistancing any sense of a hold on my mind. I turned left at a crossroads before I quite knew why, and crossed another road between fields before turning left at the next one. I was so anxious to reinforce my memories, having felt them being stolen or erased, that I was bound for the Harvest Moon.

The pub had just opened for the evening by the time I parked outside. The pony-tailed barman gave me an imprecise loose-mouthed grin from behind the bar. "What's yours today?"

I was happy to think this promised reassurance. "Just a pint of lager, thanks."

He waved a finger at the pumps in front of him, which bore dauntingly authentic names. "Nothing realer."

"I did try one last time I was here."

"You did at that." He squeezed his moustache with a thumb and forefinger, apparently an aid to recollection. "Hunt's End, wasn't it?" he said. "And you met your lady out back."

"You've a good memory."

"Never know when you're going to need it in this job," he said and levered out a pint of Viking's Valour lager. "Too real for some."

I hoped he meant the drink I'd had last time, not this one, and certainly nothing else. "That's fine," I said, the mouthful having proved palatable enough. "So did you see what happened to the house?"

He turned from checking the contents of wine bottles in a refrigerator cabinet. "Which house was that?"

I felt a sensation in my guts too much like the one that had seized my mind outside the padlocked gates. "The one we talked about when I was here."

"Remind me."

"Where you saw them taking children."

"I've got a vague memory. Some kind of home, wasn't it?" This time pinching his moustache appeared not to work too well. "It was demolished, though," he said, and I saw his eyes lose focus. "Must have been quite a while since."

"Someone has to know more. They've made the place safe and put up a notice."

"Know more about what?" As I tried to think how to respond the barman said "Hold on, I remember now."

I might have held my breath, but I had to say "Tell me."

"The council thought the road past there might be unsafe, so they closed it for a bit while they investigated. It's open now."

I could have felt defeated, but he'd prompted me to say "Unsafe how?"

"Seems like somebody reported subsidence, but they didn't find any."

Jim had reported it, of course. In a final bid for reassurance I said "You thought there was something odd about the area, if you remember. Something in the air."

"It couldn't have been much," the barman said, fingering his brow as if to demonstrate its smoothness. "It's gone."

His answers were making my brain feel attenuated, leached of substance. When I turned away I hardly knew where I was going – not where I'd met Bobby, which had a view of the Safe To Sleep site – and then I noticed a pay phone in a corner of the room. Fumbling in my pocket for change, I made for the plasterboard niche. I felt desperate to reinforce my memories, however much I might have liked to be without them. I stood the glass on a shelf beside the phone and fed coins into the slot, and listened to a bell that sounded unnecessarily distant once I'd dialled. When a voice said "Carole Ashcroft" I pushed the button, a vintage mechanism I'd encountered very little since my childhood. "Could I speak to Bobby?" I said.

The pause might have been a reply. Seconds later Carole said "Is that Dominic Sheldrake?"

"Guilty," I admitted, not much of a joke.

"What do you want with Bob this time?"

"Just to see how things are."

"I'll find out if she wants to speak to you."

Carole's tone made it plain she hoped not, and I was trying to decide if a plea would help my case when I heard Bobby in the background. "Is that Dom? Of course I'll speak to him."

I could have fancied that the plastic clatter denoted some kind of minor struggle, but surely it was just an amplified handover. "Is everything all right, Dom?" Bobby said at once.

"Pretty much," I said, which felt overstated. "I've just been to look where the Nobles were operating. There's no trace."

"I told you'd they'd gone when I came back here. I'm still sure Christian sent me off so they could leave without me."

I did my best not to hear wistfulness in her voice. I was dismayed enough to hear her calling Noble by his first name. "And you still don't know why they left so suddenly," I said.

"I told you, I didn't like to hang around any longer than I had to. You've been, so maybe you can imagine how it felt to be in there on your own when I got back that day. I'm not even sure if I was on my own. I'm fine, Carole. I want to talk, especially to Dom."

"Just remember I'm here if you want me," Carole said despite retreating audibly into another room.

"I know," Bobby called and lowered her voice. "Actually, Dom, I'm not sure it was so sudden."

"Why," I said with some unease, "have any of them been in touch?"

"Not a word. I've no idea where they are or what they may be calling themselves now. It's just that I've remembered something that was said before they went."

I couldn't help blurting "Make sure you remember."

"I don't forget anything, Dom." She sounded puzzled if not piqued, and I was wondering how much to explain when she said "It was at the end of the last sleep I took with them. I overheard it when I was coming back to myself. I thought he was talking about doing something with someone, but it wasn't that at all."

"What was it, then?"

"What we behold we summon." Lower still Bobby said "I thought he was trying to sound excited, but he seemed a bit afraid."

I felt as if the darkness of the niche had closed around my mind. To fend off at least some disquiet I said "Christian Noble did."

"No, his grandson. It was Toph."

Despite the childish hand in which the unfinished sentence had been added to my transcription of the journal, I'd hoped Bobby wouldn't say this. Ducking out of the oppressive dark, I moved to the limit of the phone cord. "Anyway," I said in a bid to contain some of my unease, "how's your writing?"

"Chugging on as always. Only, Dom..."

I experienced a qualm I felt I mightn't want to understand. "Only what?"

"Don't think too badly of me, but I won't be writing about the Nobles and their practices. Let's hope they've scared themselves enough this time to stop."

"Do you mind if I ask why?"

"Remember Eric Wharton and what may have happened to him."

More than this must have deterred her, but I suspected she would rather not remember. "I wouldn't want anything like that for you," I said.

"Thanks for understanding. And don't you or Jim provoke anything either."

I could only hope our visit to the abandoned house hadn't done so. "Let's stay in touch, the three of us," I said.

"We will. We always will."

I couldn't tell whether she was stopping short of our adolescent vow or meant to bring it back. I said goodbye and left the remains of my pint of lager on the bar. "I need to get home," I said, mostly to myself.

Soon the site of Safe To Sleep was below the horizon, which only made me feel it was lurking under the world. When the suburban streets closed in they seemed less substantial than I would have liked. Before I reached home the sun was nowhere to be seen, and the streetlamps looked clogged with dusk. I was turning the car off the road when I saw that another was parked beside Lesley's in front of the house. It belonged to Claudine's mother.

As I shut the front door Judith came out of the lounge with Lesley at her back. "Finish your game," she called, "and we'll be off."

I thought she was ensuring that her daughter spent as little time as possible anywhere near me, but then she extended a hand. "Dominic, I just wanted to say you were right to have your doubts about Safe To Sleep."

"Well, I'm—" I thought it wiser not to express gladness until I knew why. "How do you think I was?"

"Even if they cured the children, and I'm sure they did, I can't forgive them for closing the place down like that without letting anybody know. The least they could have done is contact all of us so we know where to find them if we need to."

I saw Lesley willing me to accept this, the nearest Judith was likely to come to apologising. "As you say," I said, "we don't need them any more."

I heard a giggle in the dining-room and hoped it meant only that the children were enjoying their game. "Still," Judith said, having glanced towards the sound, "if they hadn't gone to Safe To Sleep they wouldn't be friends now. That's worth the bother."

Another giggle prompted me to ask "What are they playing?"

"Claudine's teaching Toby chess. She's the youngest in the chess club at their school."

"It's not chess, mum," Claudine called. "It's our game we made up."

"Has it got a name?" I asked whoever knew.

"Trio," Toby said.

I tried to be unobtrusive as I looked into the dining-room. He and Claudine were sitting at one corner of the table, where chess pieces of both colours lay beside the board. I watched Toby move the black queen up the board and follow her with both his knights, attacking the white king from three directions at once. "I've threed you," he said.

"I'll win next time," Claudine said, and I thought she was making it sound like a ritual. "I'm coming now, mum."

Toby waved her off from the front door while Lesley and I stood behind him, and I tried not to feel we were consciously playing the family on the lit stage of the hall with the night for an audience. Toby had already dined with Claudine, and once he'd had his bath he read us a Hans Andersen tale. I saw Lesley's eyes grow moist as the ugly duckling bent his head and waited for the swans to kill him. I tried to feel nothing except pleasure when he caught sight of his transformed image in the water, but the notion of bodily change made me nervous, and I kept recalling that the author's middle name was Christian. As I kissed Toby good night I could see no darkness in his eyes, however deep into them I peered, and hoped this meant Noble had abandoned him for good.

Once I'd cleared away the game that wasn't chess Lesley brought in her casserole – beef bourgignon. As I opened a bottle of Syrah and filled our glasses I was dogged by a sense of enacting our marriage. I'd enthused about dinner, having savoured a mouthful, when Lesley said "How was your film?"

"I didn't go. I was delayed and then it was too late."

"That's annoying. What was the delay?"

"The vee cee collared me on the way to the car park. He wanted to know how we're doing."

"And you said..."

"That we're all back together." It was a statement that tried not to sound like a hope. I reached for my glass while I said "What would you have told him?"

"Just that," Lesley said but gave me a lingering blink. "Surely he didn't keep you all that time."

"No, of course not." At this point I had to leave truth behind. "I knew you'd be busy with Judith and Claudine," I said, "so I took the time to do some thinking."

"No need to make it sound as if you were excluded. That really isn't fair." When I found no answer Lesley said "What were your thoughts, then? No, I won't ask unless you want to say."

"About us," I said, which felt true enough to pass for truth, "and how I never want to be without you two again."

"Then don't give me the reasons you gave me ever again. What Judith said before, let's leave it at that," she said and reached to take my hand. "We've been through what we've been through, and now let's live for the future."

I wondered how much she had Toby's happiness in mind. I knew his pleas to her had helped keep our family together, though I wasn't sure how crucial they might have been. More than anything, the fact that we no longer monitored his sleep let me think we might be returning to normal, even achieving the normality we'd never previously had. Perhaps that was the last time I was able to delude myself.

We glanced into Toby's room on our way to bed. He was asleep, and far more importantly, lying on his side. When I joined Lesley in bed she drew my hand around her naked waist, and I thought we didn't need any more words. I let my hand stray towards her breast, but she moved it gently back where it had been. This felt like a wordless postponement rather than a rejection, and I was content, even calm for a change. Before long I was asleep.

I lurched awake with a sense that I was about to have a dream I would be desperate to escape. Perhaps I was already dreaming, since although my hand was still on Lesley's waist, I couldn't make it work. I wanted to cling to her to hold myself back from the imminent nightmare, but my hand, not to mention the arm, hardly felt present at all. The harder I strove to hold on, the more remote the useless object grew. It wasn't merely distant but insubstantial, and as my sense of it fled beyond reach I knew I wasn't dreaming. I would have needed my body to dream.

I was outside in the night, where countless lights did far too little to dispel the dark. I thought I might be snatched into the black sky, but I was racing breathlessly – with no breath at all – above the streets. Now and then dogs barked as if they sensed my passing. The last streets gave way to empty darkness, and I was terrified to think I knew where I was bound. I managed to stave off the prospect until I saw the padlocked gates that used to lead to Safe To Sleep.

I swooped along the avenue of fallen trees and then, unable to find any way to prevent myself, slid into the ground like a worm. I could have thought the denizen was waiting for me, because its unnatural hunger drew me deep into the earth. I was slipping, blind and helpless, down a spiral that might never end. Certainly the descent seemed to leave time behind. I wasn't even protected from sensations; I could feel how soft and slimy the walls were, and crawling with some form of life. The swarming mass was their actual substance, and it was starting to become mine. At some point I realised that I'd passed through the centre of the spiral, but its geometry was so abnormal that it simply led further into its own kind of darkness. I no longer knew whether I was rushing up or down. All that was clear was that I might never escape.

I felt the spiral begin to reveal more of its dreadful nature, mouthing at me like a colossal deformed maw that might have been eager to consume its victim or to deliver a monstrous welcoming kiss if not both, before I was released. It was made plain to me that the denizen hadn't been my summoner. Then I was above the faintly luminous fields, and after those the lit streets of the city, and by no means soon enough in bed with Lesley, where I had to remember how to take a breath. No doubt my body had kept up the process in my absence. I managed to relax my grip on Lesley's waist before it could waken her, though she murmured a sleepy complaint that fell short of words. However fiercely I might have clung to her, it wouldn't have made me feel safe. I was still hearing the voice I'd heard in my mind as my captor let me go — Toph's voice, sounding less than ever like a child and yet childishly gleeful. "You're ours when we want," it said.

ACKNOWLEDGEMENTS

Jenny was first, as ever – first to read the book chapter by chapter, and first in my life. We and the novel travelled a good deal. It was worked upon at the gracious Grand Hotel Bonnano in Pisa, the fine Blue Sky Hotel in Petra on Lesvos, the likeably quirky Hotel Il Girasole in Milan (where I was a guest at Stranimondi at the invitation of the good Barbra Bucci), the splendid Pan Pacific in Singapore (where the breakfast buffet seemed boundless) and the fine Pathumwan Princess in Bangkok. Come to that, it went to Fantasycon in Scarborough and the Festival of Fantastic Films in Manchester.

Michael Wesley lent me his nightmare for the finale of this volume. Richard Hill gave me insights into academia. My old friend Keith Ravenscroft kept me supplied with good things, and also with the Blu-ray of *A.P.E.*... My choice, and I'm perversely glad. In South Korea it was apparently released as *The Great Counterattack of King Kong*.

FLAME TREE PRESS
FICTION WITHOUT FRONTIERS
Award-Winning Authors & Original Voices

Flame Tree Press is the trade fiction imprint of Flame Tree Publishing, focusing on excellent writing in horror and the supernatural, crime and mystery, science fiction and fantasy. Our aim is to explore beyond the boundaries of the everyday, with tales from both award-winning authors and original voices.

•

The First Book of the *Three Births of Daoloth* series:
The Searching Dead
Other titles available by Ramsey Campbell:
Thirteen Days by Sunset Beach
Think Yourself Lucky
The Hungry Moon
The Influence
The Wise Friend
Somebody's Voice

Other horror and suspense titles available include:
Snowball by Gregory Bastianelli
The Haunting of Henderson Close by Catherine Cavendish
The Garden of Bewitchment by Catherine Cavendish
The House by the Cemetery by John Everson
The Devil's Equinox by John Everson
Hellrider by JG Faherty
The Toy Thief by D.W. Gillespie
One By One by D.W. Gillespie
Black Wings by Megan Hart
The Playing Card Killer by Russell James
The Sorrows by Jonathan Janz
Will Haunt You by Brian Kirk
We Are Monsters by Brian Kirk
Hearthstone Cottage by Frazer Lee
Those Who Came Before by J.H. Moncrieff
Stoker's Wilde by Steven Hopstaken & Melissa Prusi
Creature by Hunter Shea
Ghost Mine by Hunter Shea
Slash by Hunter Shea

•

Join our mailing list for free short stories, new release details, news about our authors and special promotions:

flametreepress.com